MIKE MAIHAC

CLEOPATRA IN SPACE

BOOK ONE
TARGET PRACTICE

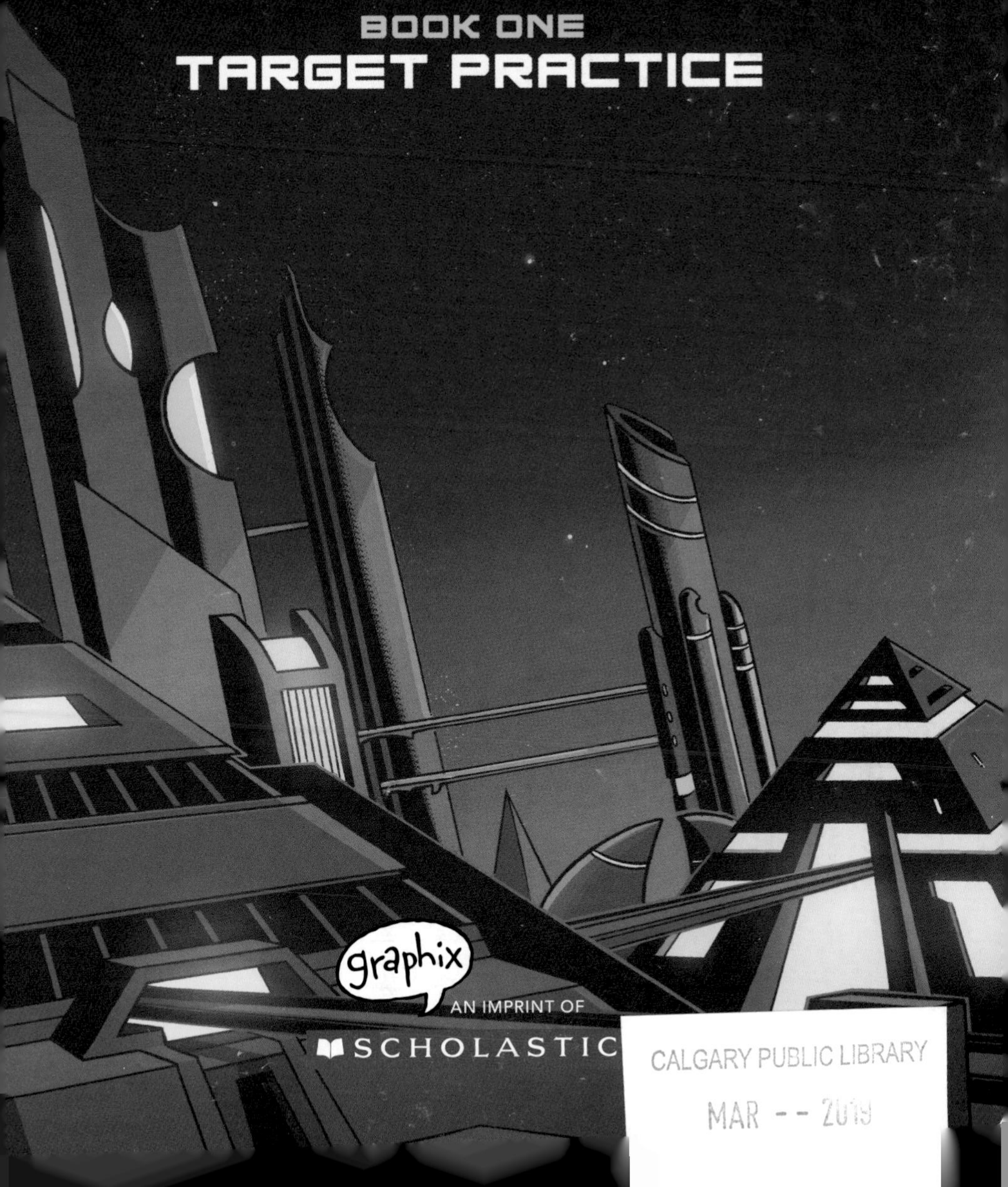

graphix

AN IMPRINT OF

SCHOLASTIC

Library of Congress Control Number: 2013934374

ISBN 978-0-545-52842-9 (hardcover)
ISBN 978-0-545-52843-6 (paperback)

10 9 8   18
First edition, May 2014
Edited by Cassandra Pelham
Book design by Phil Falco
Creative Director: David Saylor
Printed in Malaysia   108

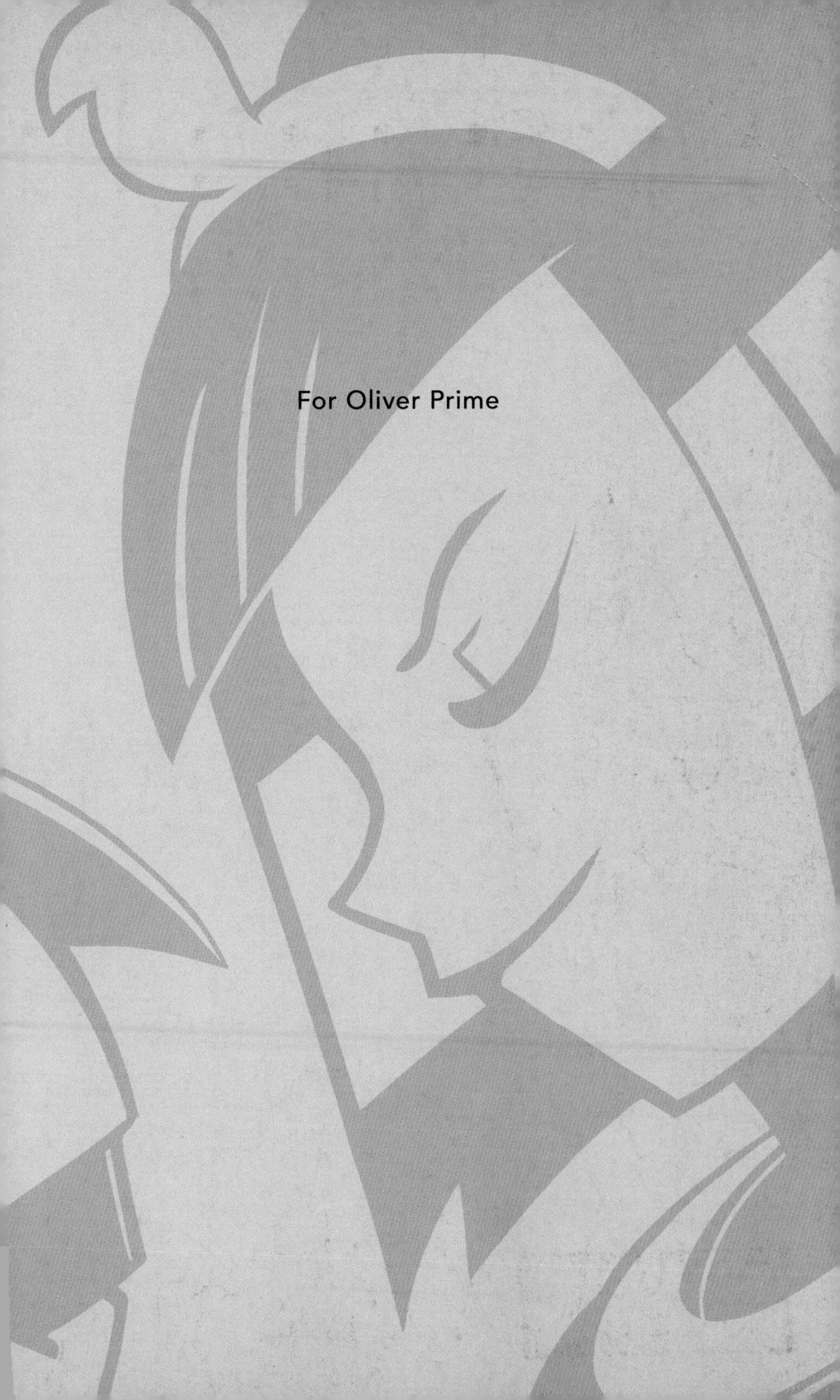

For Oliver Prime

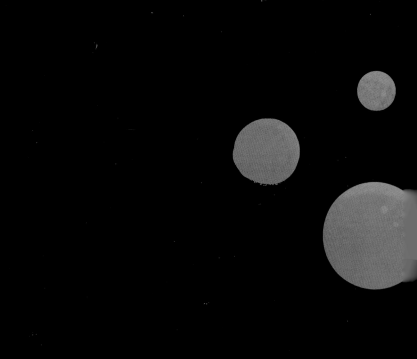

CHAPTER ONE

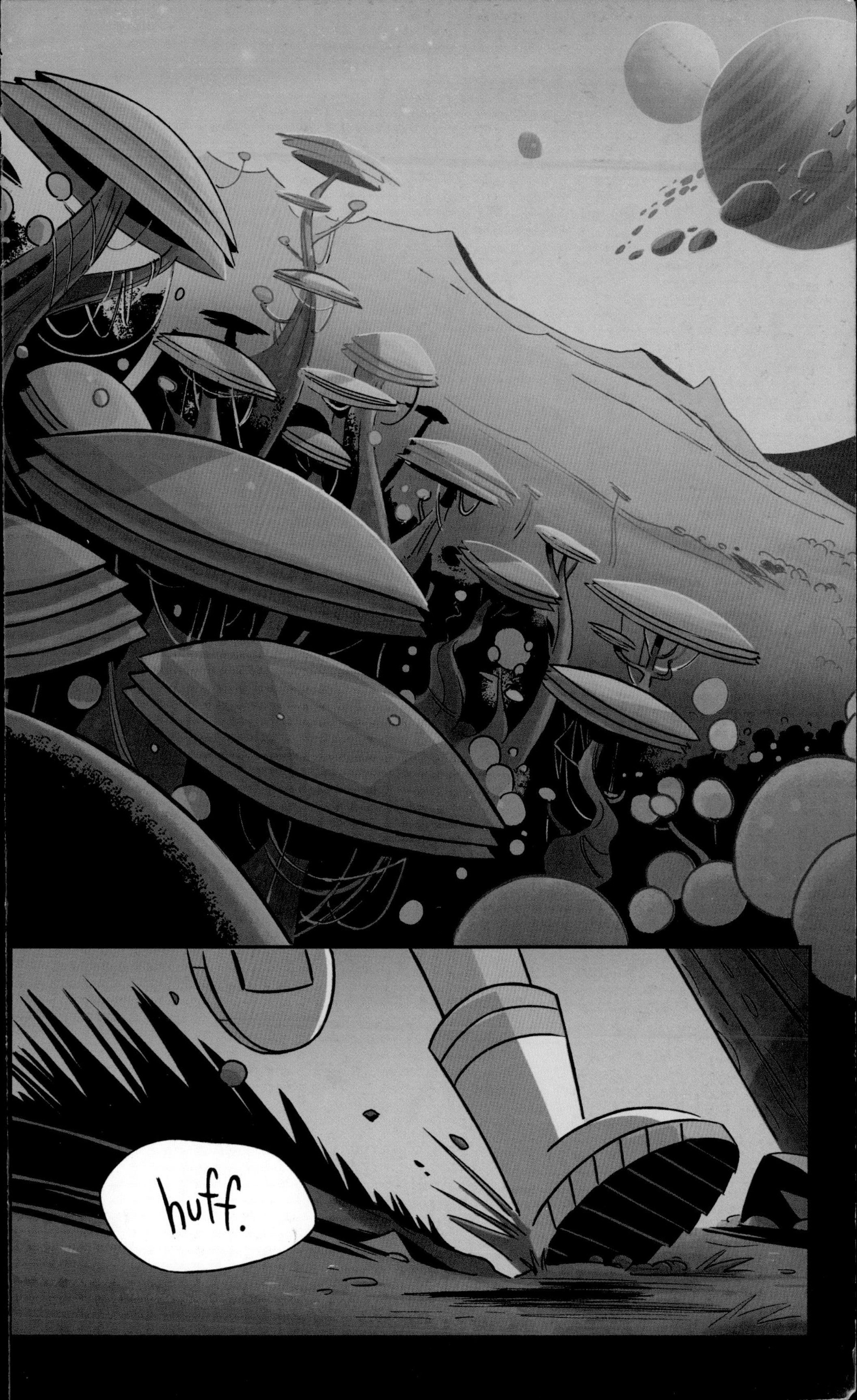
huff.

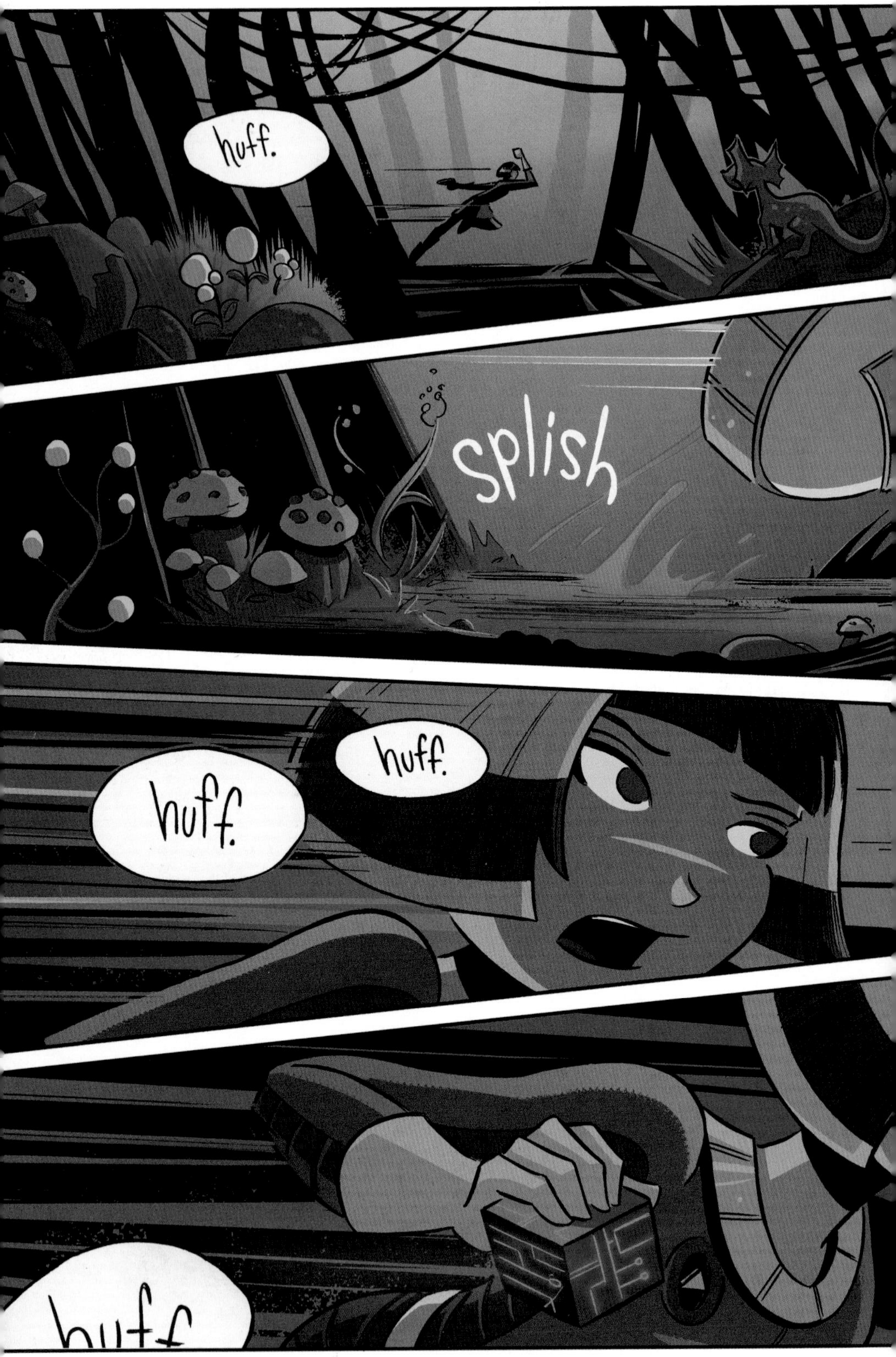
huff.
splish
huff.
huff.

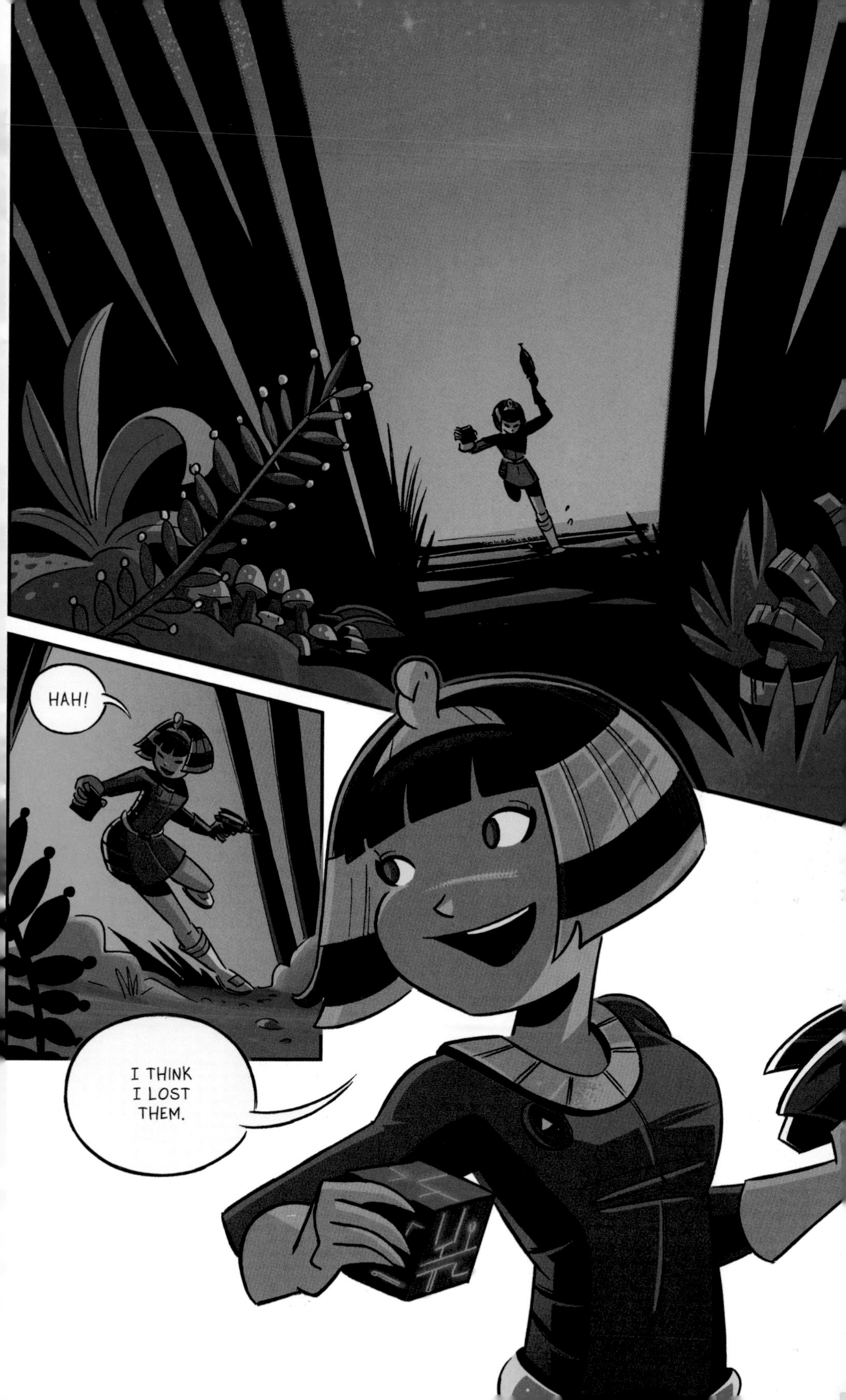
HAH!
I THINK I LOST THEM.

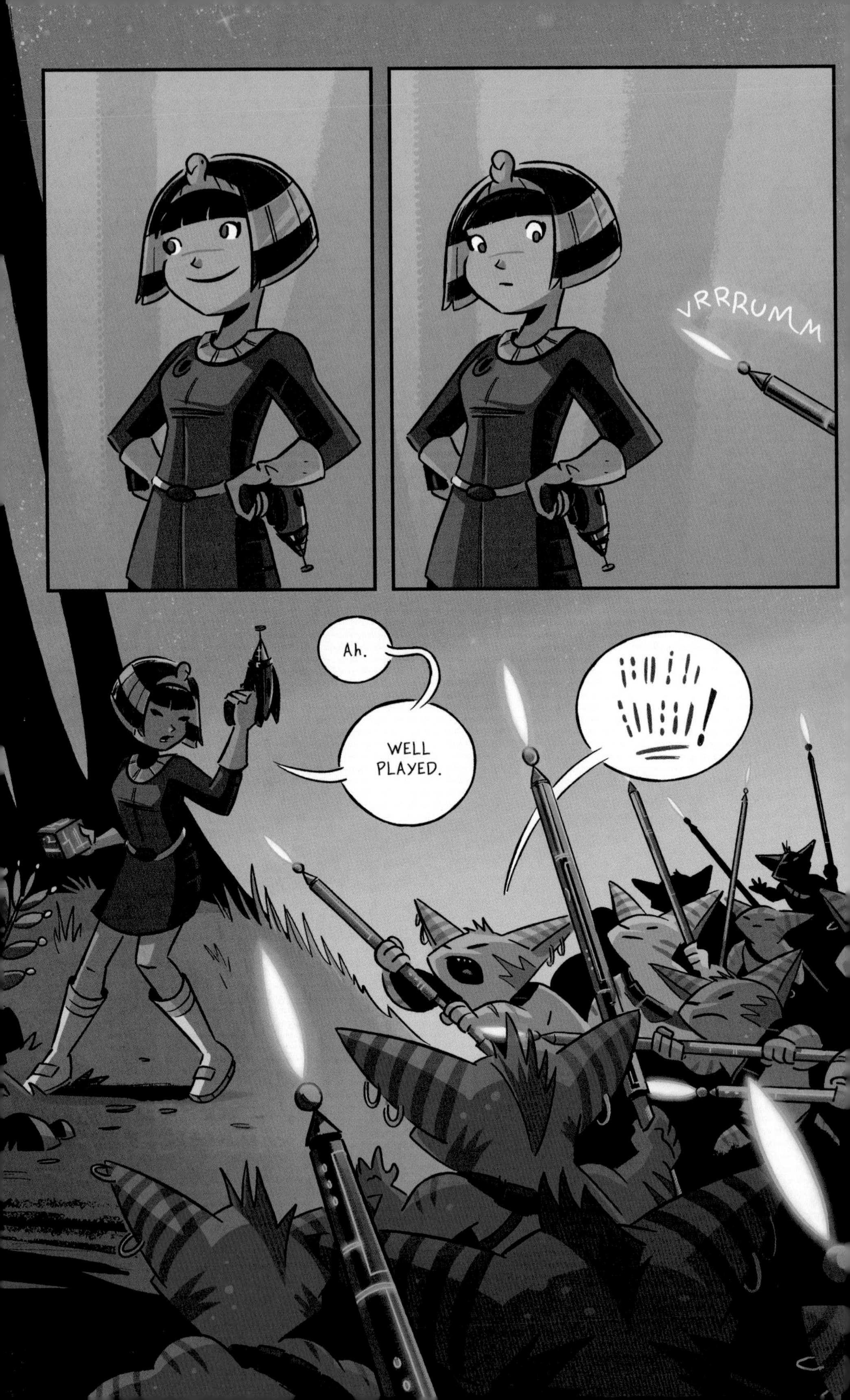
VRRRUMM
Ah.
WELL PLAYED.
!!!!!!!!!

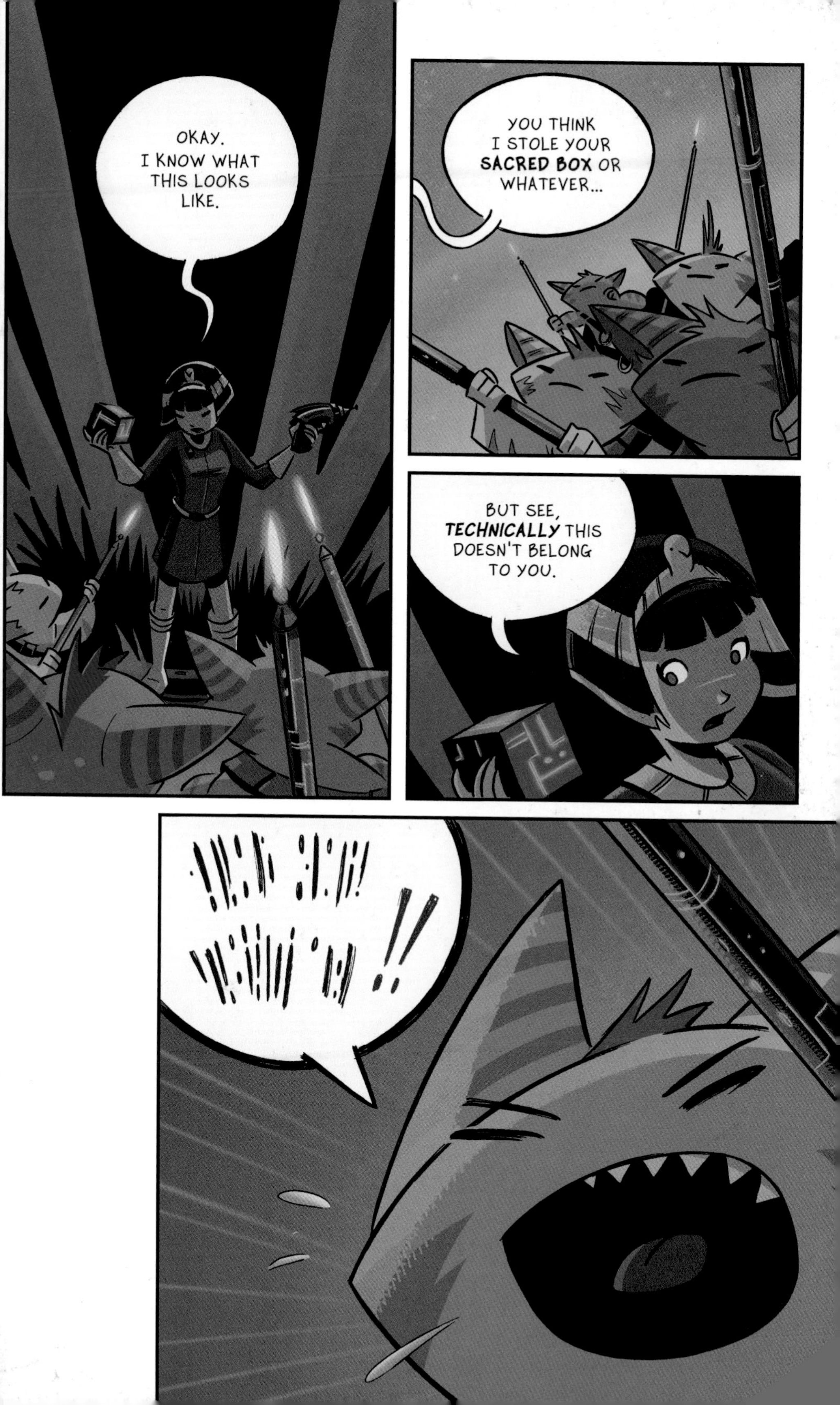
OKAY. I KNOW WHAT THIS LOOKS LIKE.
YOU THINK I STOLE YOUR **SACRED BOX** OR WHATEVER...
BUT SEE, ***TECHNICALLY*** THIS DOESN'T BELONG TO YOU.

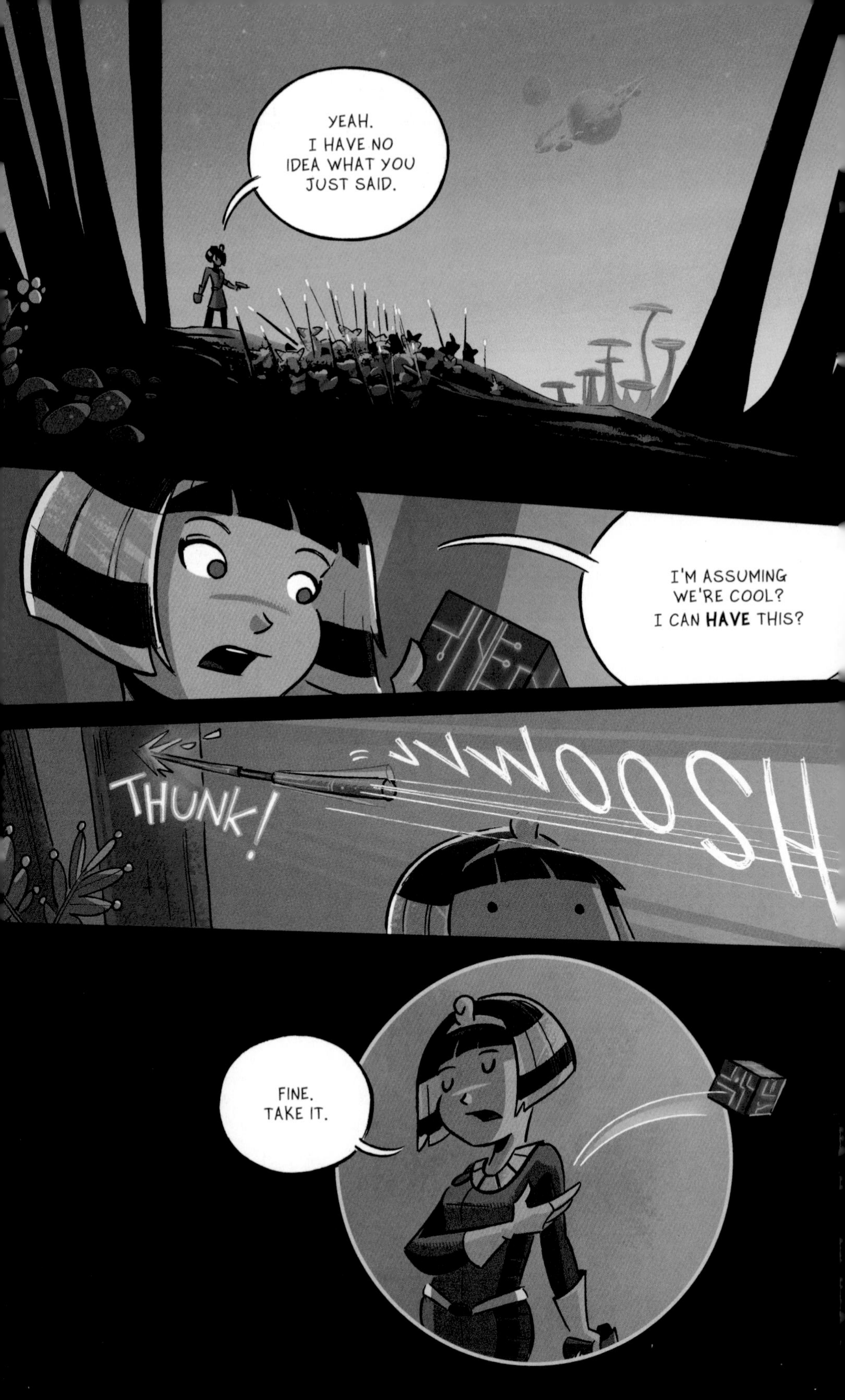
YEAH. I HAVE NO IDEA WHAT YOU JUST SAID.
I'M ASSUMING WE'RE COOL? I CAN **HAVE** THIS?
THUNK!
VVWOOSH
FINE. TAKE IT.

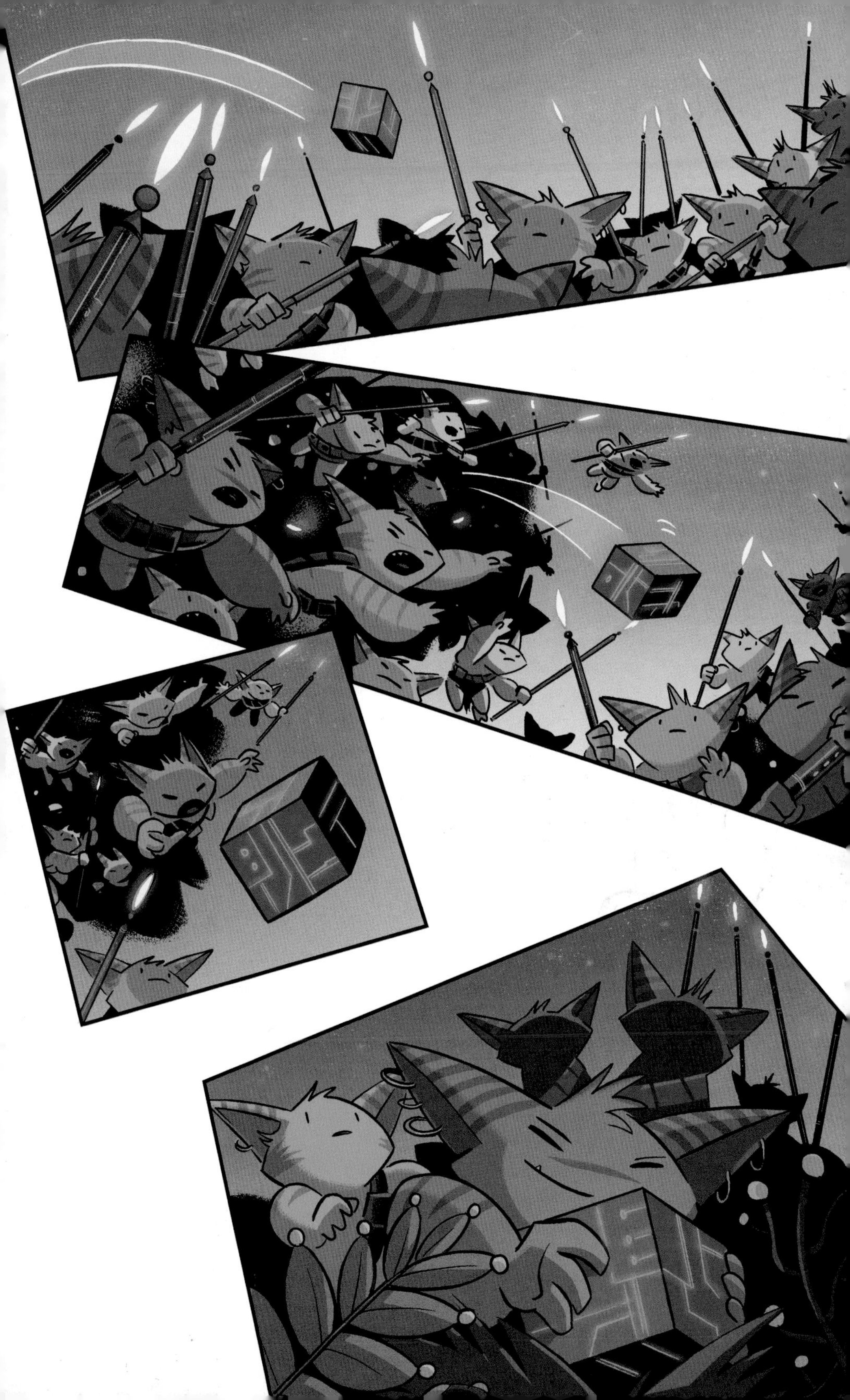

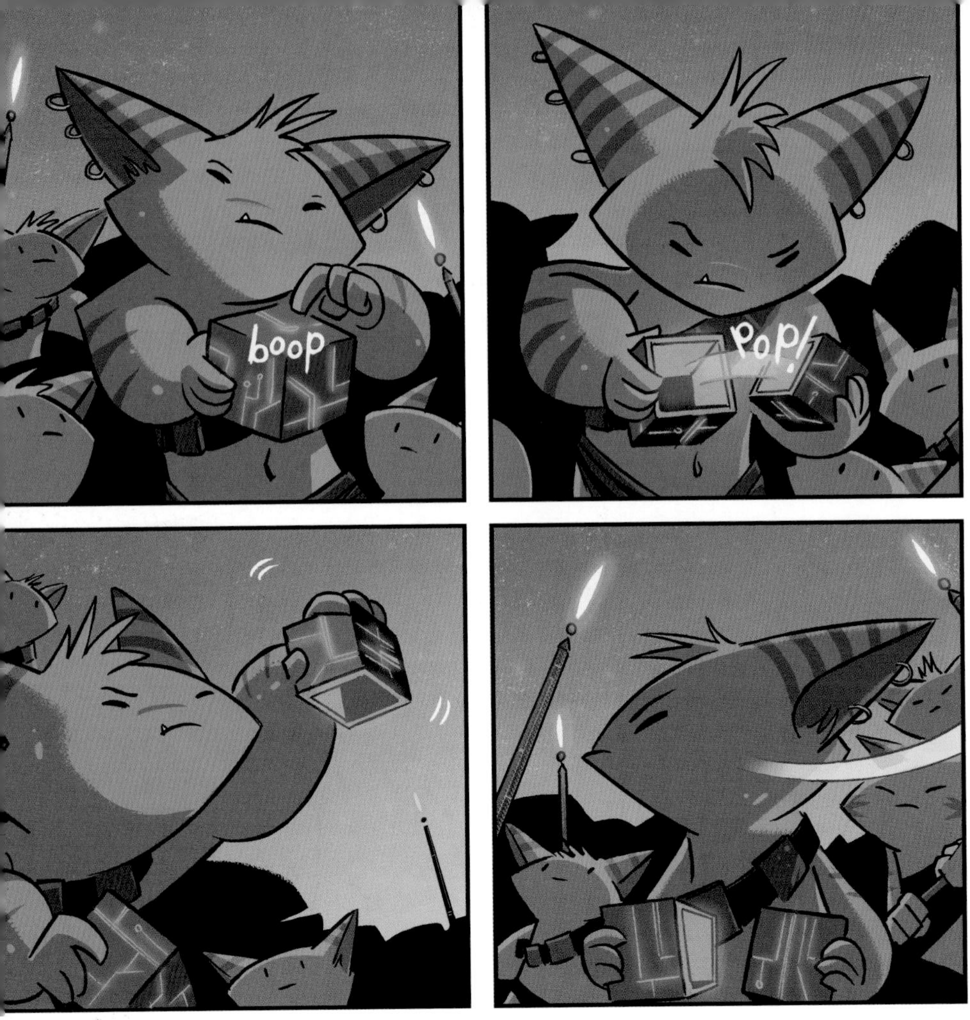
boop
pop!

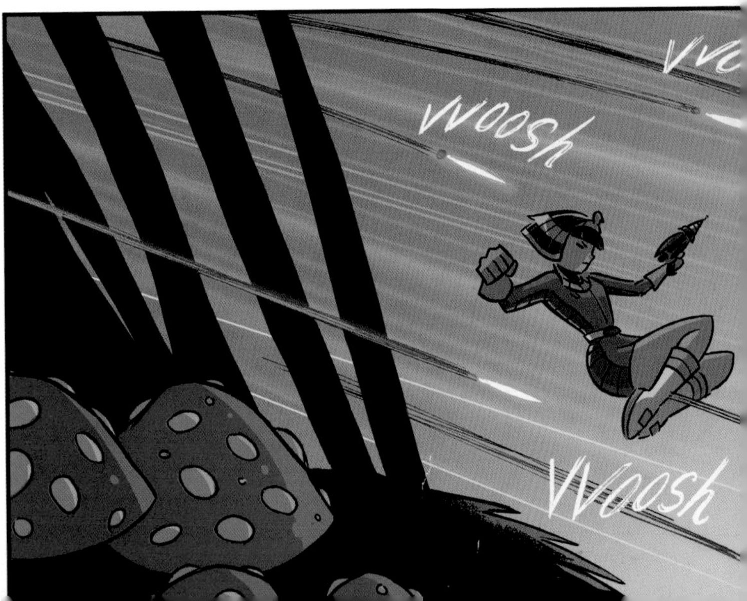
VVOOSH
VVOOSH

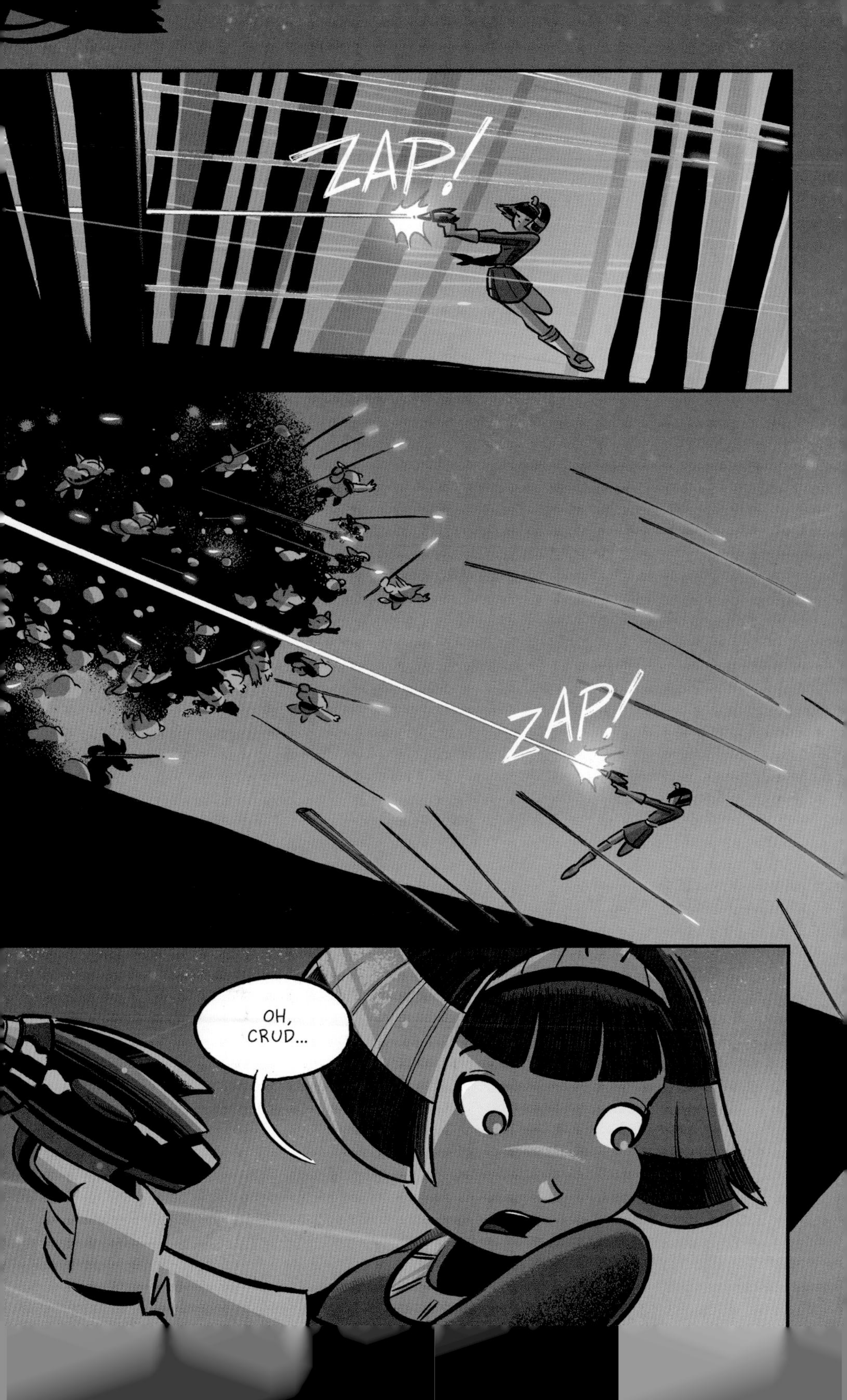
ZAP!
ZAP!
OH, CRUD...

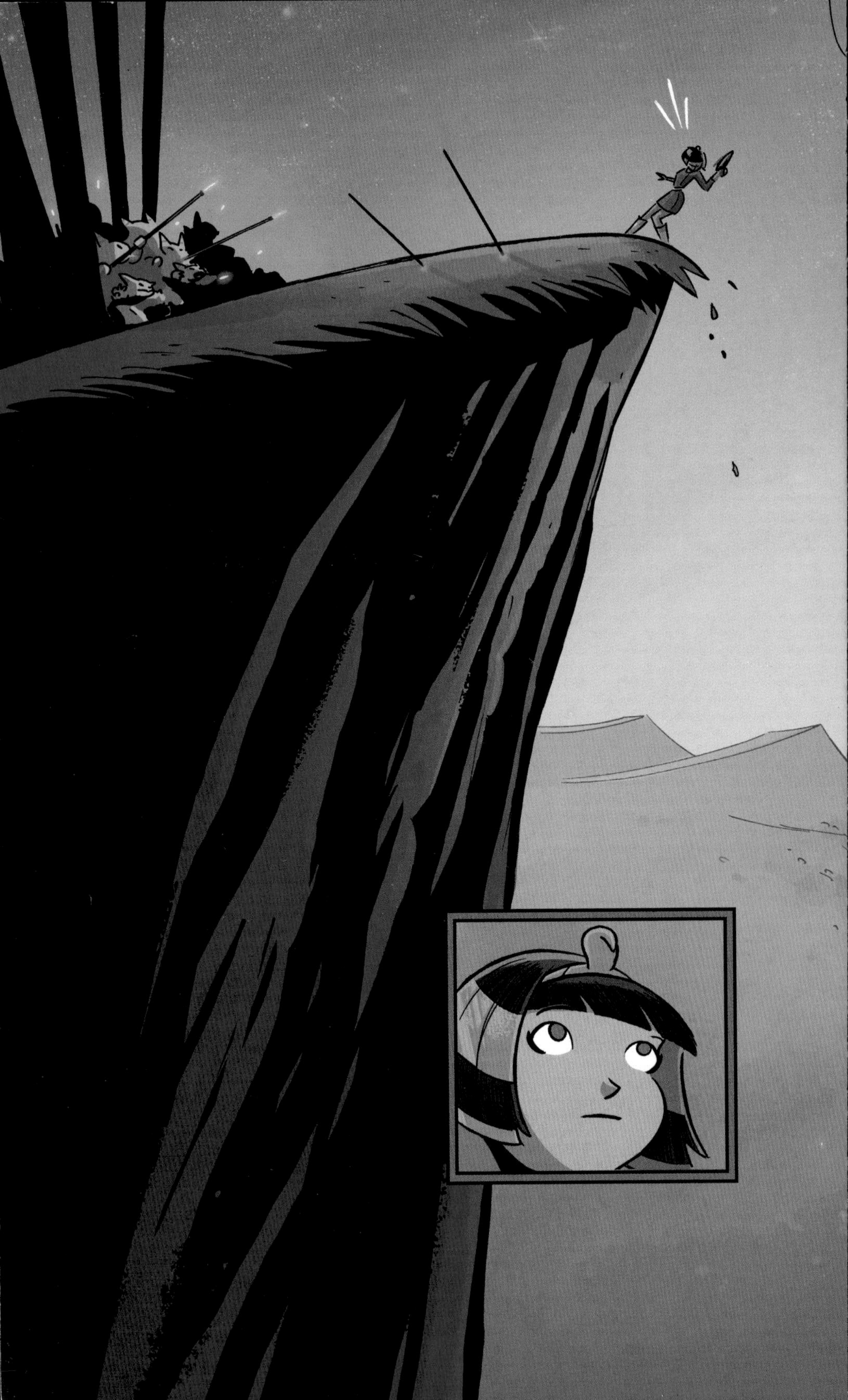

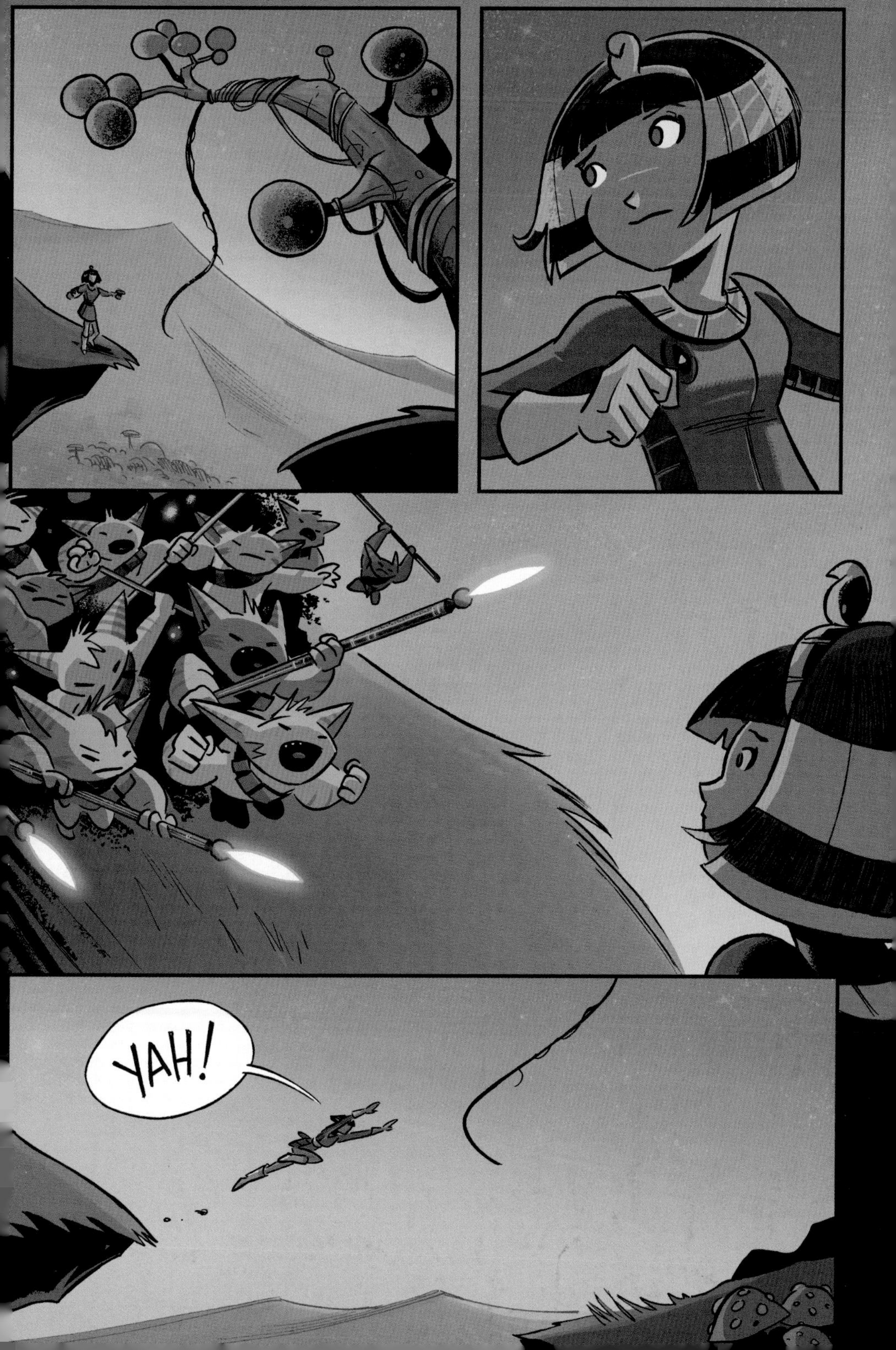
YAH!

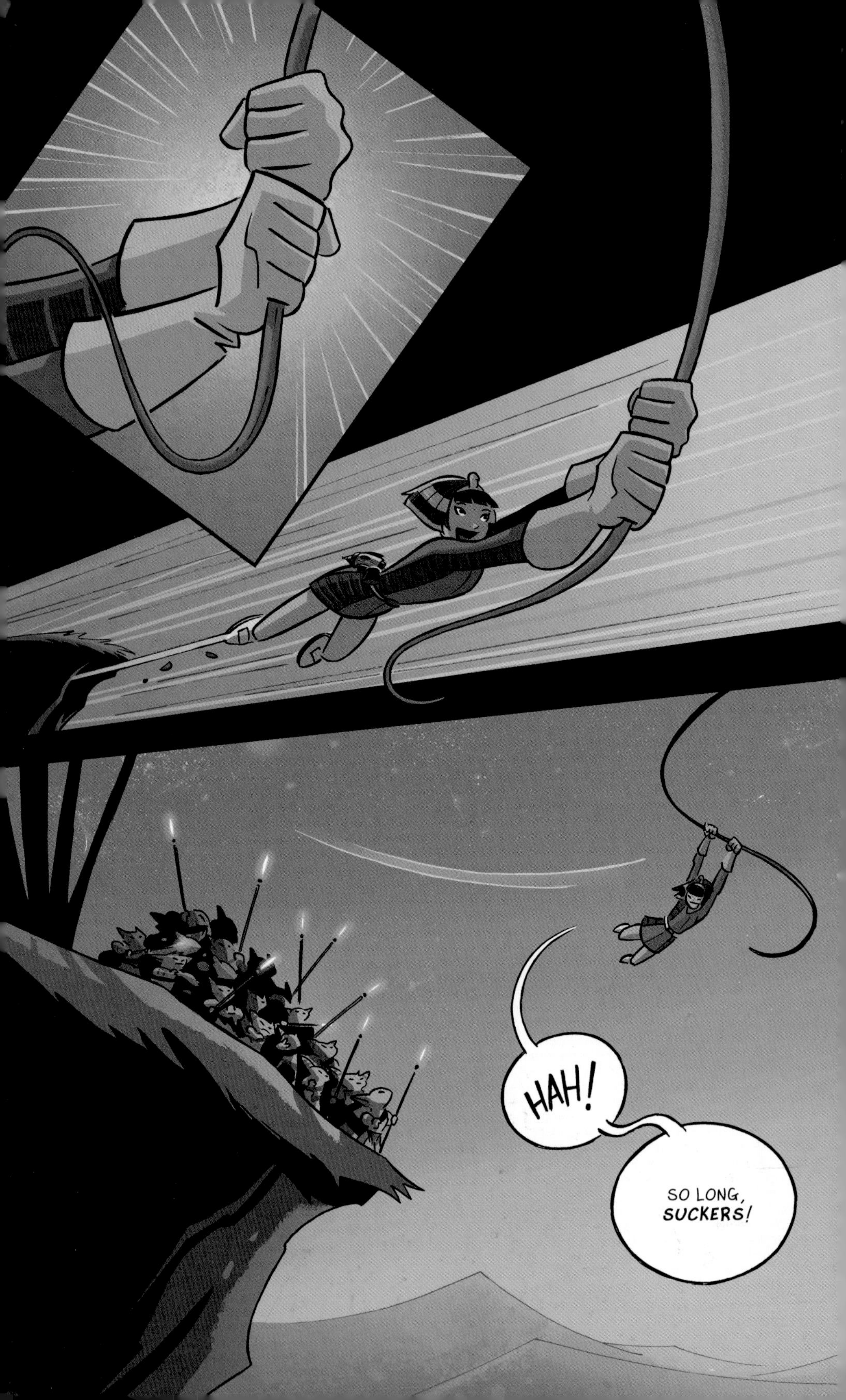
HAH!
SO LONG, SUCKERS!

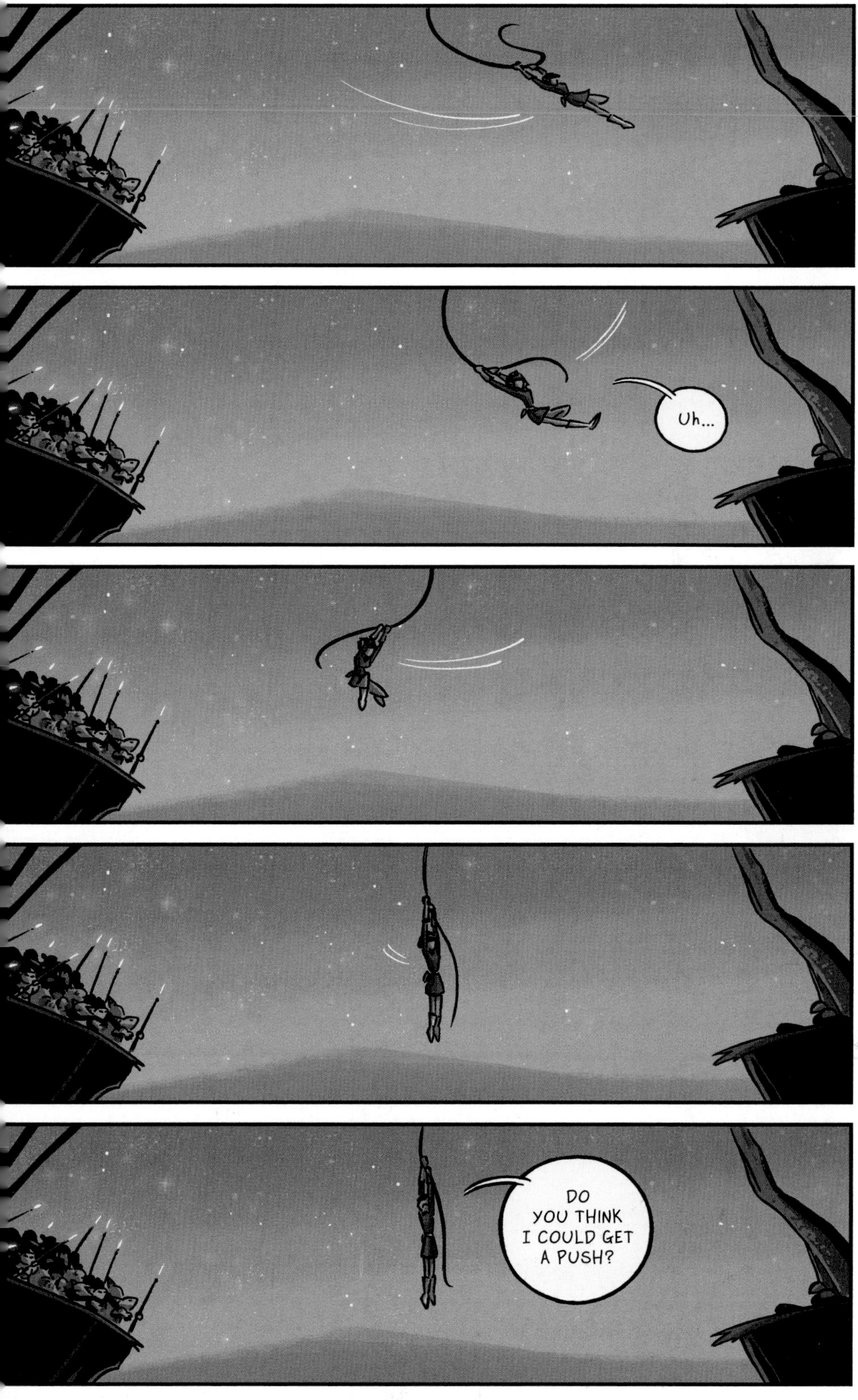
Uh...
DO YOU THINK I COULD GET A PUSH?

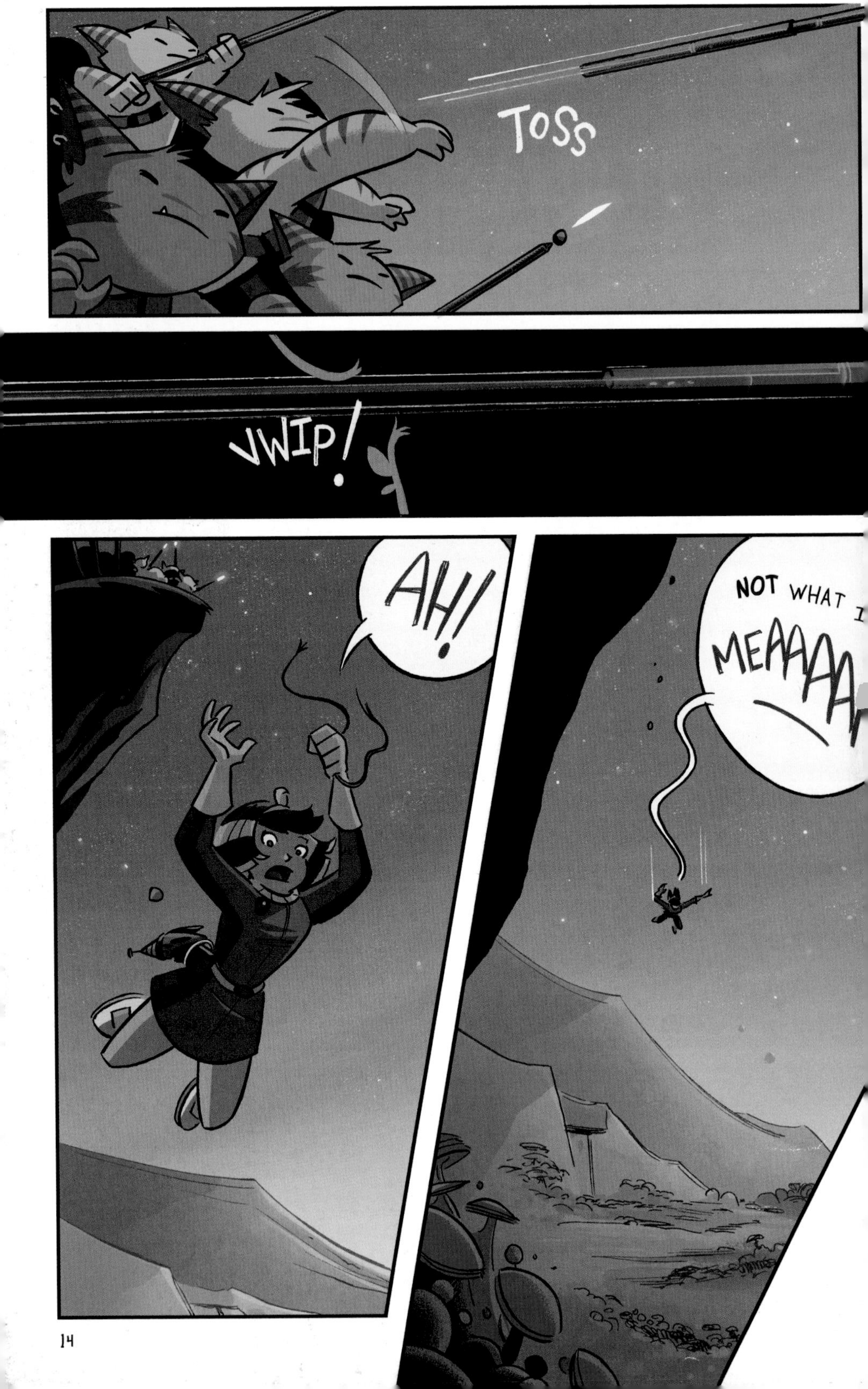
TOSS
VWIP!
AH!
NOT WHAT I
MEAAAA

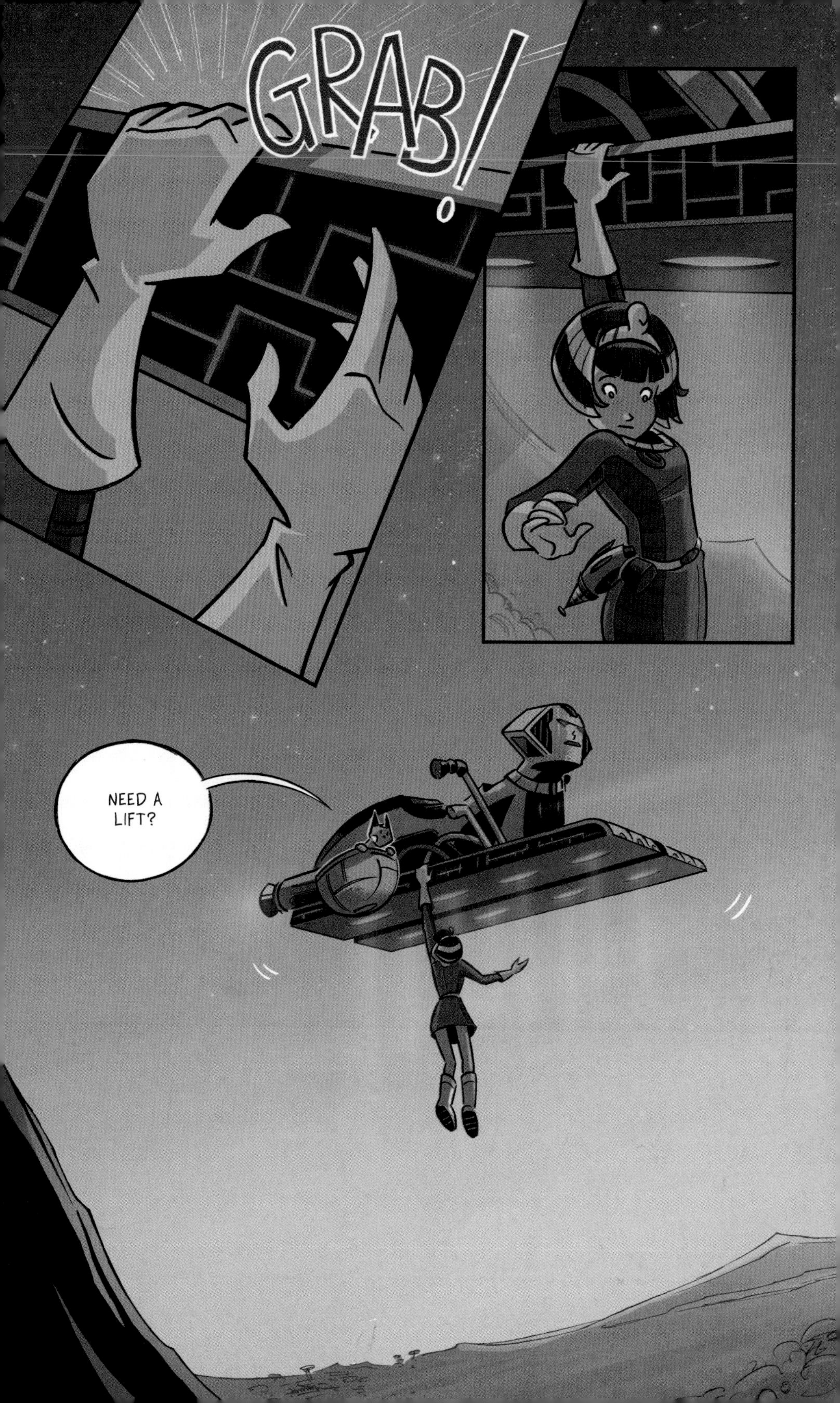
GRAB!
NEED A LIFT?

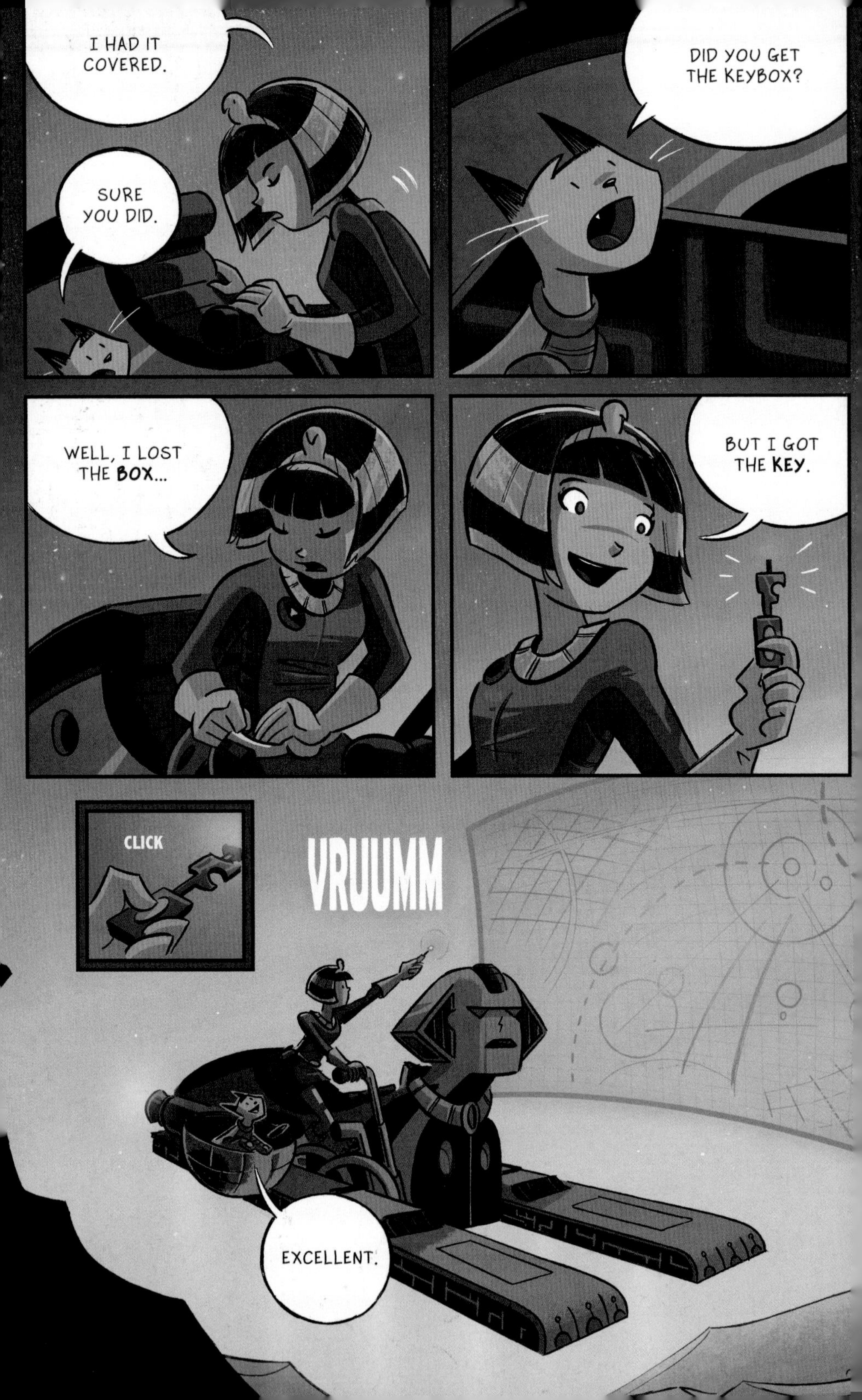
I HAD IT COVERED.
SURE YOU DID.
DID YOU GET THE KEYBOX?
WELL, I LOST THE **BOX**...
BUT I GOT THE **KEY**.
CLICK
VRUUMM
EXCELLENT.

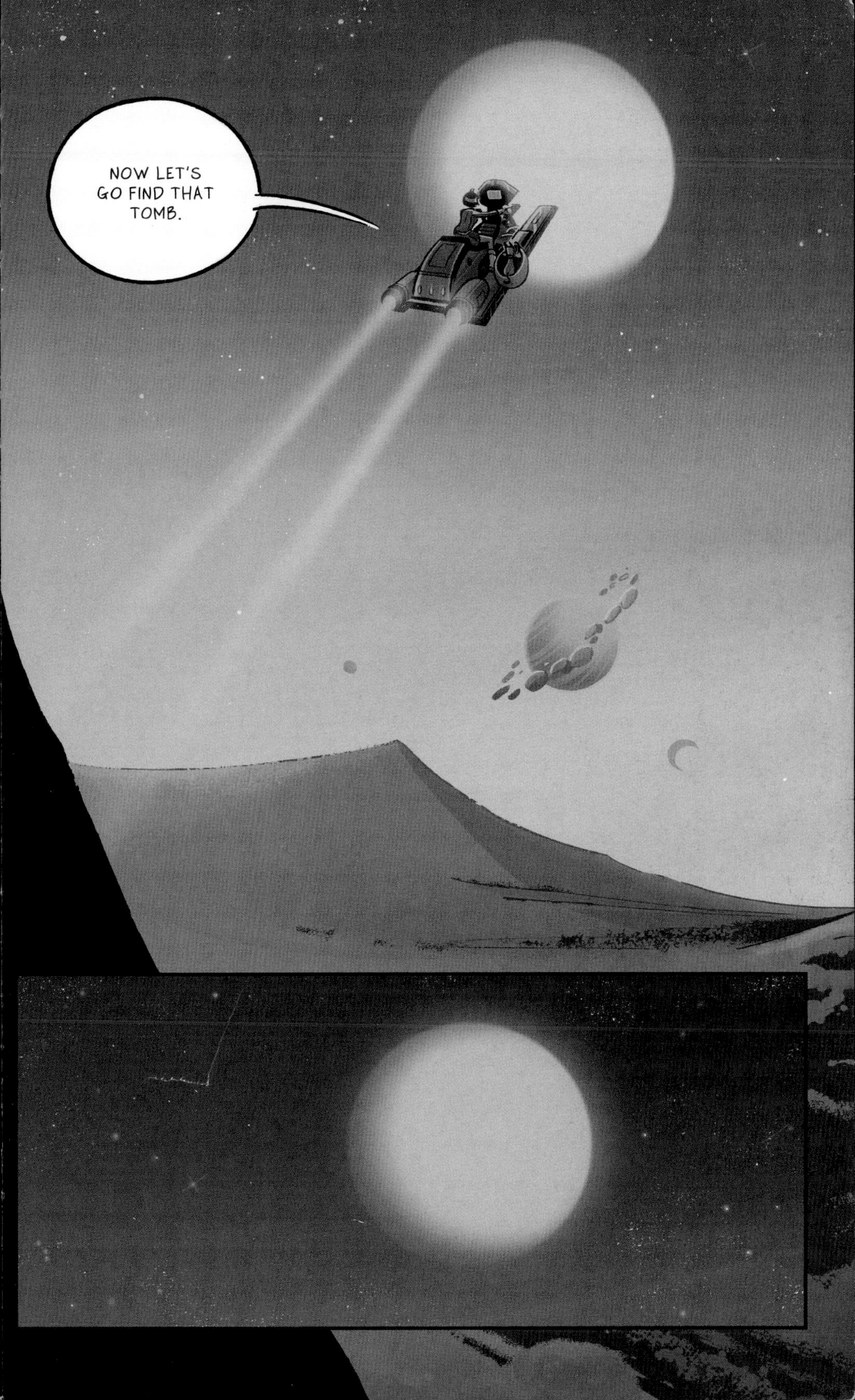
NOW LET'S GO FIND THAT TOMB.

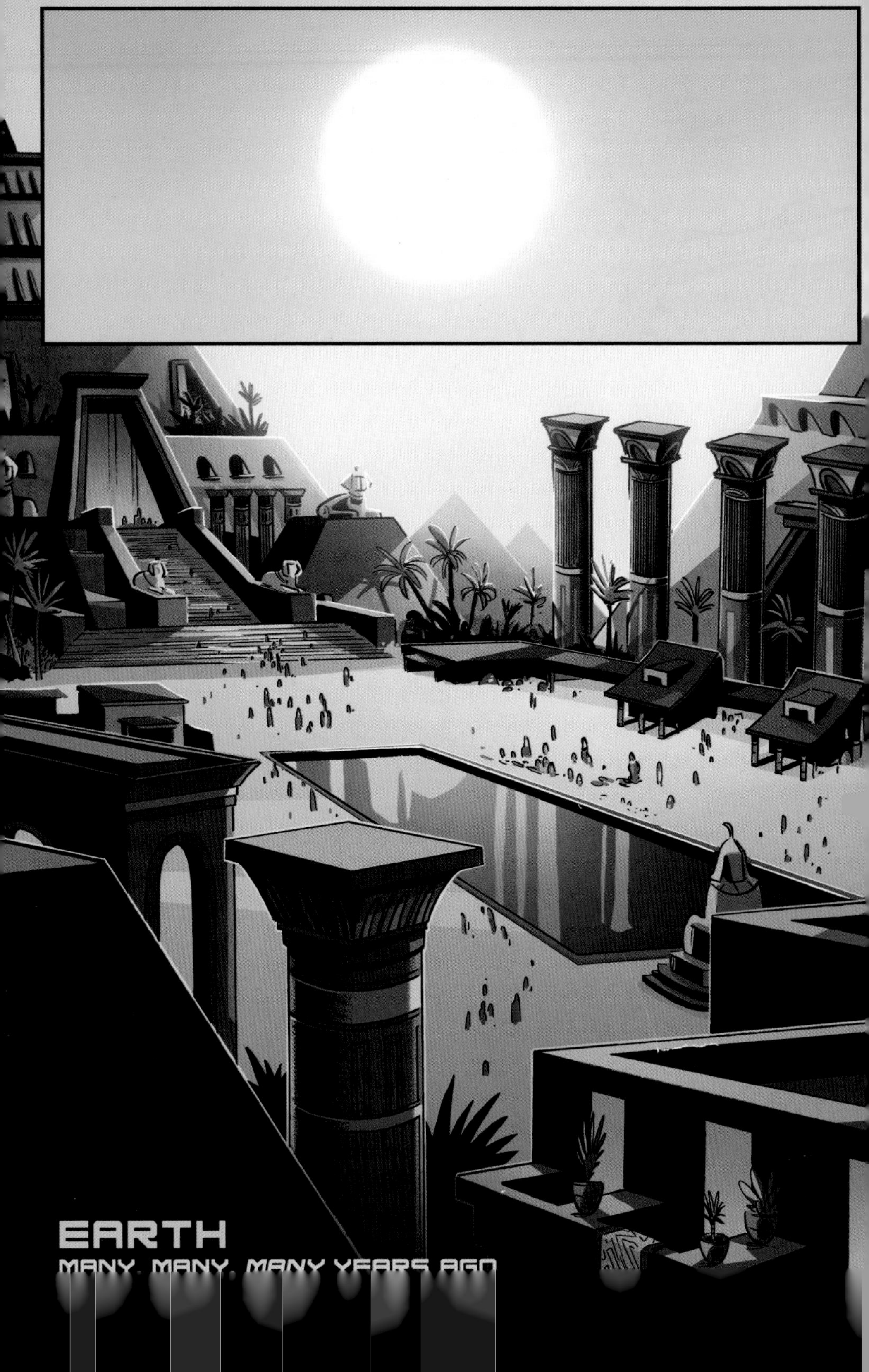
EARTH
MANY, MANY, MANY YEARS AGO

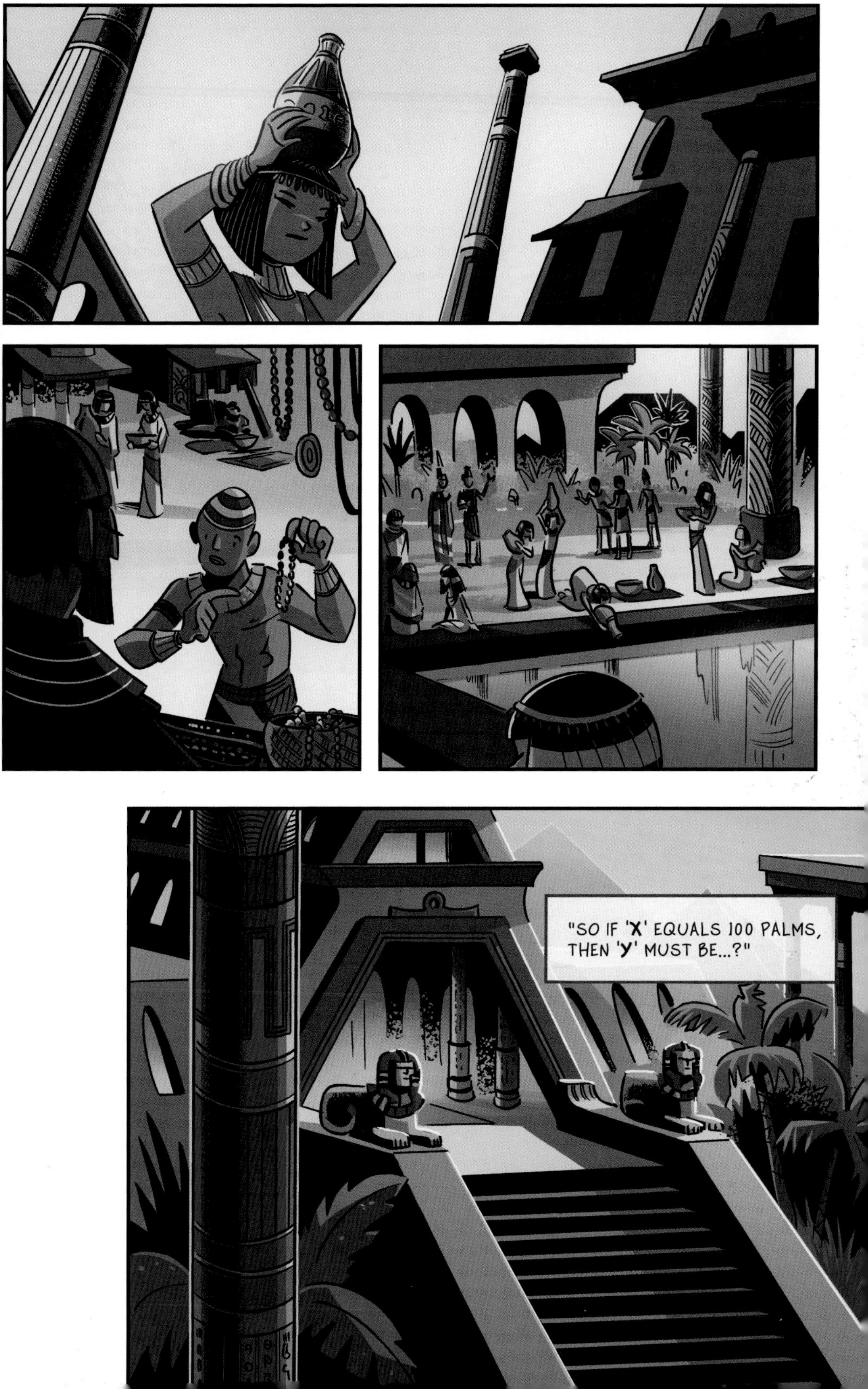
"SO IF 'X' EQUALS 100 PALMS, THEN 'Y' MUST BE...?"

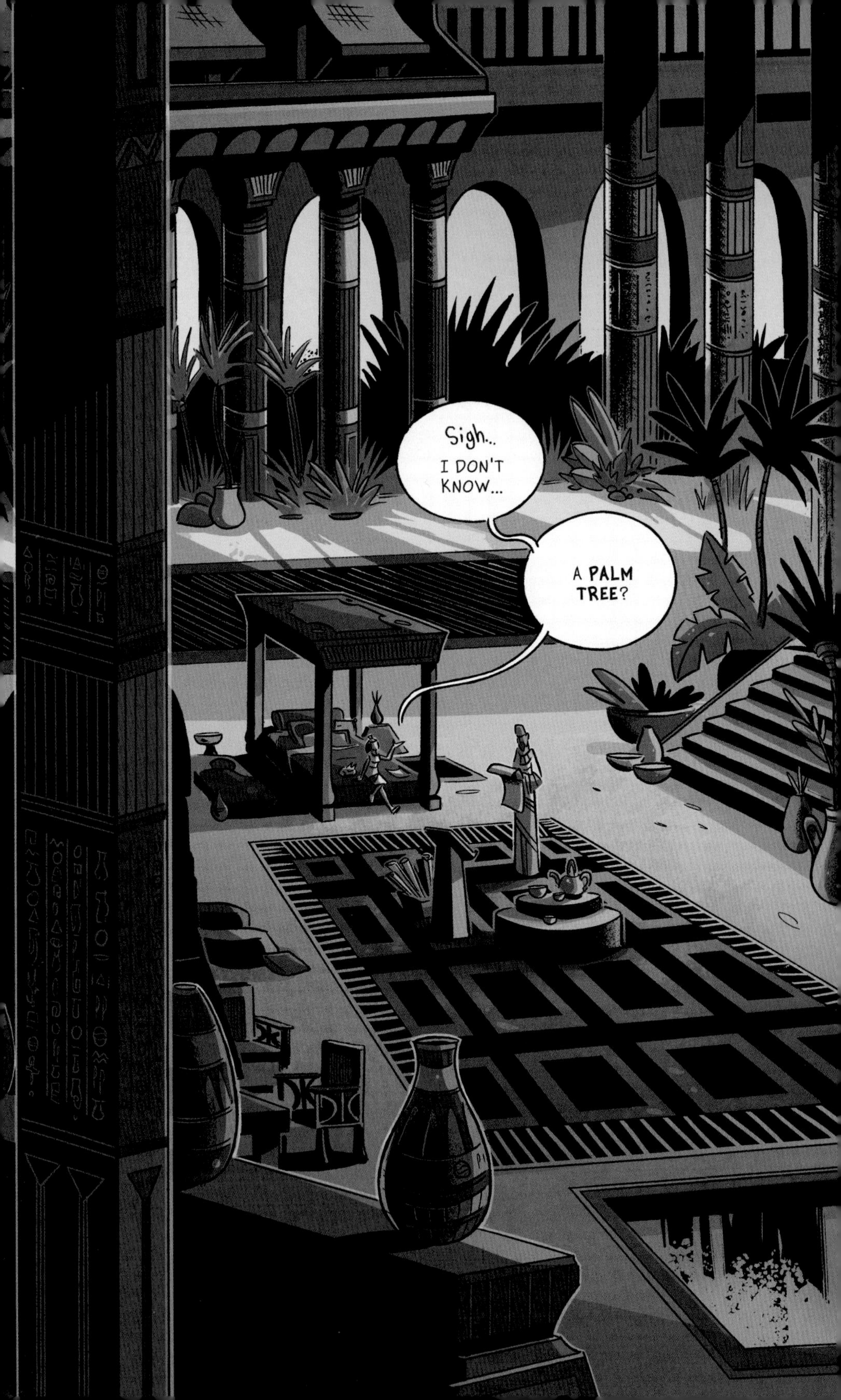
Sigh.. I DON'T KNOW...
A PALM TREE?

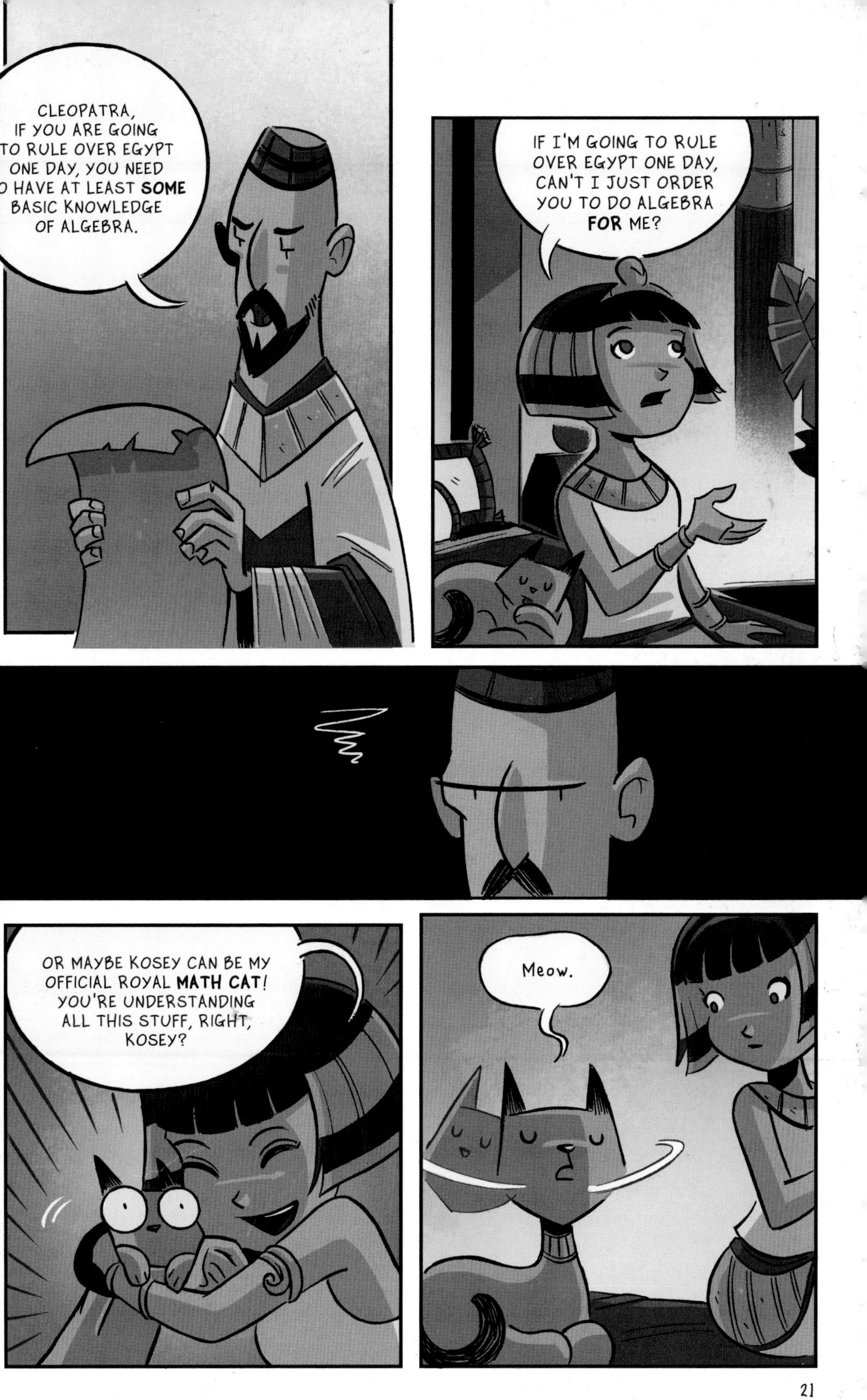
CLEOPATRA, IF YOU ARE GOING TO RULE OVER EGYPT ONE DAY, YOU NEED O HAVE AT LEAST SOME BASIC KNOWLEDGE OF ALGEBRA.
IF I'M GOING TO RULE OVER EGYPT ONE DAY, CAN'T I JUST ORDER YOU TO DO ALGEBRA FOR ME?
OR MAYBE KOSEY CAN BE MY OFFICIAL ROYAL MATH CAT! YOU'RE UNDERSTANDING ALL THIS STUFF, RIGHT, KOSEY?
Meow.

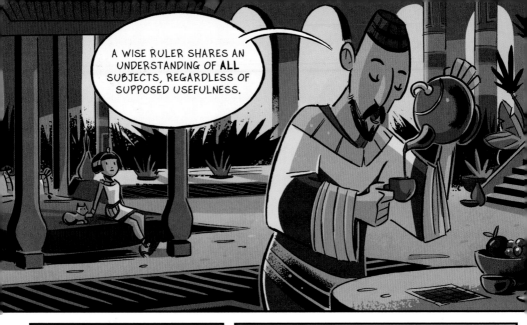

A WISE RULER SHARES AN UNDERSTANDING OF **ALL** SUBJECTS, REGARDLESS OF SUPPOSED USEFULNESS.

Sip.

YOUR FATHER--

MY FATHER IS BUSY **DELEGATING** SUBJECTS ON THE ASSEMBLY OF MY BIRTHDAY CELEBRATION RIGHT NOW, BAKARI.

AND YOU AREN'T EXCITED ABOUT TONIGHT'S FESTIVITIES?

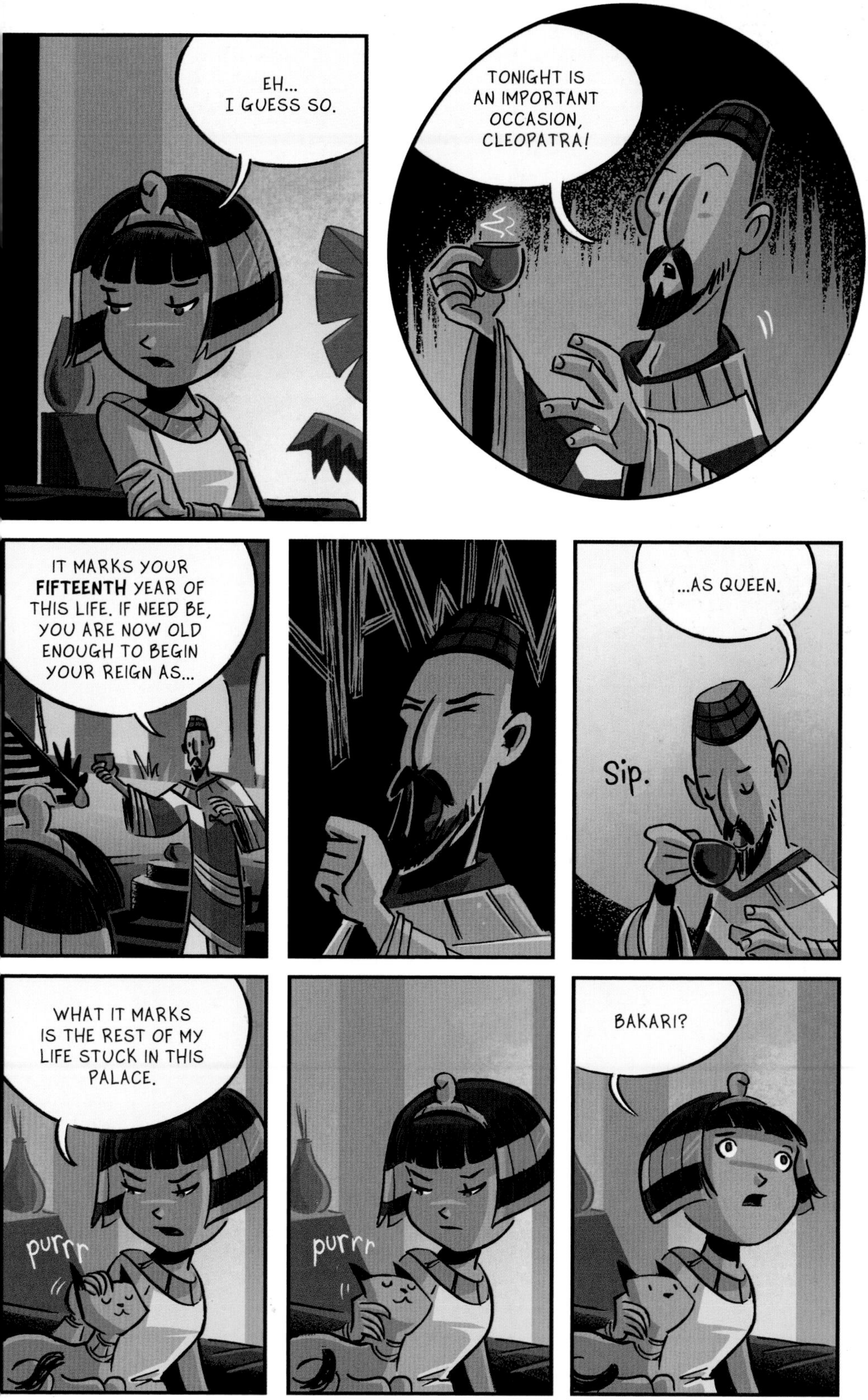
EH... I GUESS SO.
TONIGHT IS AN IMPORTANT OCCASION, CLEOPATRA!
IT MARKS YOUR **FIFTEENTH** YEAR OF THIS LIFE. IF NEED BE, YOU ARE NOW OLD ENOUGH TO BEGIN YOUR REIGN AS...
...AS QUEEN.
Sip.
WHAT IT MARKS IS THE REST OF MY LIFE STUCK IN THIS PALACE.
purrr
purrr
BAKARI?

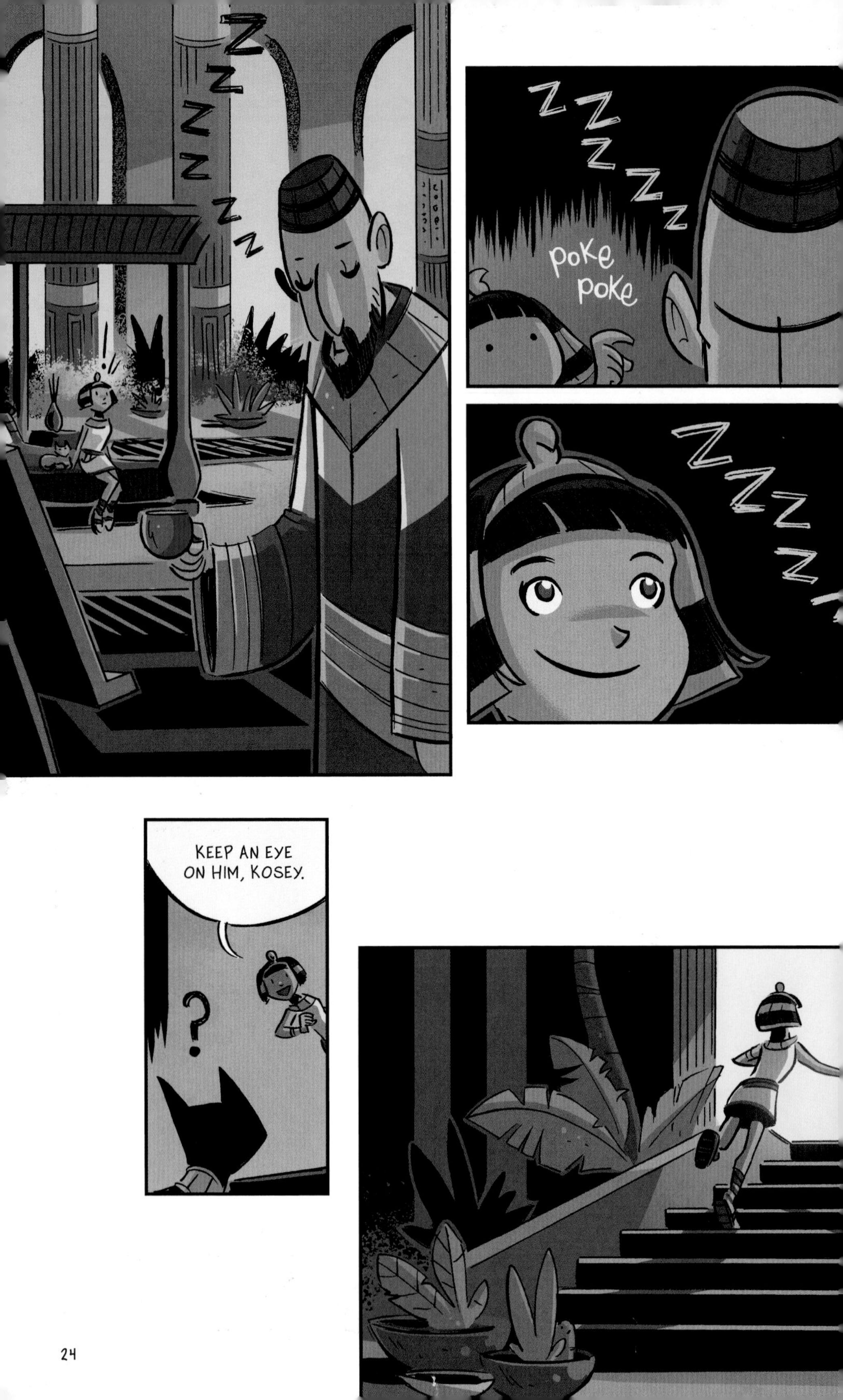

ZZZZZZZ
ZZZZZ
POKE POKE
ZZZZZ
?
KEEP AN EYE ON HIM, KOSEY.

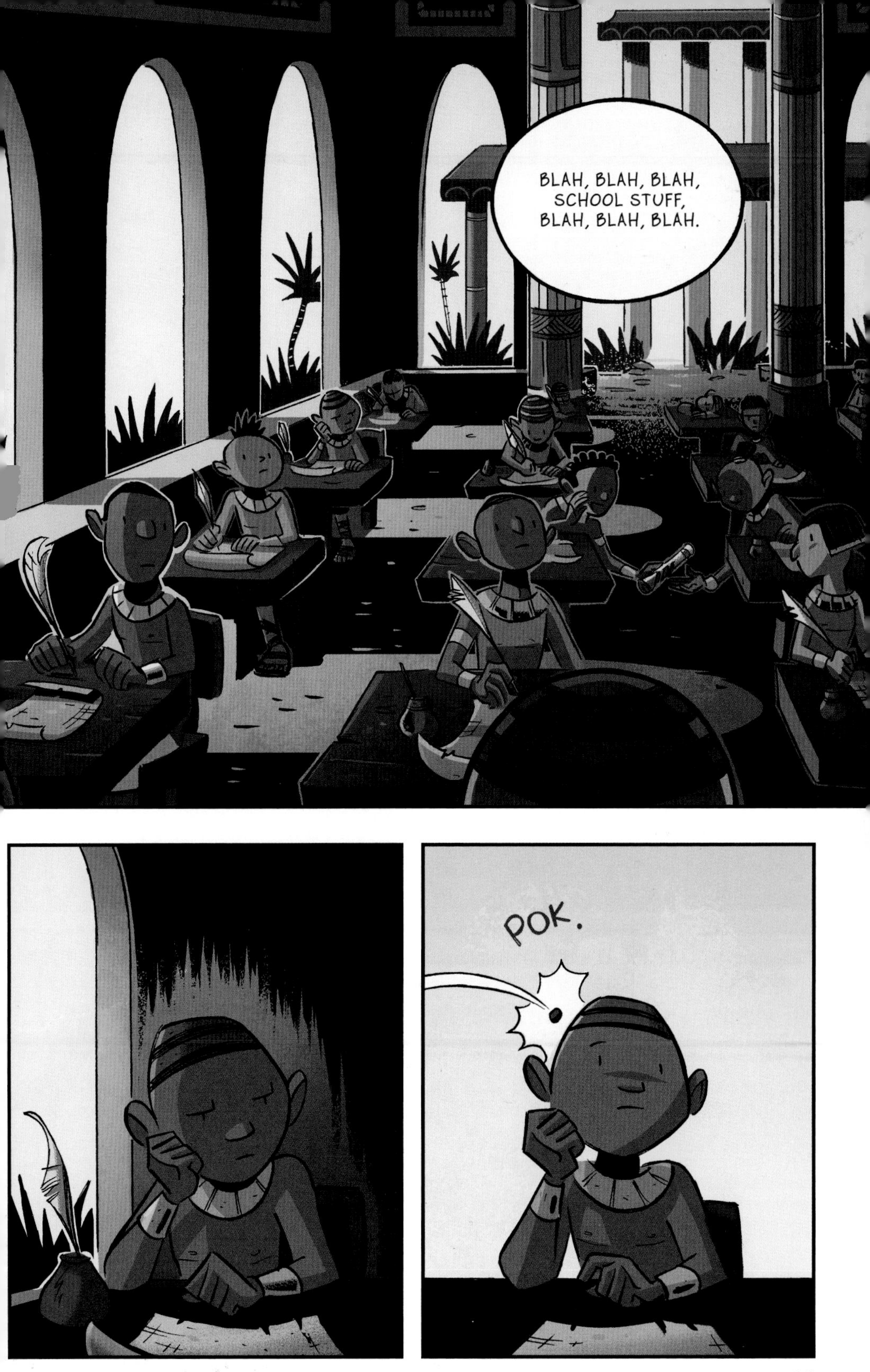
BLAH, BLAH, BLAH,
SCHOOL STUFF,
BLAH, BLAH, BLAH.
POK.

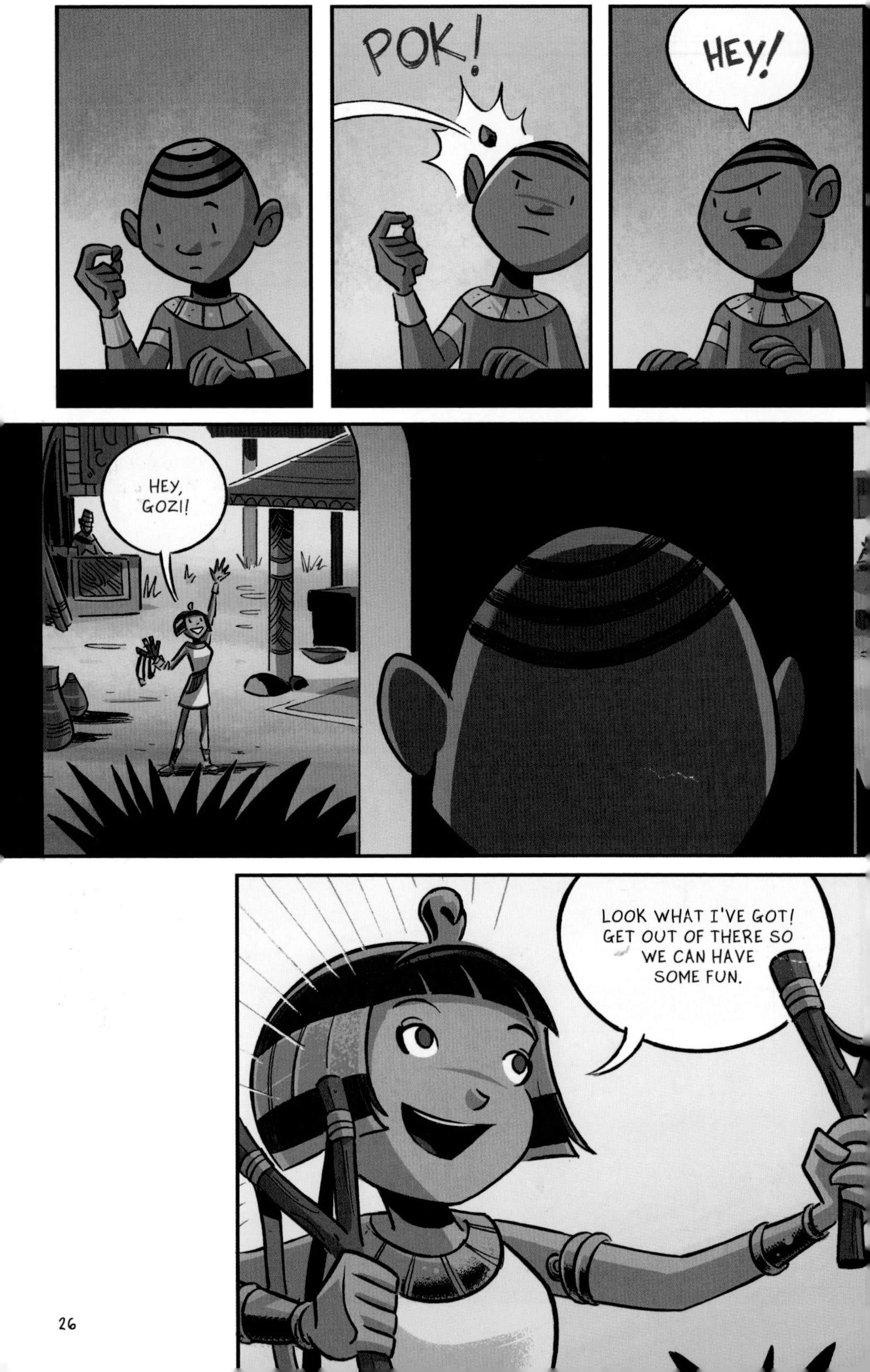
POK!
HEY!
HEY, GOZI!
LOOK WHAT I'VE GOT! GET OUT OF THERE SO WE CAN HAVE SOME FUN.

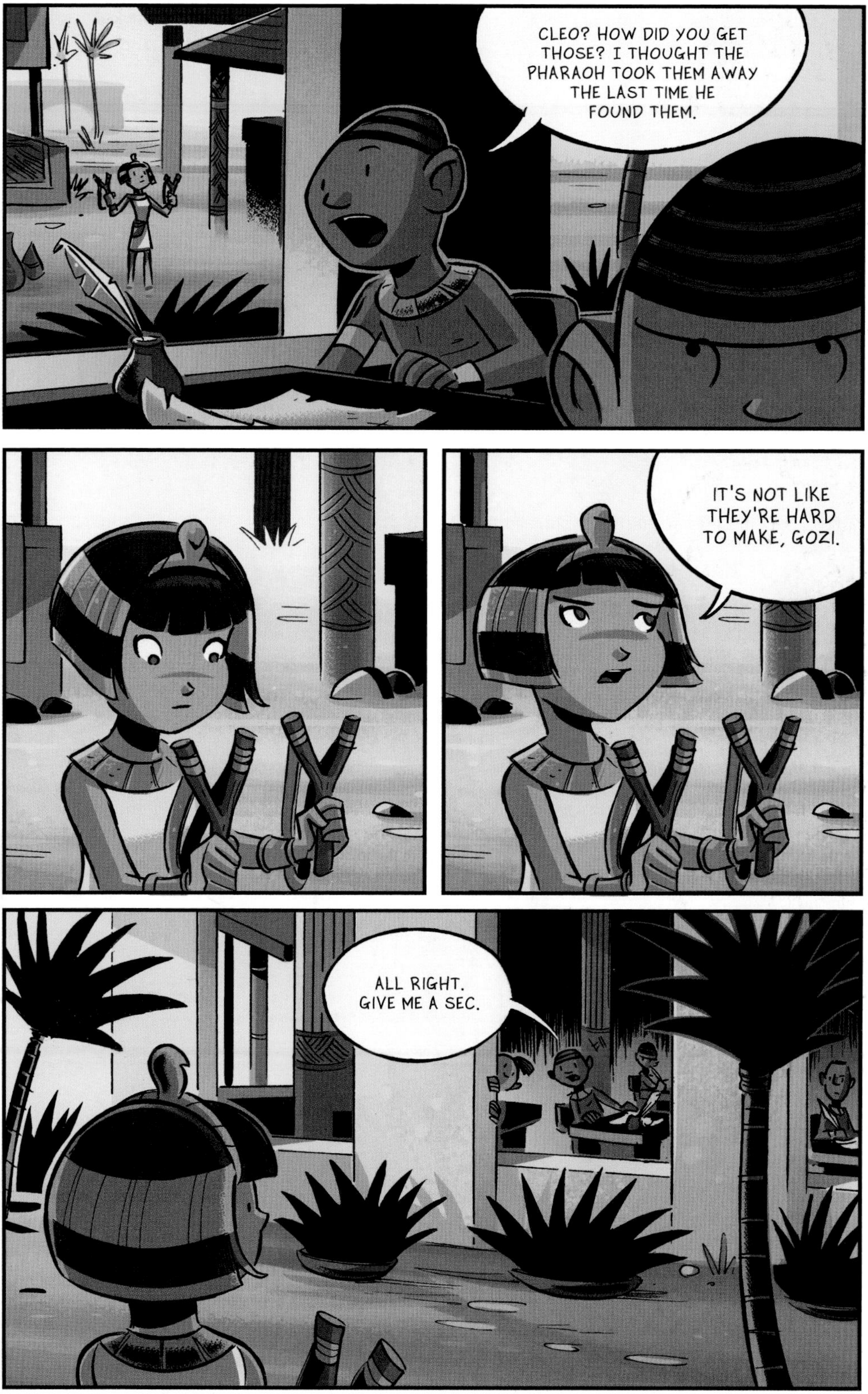
CLEO? HOW DID YOU GET THOSE? I THOUGHT THE PHARAOH TOOK THEM AWAY THE LAST TIME HE FOUND THEM.
IT'S NOT LIKE THEY'RE HARD TO MAKE, GOZI.
ALL RIGHT. GIVE ME A SEC.

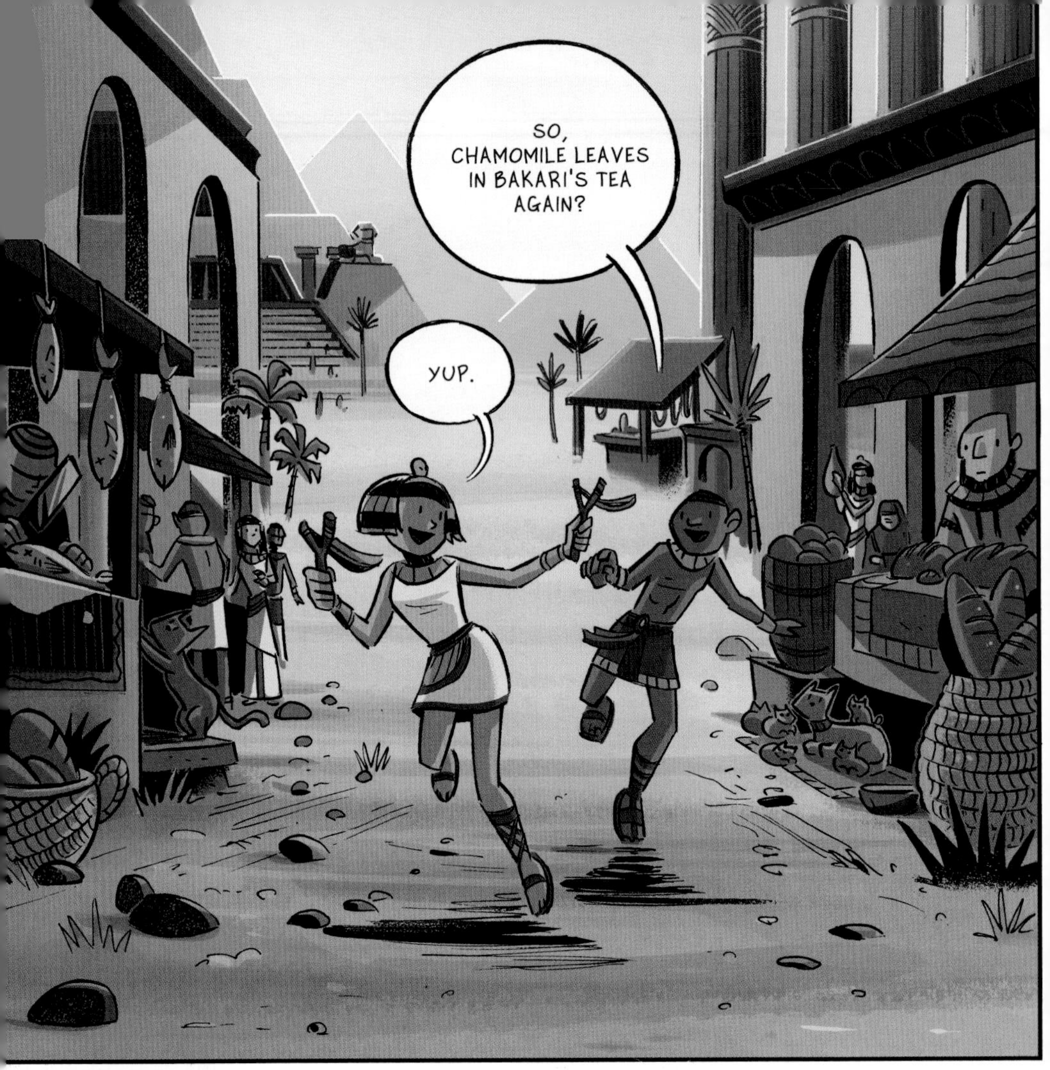
SO, CHAMOMILE LEAVES IN BAKARI'S TEA AGAIN?
YUP.

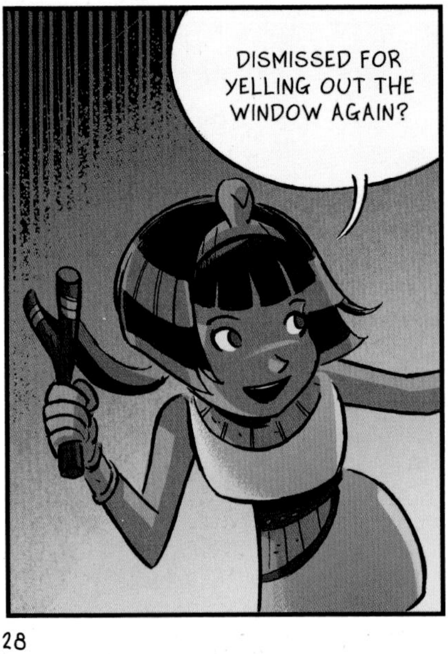
DISMISSED FOR YELLING OUT THE WINDOW AGAIN?

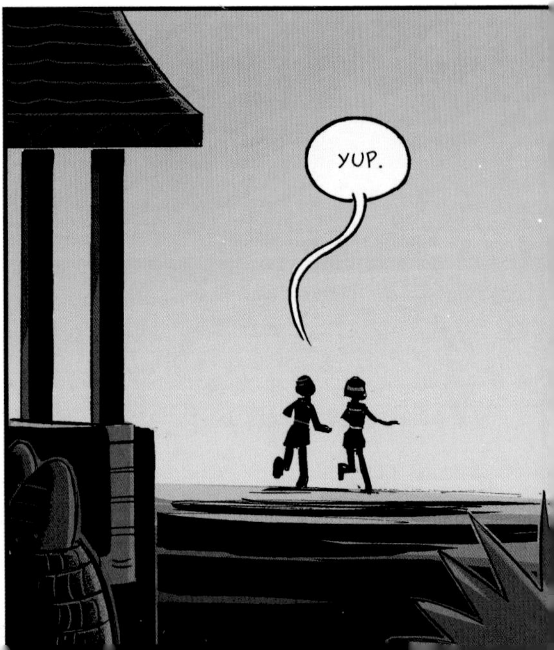
YUP.

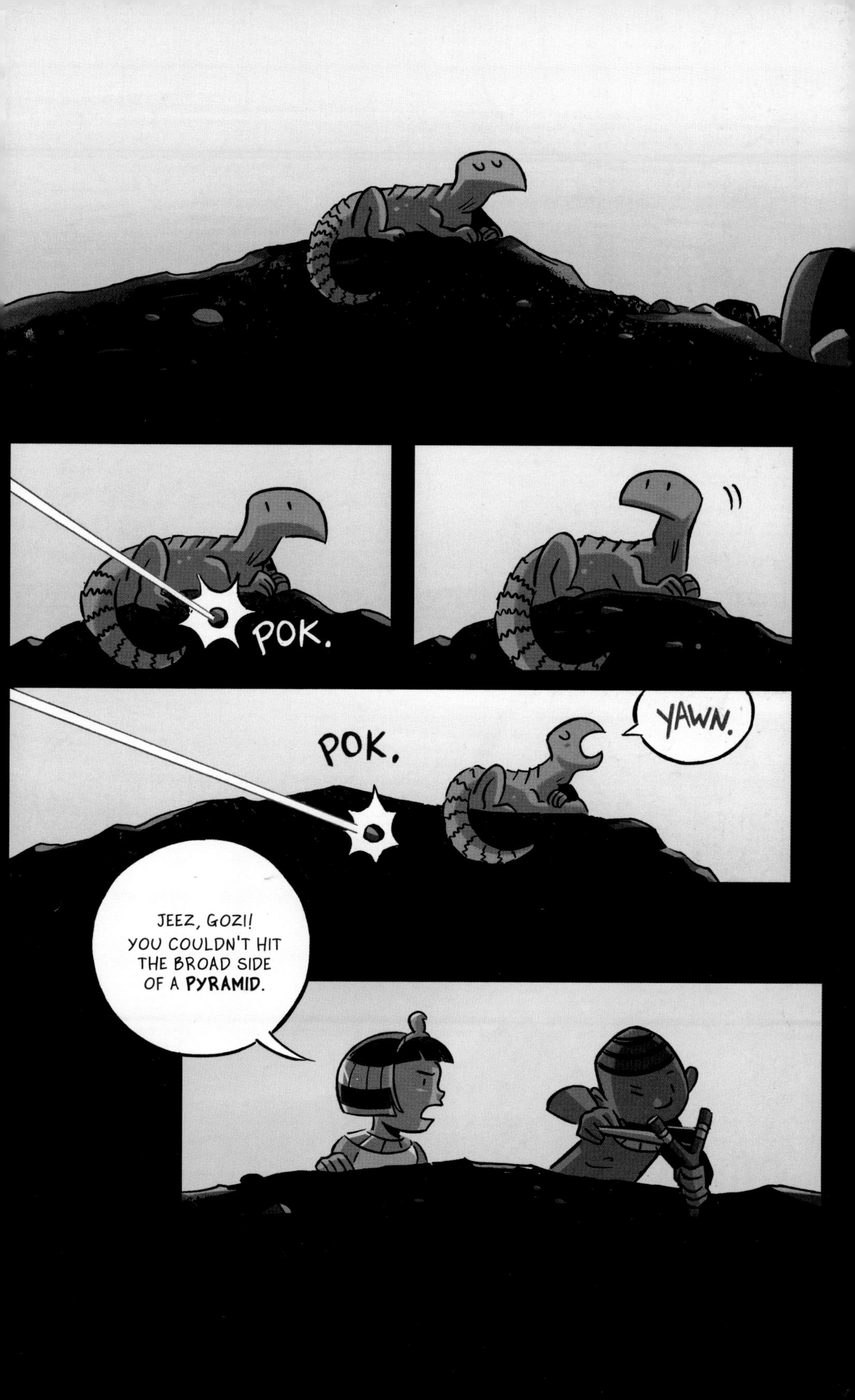
POK.
POK.
YAWN.
JEEZ, GOZI! YOU COULDN'T HIT THE BROAD SIDE OF A PYRAMID.

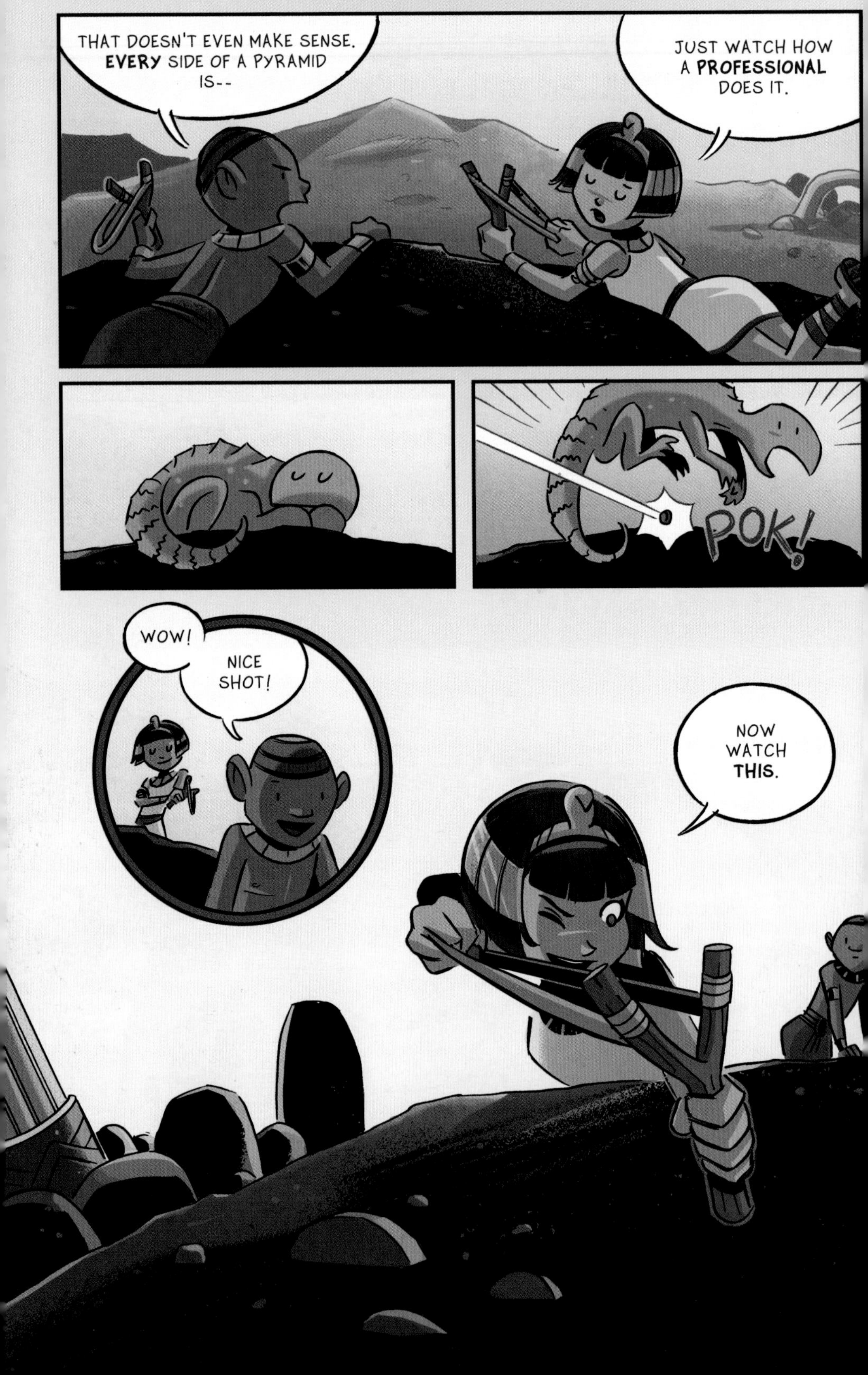
THAT DOESN'T EVEN MAKE SENSE. **EVERY** SIDE OF A PYRAMID IS--
JUST WATCH HOW A **PROFESSIONAL** DOES IT.
POK!
WOW!
NICE SHOT!
NOW WATCH **THIS**.

POK
POK
POK
POK
POK

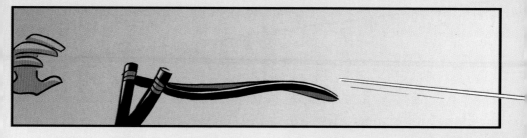

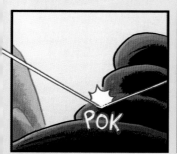

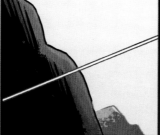

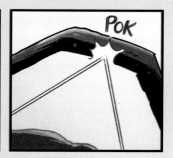

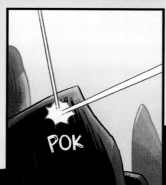

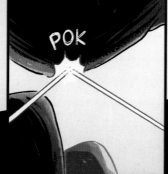

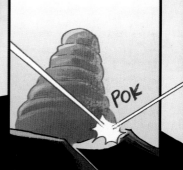

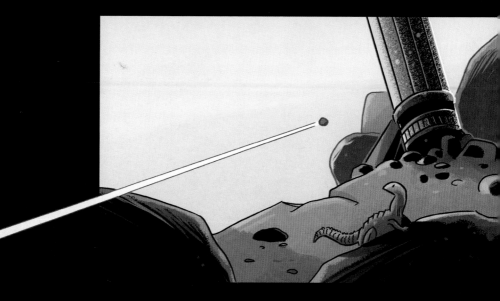

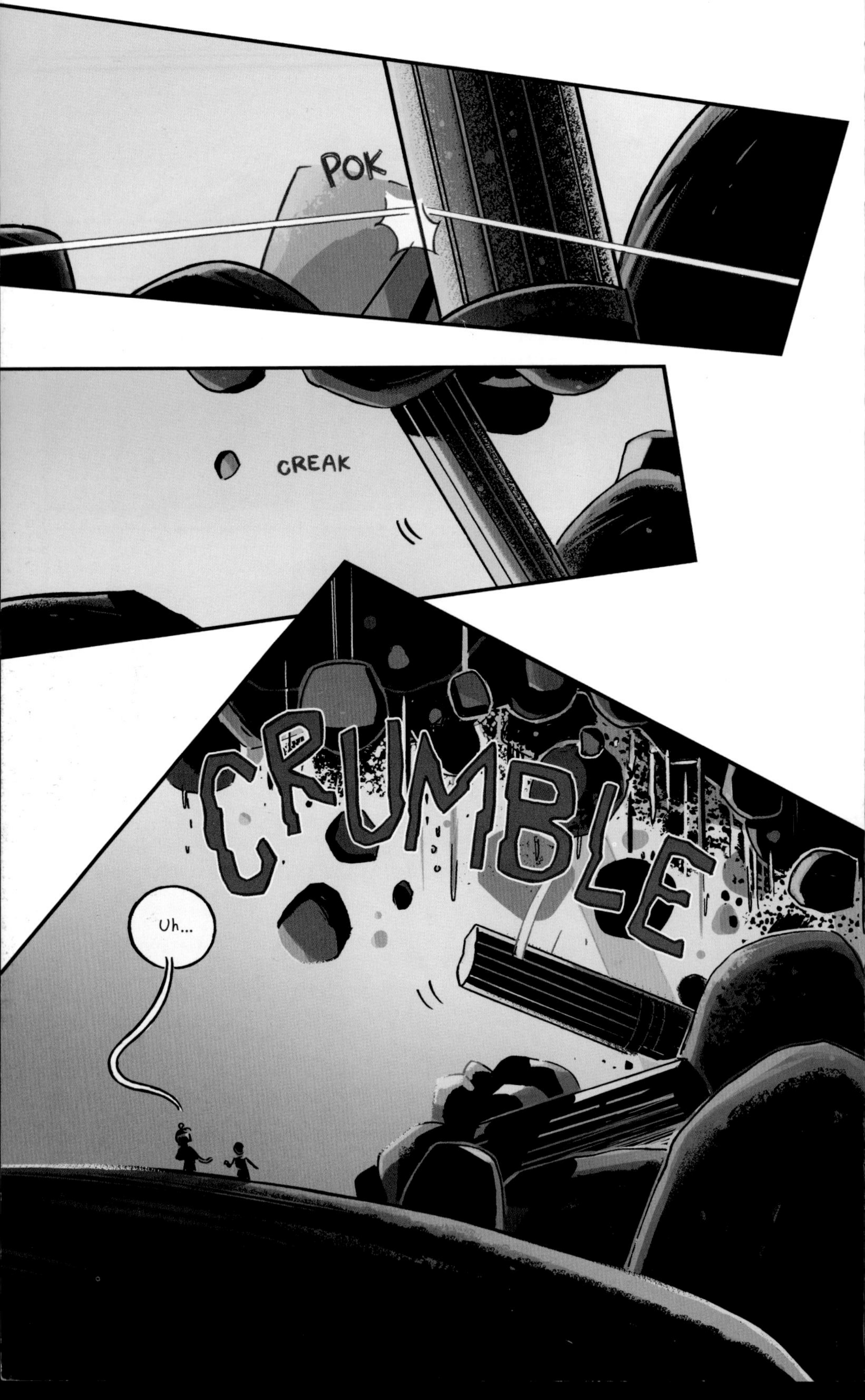
POK
CREAK
CRUMBLE
Uh...

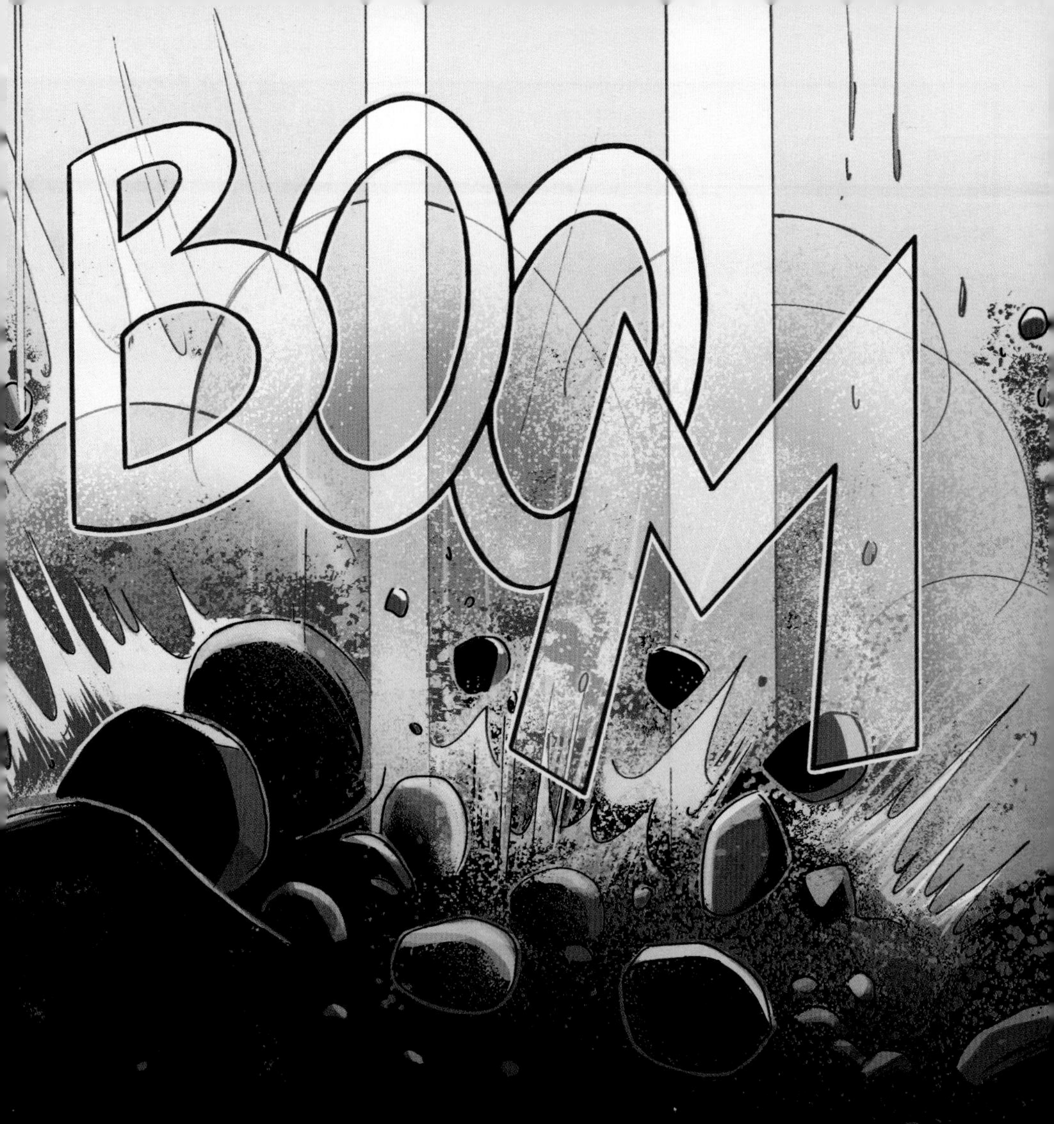
BOOM

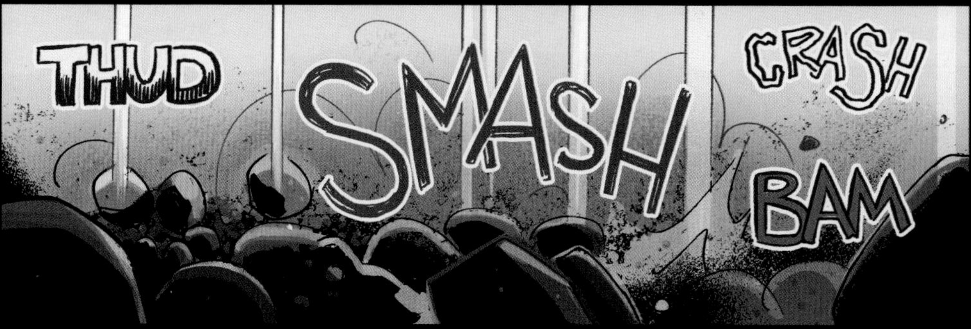
THUD
SMASH
CRASH
BAM

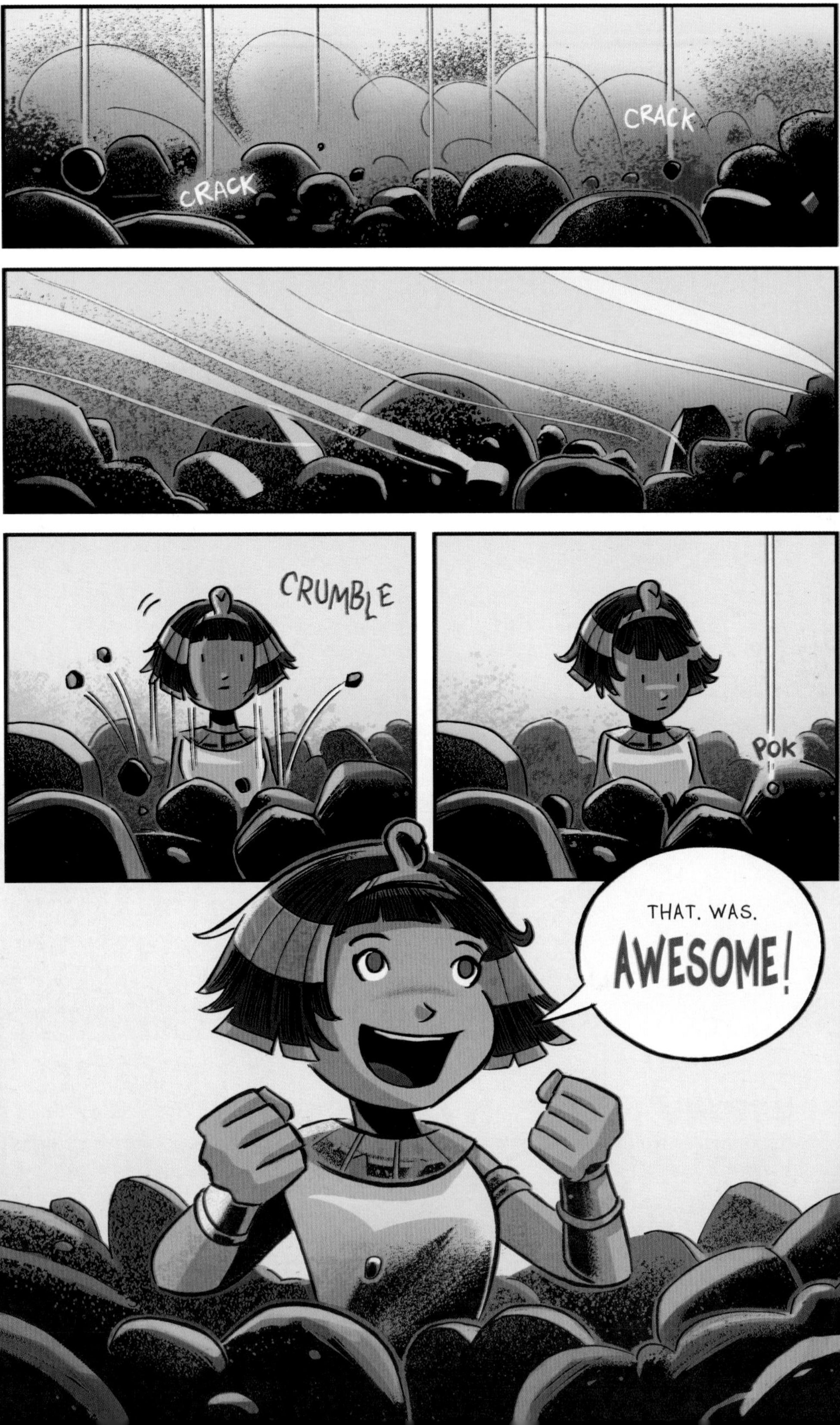
CRACK
CRACK
CRUMBLE
POK
THAT. WAS.
AWESOME!

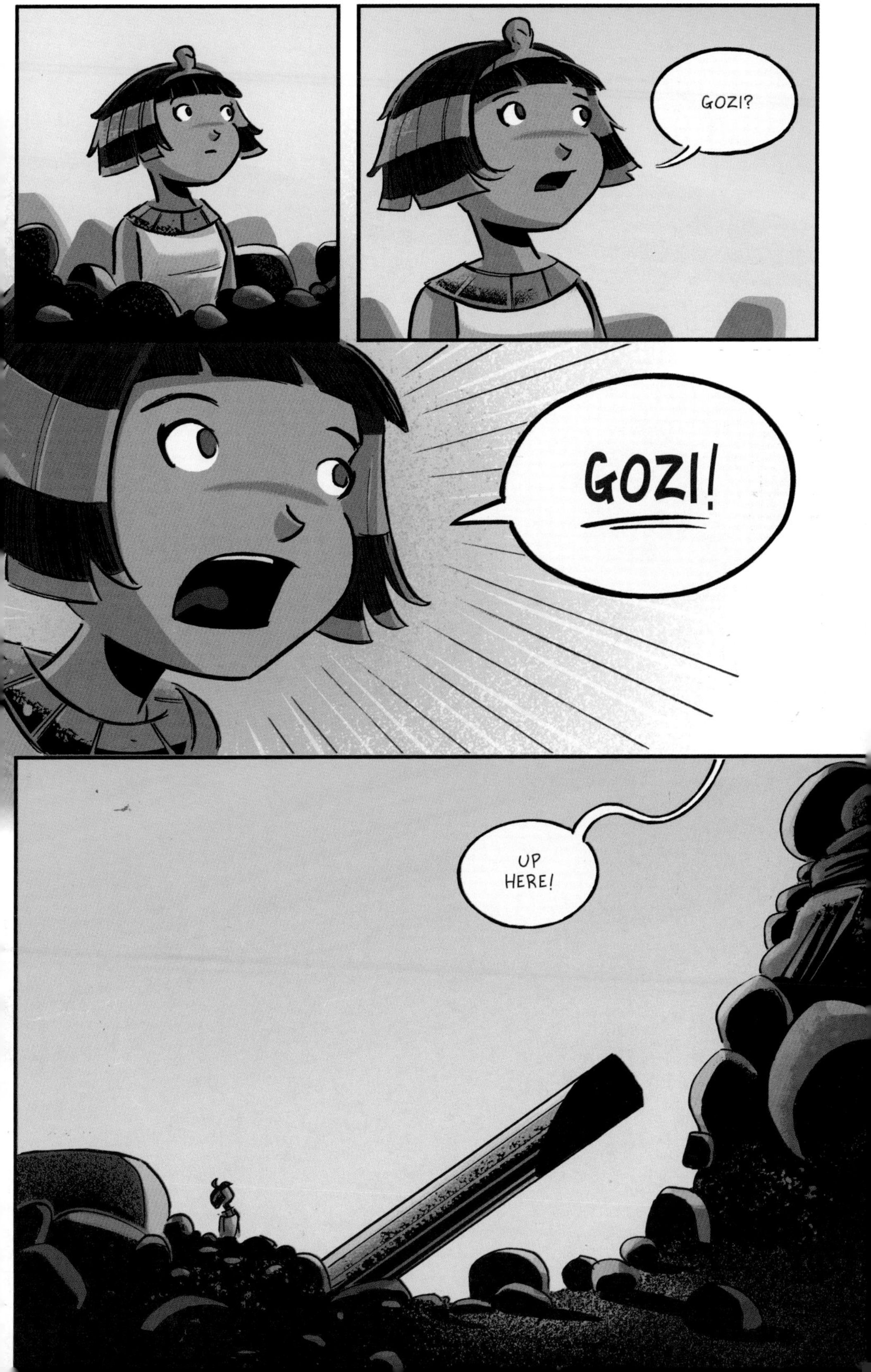
GOZI?
GOZI!
UP HERE!

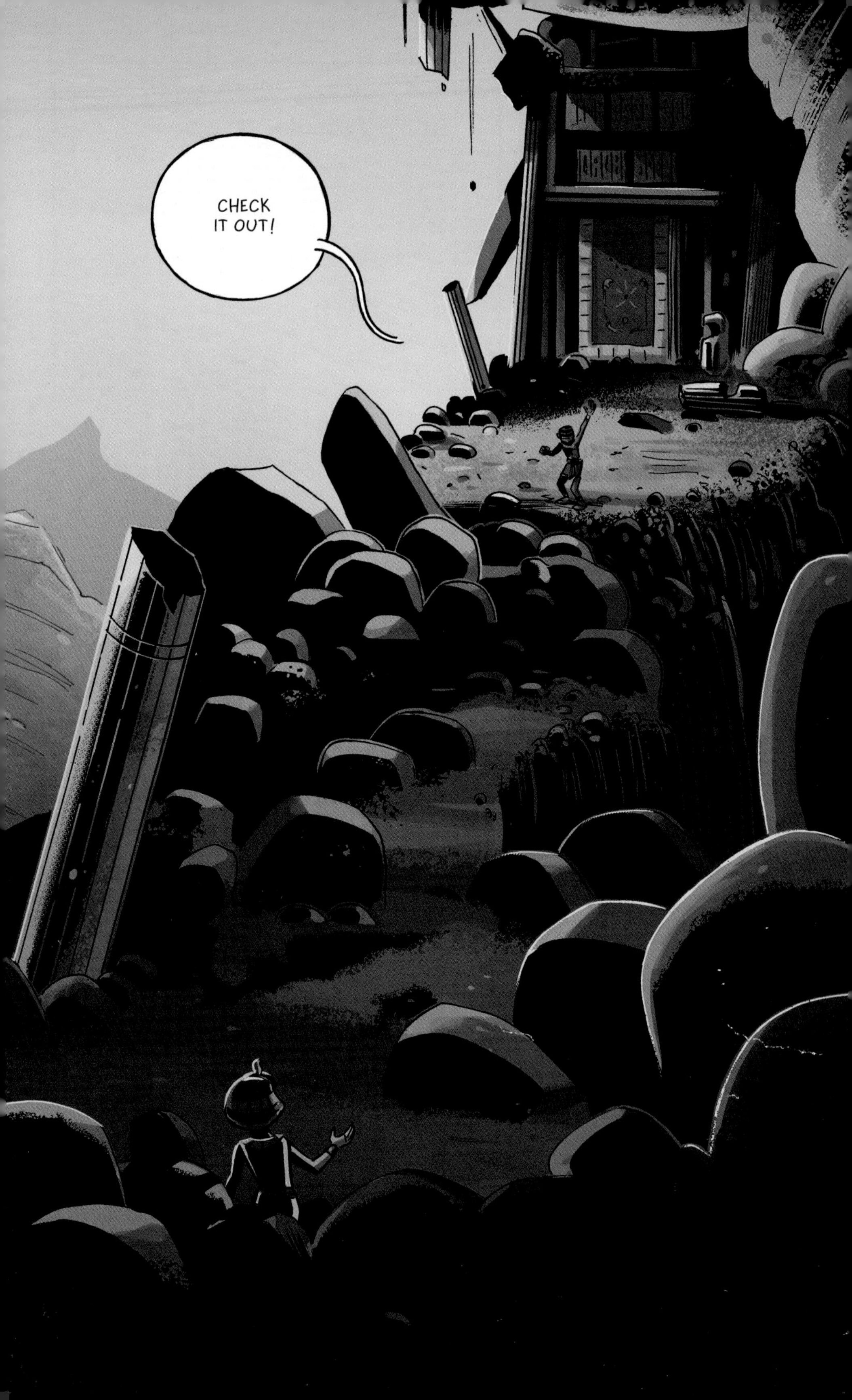
CHECK IT OUT!

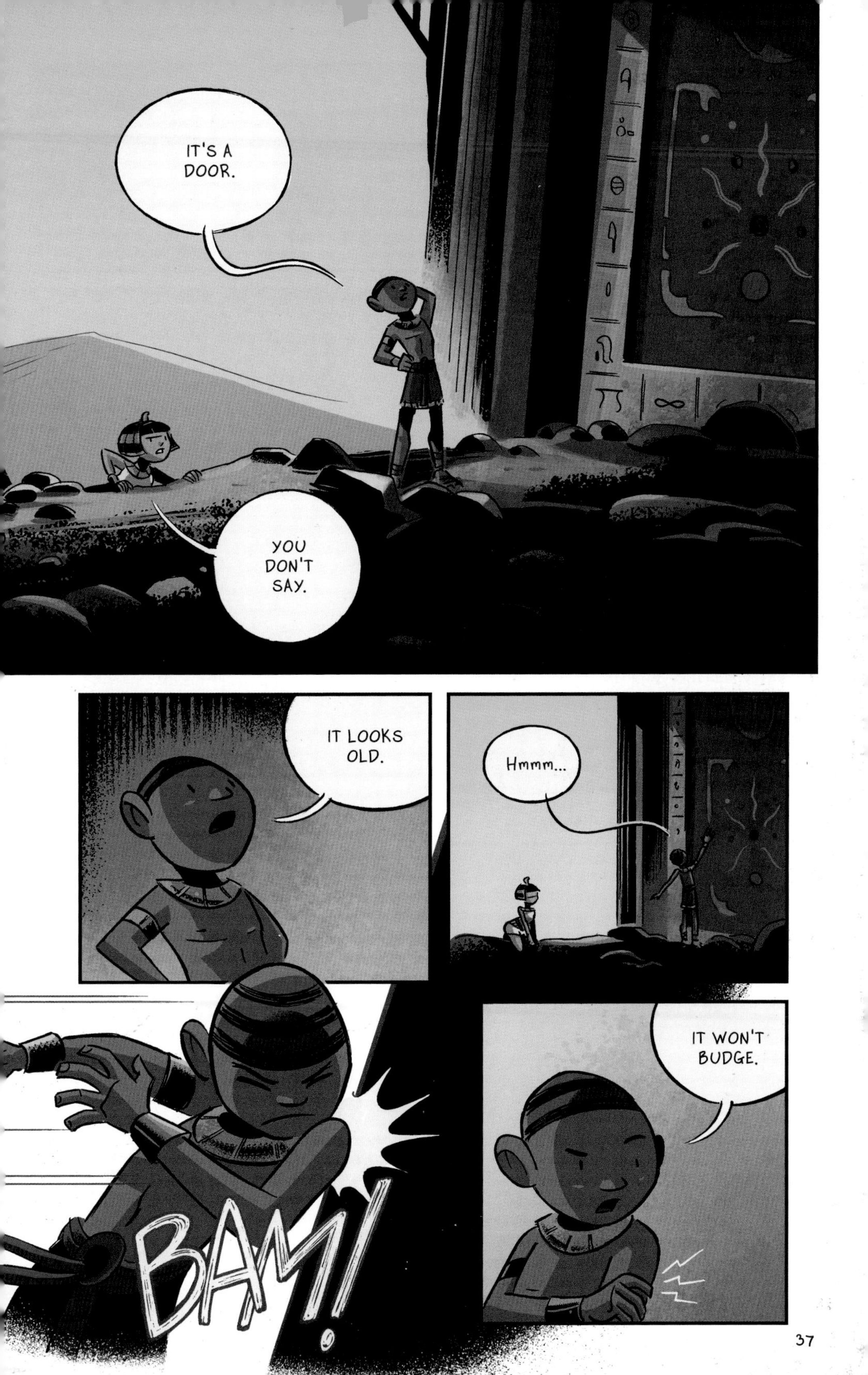
IT'S A DOOR.
YOU DON'T SAY.
IT LOOKS OLD.
Hmmm...
BAM!
IT WON'T BUDGE.

HERE.

LET **ME** SEE.

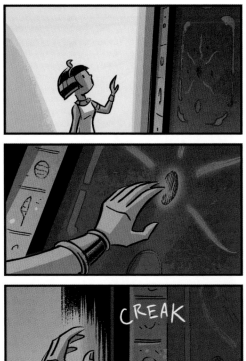

CREAK

SWING

HUH.

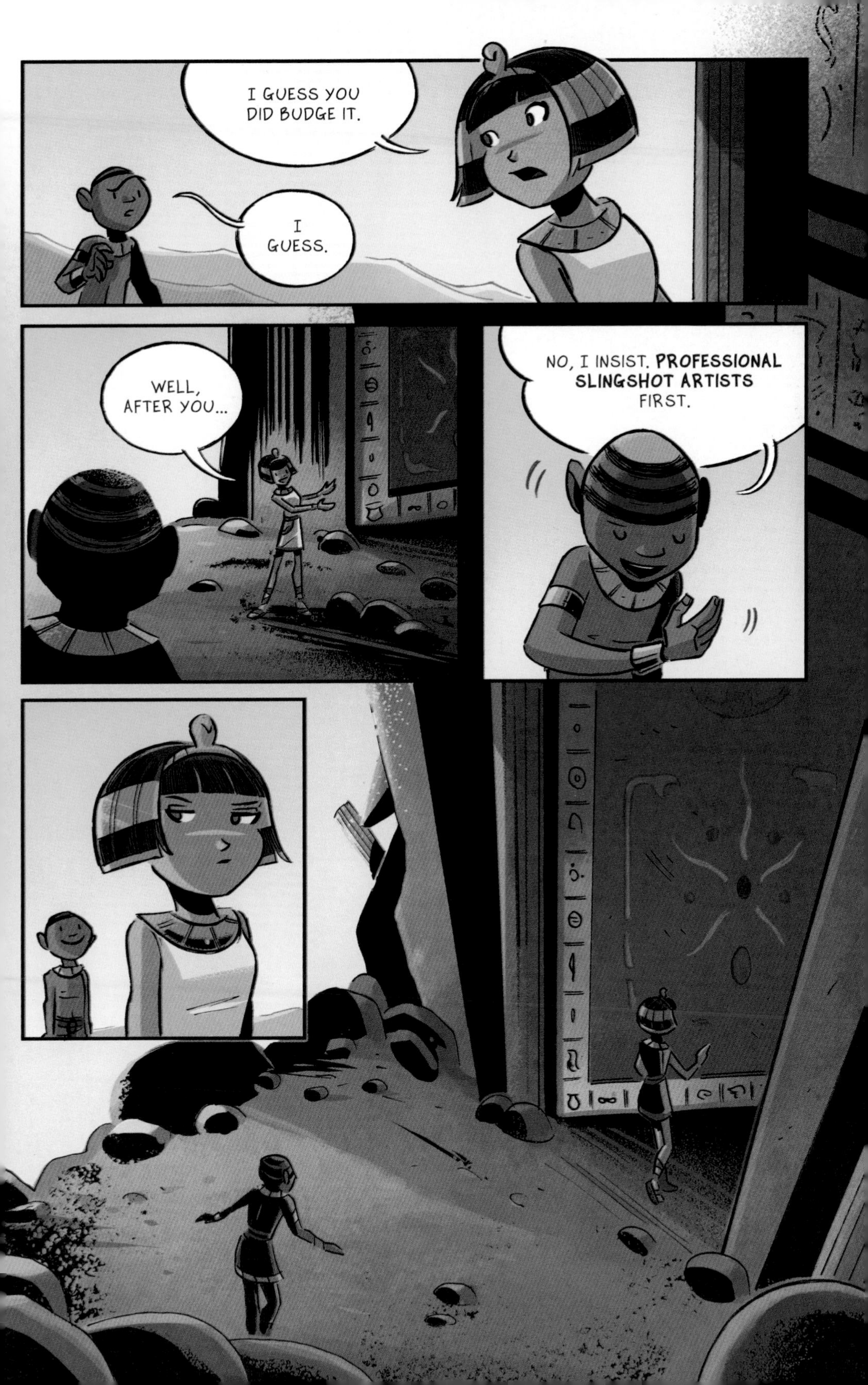
I GUESS YOU DID BUDGE IT.
I GUESS.
WELL, AFTER YOU...
NO, I INSIST. **PROFESSIONAL SLINGSHOT ARTISTS** FIRST.

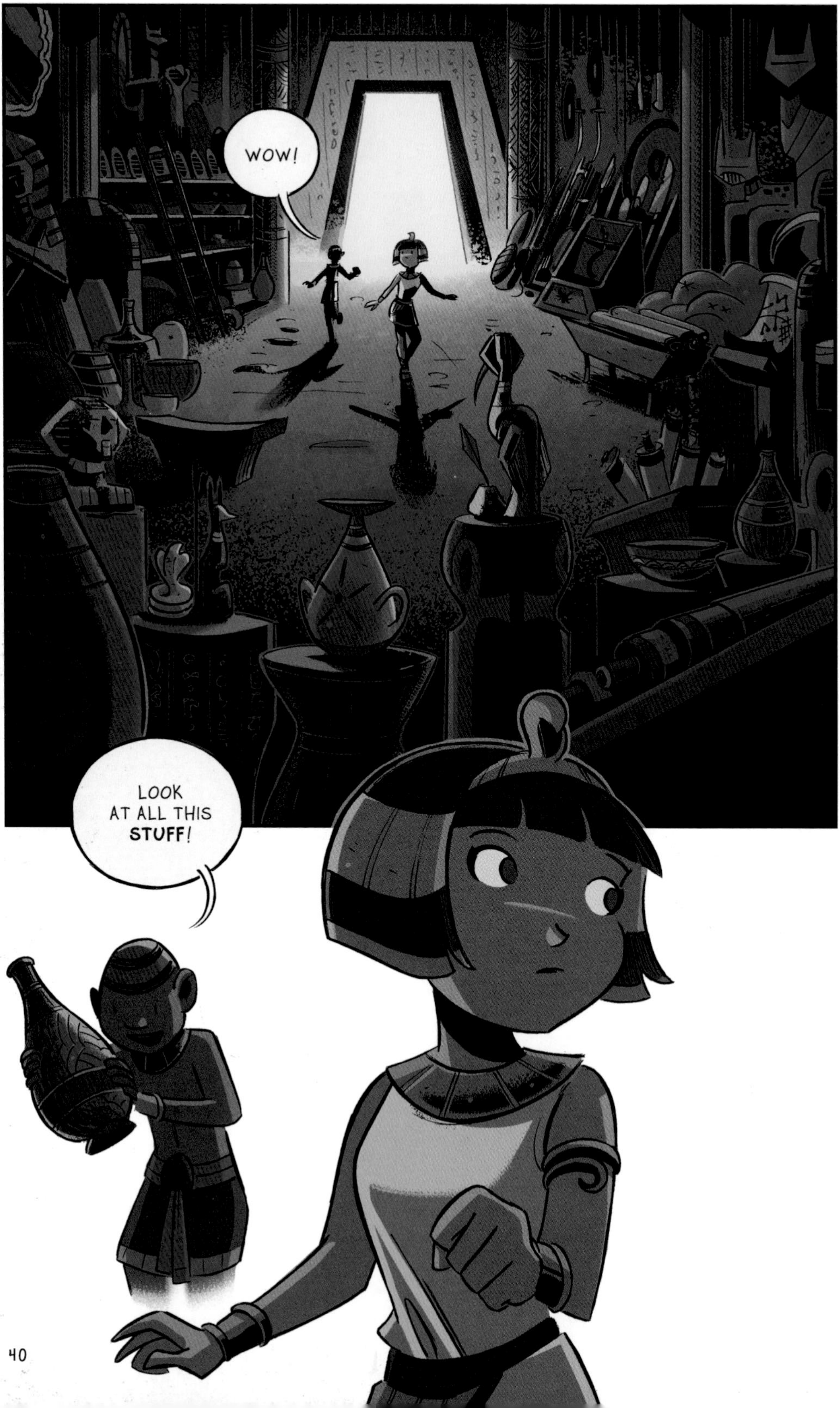
WOW!
LOOK AT ALL THIS **STUFF**!

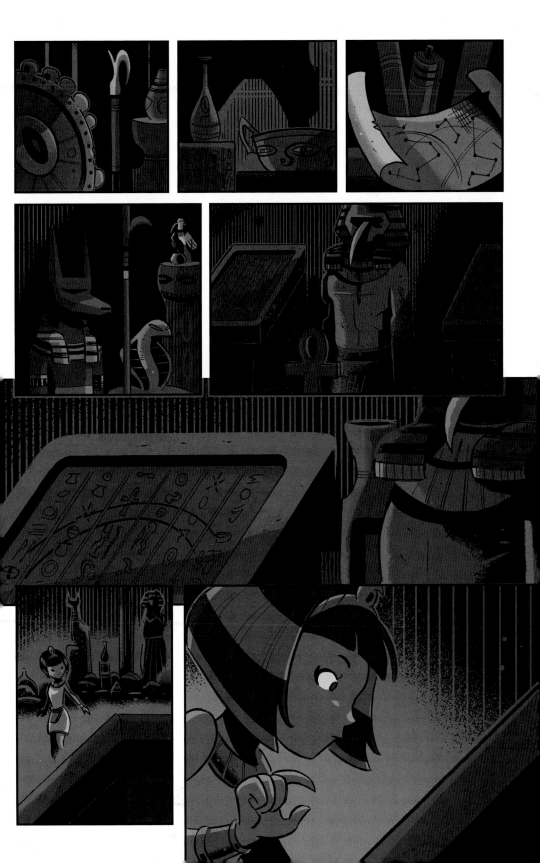

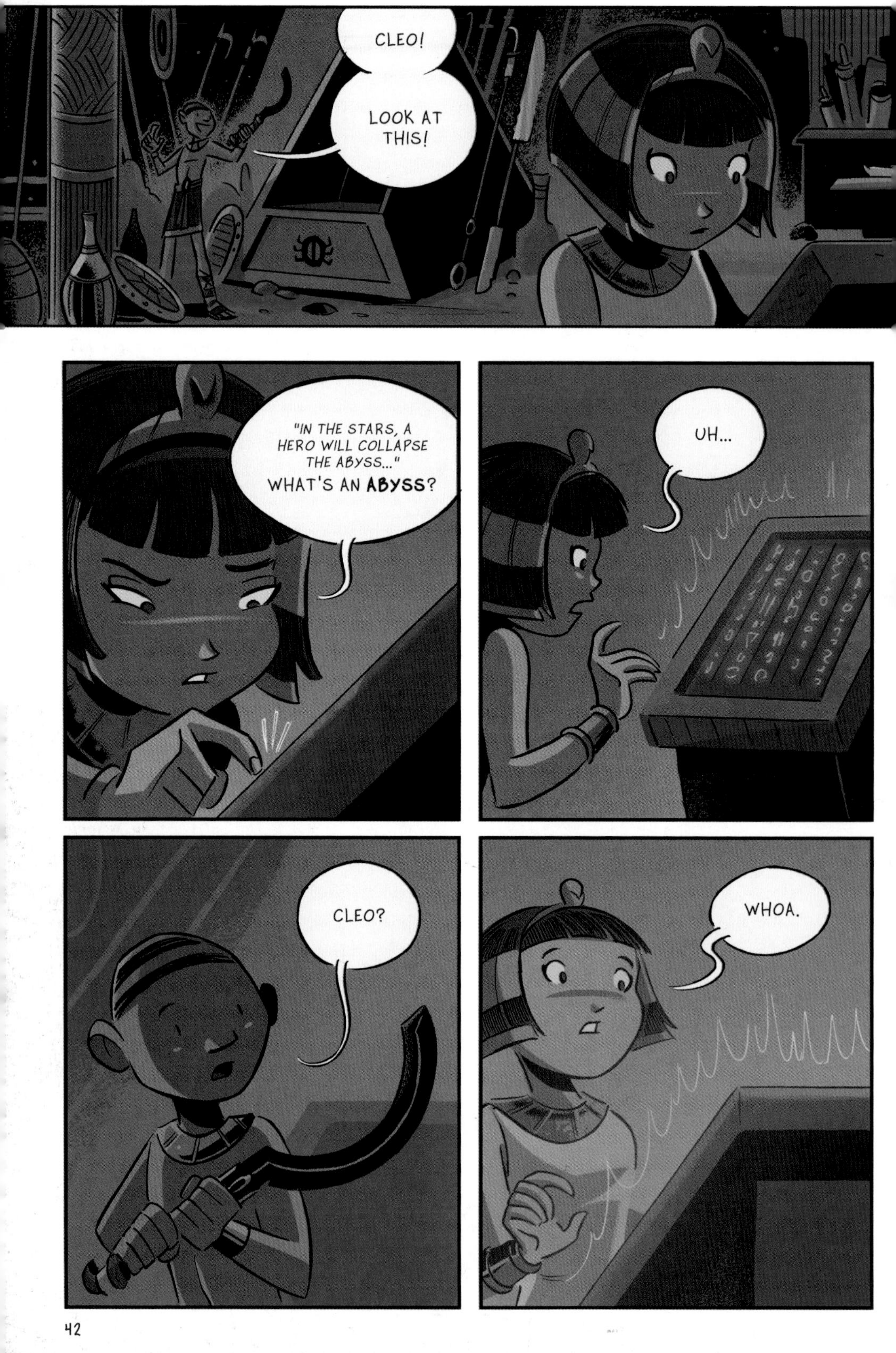
CLEO!
LOOK AT THIS!
"IN THE STARS, A HERO WILL COLLAPSE THE ABYSS..." WHAT'S AN **ABYSS**?
UH...
CLEO?
WHOA.

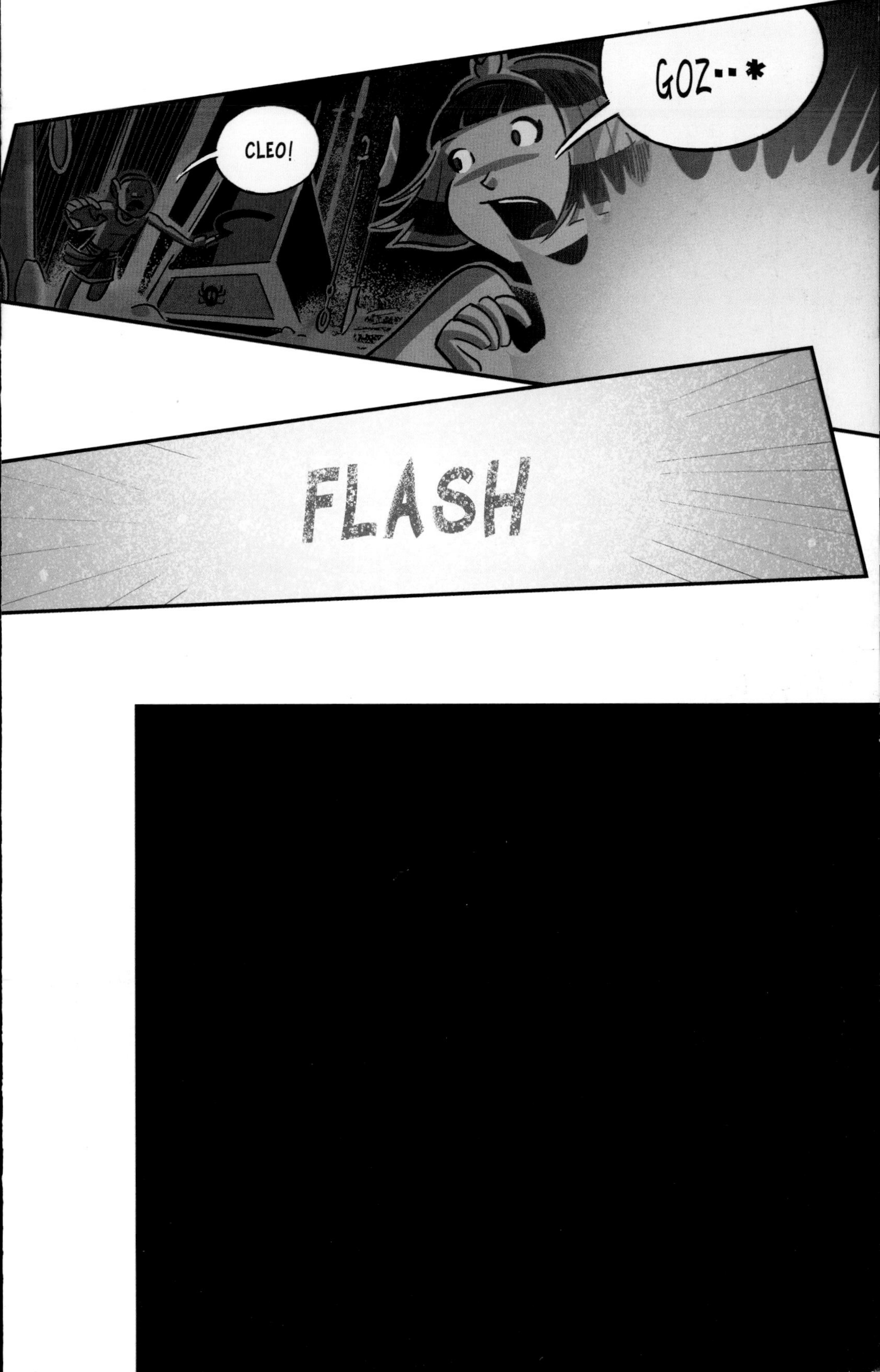
CLEO!
GOZ..*
FLASH

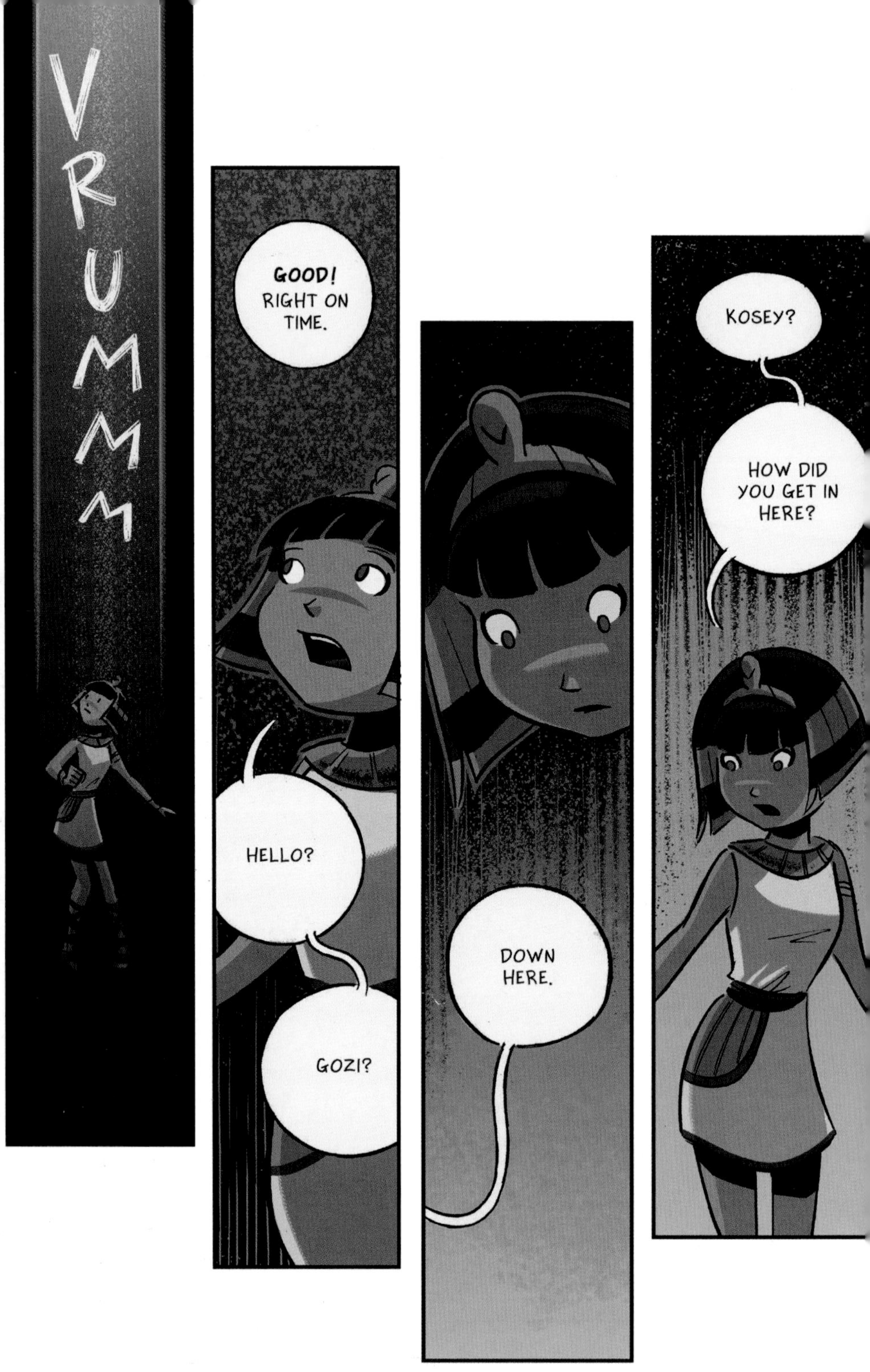
VRUMMM
GOOD! RIGHT ON TIME.
HELLO?
GOZI?
DOWN HERE.
KOSEY?
HOW DID YOU GET IN HERE?

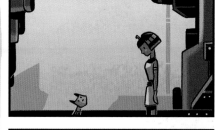

ACTUALLY, THE NAME'S **KHENSU**. BUT I DID HAVE A GREAT-GREAT-GREAT-MANY GREATS-GRANDFATHER NAMED KOSEY.

TALKING. CAT.

I'M **DEAD**, AREN'T I?

DEAD? WHAT?

NO, YOU'RE--

AH! SHE'S **HERE**.

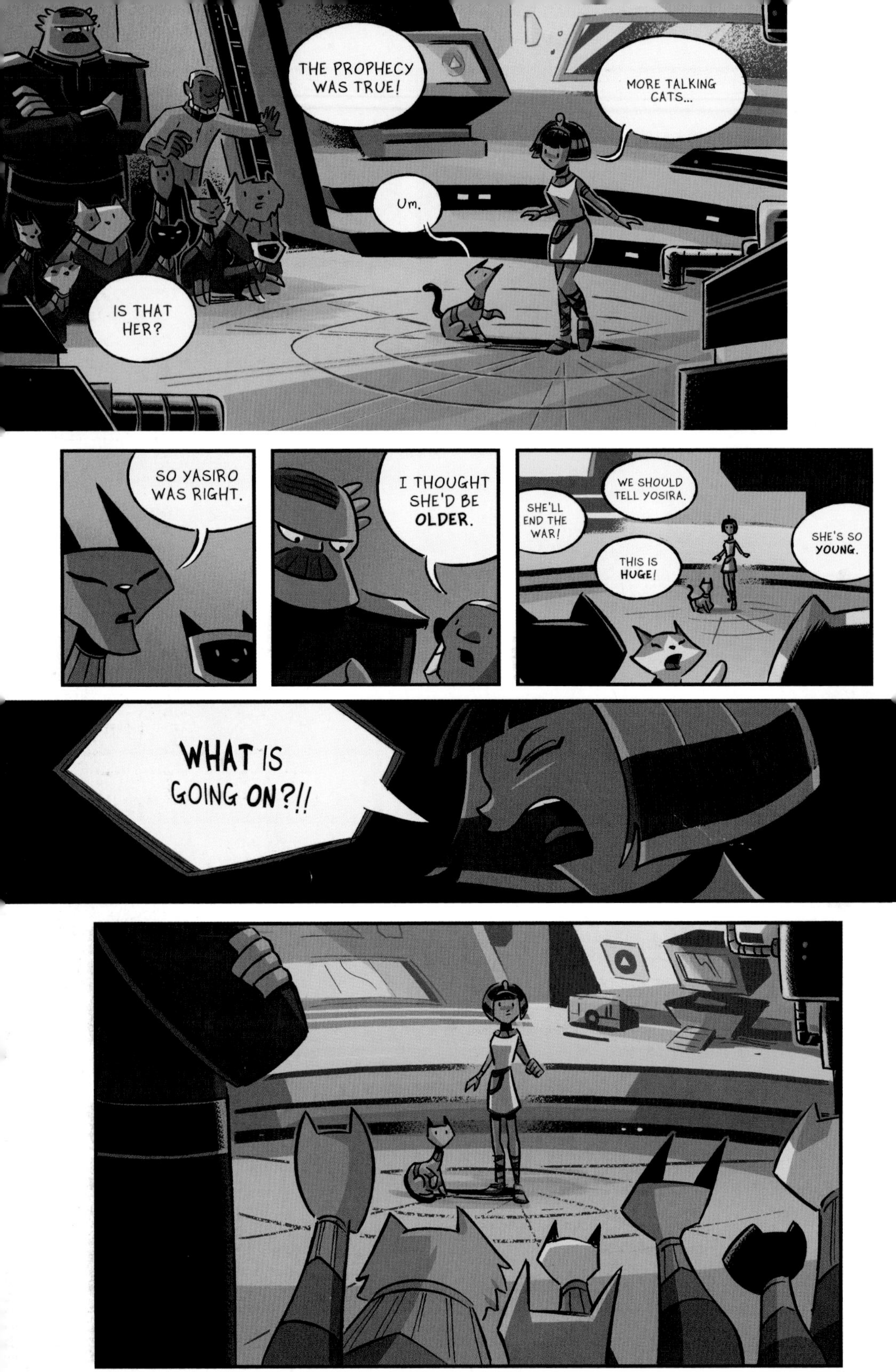
THE PROPHECY WAS TRUE!
MORE TALKING CATS...
Um.
IS THAT HER?
SO YASIRO WAS RIGHT.
I THOUGHT SHE'D BE **OLDER**.
WE SHOULD TELL YOSIRA.
SHE'LL END THE WAR!
THIS IS **HUGE**!
SHE'S SO **YOUNG**.
WHAT IS GOING **ON**?!!

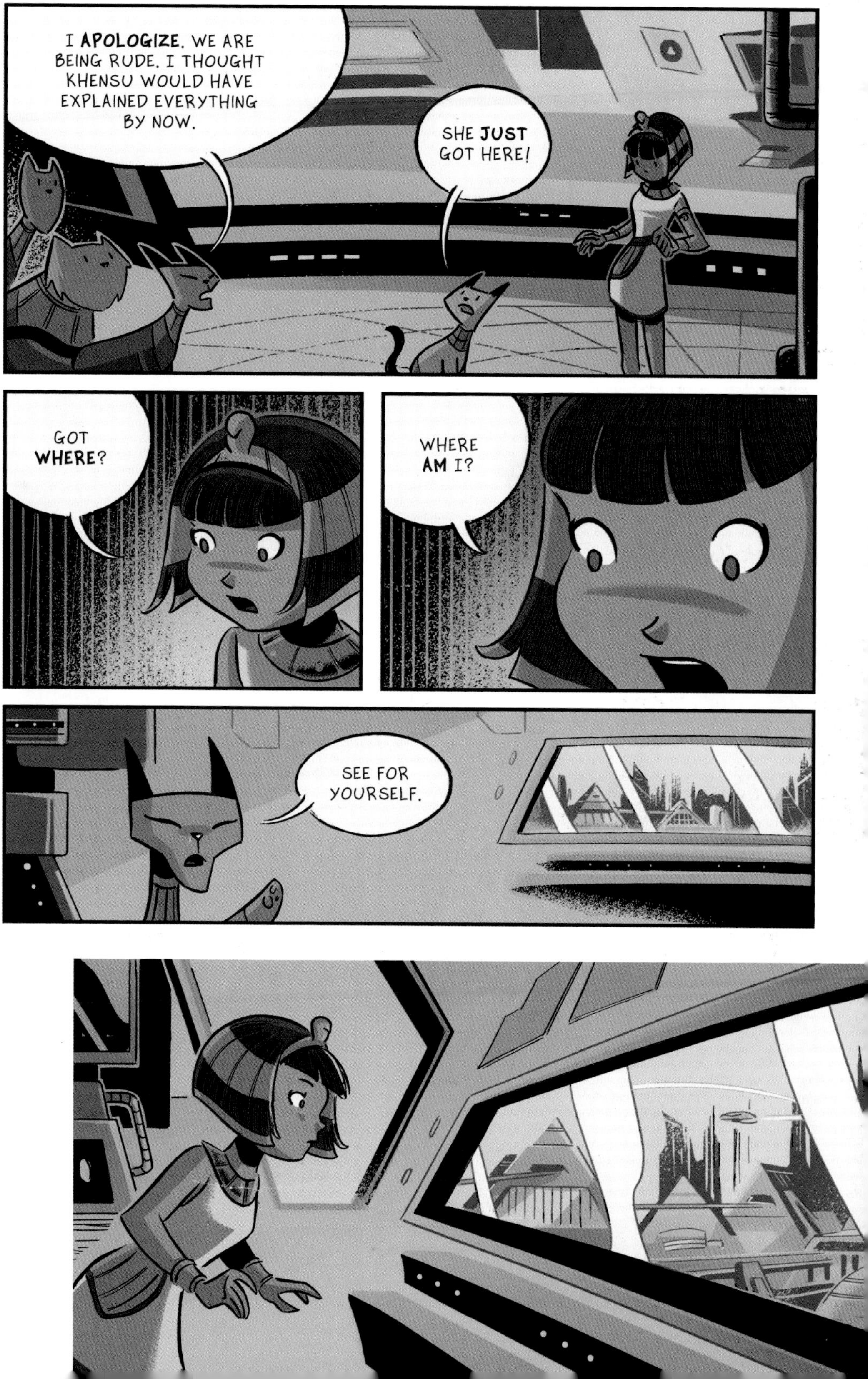
I **APOLOGIZE.** WE ARE BEING RUDE. I THOUGHT KHENSU WOULD HAVE EXPLAINED EVERYTHING BY NOW.
SHE **JUST** GOT HERE!
GOT **WHERE**?
WHERE **AM** I?
SEE FOR YOURSELF.

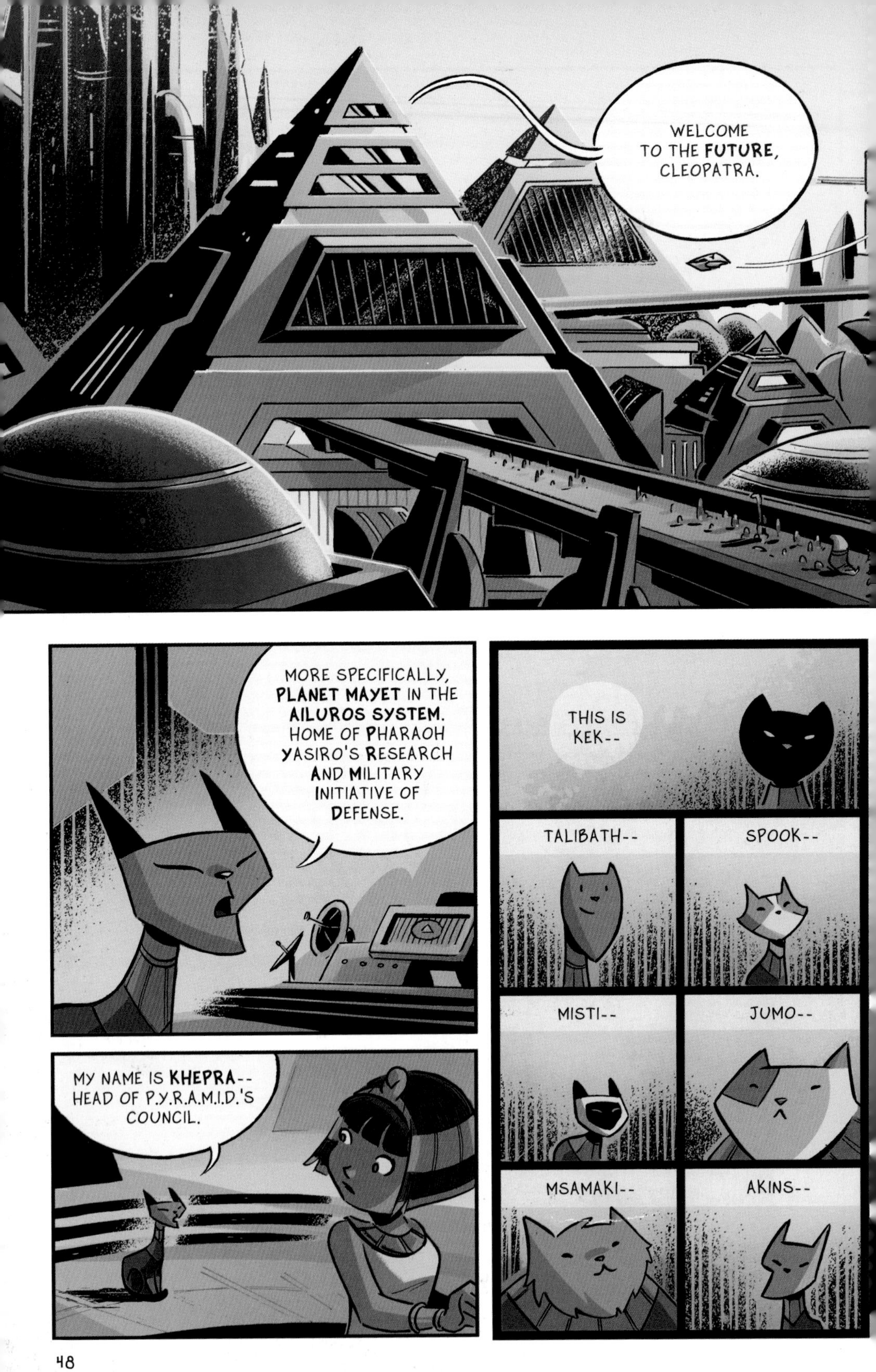
WELCOME TO THE **FUTURE**, CLEOPATRA.
MORE SPECIFICALLY, **PLANET MAYET** IN THE **AILUROS SYSTEM**. HOME OF PHARAOH YASIRO'S RESEARCH AND MILITARY INITIATIVE OF DEFENSE.
THIS IS KEK--
TALIBATH--
SPOOK--
MISTI--
JUMO--
MY NAME IS **KHEPRA**-- HEAD OF P.Y.R.A.M.I.D.'S COUNCIL.
MSAMAKI--
AKINS--

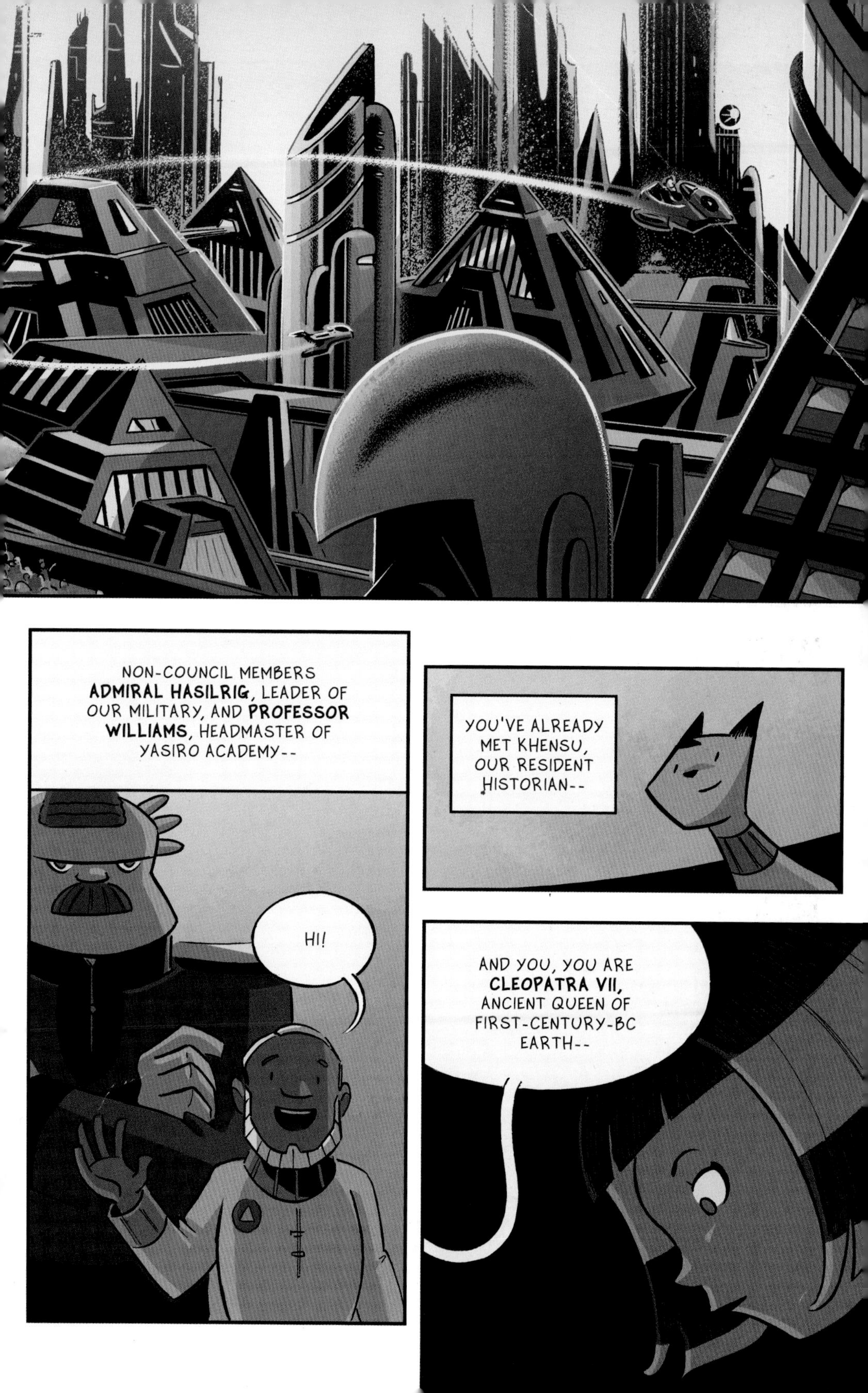

NON-COUNCIL MEMBERS **ADMIRAL HASILRIG**, LEADER OF OUR MILITARY, AND **PROFESSOR WILLIAMS**, HEADMASTER OF YASIRO ACADEMY--
HI!
YOU'VE ALREADY MET KHENSU, OUR RESIDENT HISTORIAN--
AND YOU, YOU ARE **CLEOPATRA VII,** ANCIENT QUEEN OF FIRST-CENTURY-BC EARTH--

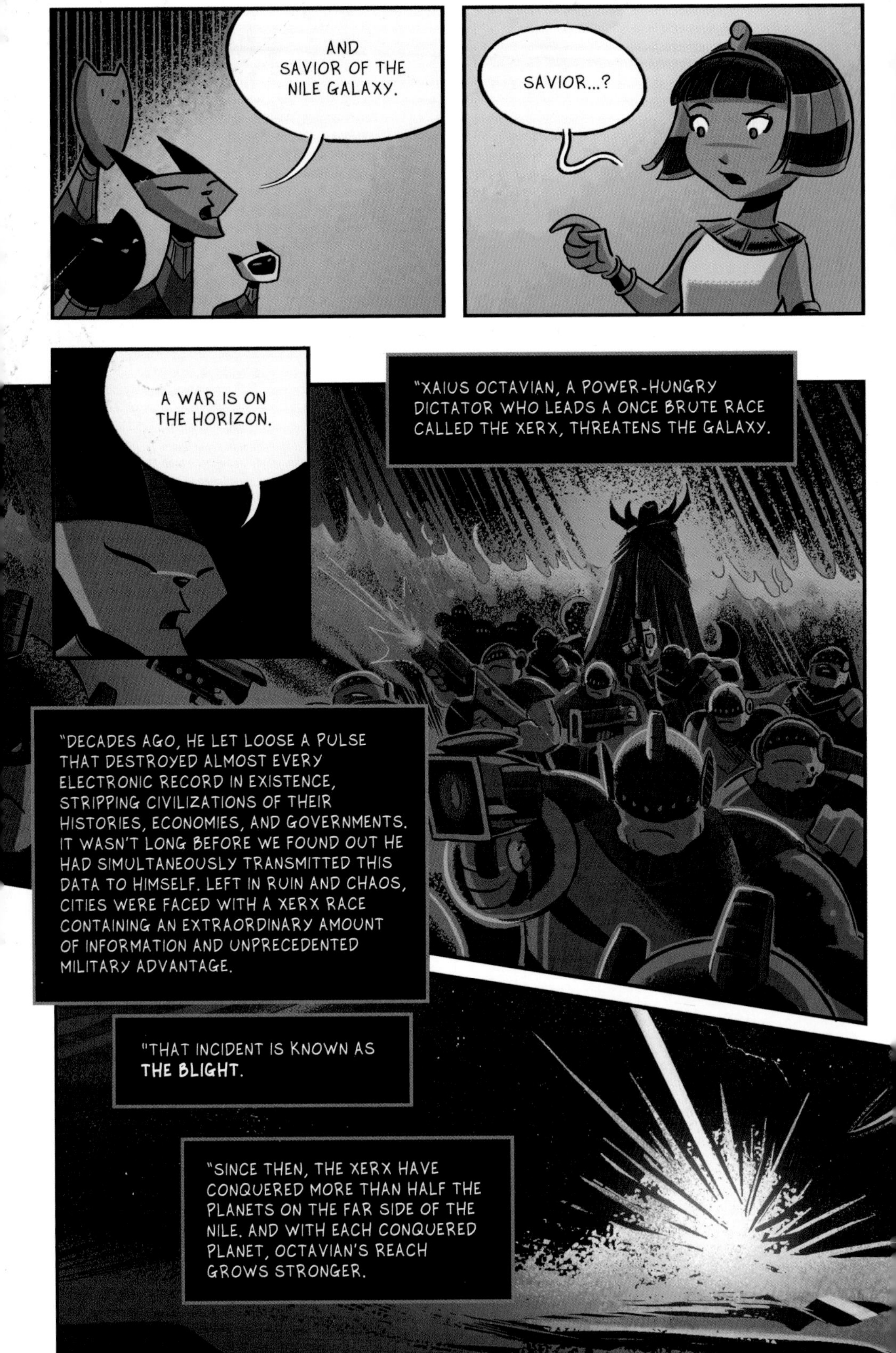
AND SAVIOR OF THE NILE GALAXY.
SAVIOR...?
A WAR IS ON THE HORIZON.
"XAIUS OCTAVIAN, A POWER-HUNGRY DICTATOR WHO LEADS A ONCE BRUTE RACE CALLED THE XERX, THREATENS THE GALAXY.
"DECADES AGO, HE LET LOOSE A PULSE THAT DESTROYED ALMOST EVERY ELECTRONIC RECORD IN EXISTENCE, STRIPPING CIVILIZATIONS OF THEIR HISTORIES, ECONOMIES, AND GOVERNMENTS. IT WASN'T LONG BEFORE WE FOUND OUT HE HAD SIMULTANEOUSLY TRANSMITTED THIS DATA TO HIMSELF. LEFT IN RUIN AND CHAOS, CITIES WERE FACED WITH A XERX RACE CONTAINING AN EXTRAORDINARY AMOUNT OF INFORMATION AND UNPRECEDENTED MILITARY ADVANTAGE.
"THAT INCIDENT IS KNOWN AS **THE BLIGHT**.
"SINCE THEN, THE XERX HAVE CONQUERED MORE THAN HALF THE PLANETS ON THE FAR SIDE OF THE NILE. AND WITH EACH CONQUERED PLANET, OCTAVIAN'S REACH GROWS STRONGER.

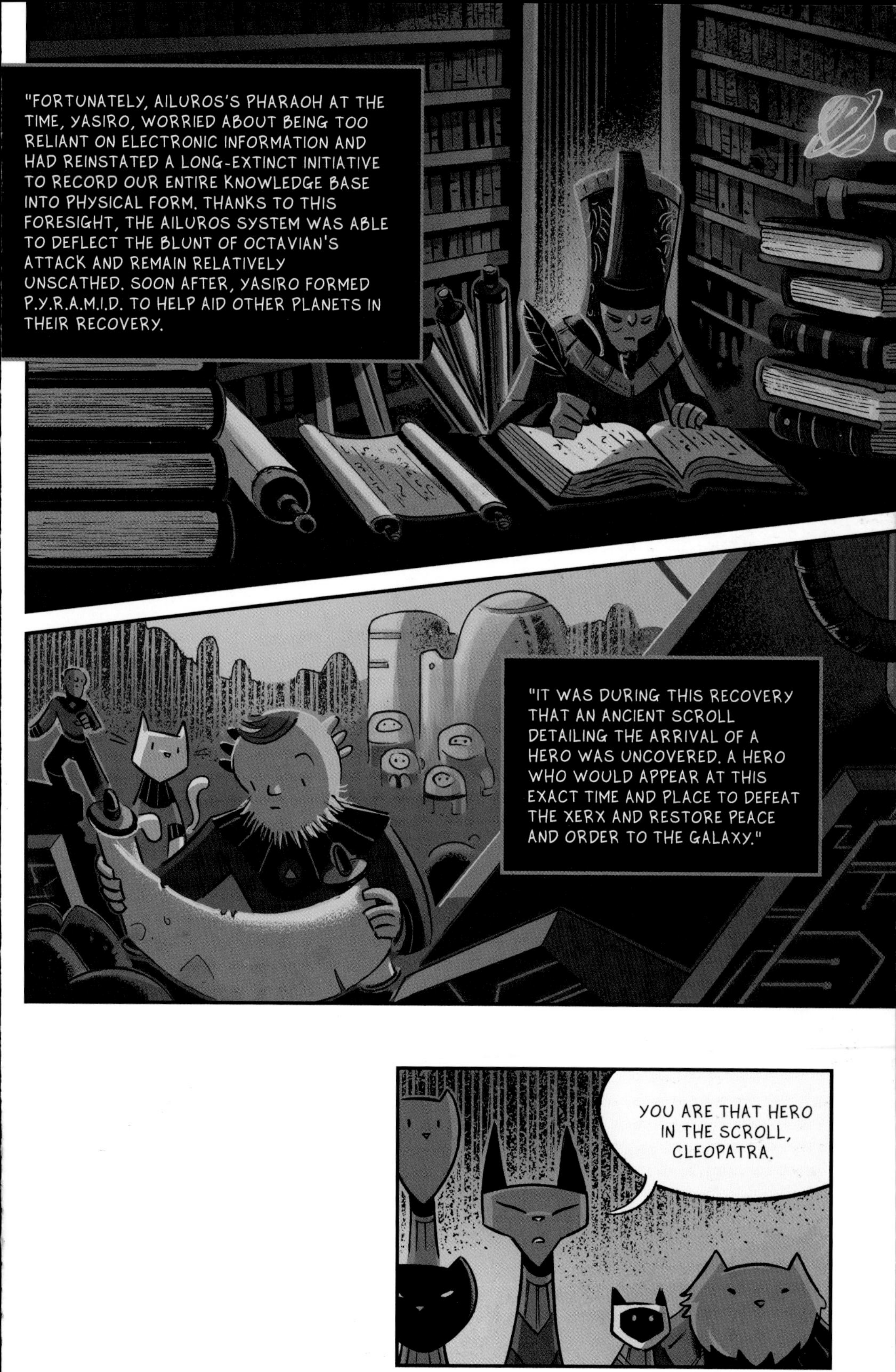
"FORTUNATELY, AILUROS'S PHARAOH AT THE TIME, YASIRO, WORRIED ABOUT BEING TOO RELIANT ON ELECTRONIC INFORMATION AND HAD REINSTATED A LONG-EXTINCT INITIATIVE TO RECORD OUR ENTIRE KNOWLEDGE BASE INTO PHYSICAL FORM. THANKS TO THIS FORESIGHT, THE AILUROS SYSTEM WAS ABLE TO DEFLECT THE BLUNT OF OCTAVIAN'S ATTACK AND REMAIN RELATIVELY UNSCATHED. SOON AFTER, YASIRO FORMED P.Y.R.A.M.I.D. TO HELP AID OTHER PLANETS IN THEIR RECOVERY.
"IT WAS DURING THIS RECOVERY THAT AN ANCIENT SCROLL DETAILING THE ARRIVAL OF A HERO WAS UNCOVERED. A HERO WHO WOULD APPEAR AT THIS EXACT TIME AND PLACE TO DEFEAT THE XERX AND RESTORE PEACE AND ORDER TO THE GALAXY."
YOU ARE THAT HERO IN THE SCROLL, CLEOPATRA.

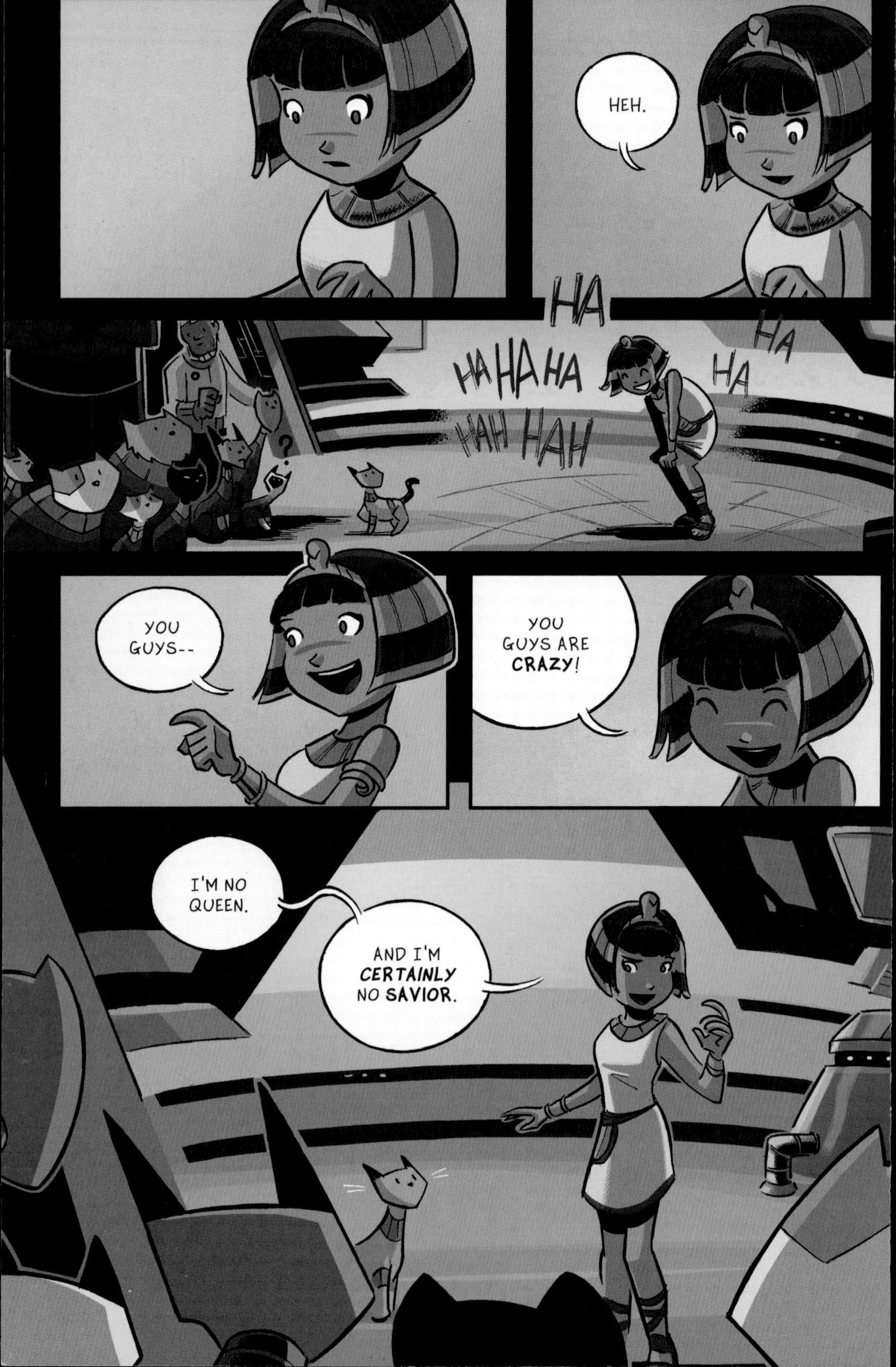
HEH.
HA
HAHAHA
HA
HA
HAH HAH
?
YOU GUYS--
YOU GUYS ARE **CRAZY**!
I'M NO QUEEN.
AND I'M **CERTAINLY** NO **SAVIOR**.

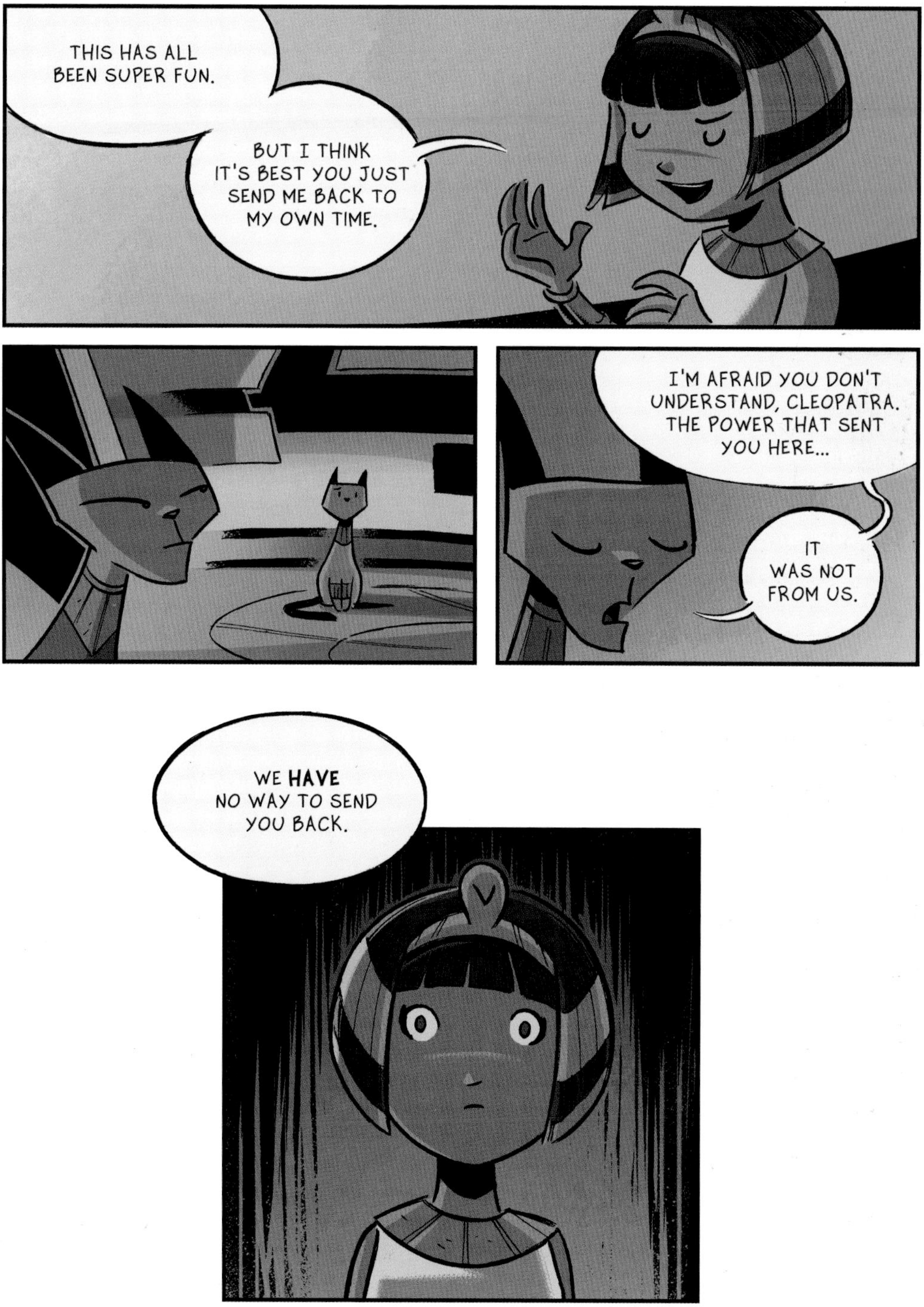
THIS HAS ALL BEEN SUPER FUN.
BUT I THINK IT'S BEST YOU JUST SEND ME BACK TO MY OWN TIME.
I'M AFRAID YOU DON'T UNDERSTAND, CLEOPATRA. THE POWER THAT SENT YOU HERE...
IT WAS NOT FROM US.
WE **HAVE** NO WAY TO SEND YOU BACK.

CHAPTER TWO

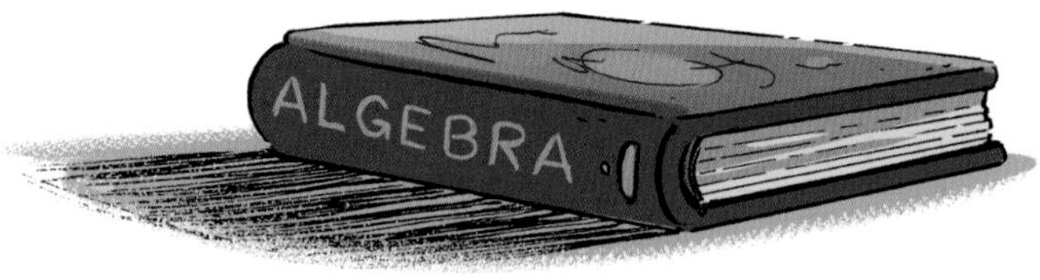
ALGEBRA

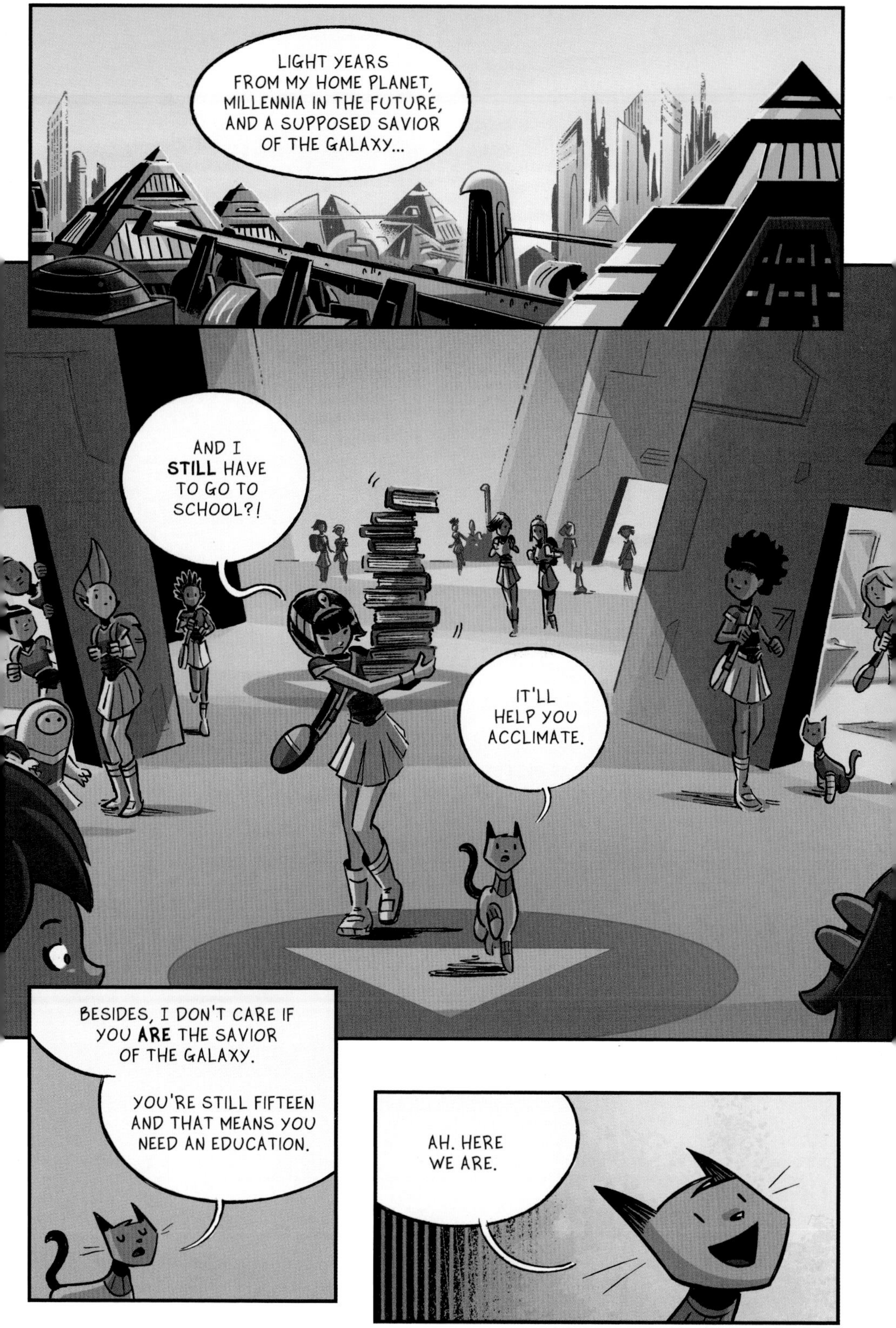
LIGHT YEARS FROM MY HOME PLANET, MILLENNIA IN THE FUTURE, AND A SUPPOSED SAVIOR OF THE GALAXY...
AND I **STILL** HAVE TO GO TO SCHOOL?!
IT'LL HELP YOU ACCLIMATE.
BESIDES, I DON'T CARE IF YOU **ARE** THE SAVIOR OF THE GALAXY.
YOU'RE STILL FIFTEEN AND THAT MEANS YOU NEED AN EDUCATION.
AH. HERE WE ARE.

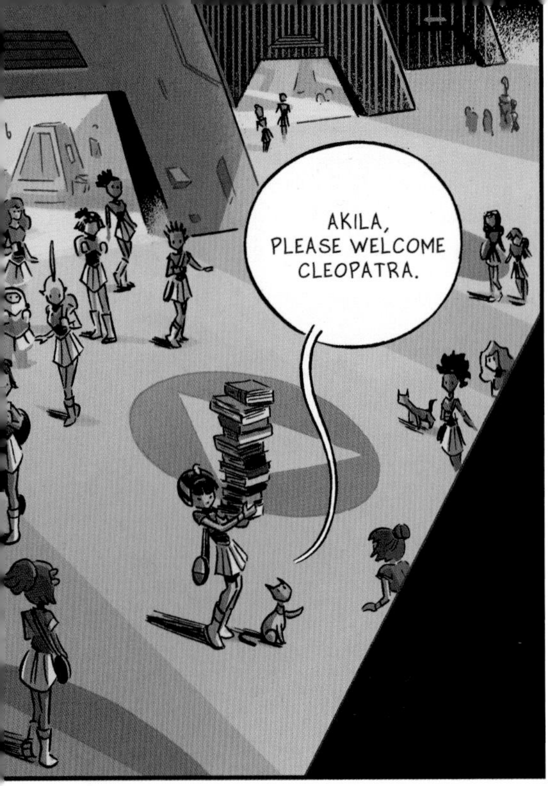
AKILA, PLEASE WELCOME CLEOPATRA.
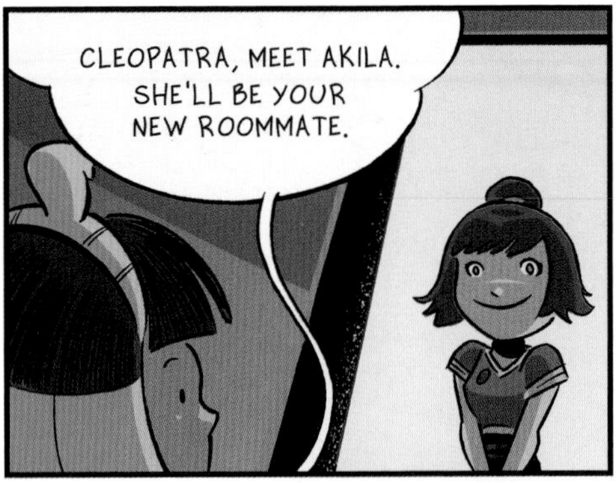
CLEOPATRA, MEET AKILA. SHE'LL BE YOUR NEW ROOMMATE.
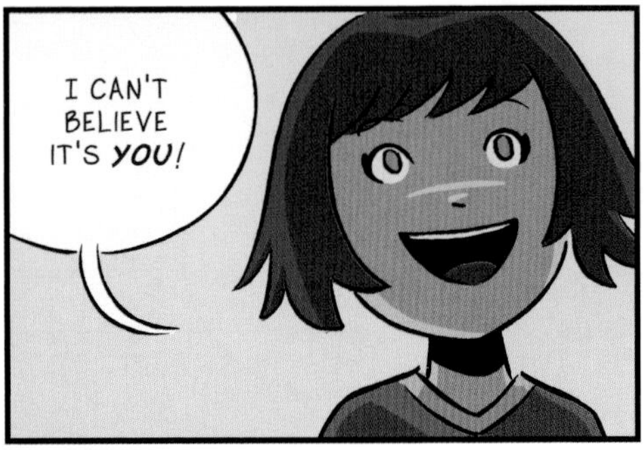
I CAN'T BELIEVE IT'S *YOU*!
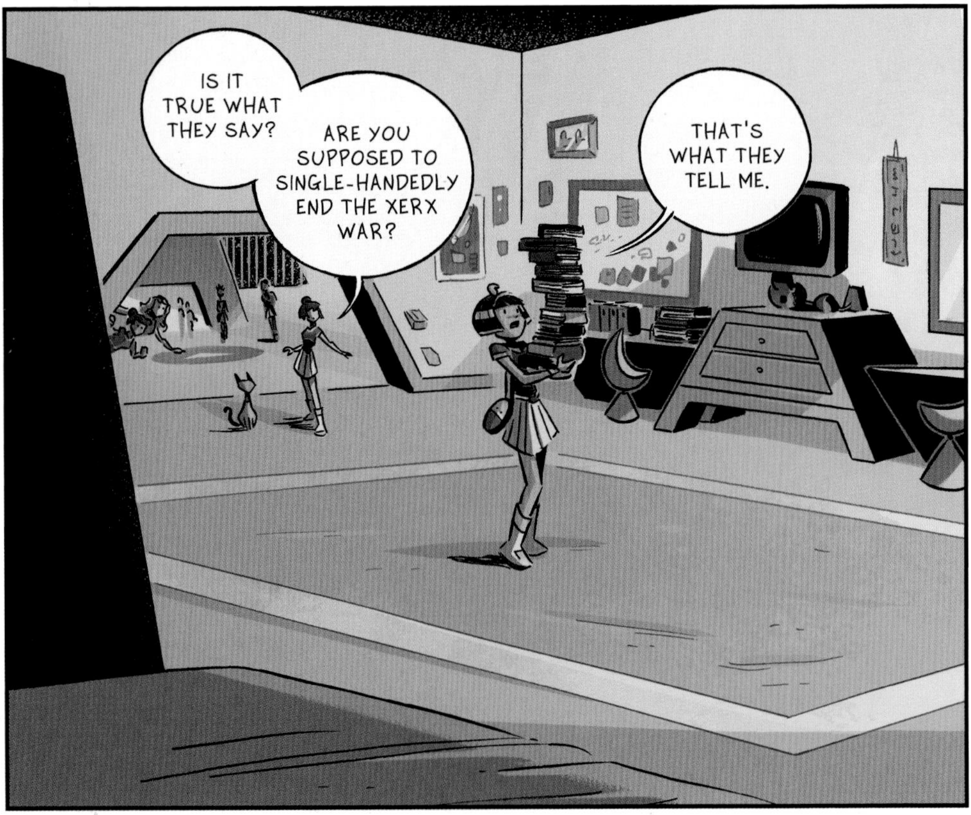
IS IT TRUE WHAT THEY SAY?
ARE YOU SUPPOSED TO SINGLE-HANDEDLY END THE XERX WAR?
THAT'S WHAT THEY TELL ME.

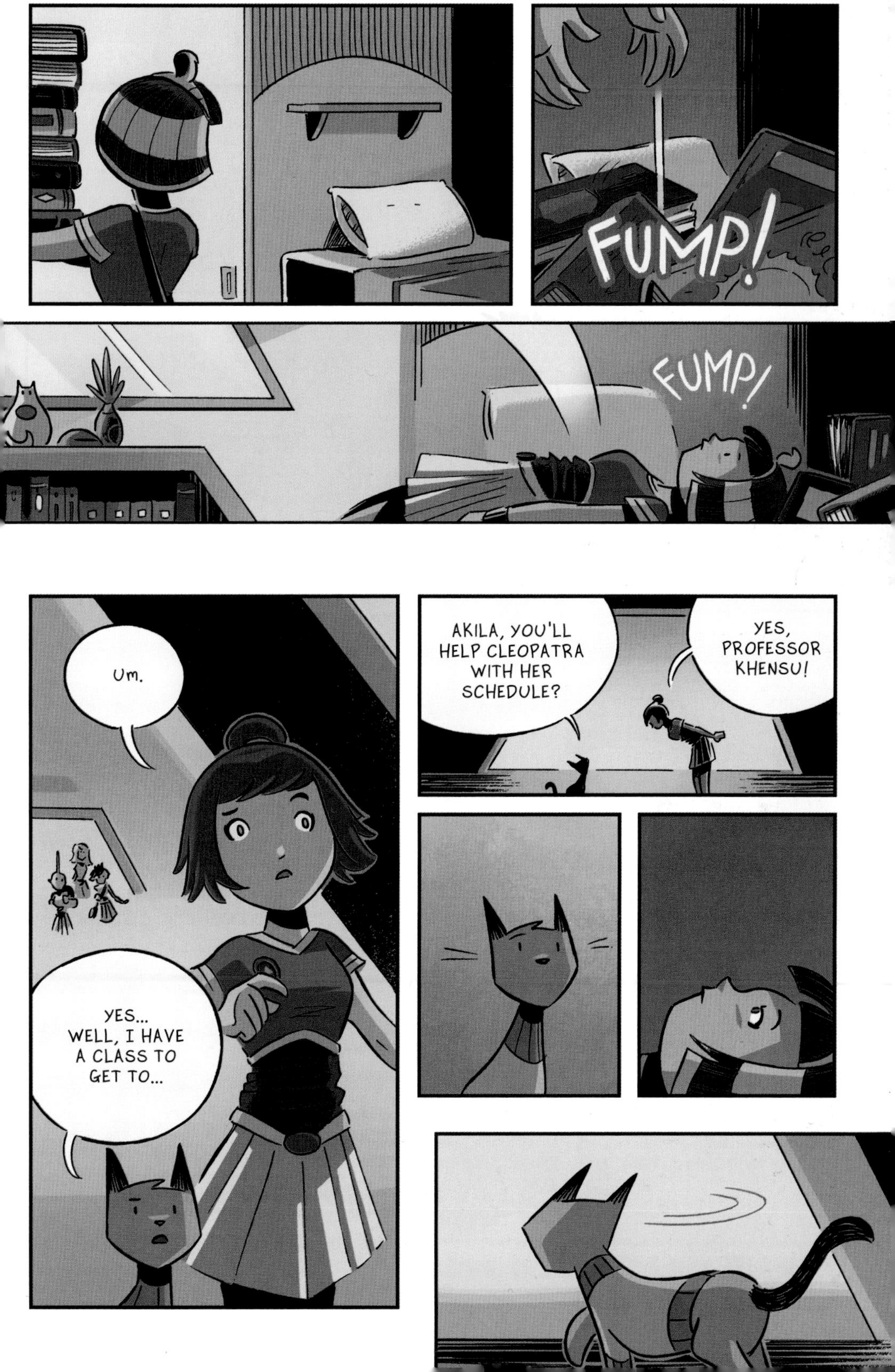
FUMP!
FUMP!
Um.
YES... WELL, I HAVE A CLASS TO GET TO...
AKILA, YOU'LL HELP CLEOPATRA WITH HER SCHEDULE?
YES, PROFESSOR KHENSU!

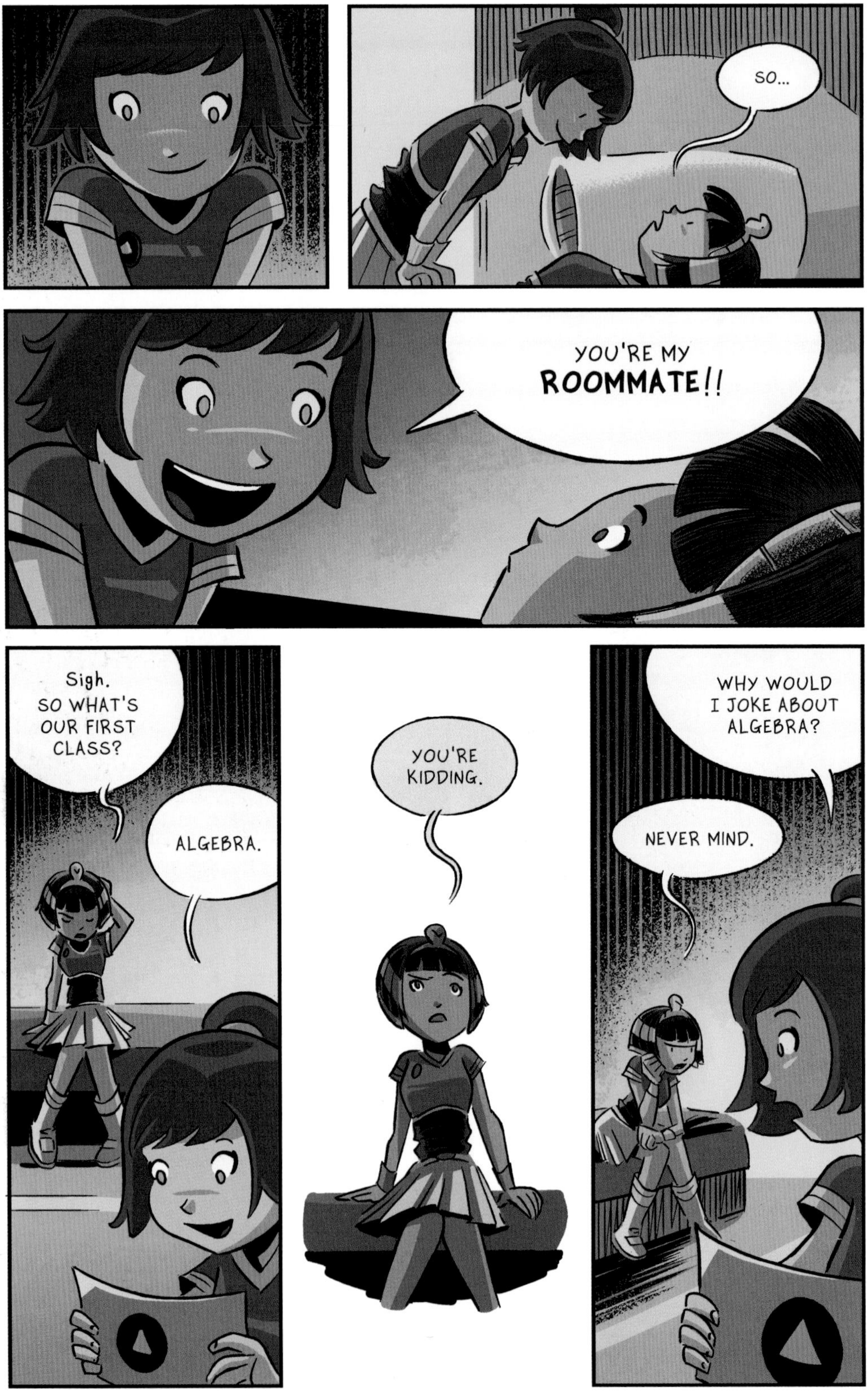
SO...
YOU'RE MY **ROOMMATE**!!
Sigh. SO WHAT'S OUR FIRST CLASS?
ALGEBRA.
YOU'RE KIDDING.
WHY WOULD I JOKE ABOUT ALGEBRA?
NEVER MIND.

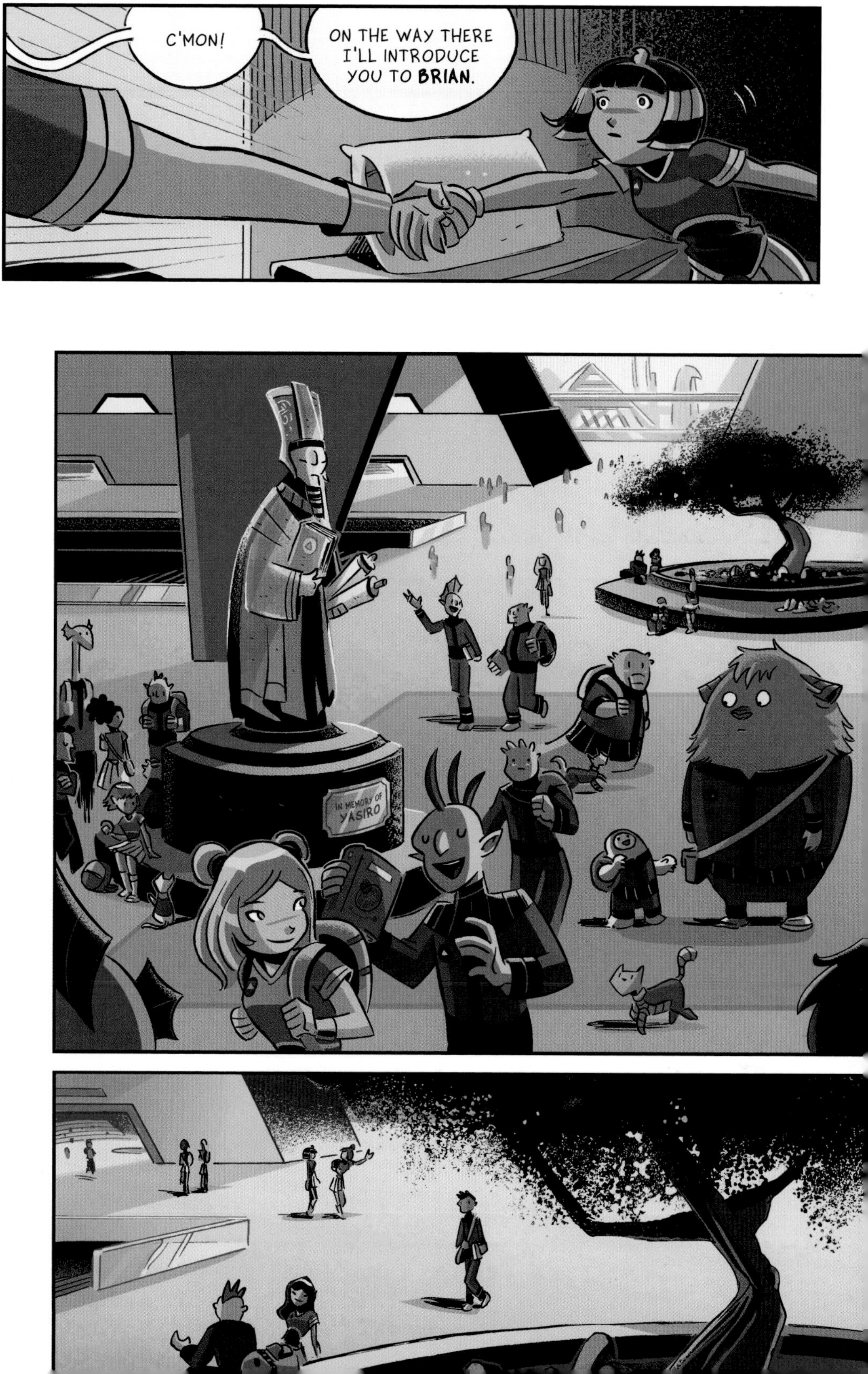
C'MON!
ON THE WAY THERE I'LL INTRODUCE YOU TO **BRIAN**.
IN MEMORY OF YASIRO

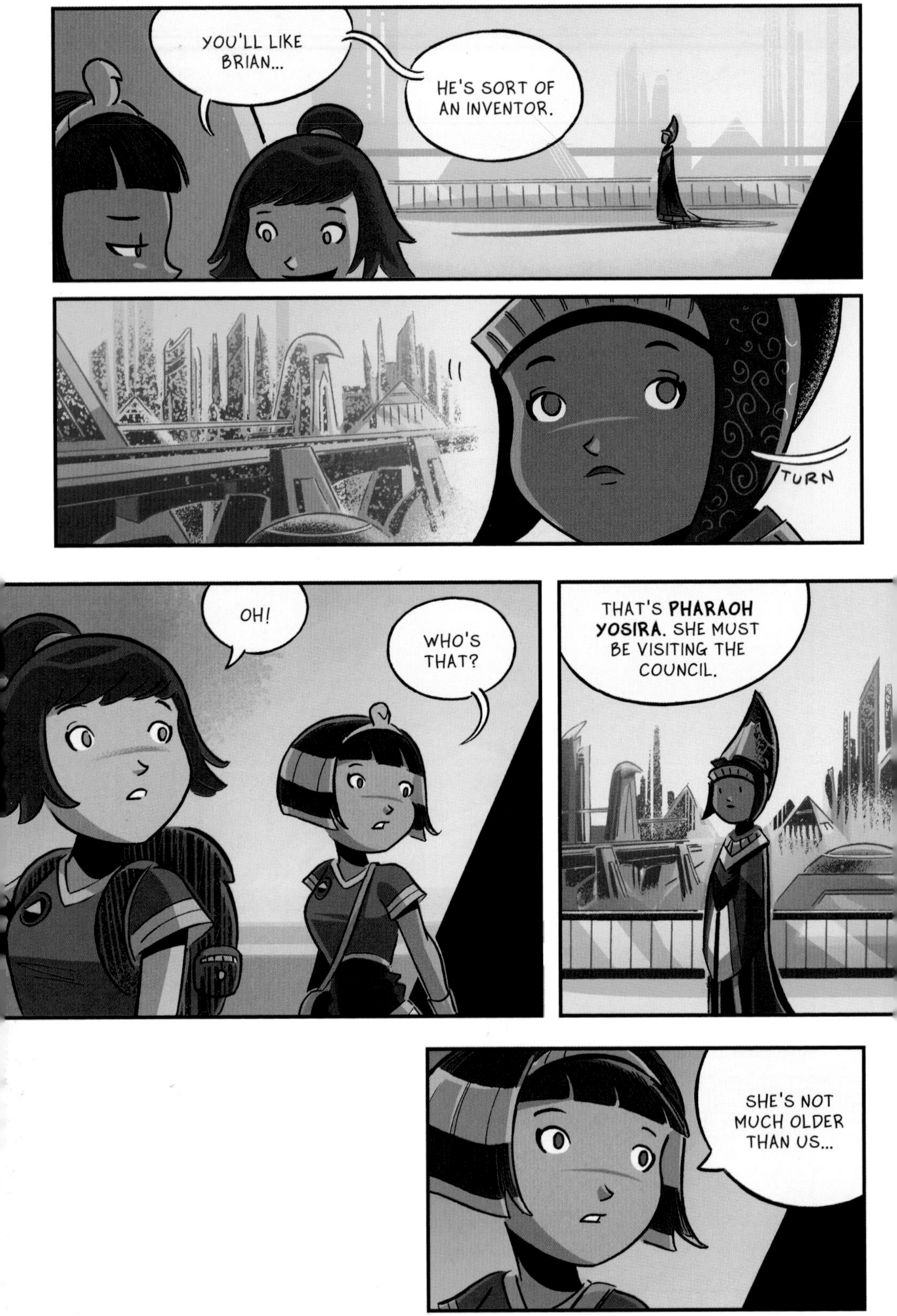
YOU'LL LIKE BRIAN...
HE'S SORT OF AN INVENTOR.
TURN
OH!
WHO'S THAT?
THAT'S **PHARAOH YOSIRA**. SHE MUST BE VISITING THE COUNCIL.
SHE'S NOT MUCH OLDER THAN US...

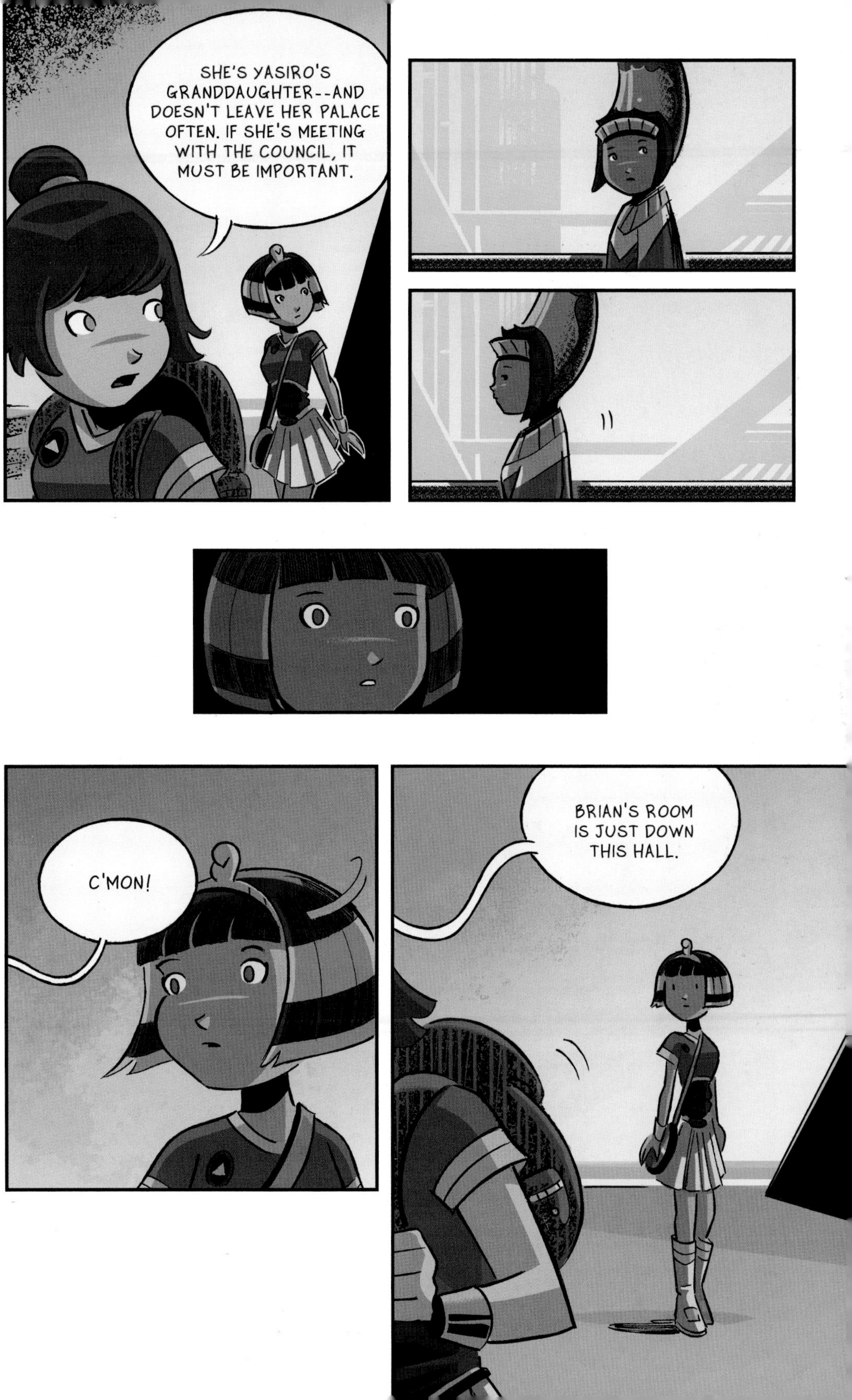
SHE'S YASIRO'S GRANDDAUGHTER--AND DOESN'T LEAVE HER PALACE OFTEN. IF SHE'S MEETING WITH THE COUNCIL, IT MUST BE IMPORTANT.
C'MON!
BRIAN'S ROOM IS JUST DOWN THIS HALL.

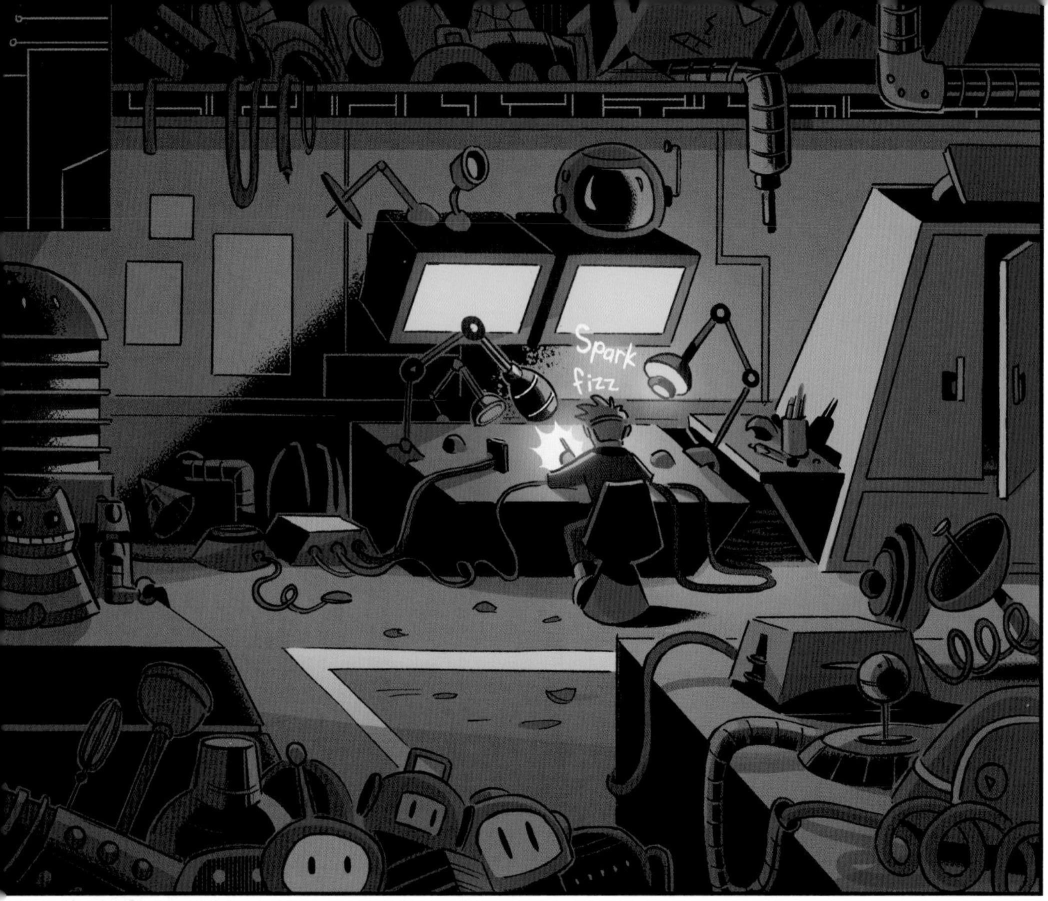
Spark
fizz

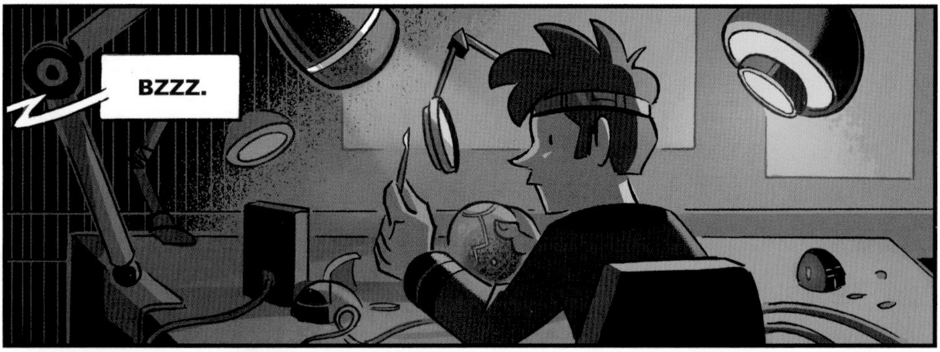
BZZZ.

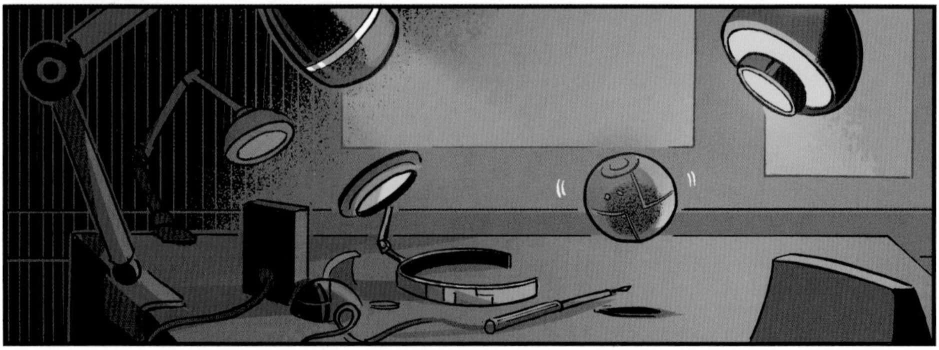

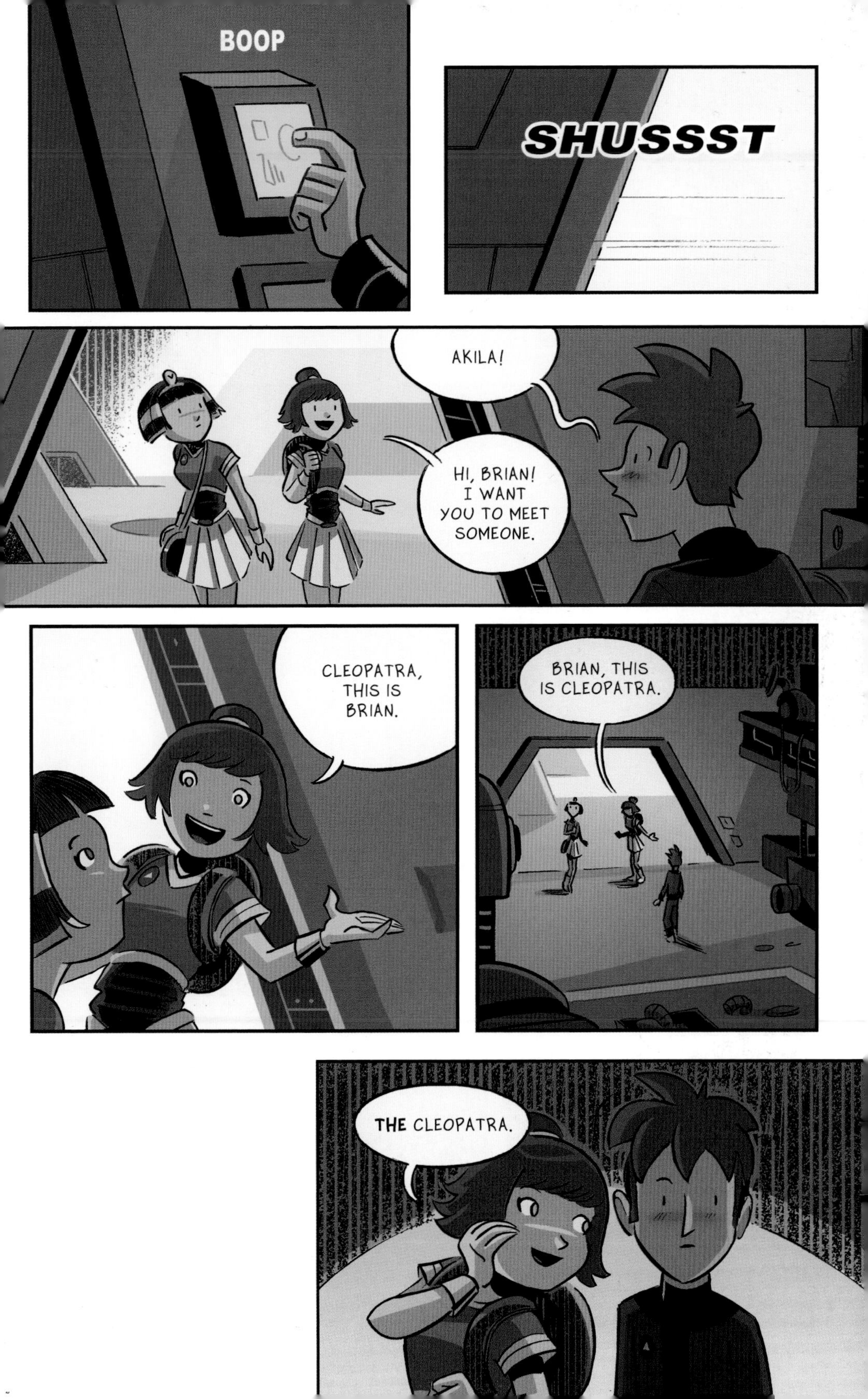
BOOP
SHUSSST
AKILA!
HI, BRIAN! I WANT YOU TO MEET SOMEONE.
CLEOPATRA, THIS IS BRIAN.
BRIAN, THIS IS CLEOPATRA.
THE CLEOPATRA.

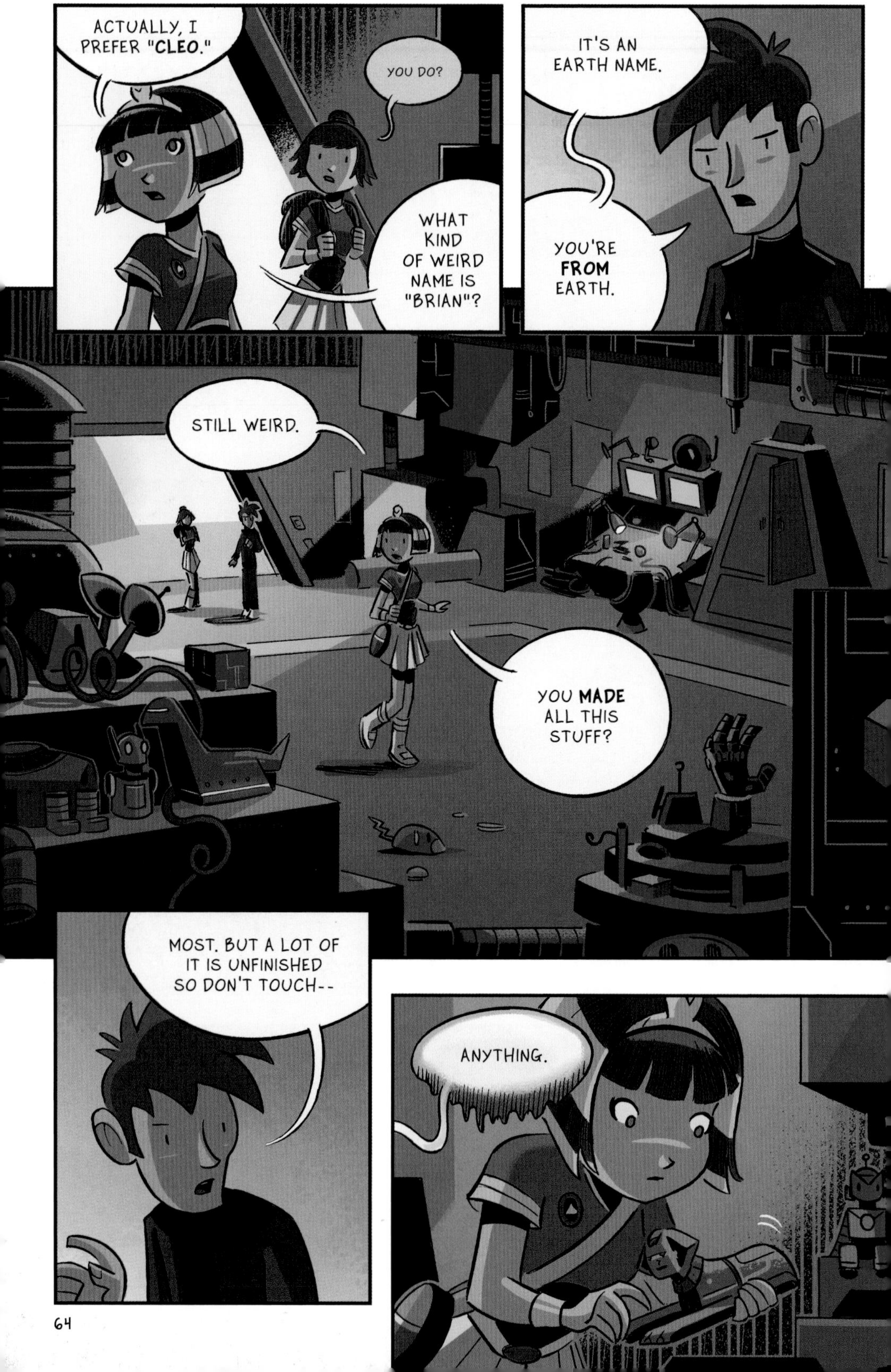
ACTUALLY, I PREFER "CLEO."
YOU DO?
WHAT KIND OF WEIRD NAME IS "BRIAN"?
IT'S AN EARTH NAME.
YOU'RE FROM EARTH.
STILL WEIRD.
YOU MADE ALL THIS STUFF?
MOST. BUT A LOT OF IT IS UNFINISHED SO DON'T TOUCH--
ANYTHING.

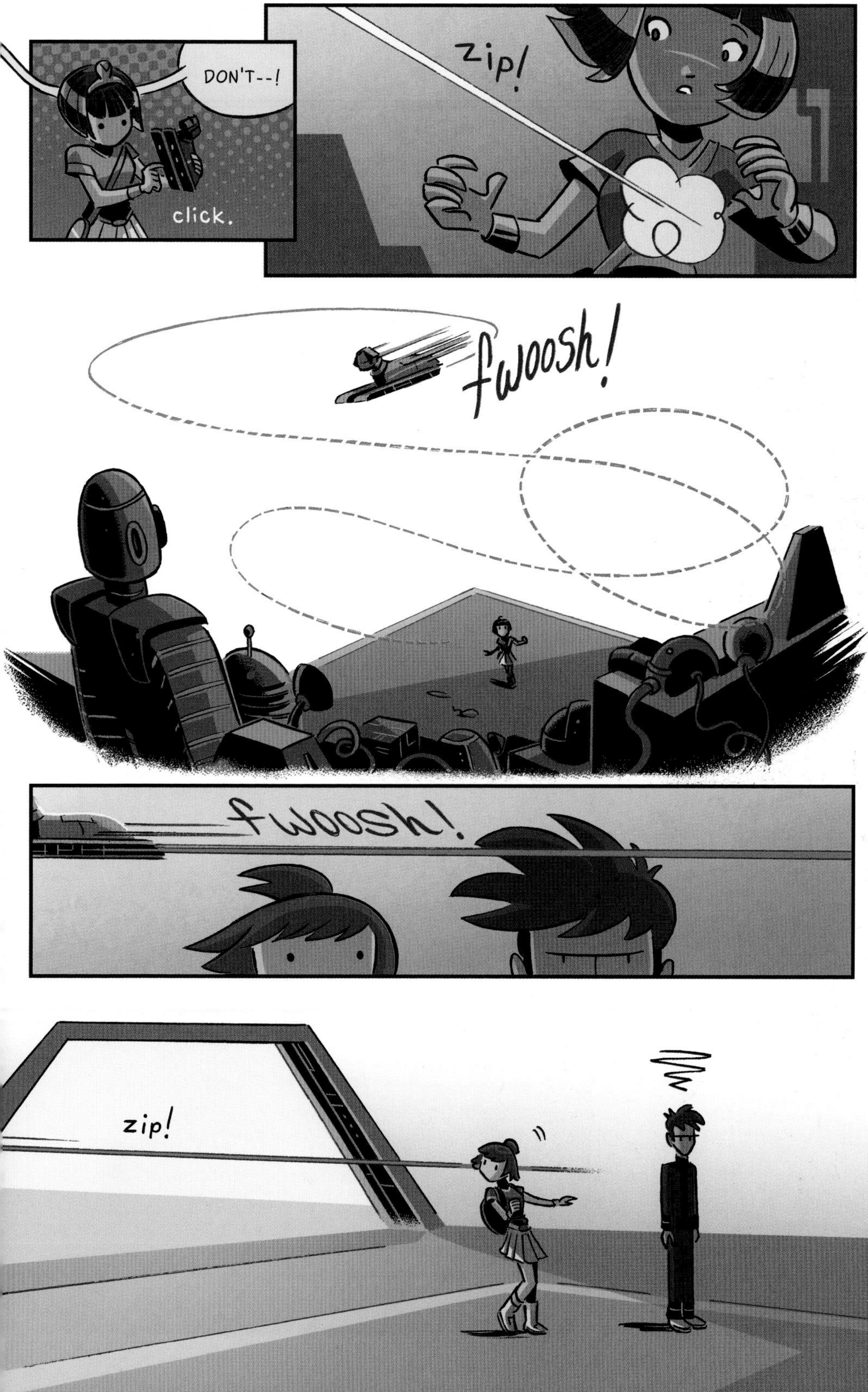
DON'T--!
click.
zip!
fwoosh!
fwoosh!
zip!

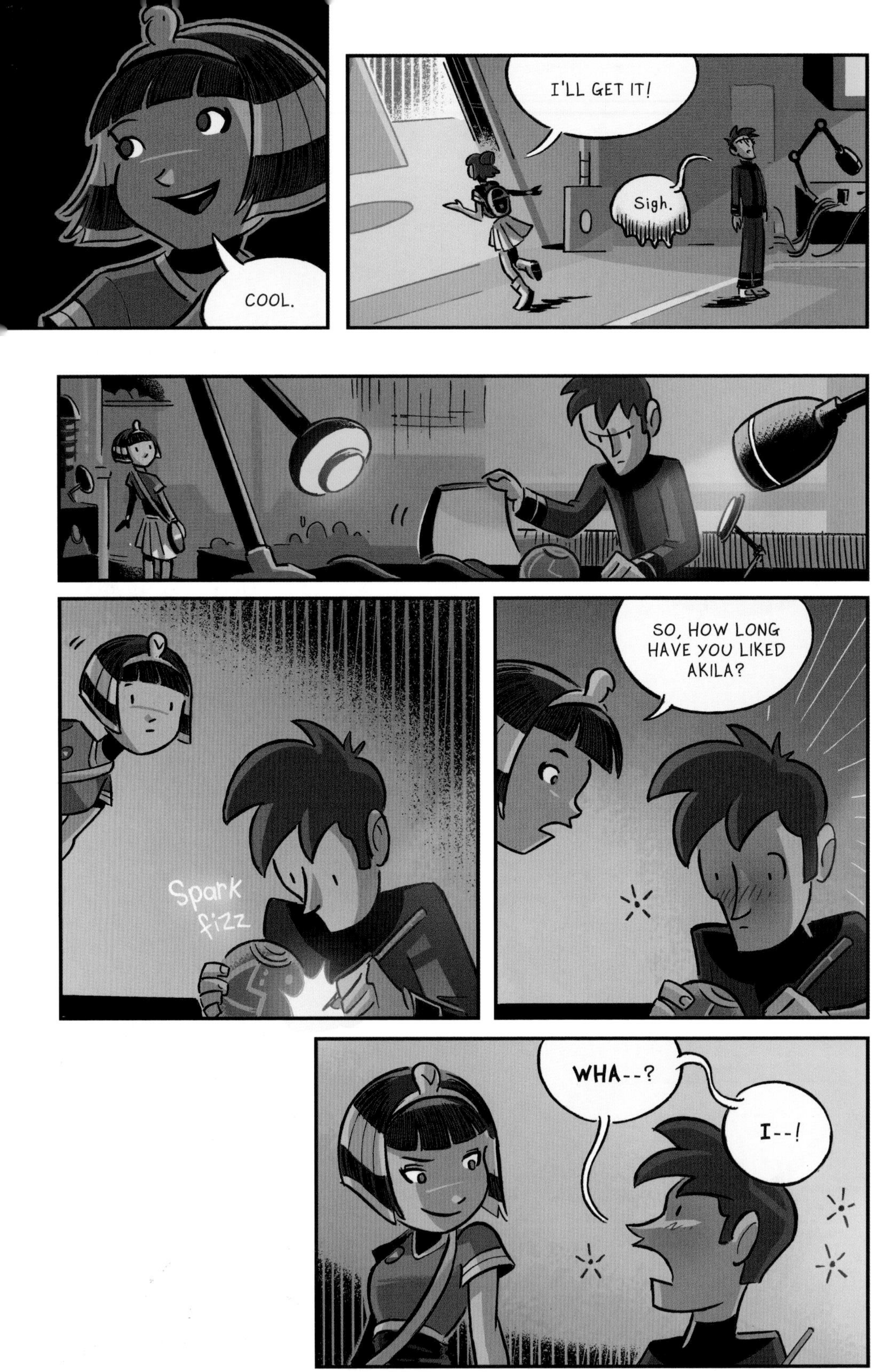
COOL.
I'LL GET IT!
Sigh.
Spark
fizz
SO, HOW LONG HAVE YOU LIKED AKILA?
WHA--?
I--!

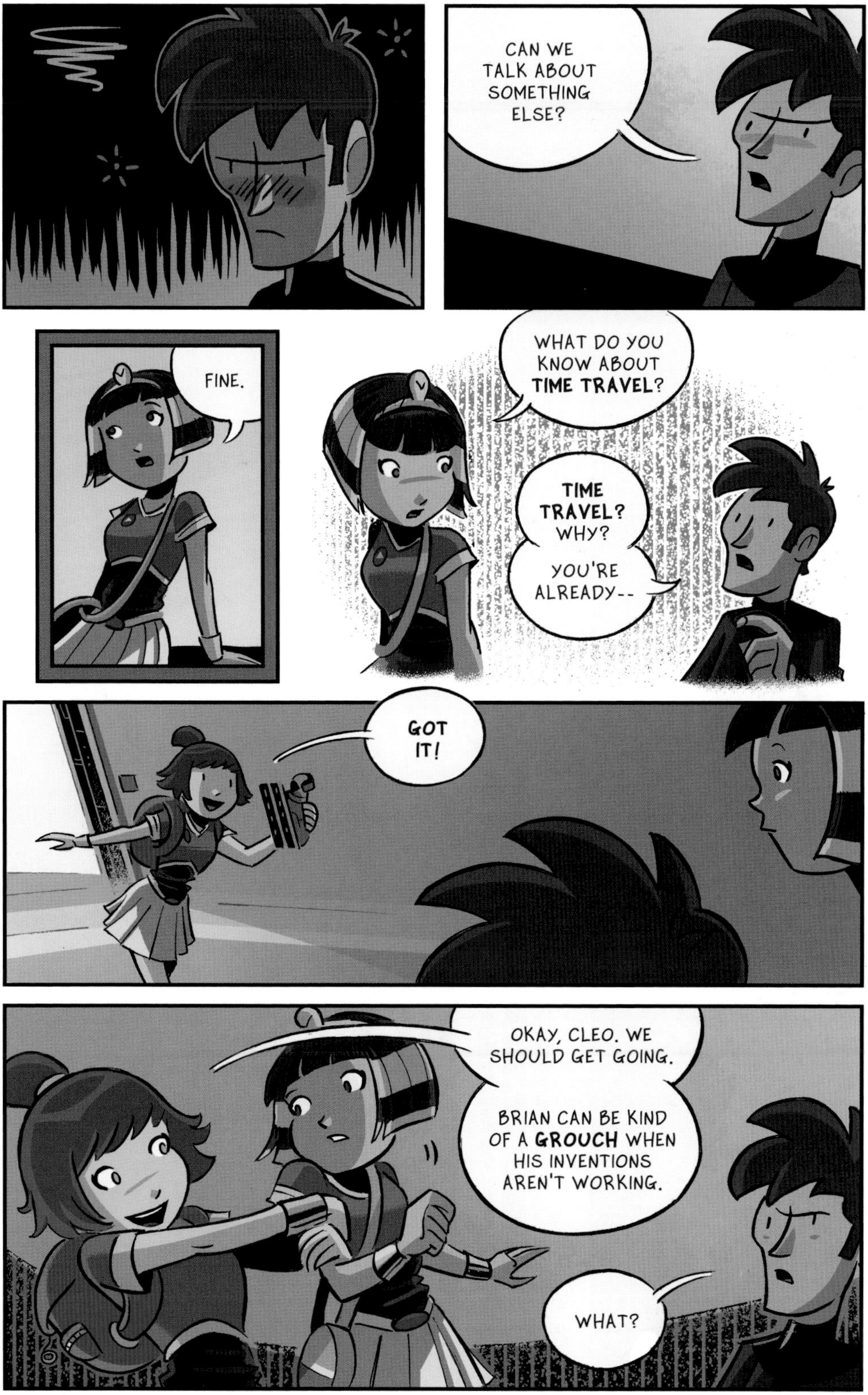
CAN WE TALK ABOUT SOMETHING ELSE?
FINE.
WHAT DO YOU KNOW ABOUT TIME TRAVEL?
TIME TRAVEL? WHY?
YOU'RE ALREADY--
GOT IT!
OKAY, CLEO. WE SHOULD GET GOING.
BRIAN CAN BE KIND OF A GROUCH WHEN HIS INVENTIONS AREN'T WORKING.
WHAT?

MY INVENTIONS ARE WORKING.

BLEEP

VZZZZZSH

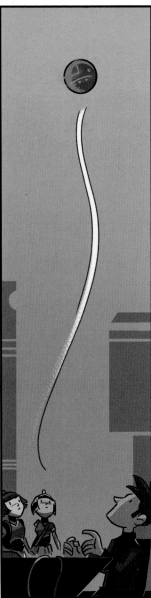

Sputter

FIZZ

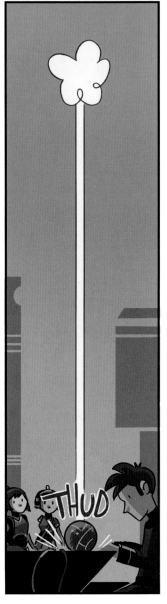

THUD

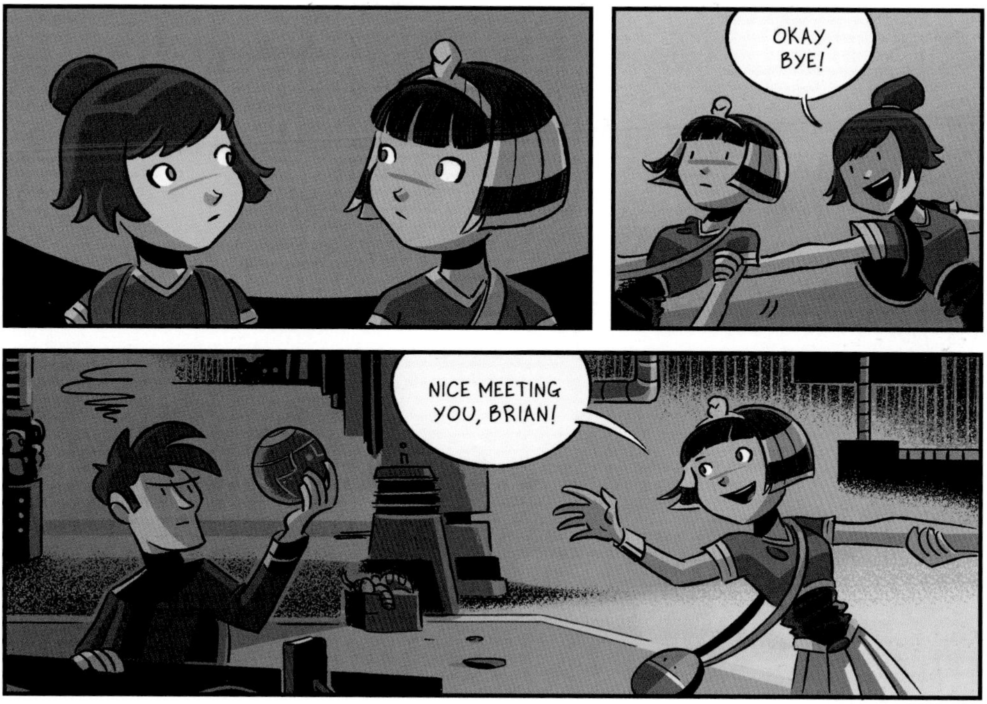
OKAY, BYE!
NICE MEETING YOU, BRIAN!

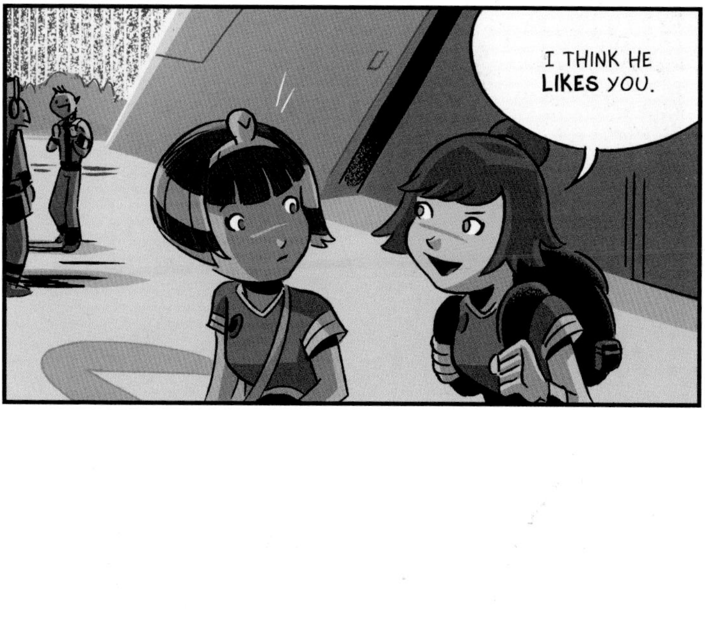
I THINK HE **LIKES** YOU.

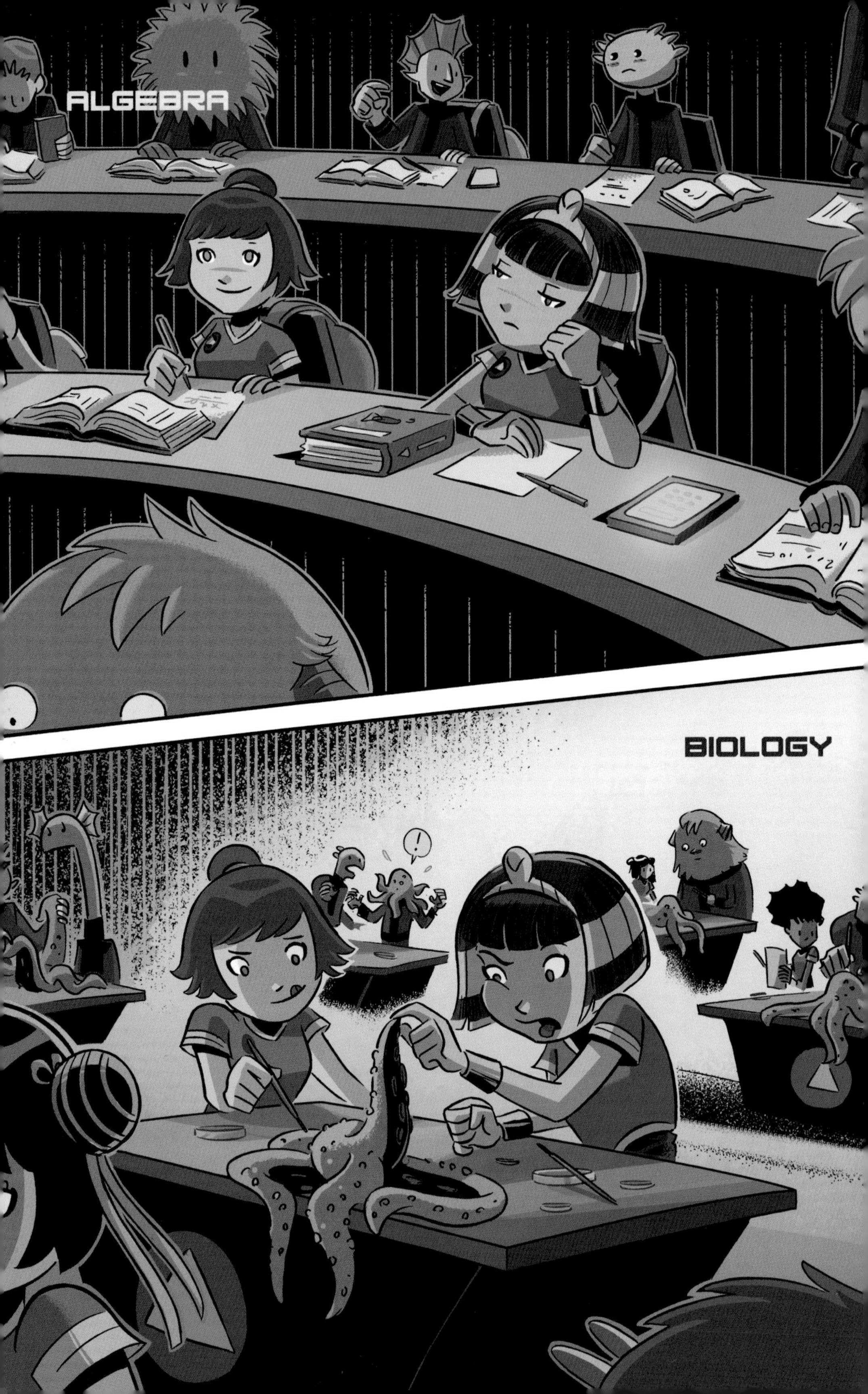
ALGEBRA
BIOLOGY
!

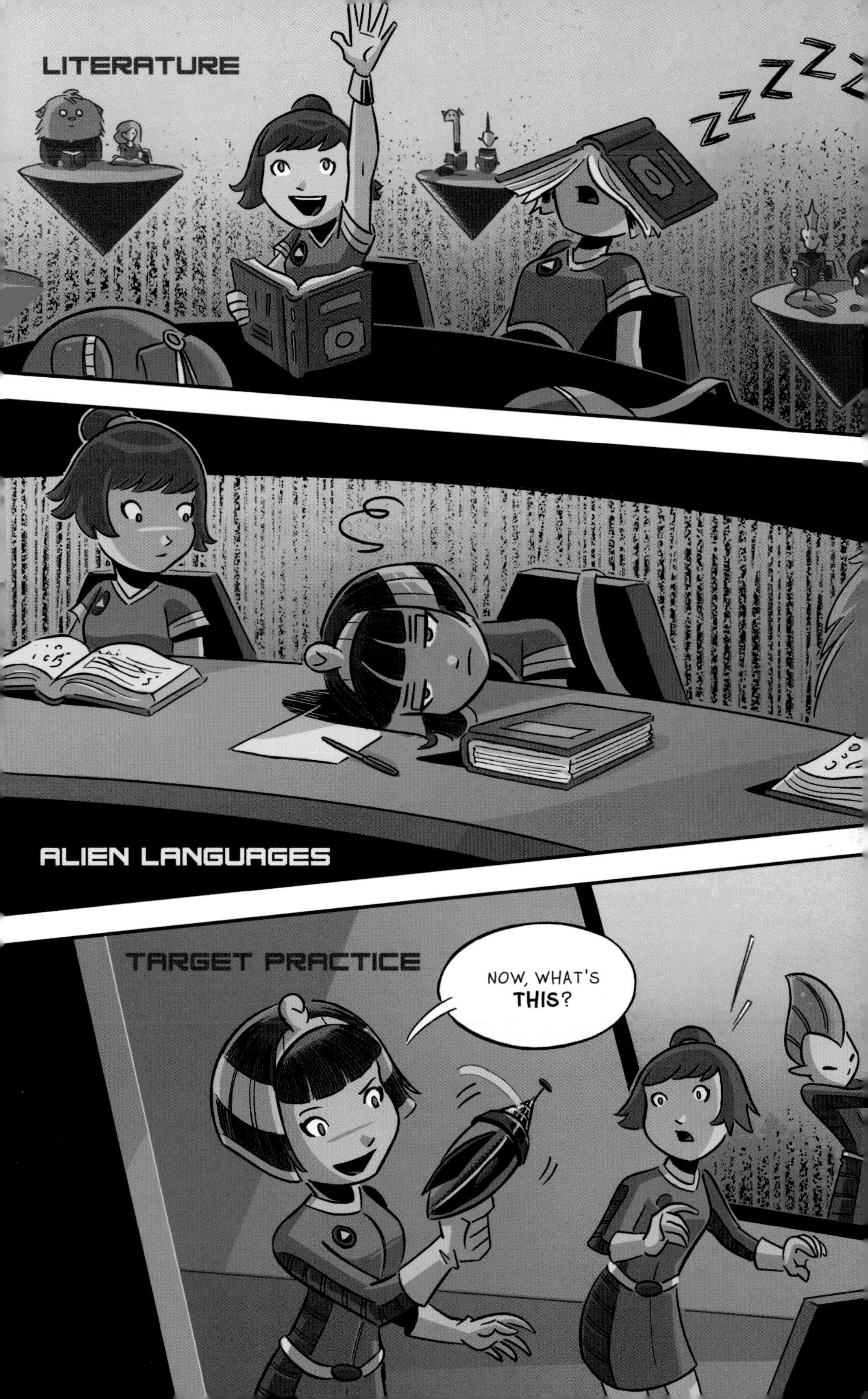
LITERATURE
ZZZZZZ
ALIEN LANGUAGES
TARGET PRACTICE
NOW, WHAT'S THIS?

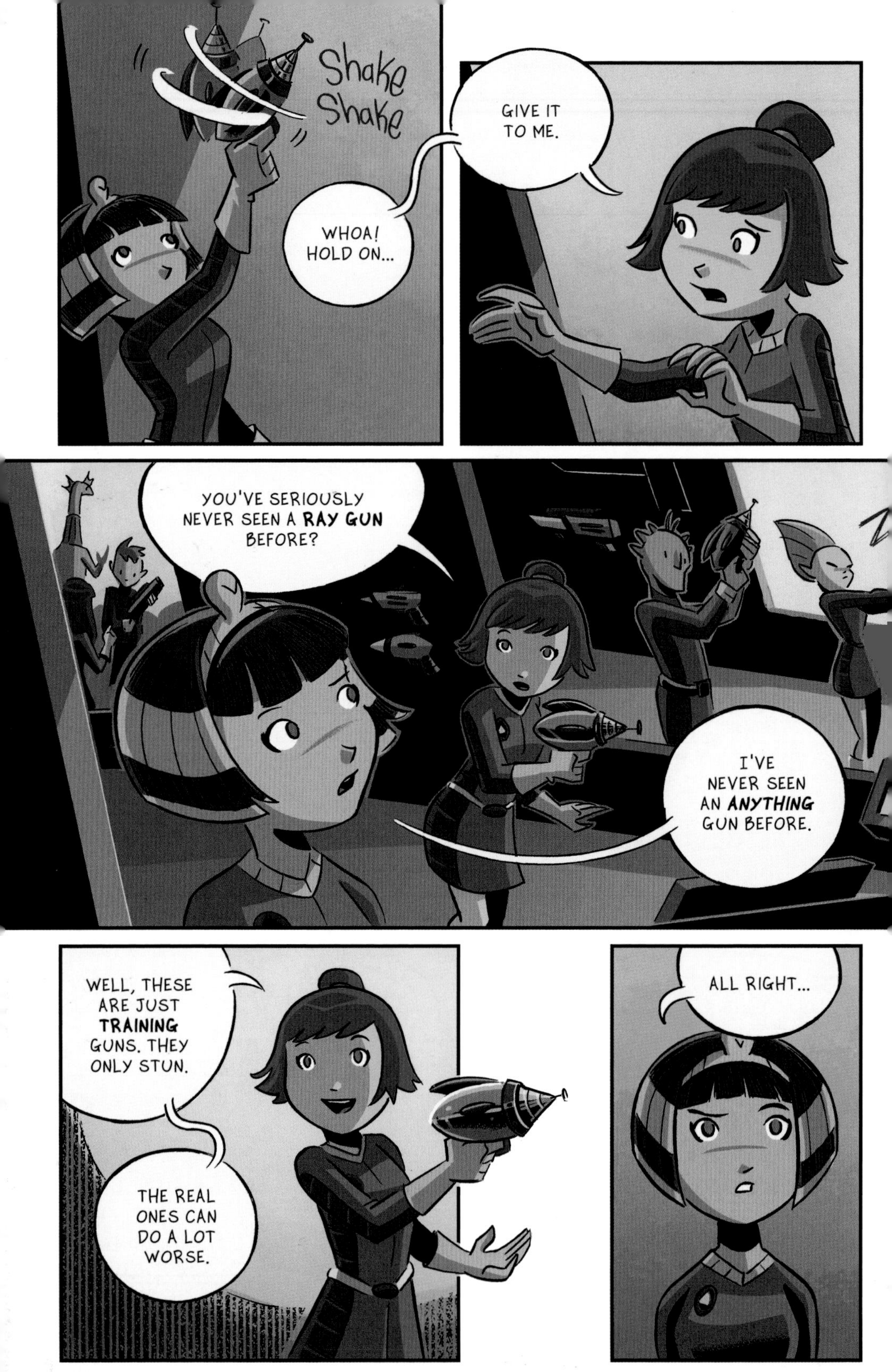
Shake
Shake
GIVE IT TO ME.
WHOA! HOLD ON...
YOU'VE SERIOUSLY NEVER SEEN A **RAY GUN** BEFORE?
I'VE NEVER SEEN AN **ANYTHING** GUN BEFORE.
WELL, THESE ARE JUST **TRAINING** GUNS. THEY ONLY STUN.
THE REAL ONES CAN DO A LOT WORSE.
ALL RIGHT...

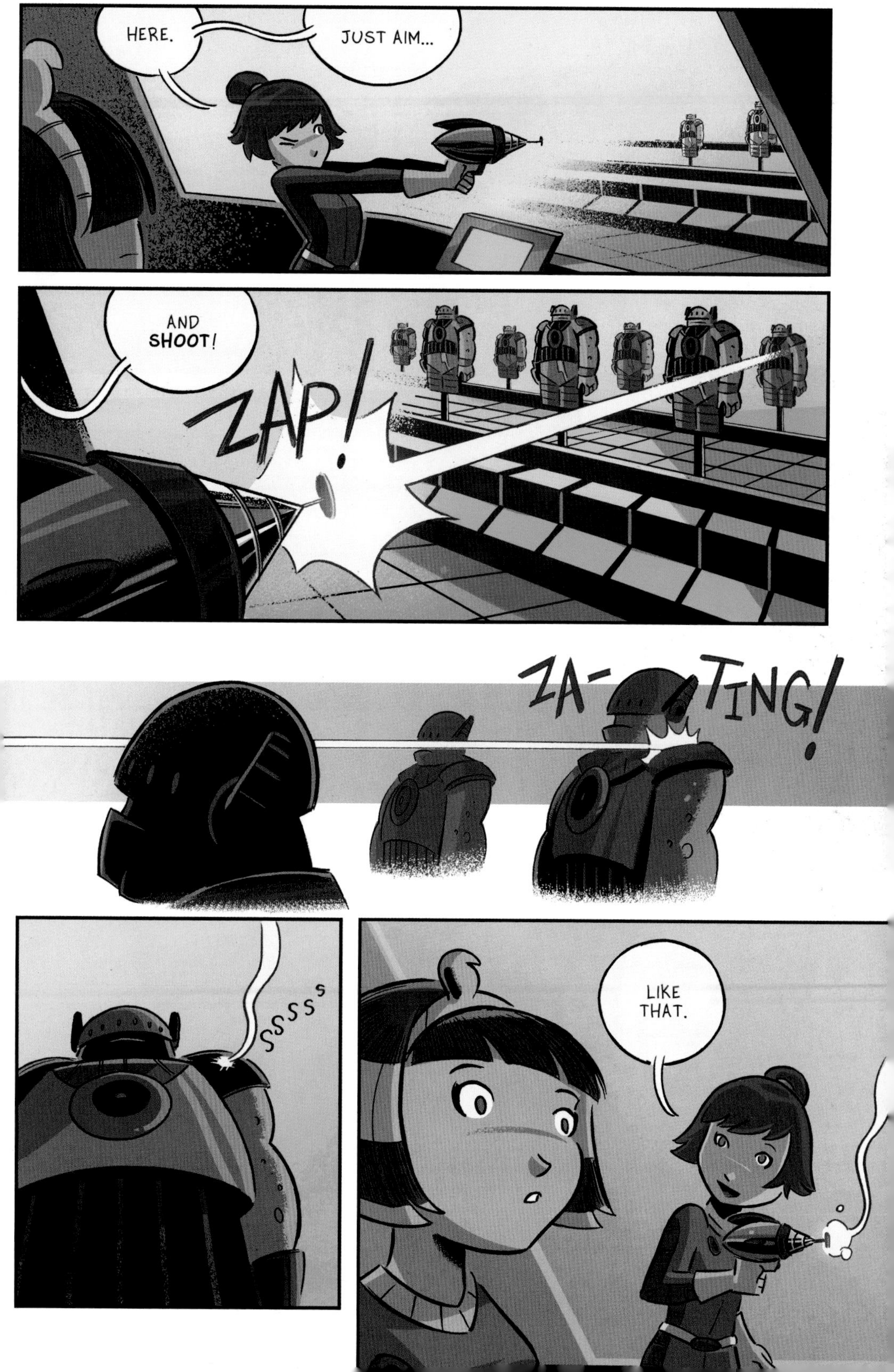
HERE.
JUST AIM...
AND SHOOT!
ZAP!
ZA-TING!
SSSSS
LIKE THAT.

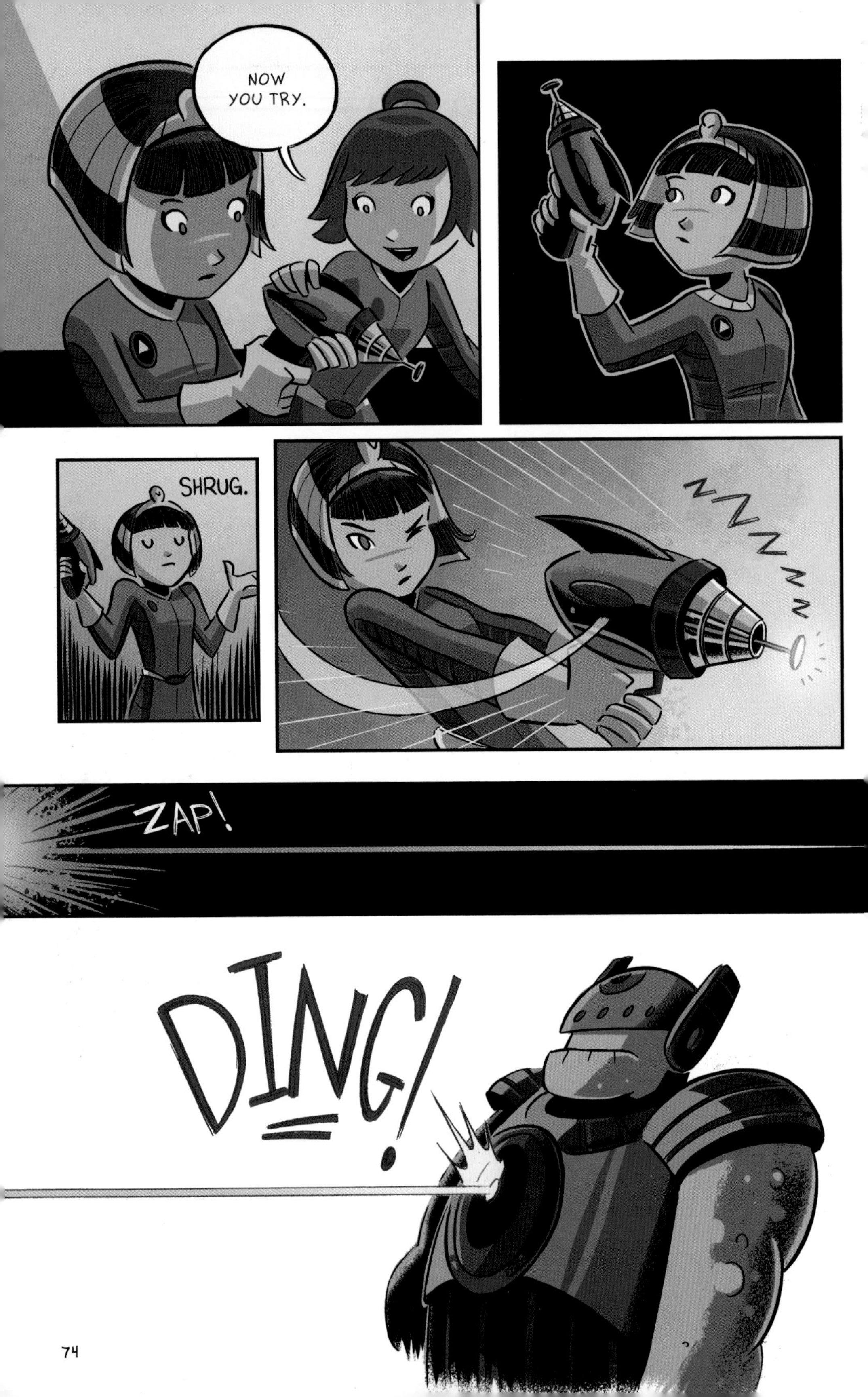
NOW YOU TRY.
SHRUG.
ZNNNN
ZAP!
DING!

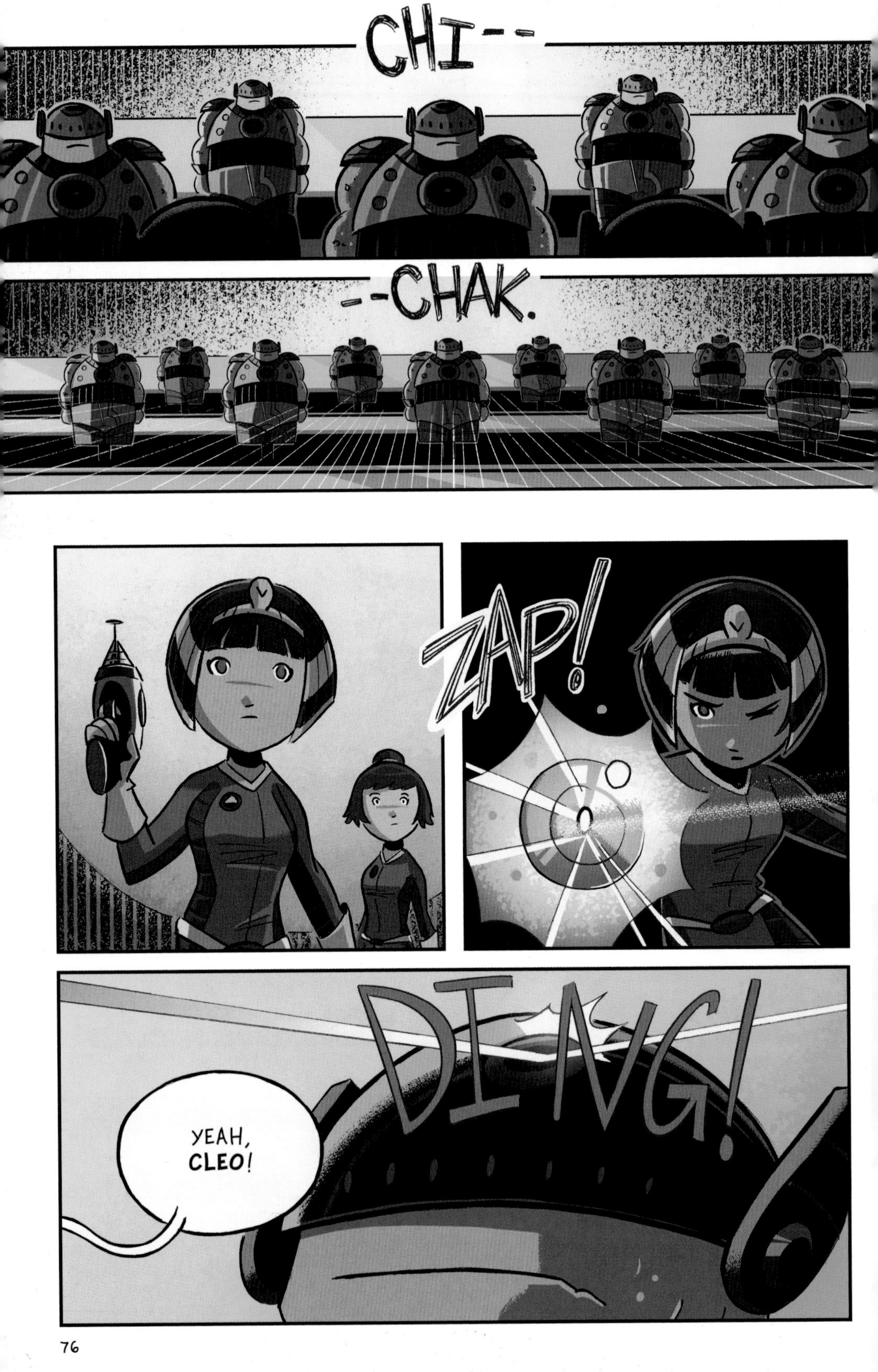
CHI--
--CHAK.
ZAP!
DING!
YEAH, CLEO!

SHOOM SHOOM SHOOM SHOOM SHOOM SHOOM SHOOM SHOOM

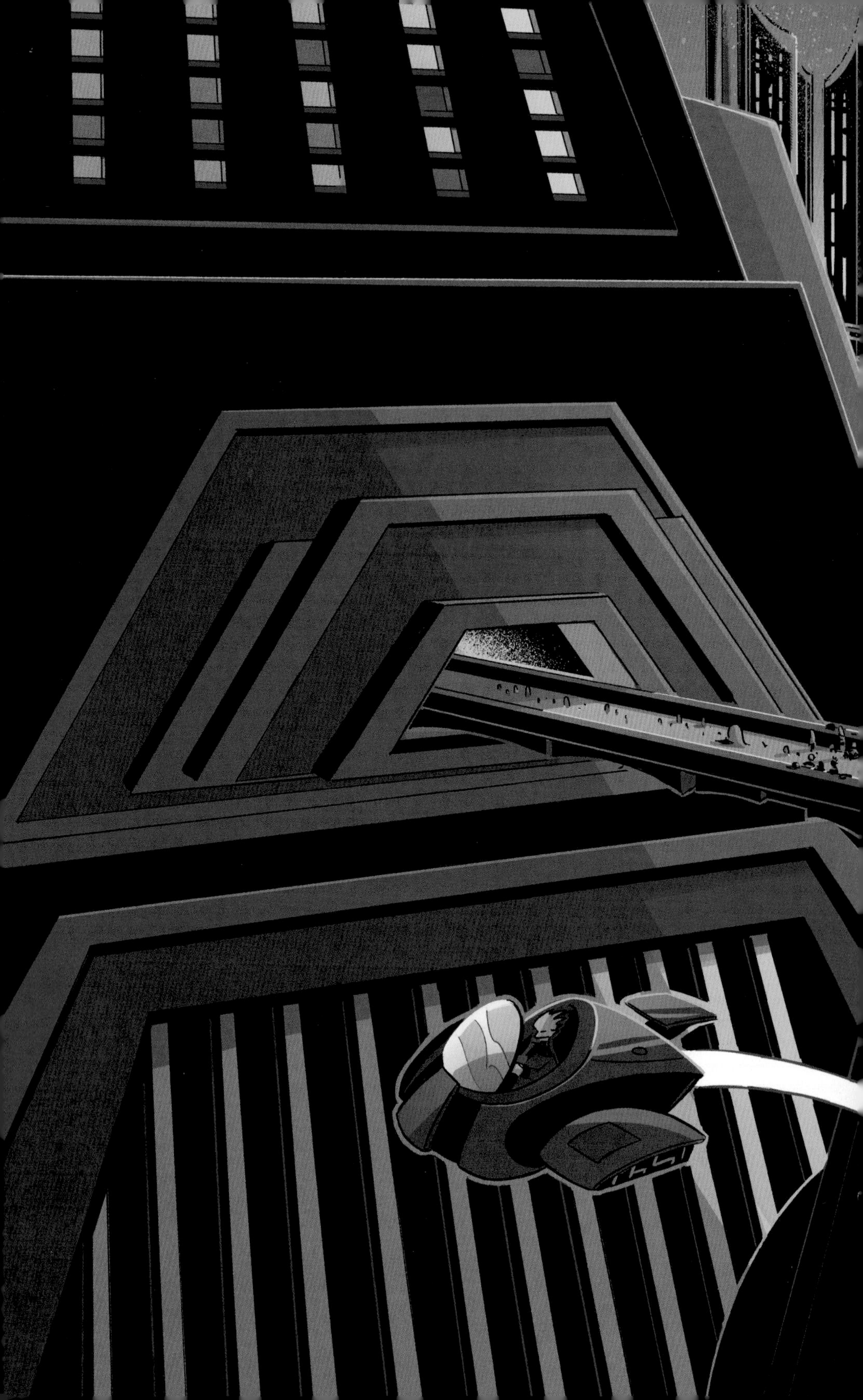

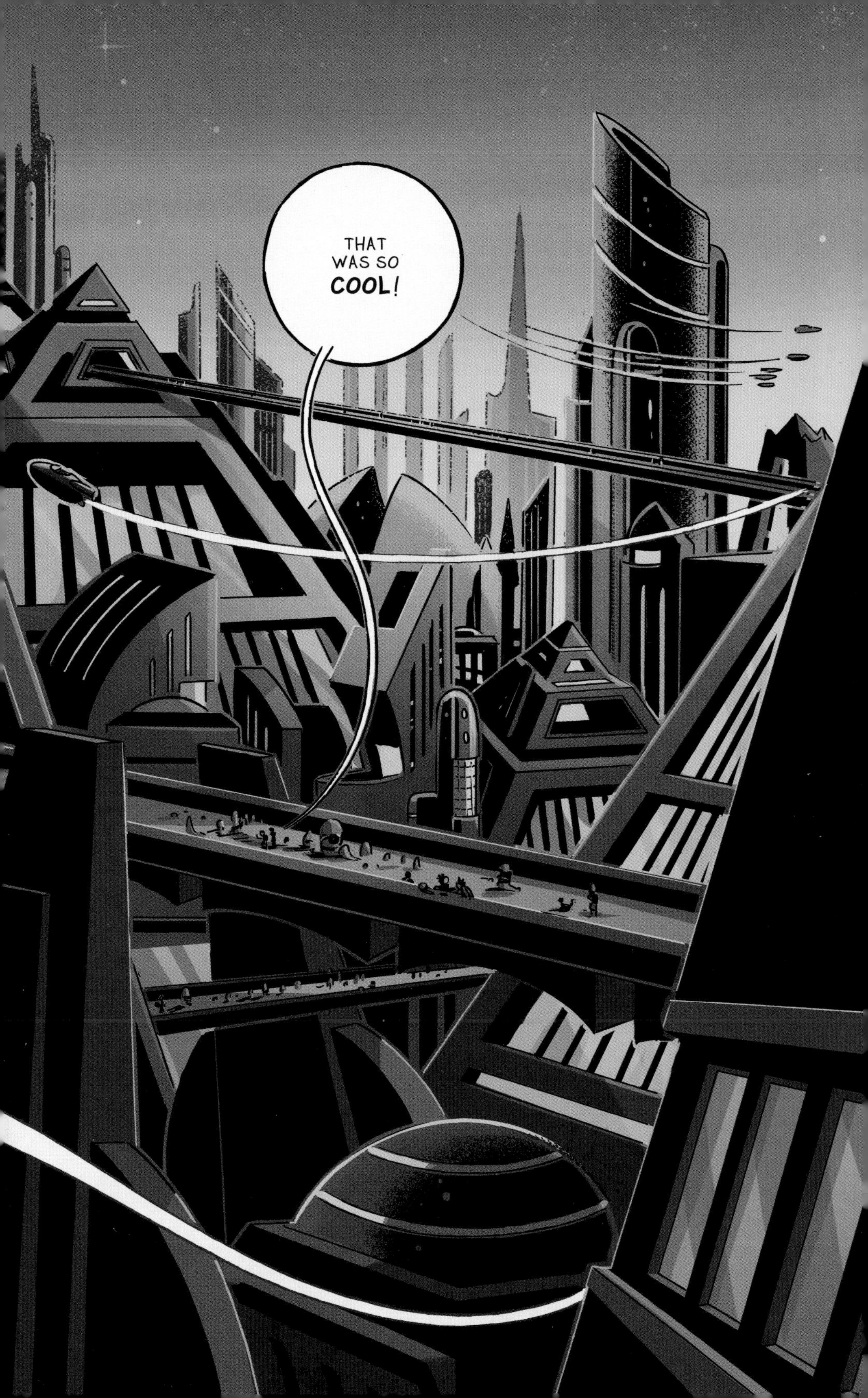
THAT WAS SO **COOL**!

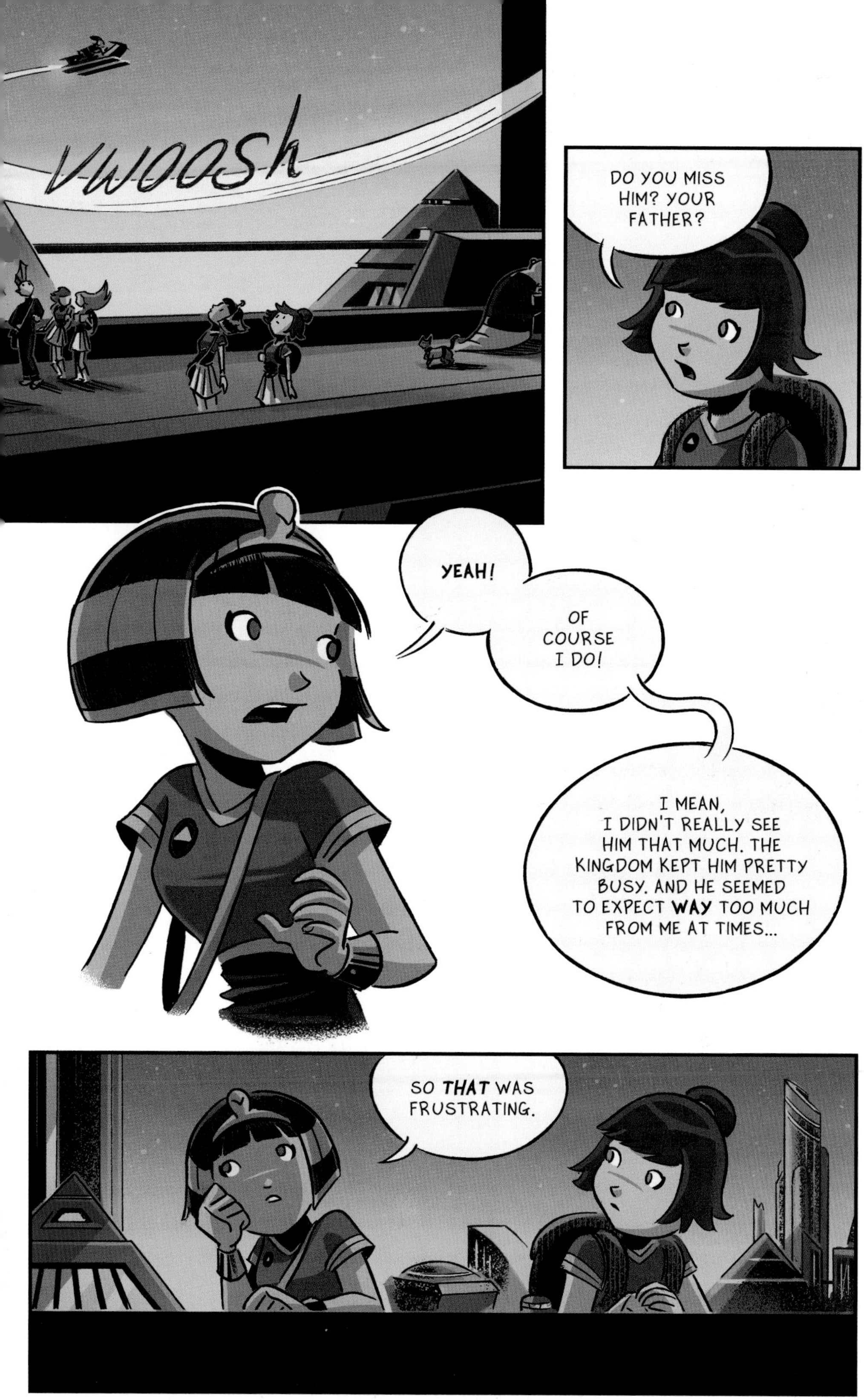
VWOOSH
DO YOU MISS HIM? YOUR FATHER?
YEAH!
OF COURSE I DO!
I MEAN, I DIDN'T REALLY SEE HIM THAT MUCH. THE KINGDOM KEPT HIM PRETTY BUSY. AND HE SEEMED TO EXPECT **WAY** TOO MUCH FROM ME AT TIMES...
SO **THAT** WAS FRUSTRATING.

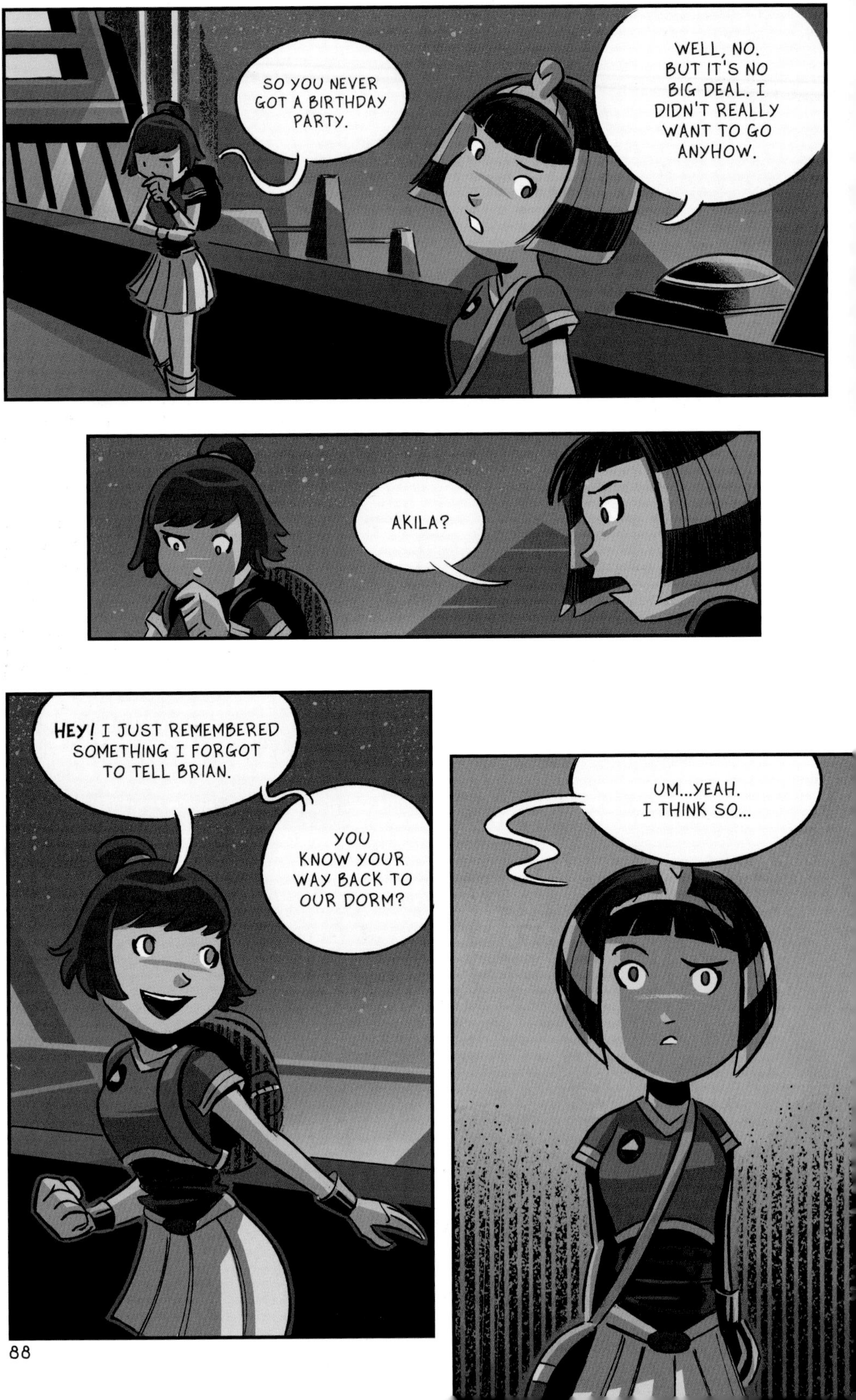
SO YOU NEVER GOT A BIRTHDAY PARTY.
WELL, NO. BUT IT'S NO BIG DEAL. I DIDN'T REALLY WANT TO GO ANYHOW.
AKILA?
HEY! I JUST REMEMBERED SOMETHING I FORGOT TO TELL BRIAN.
YOU KNOW YOUR WAY BACK TO OUR DORM?
UM...YEAH. I THINK SO...

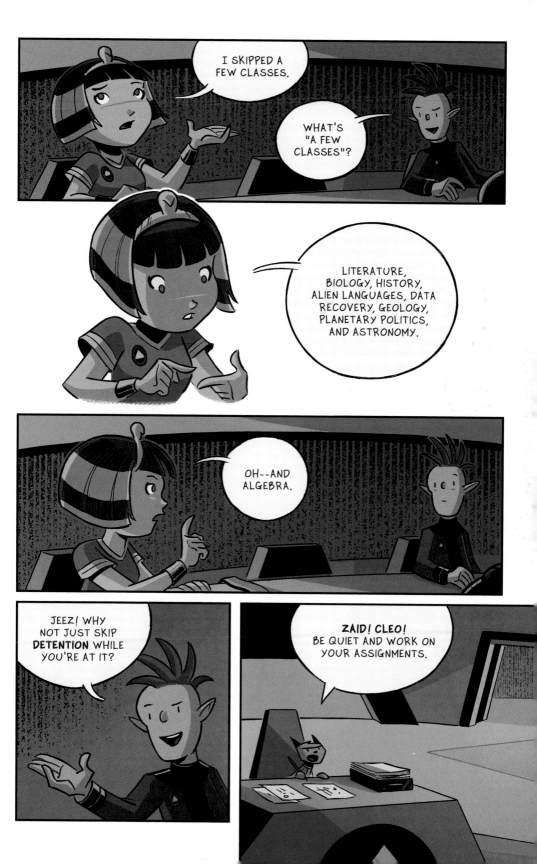

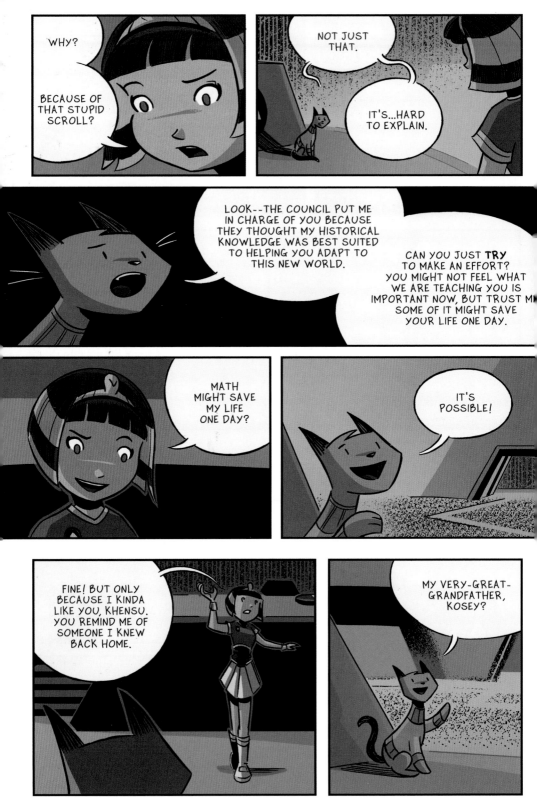

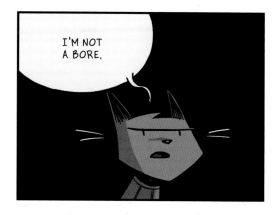

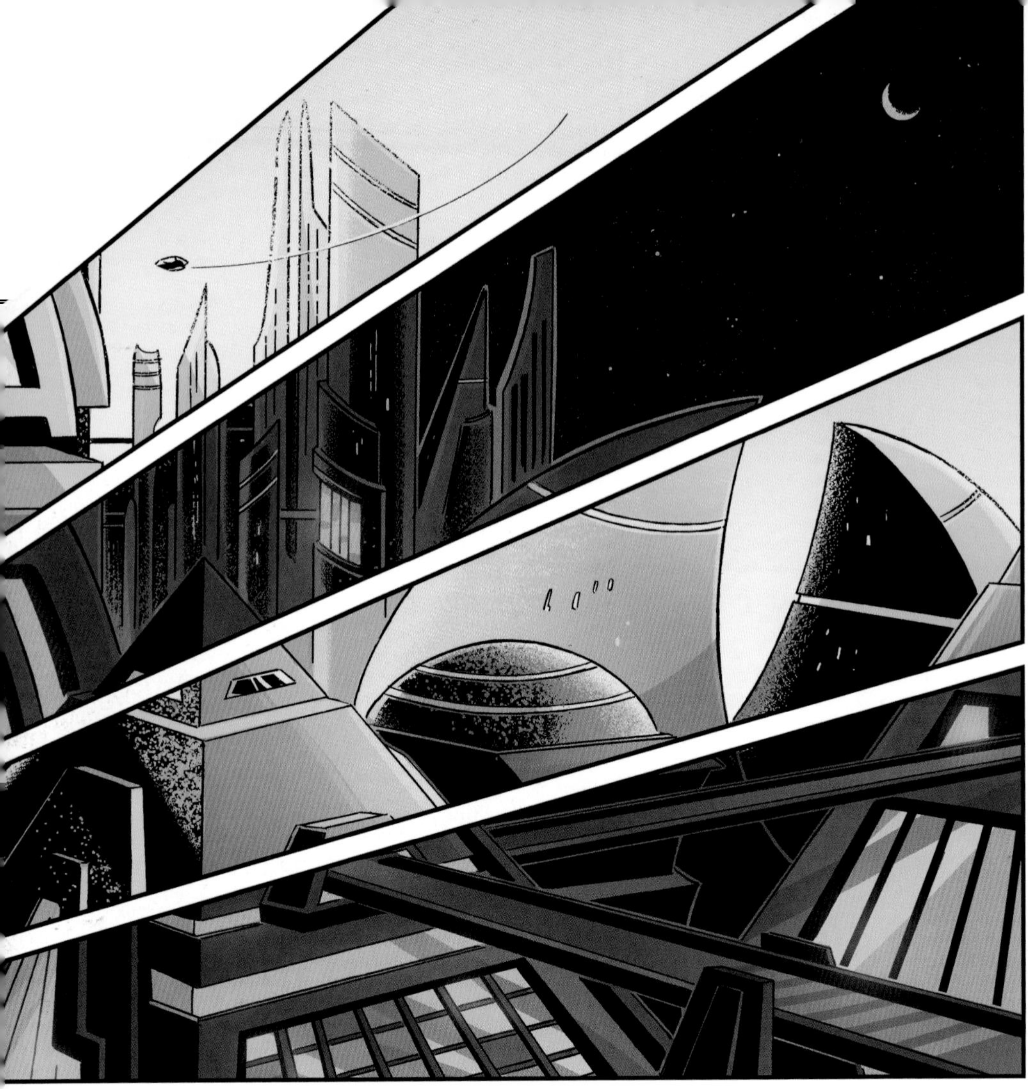

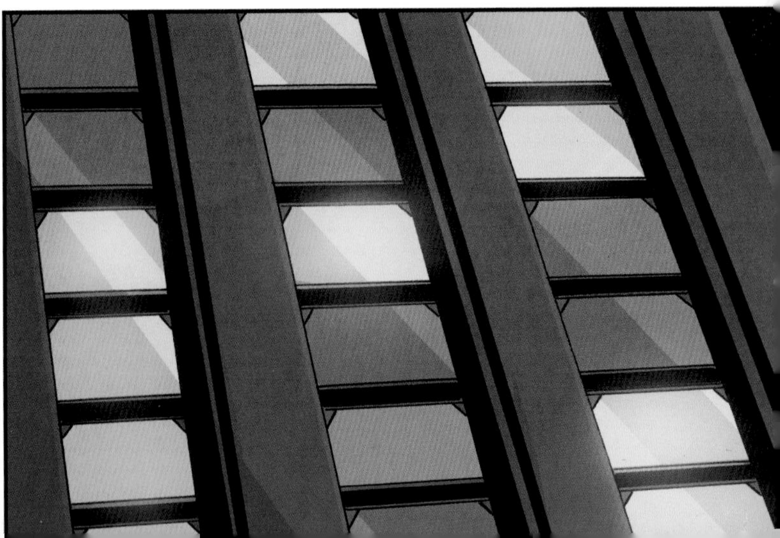

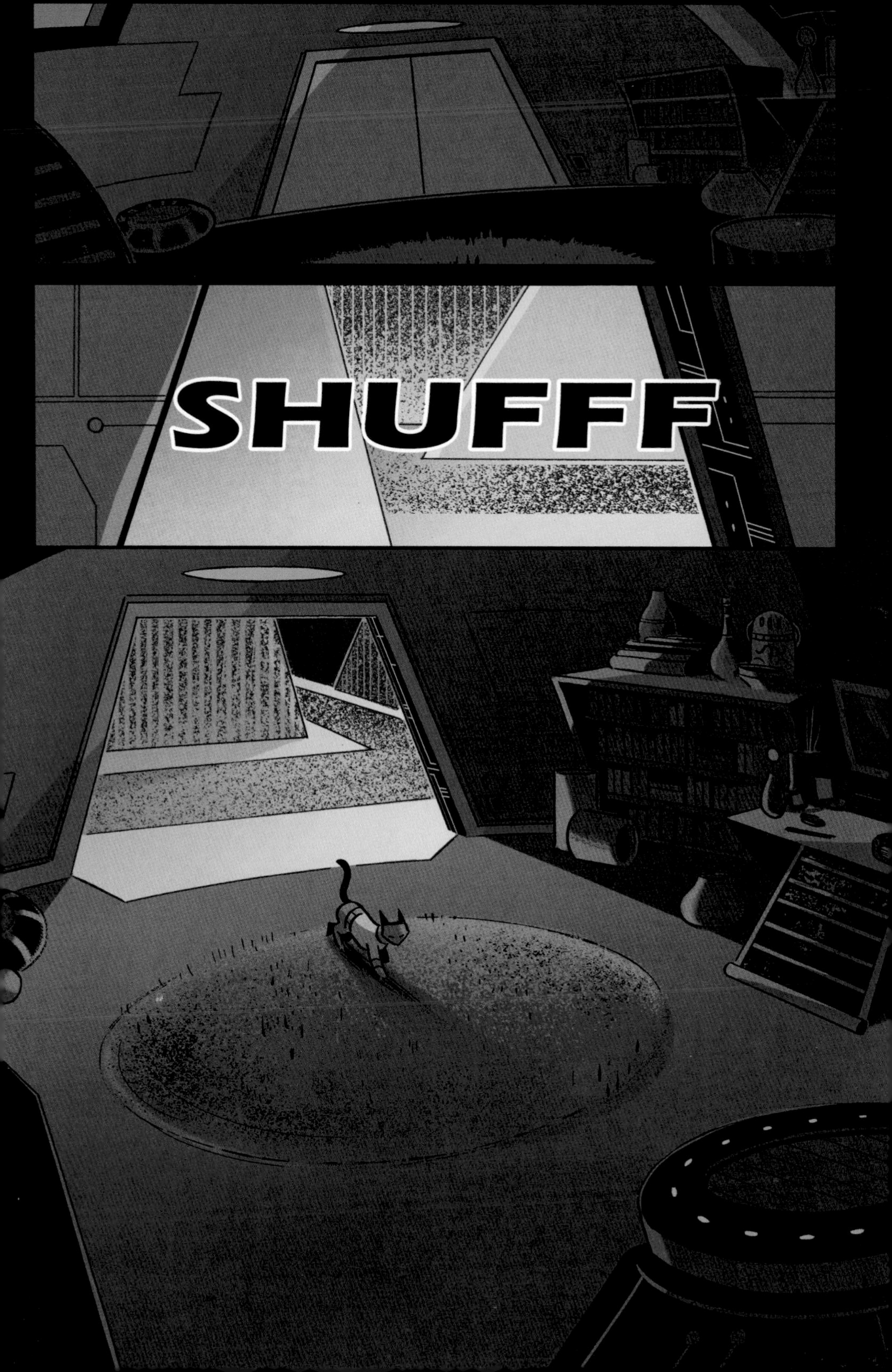
SHUFFF

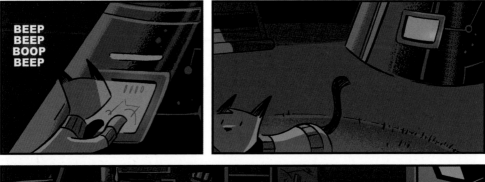

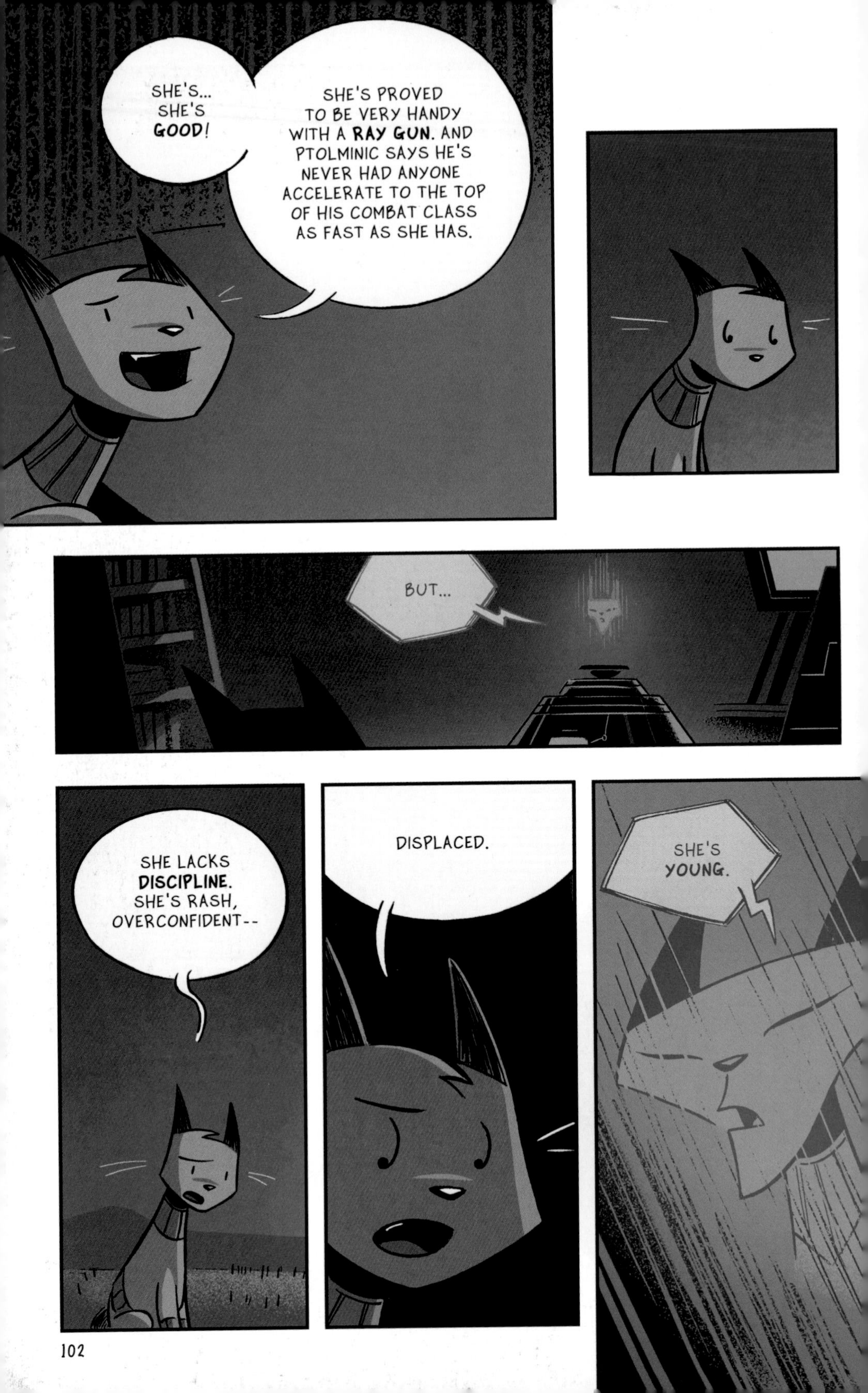
SHE'S... SHE'S **GOOD**!
SHE'S PROVED TO BE VERY HANDY WITH A **RAY GUN**. AND PTOLMINIC SAYS HE'S NEVER HAD ANYONE ACCELERATE TO THE TOP OF HIS COMBAT CLASS AS FAST AS SHE HAS.
BUT...
SHE LACKS **DISCIPLINE**. SHE'S RASH, OVERCONFIDENT--
DISPLACED.
SHE'S **YOUNG**.

VZZZSH

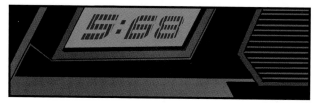

ALMOST FORGOT!

SHUFFF

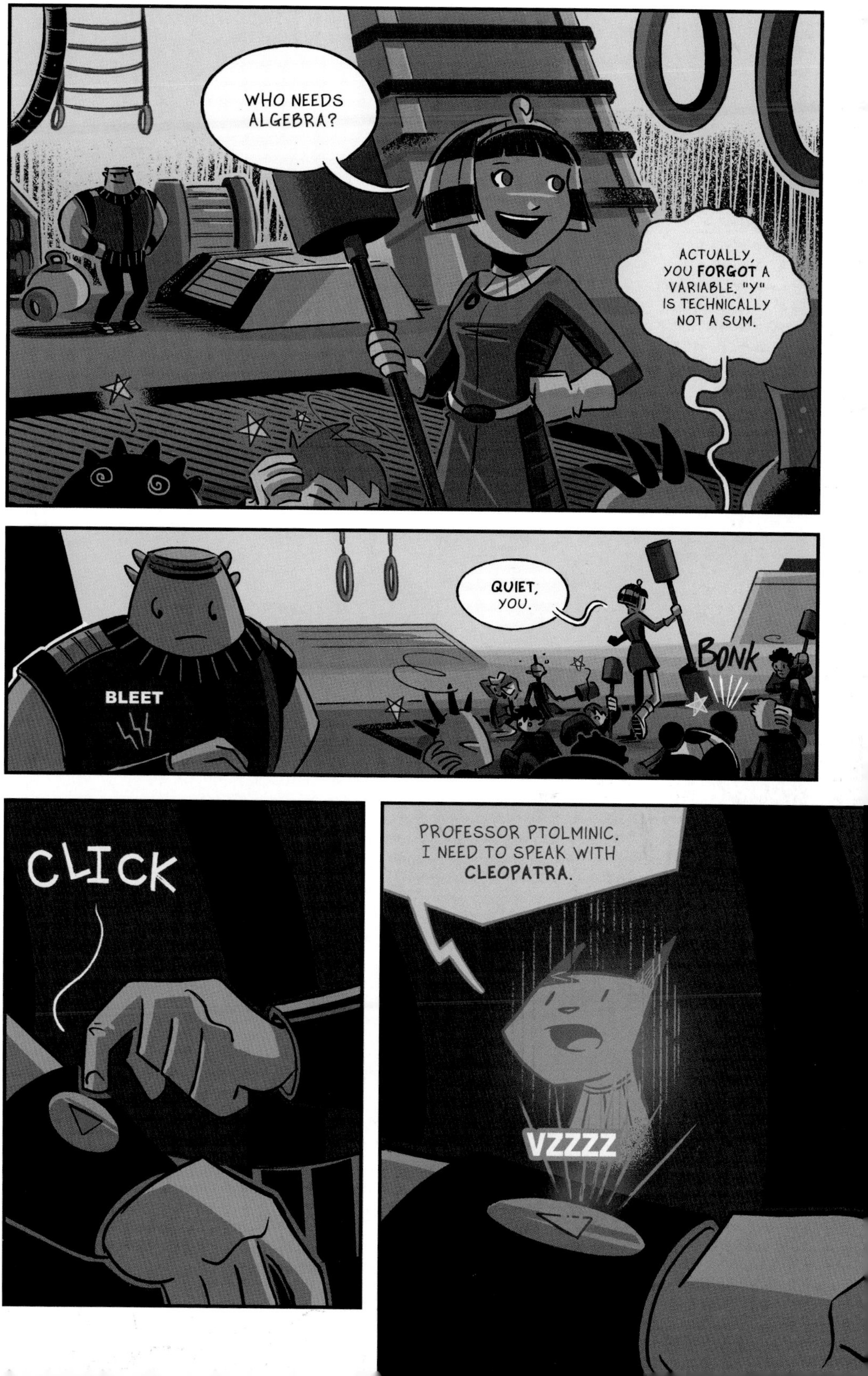
WHO NEEDS ALGEBRA?
ACTUALLY, YOU FORGOT A VARIABLE. "Y" IS TECHNICALLY NOT A SUM.
QUIET, YOU.
BLEET
BONK
CLICK
PROFESSOR PTOLMINIC. I NEED TO SPEAK WITH CLEOPATRA.
VZZZZ

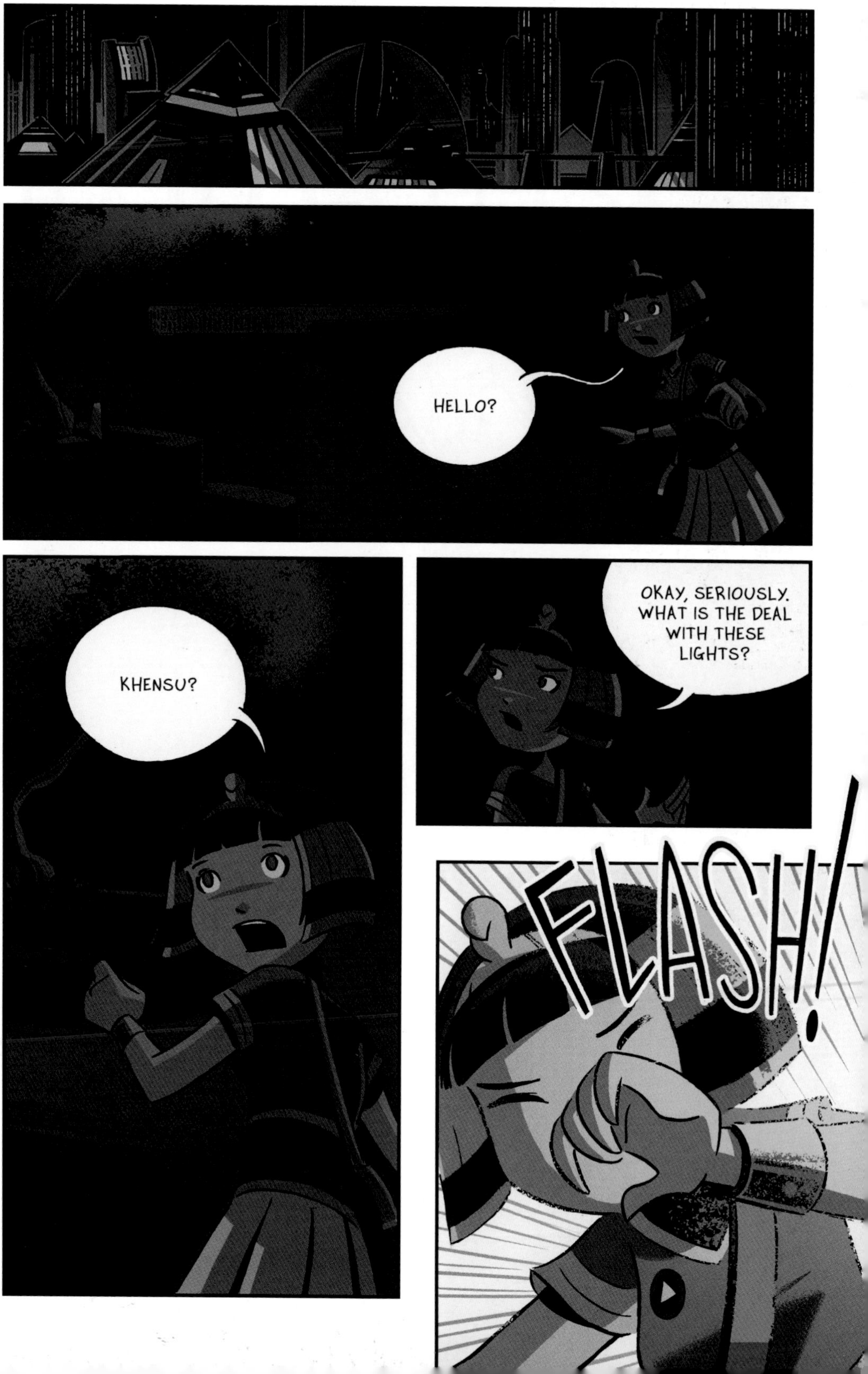
HELLO?
KHENSU?
OKAY, SERIOUSLY. WHAT IS THE DEAL WITH THESE LIGHTS?
FLASH!

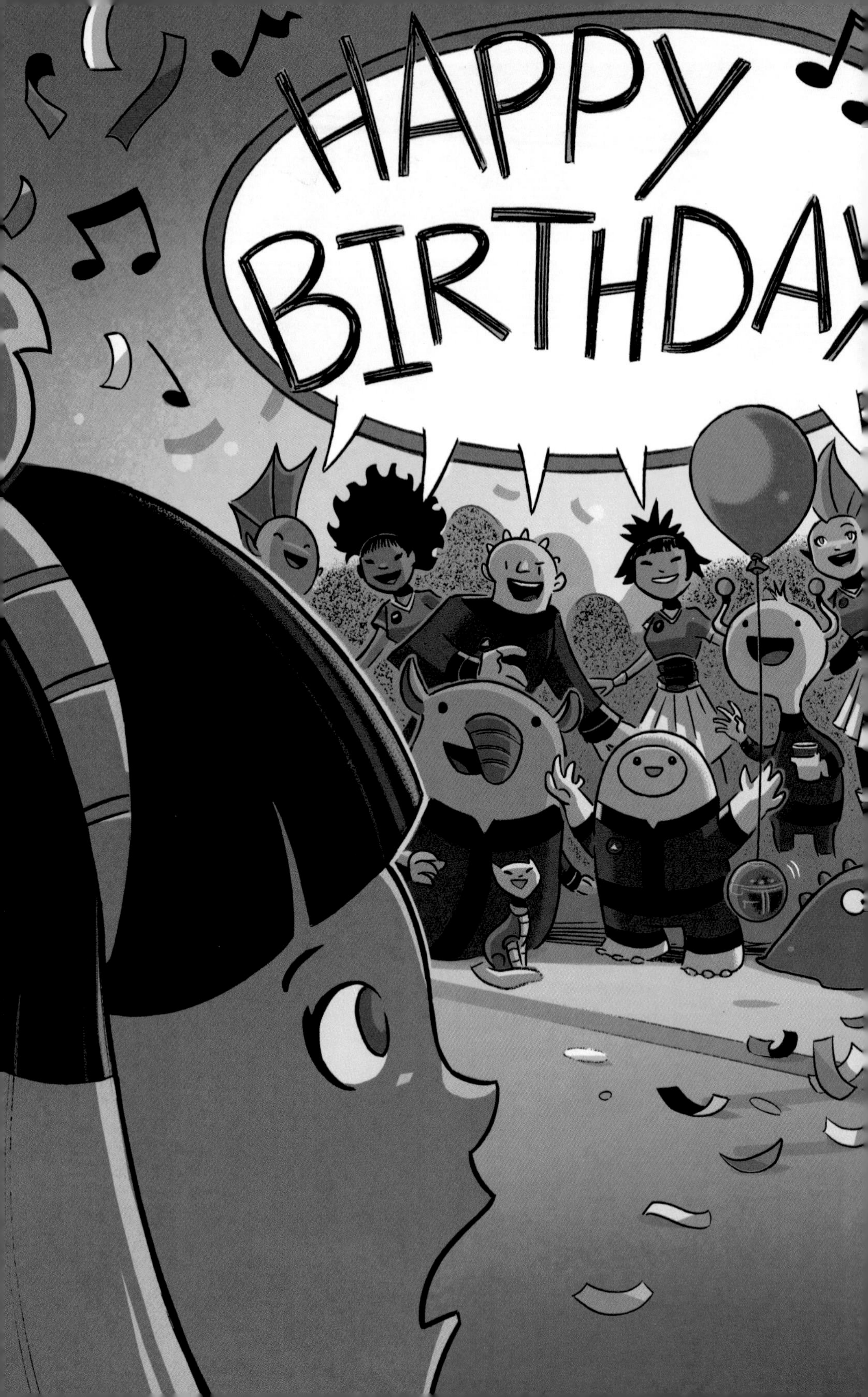
HAPPY BIRTHDAY

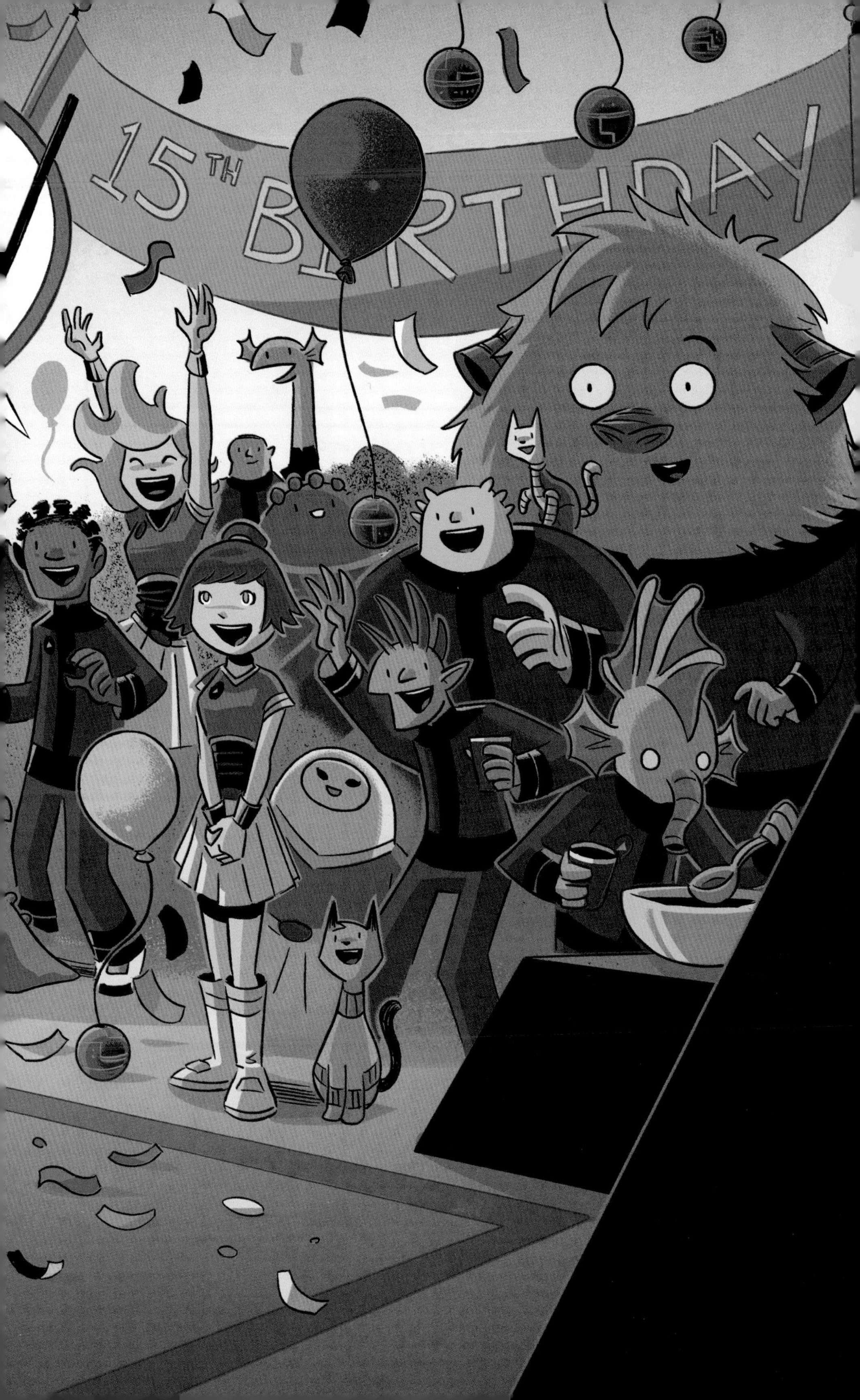
15TH BIRTHDAY

CHAPTER THREE

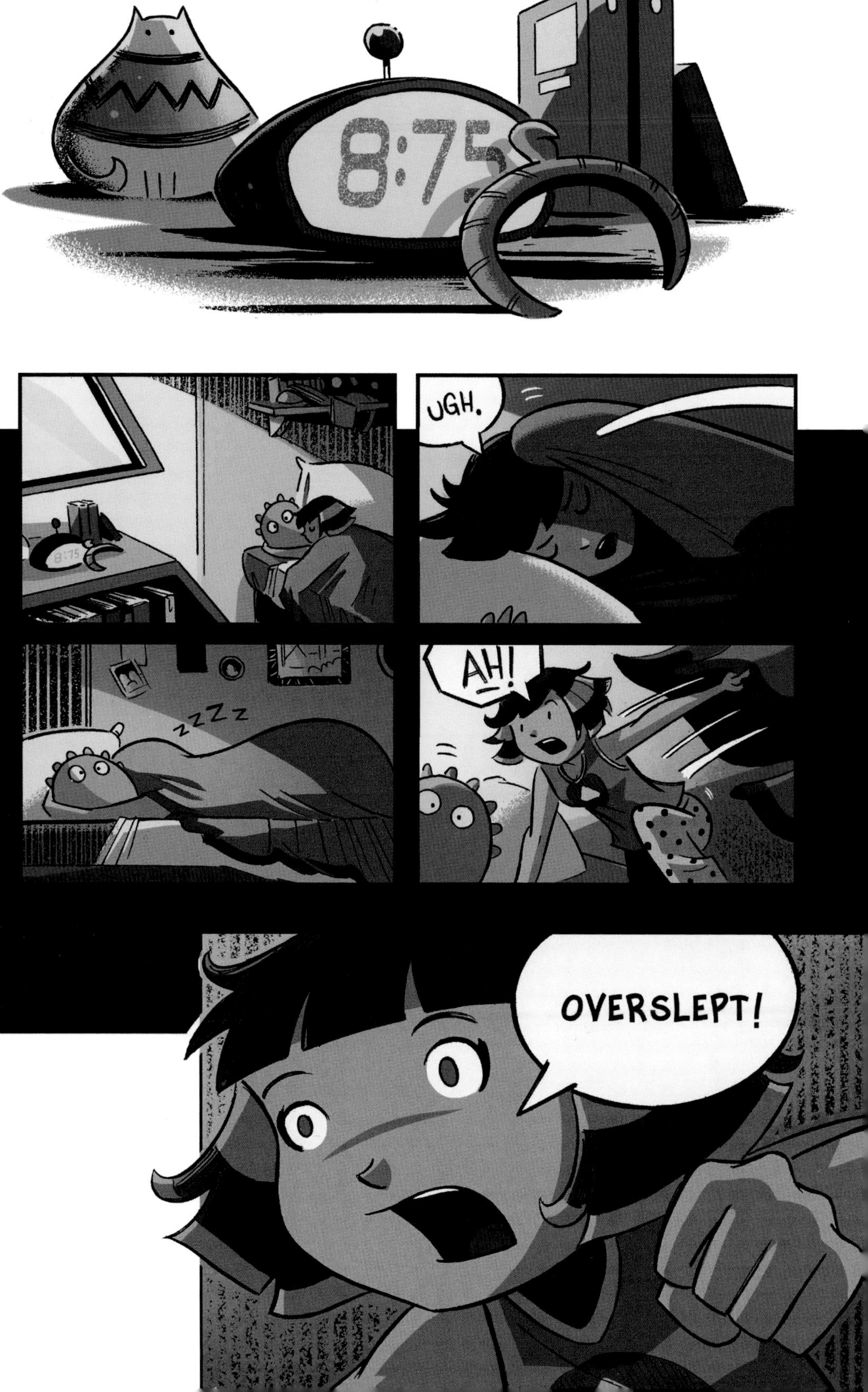
8:75
UGH.
AH!
OVERSLEPT!

FIRST OFF, IT'S A SCHOOL **ASSIGNMENT**, NOT A MISSION.

SECOND OFF, RELAX! THESE FIRST SOLO ONES ARE **EASY**. USUALLY IT'S JUST ABOUT RECOVERING SOME HISTORICAL DATA FROM SOMEWHERE.

OH-- YOU CAN'T EVEN **SEE** MY SOCKS...

I DIDN'T HAVE TO LEAVE THE SCHOOL GROUNDS FOR MINE. JUST SPENT THE ENTIRE DAY IN THE LIBRARY.

IT WAS **AMAZING**.

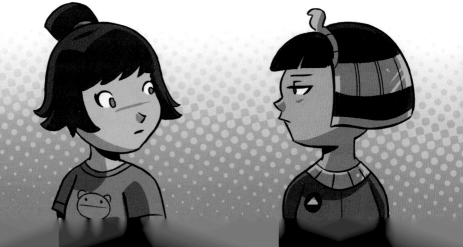

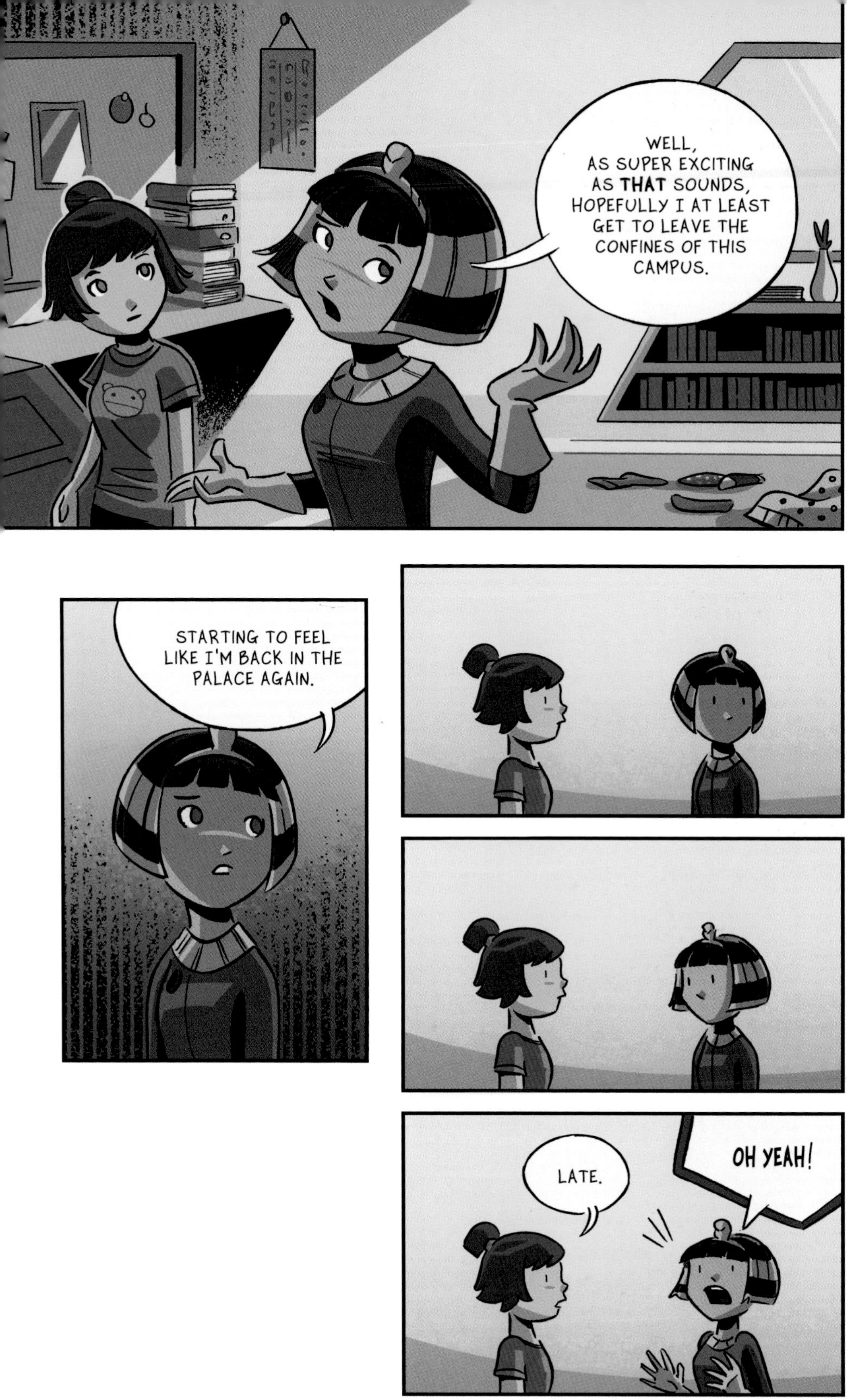
WELL, AS SUPER EXCITING AS THAT SOUNDS, HOPEFULLY I AT LEAST GET TO LEAVE THE CONFINES OF THIS CAMPUS.
STARTING TO FEEL LIKE I'M BACK IN THE PALACE AGAIN.
LATE.
OH YEAH!

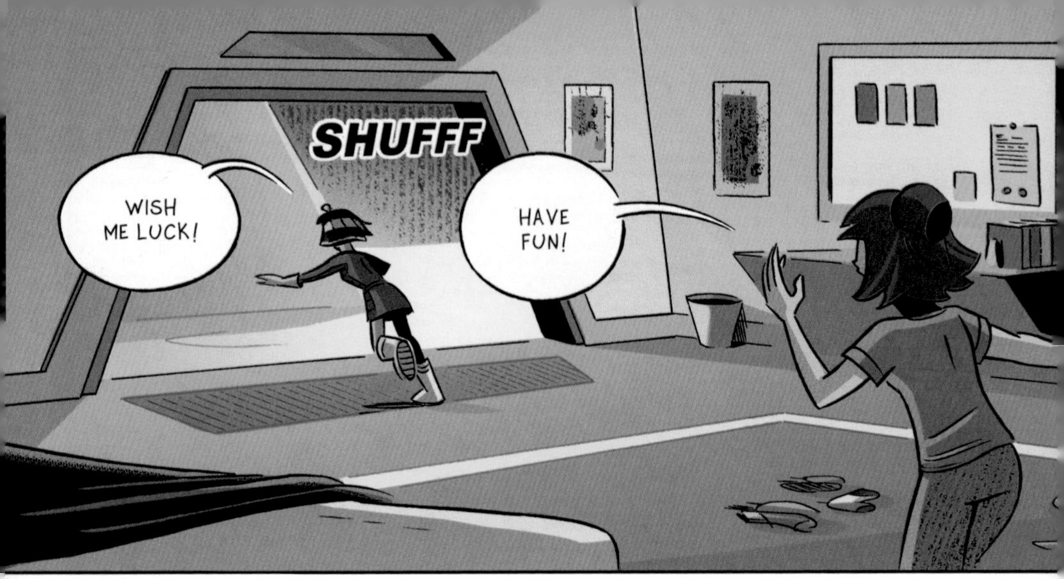
SHUFFF
WISH ME LUCK!
HAVE FUN!

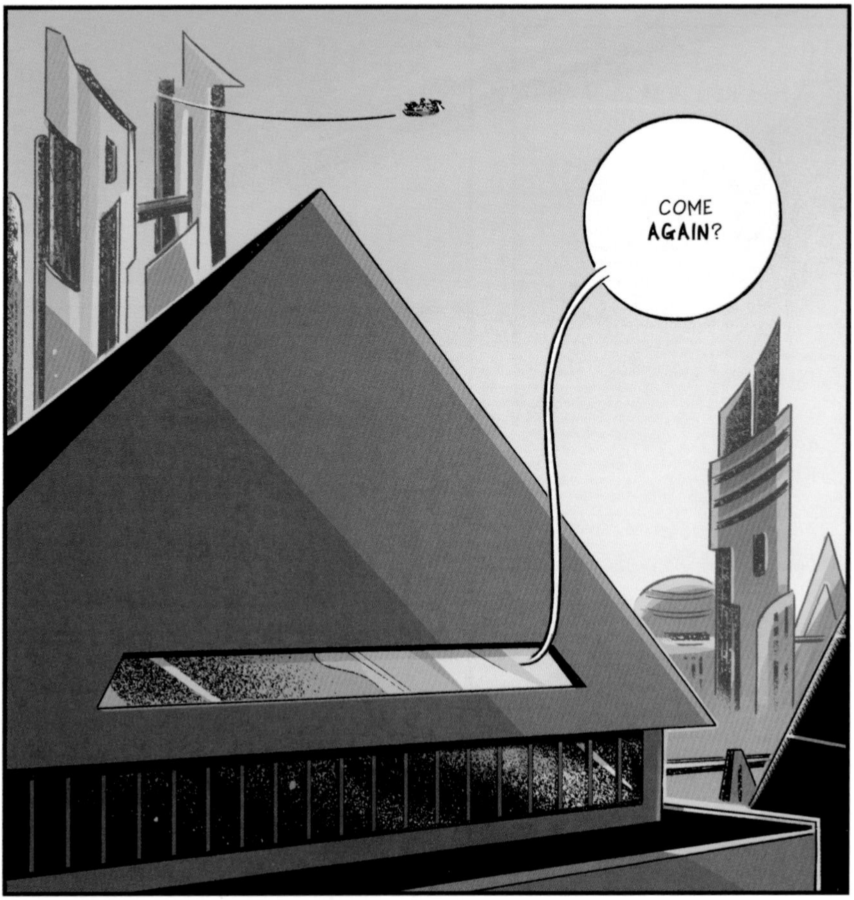
COME AGAIN?

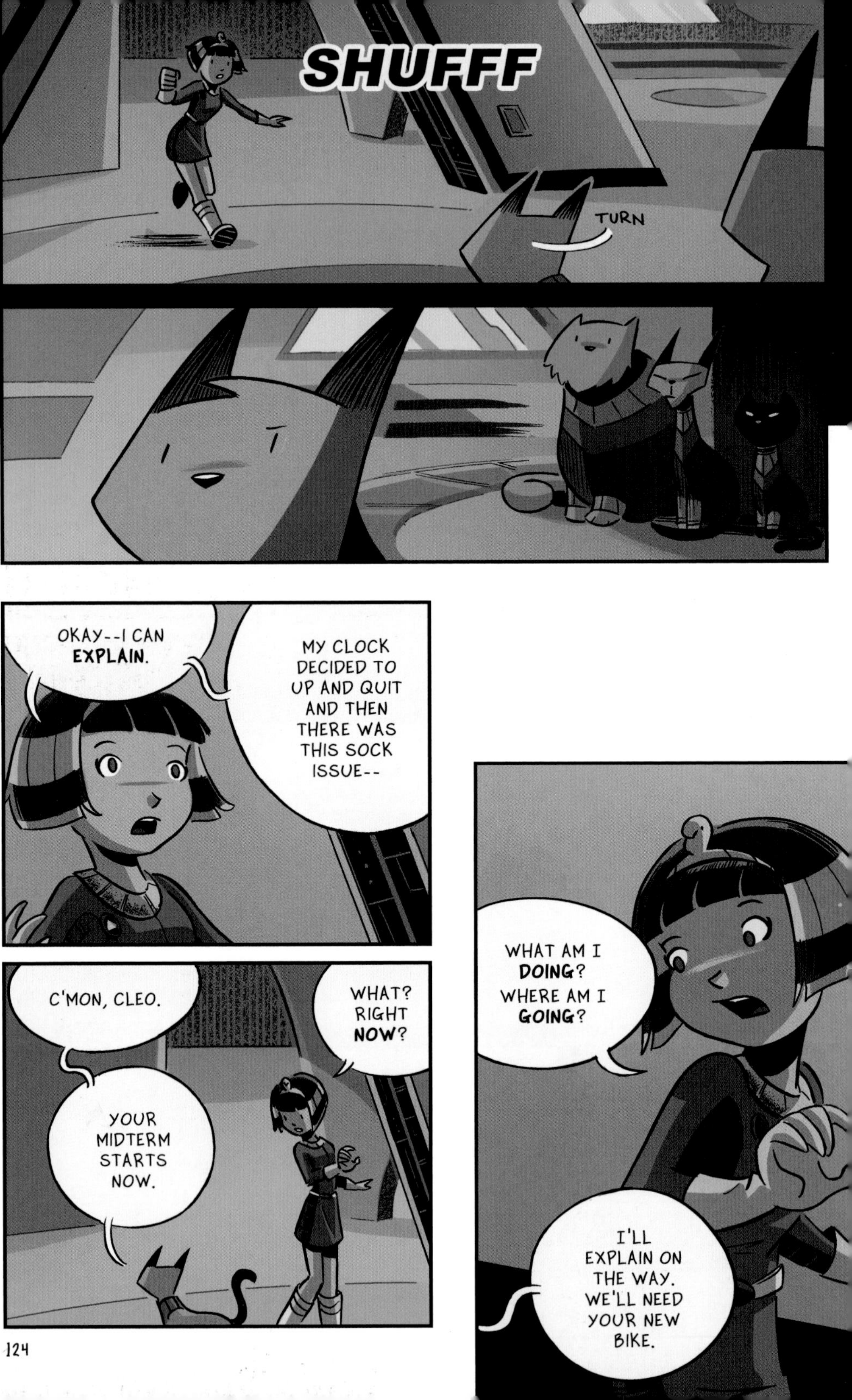
SHUFFF
TURN
OKAY--I CAN EXPLAIN.
MY CLOCK DECIDED TO UP AND QUIT AND THEN THERE WAS THIS SOCK ISSUE--
C'MON, CLEO.
YOUR MIDTERM STARTS NOW.
WHAT? RIGHT NOW?
WHAT AM I DOING? WHERE AM I GOING?
I'LL EXPLAIN ON THE WAY. WE'LL NEED YOUR NEW BIKE.

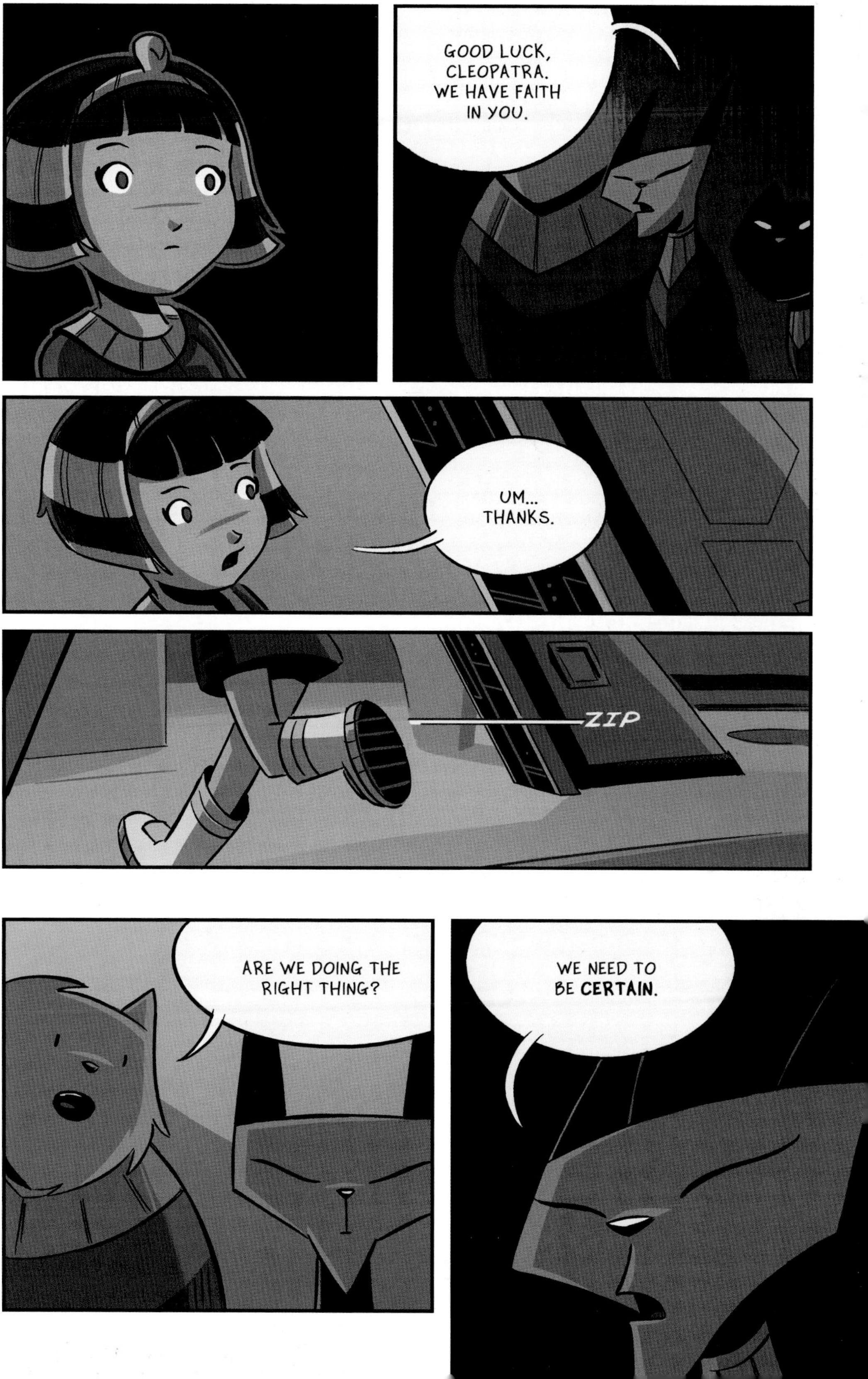
GOOD LUCK, CLEOPATRA. WE HAVE FAITH IN YOU.
UM... THANKS.
ZIP
ARE WE DOING THE RIGHT THING?
WE NEED TO BE **CERTAIN**.

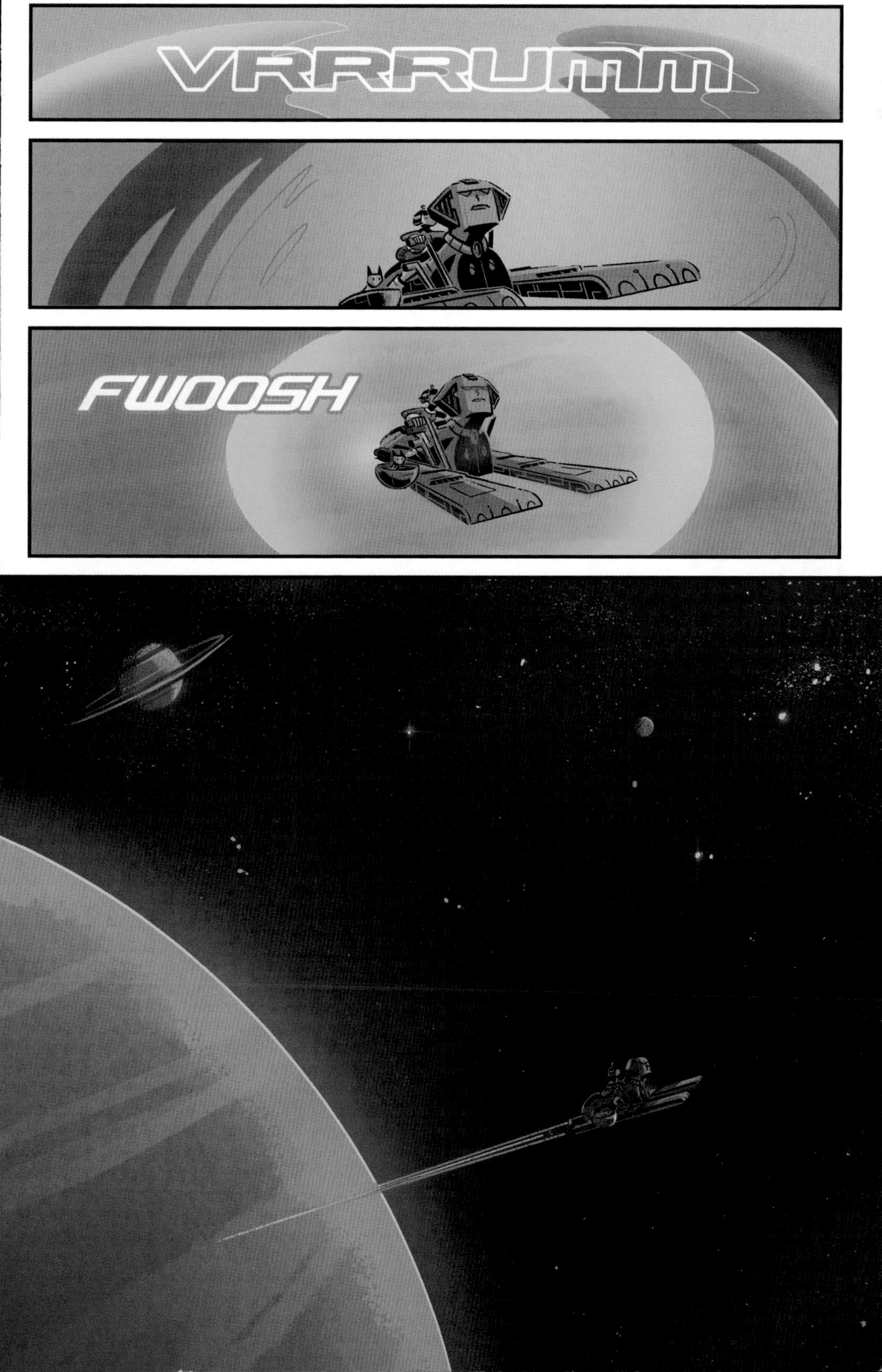
VRRRUMM
FWOOSH

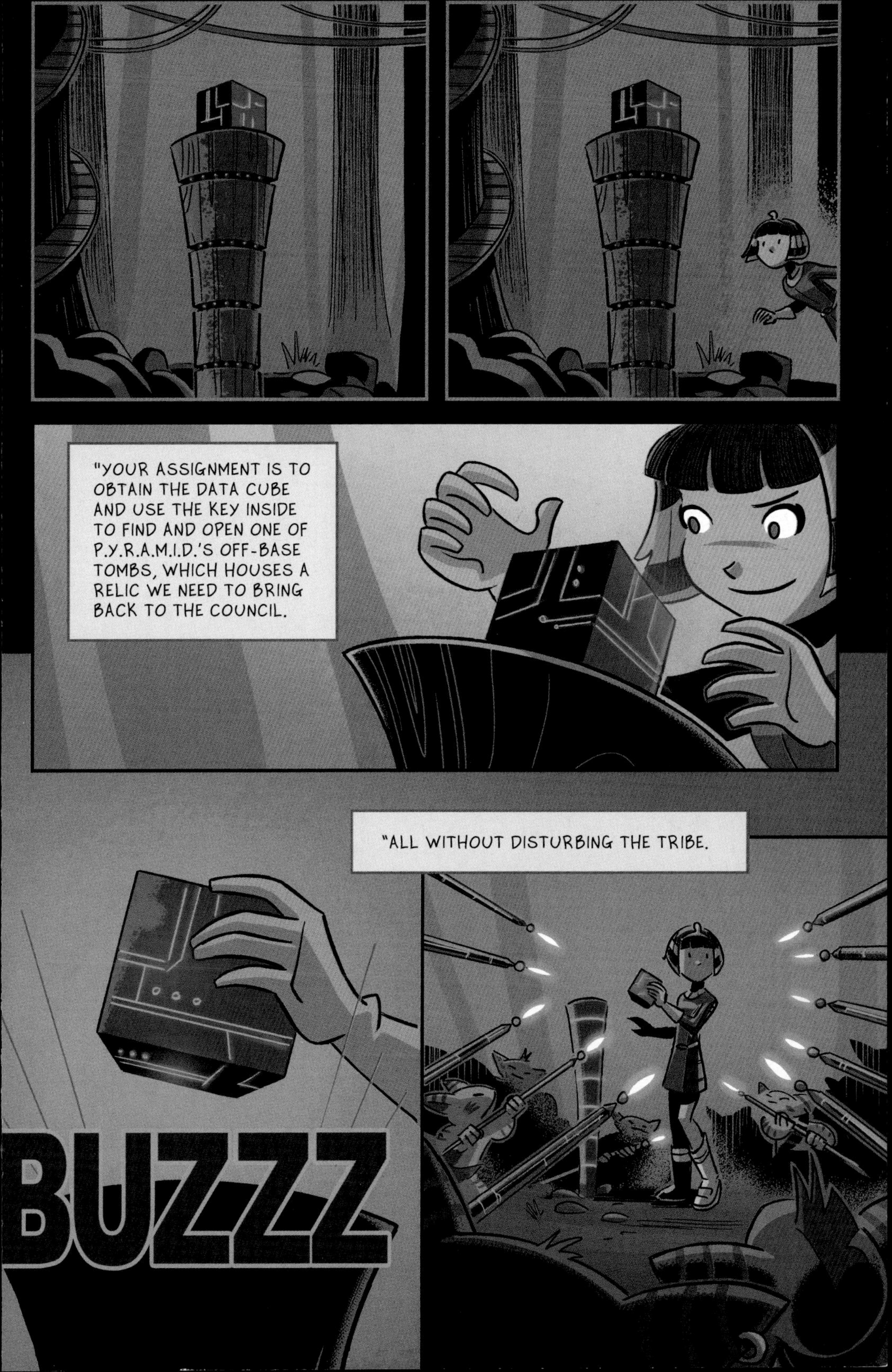
"YOUR ASSIGNMENT IS TO OBTAIN THE DATA CUBE AND USE THE KEY INSIDE TO FIND AND OPEN ONE OF P.Y.R.A.M.I.D.'S OFF-BASE TOMBS, WHICH HOUSES A RELIC WE NEED TO BRING BACK TO THE COUNCIL.
"ALL WITHOUT DISTURBING THE TRIBE.
BUZZZ

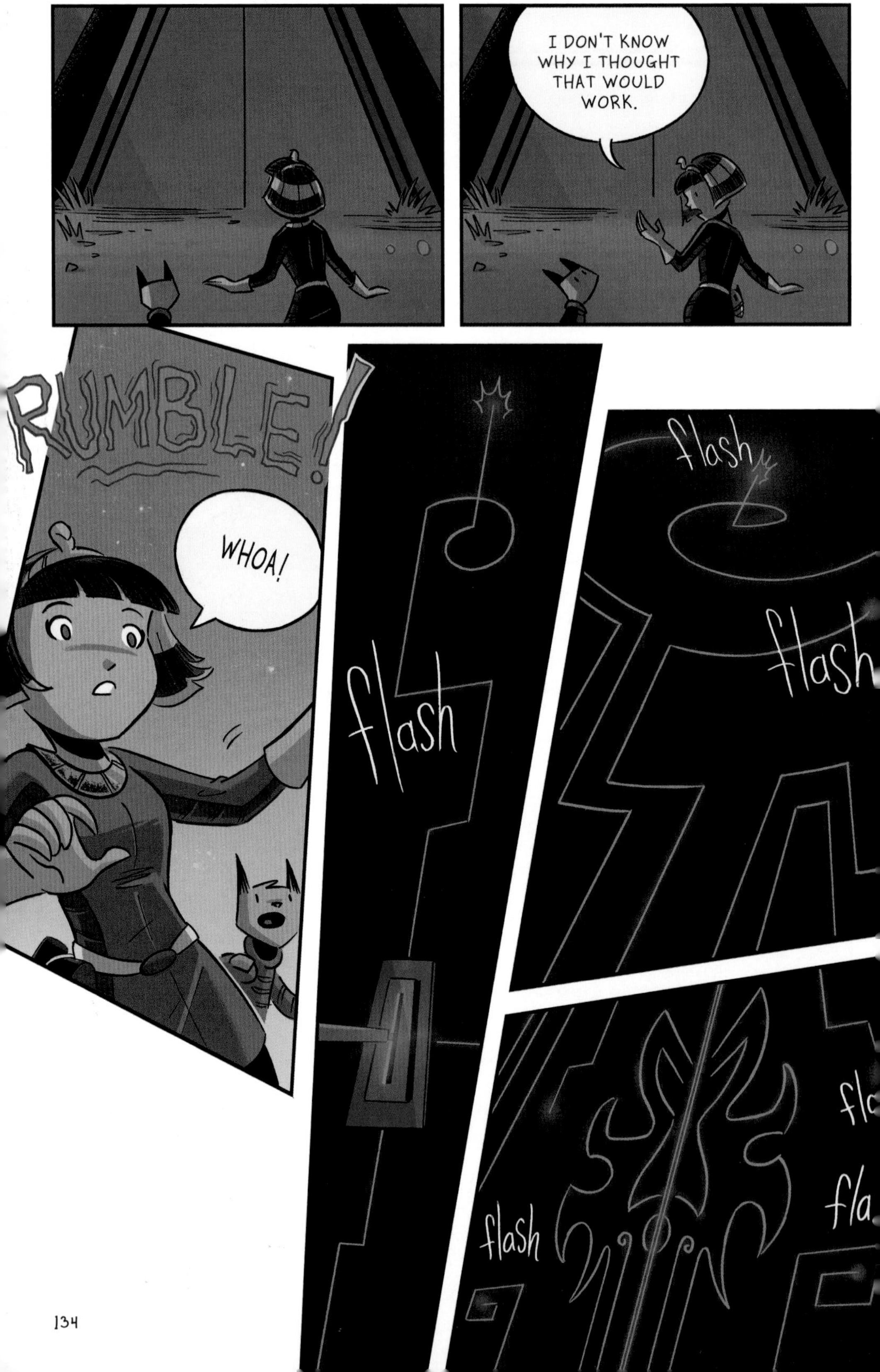

I DON'T KNOW WHY I THOUGHT THAT WOULD WORK.
RUMBLE!
WHOA!
flash
flash
flash
flash

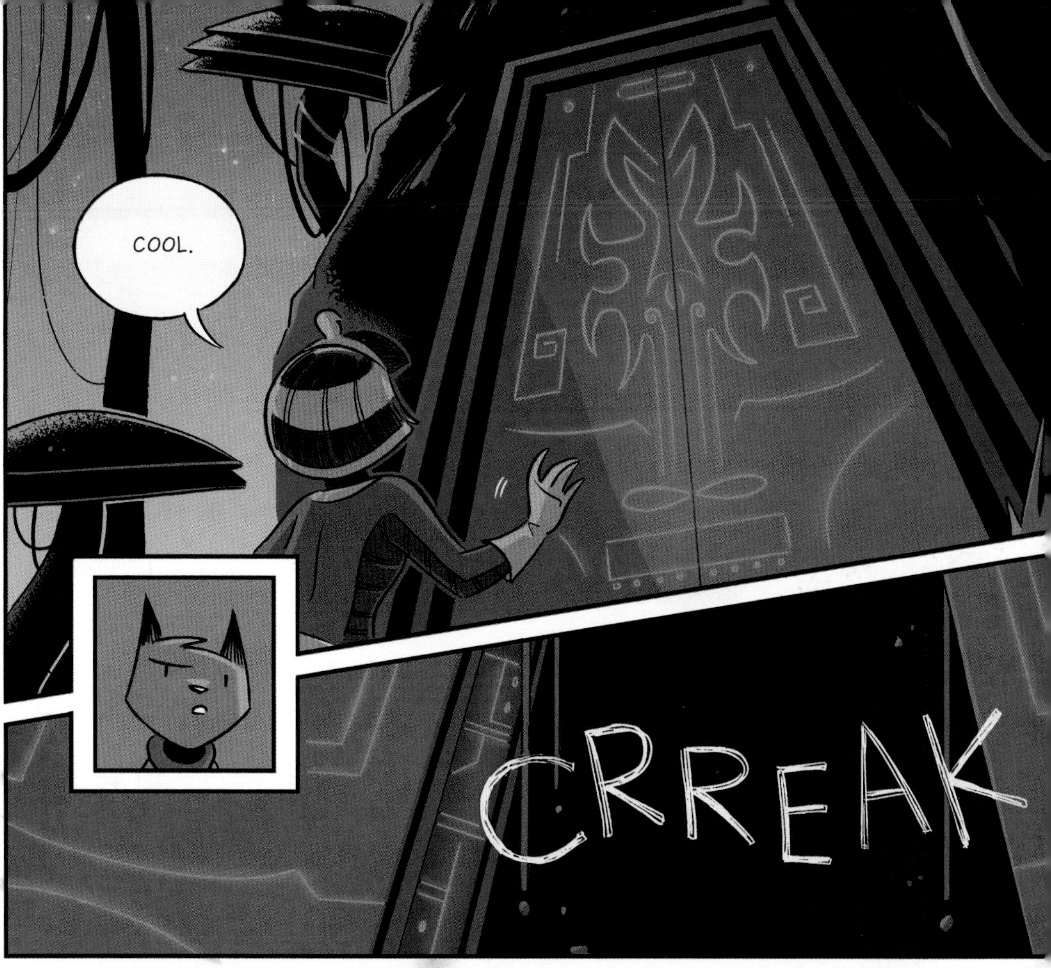
COOL.
CRREAK

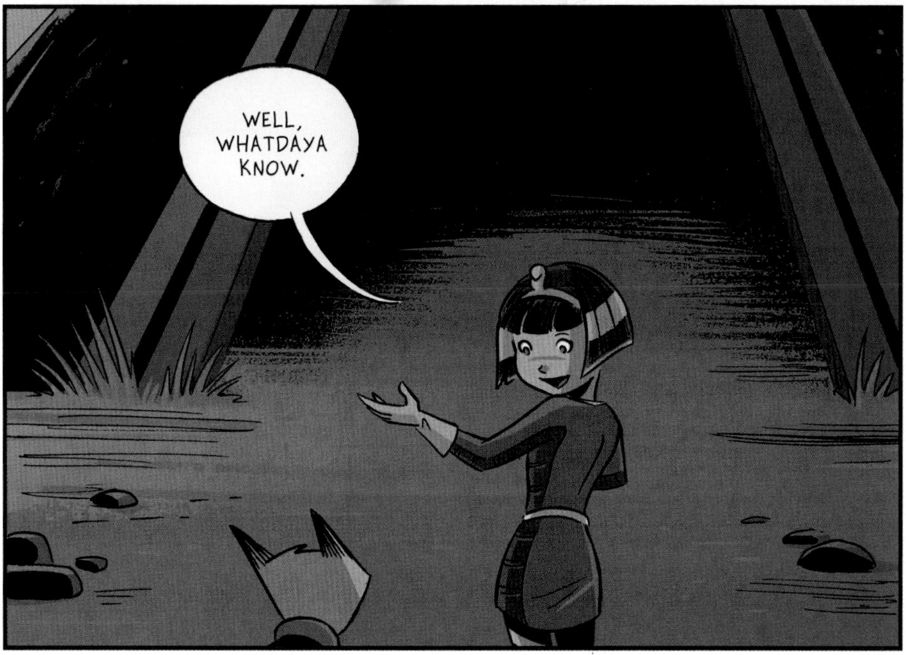
WELL, WHATDAYA KNOW.

VVRRRUMMMMM

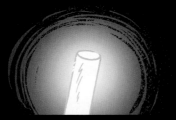

IT'S UPSETTING THAT I'M NOT EVEN **SIXTEEN** YET AND I'VE ALREADY BEEN IN MORE TOMBS THAN ANYONE SHOULD BE IN FOR **ONE** LIFETIME.

THAT'S **RIGHT**. TOMBS WERE MUCH DIFFERENT IN YOUR TIME.

WHY CALL THEM TOMBS NOW?

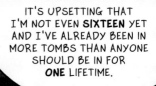

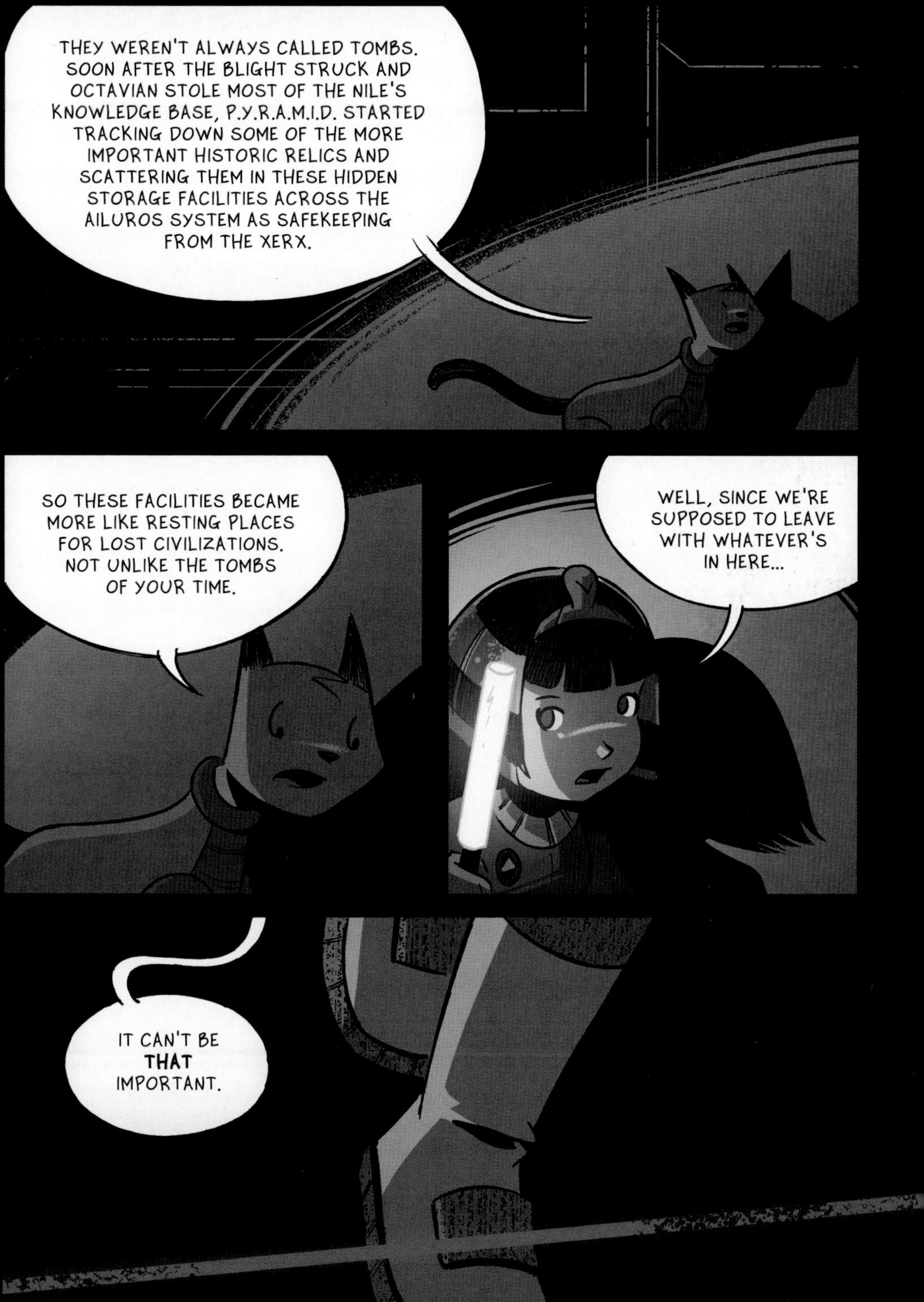
THEY WEREN'T ALWAYS CALLED TOMBS. SOON AFTER THE BLIGHT STRUCK AND OCTAVIAN STOLE MOST OF THE NILE'S KNOWLEDGE BASE, P.Y.R.A.M.I.D. STARTED TRACKING DOWN SOME OF THE MORE IMPORTANT HISTORIC RELICS AND SCATTERING THEM IN THESE HIDDEN STORAGE FACILITIES ACROSS THE AILUROS SYSTEM AS SAFEKEEPING FROM THE XERX.
SO THESE FACILITIES BECAME MORE LIKE RESTING PLACES FOR LOST CIVILIZATIONS. NOT UNLIKE THE TOMBS OF YOUR TIME.
WELL, SINCE WE'RE SUPPOSED TO LEAVE WITH WHATEVER'S IN HERE...
IT CAN'T BE **THAT** IMPORTANT.

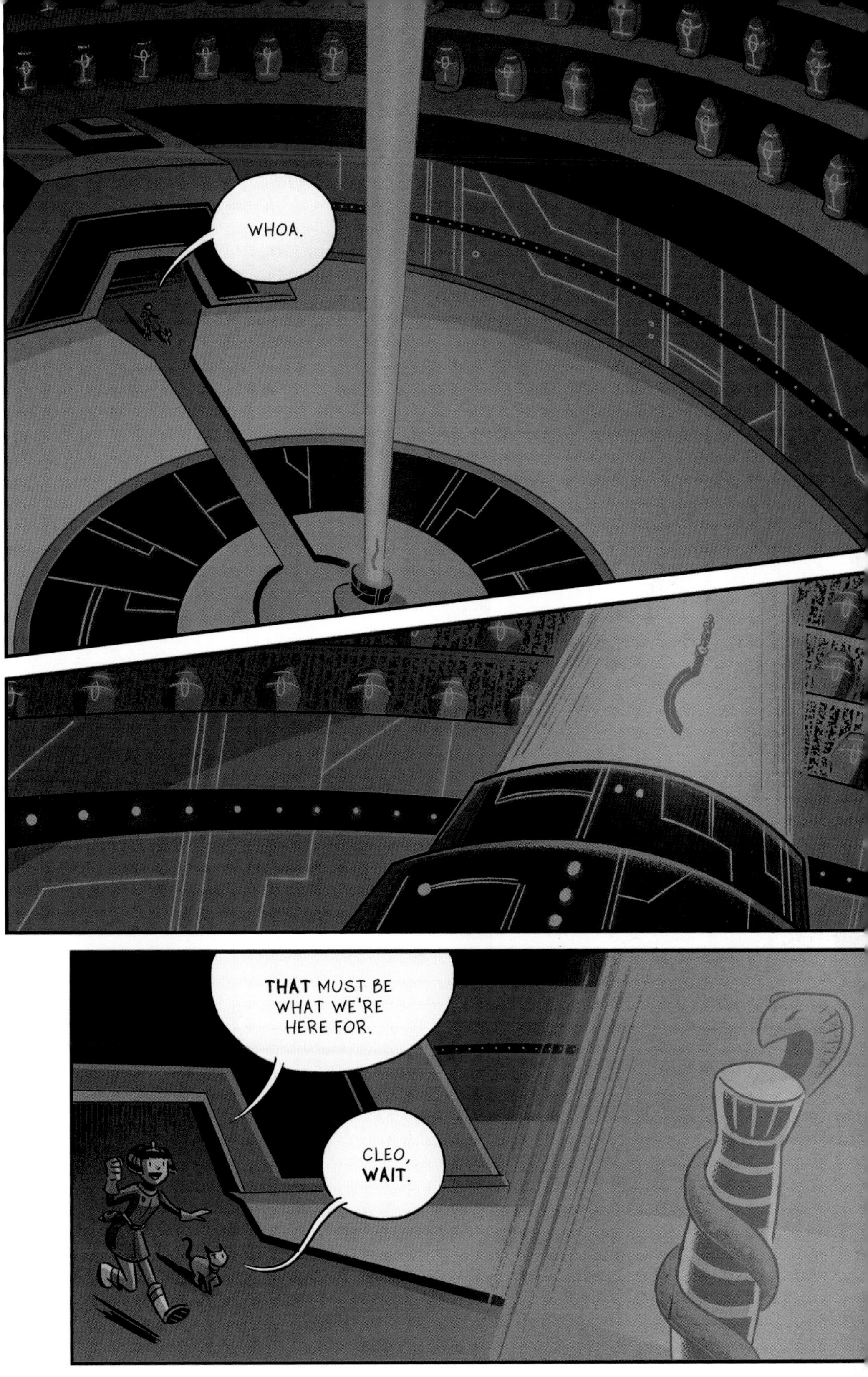
WHOA.
THAT MUST BE WHAT WE'RE HERE FOR.
CLEO, WAIT.

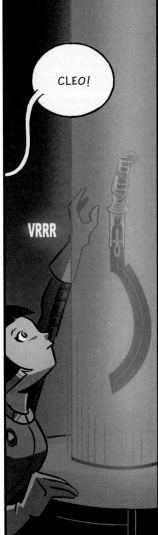

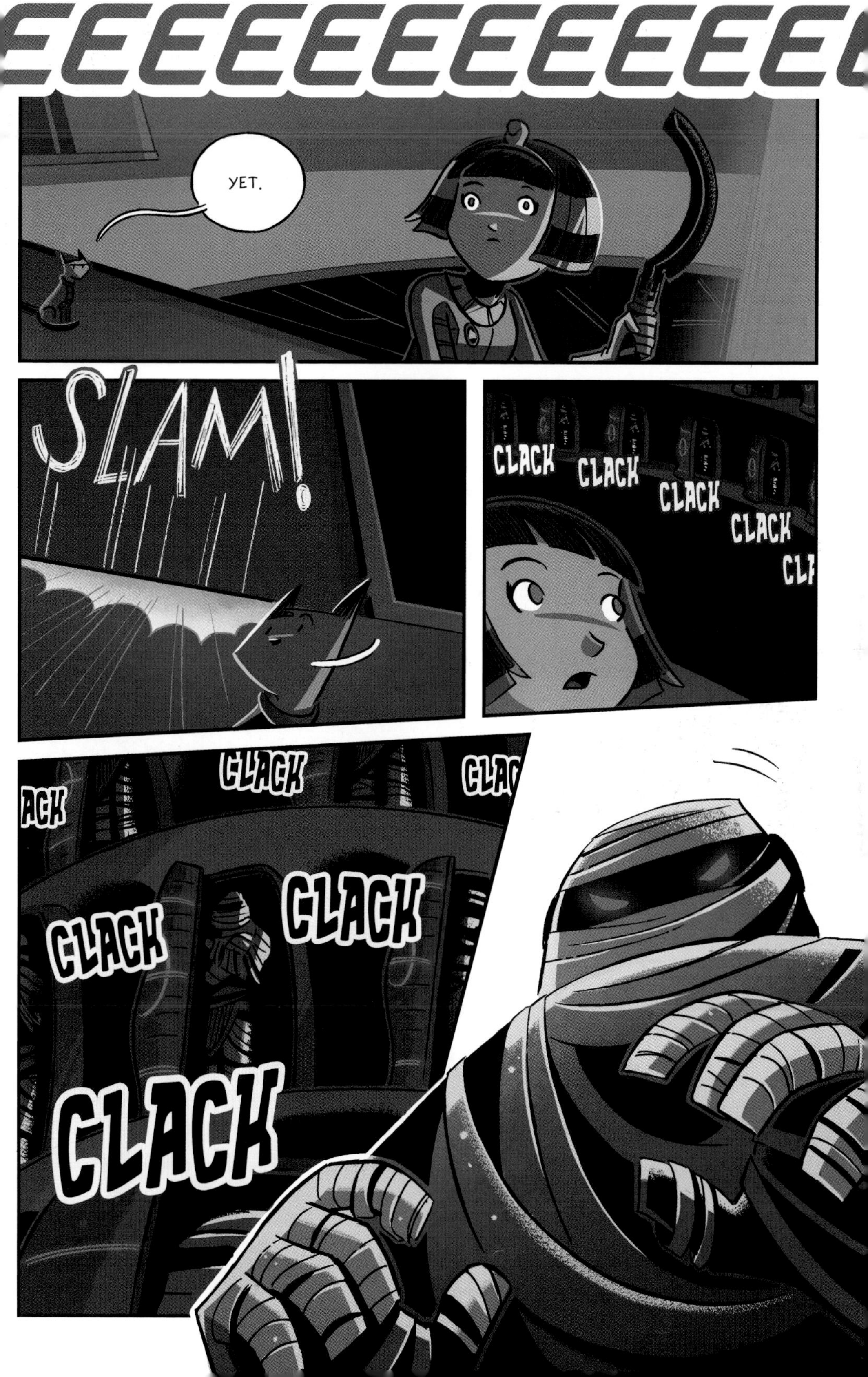

EEEEEEEEEEEE
YET.
SLAM!
CLACK
CLACK
CLACK
CLACK
ACK
CLACK
CLACK
CLACK
CLACK

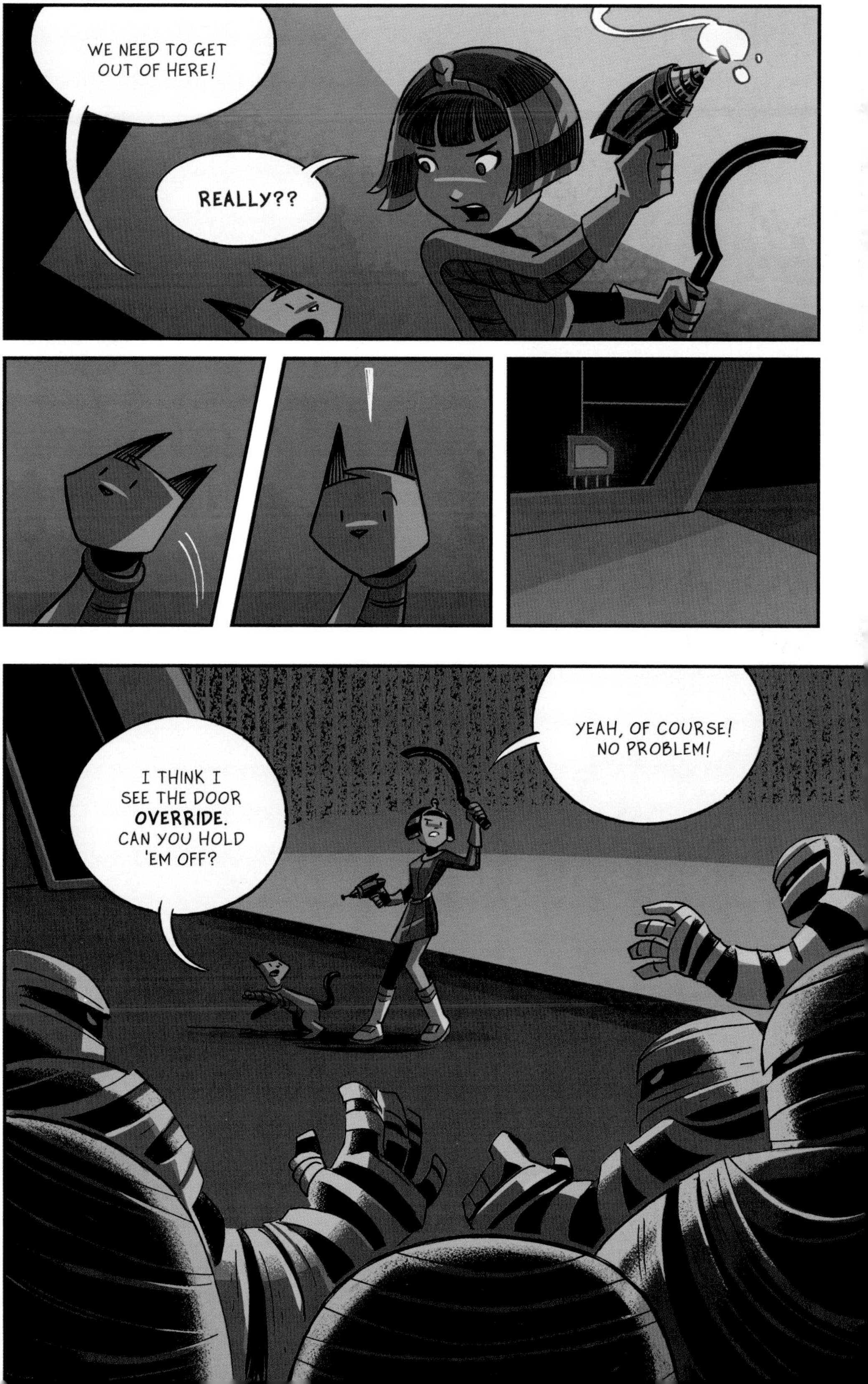
WE NEED TO GET OUT OF HERE!
REALLY??
I THINK I SEE THE DOOR **OVERRIDE.** CAN YOU HOLD 'EM OFF?
YEAH, OF COURSE! NO PROBLEM!

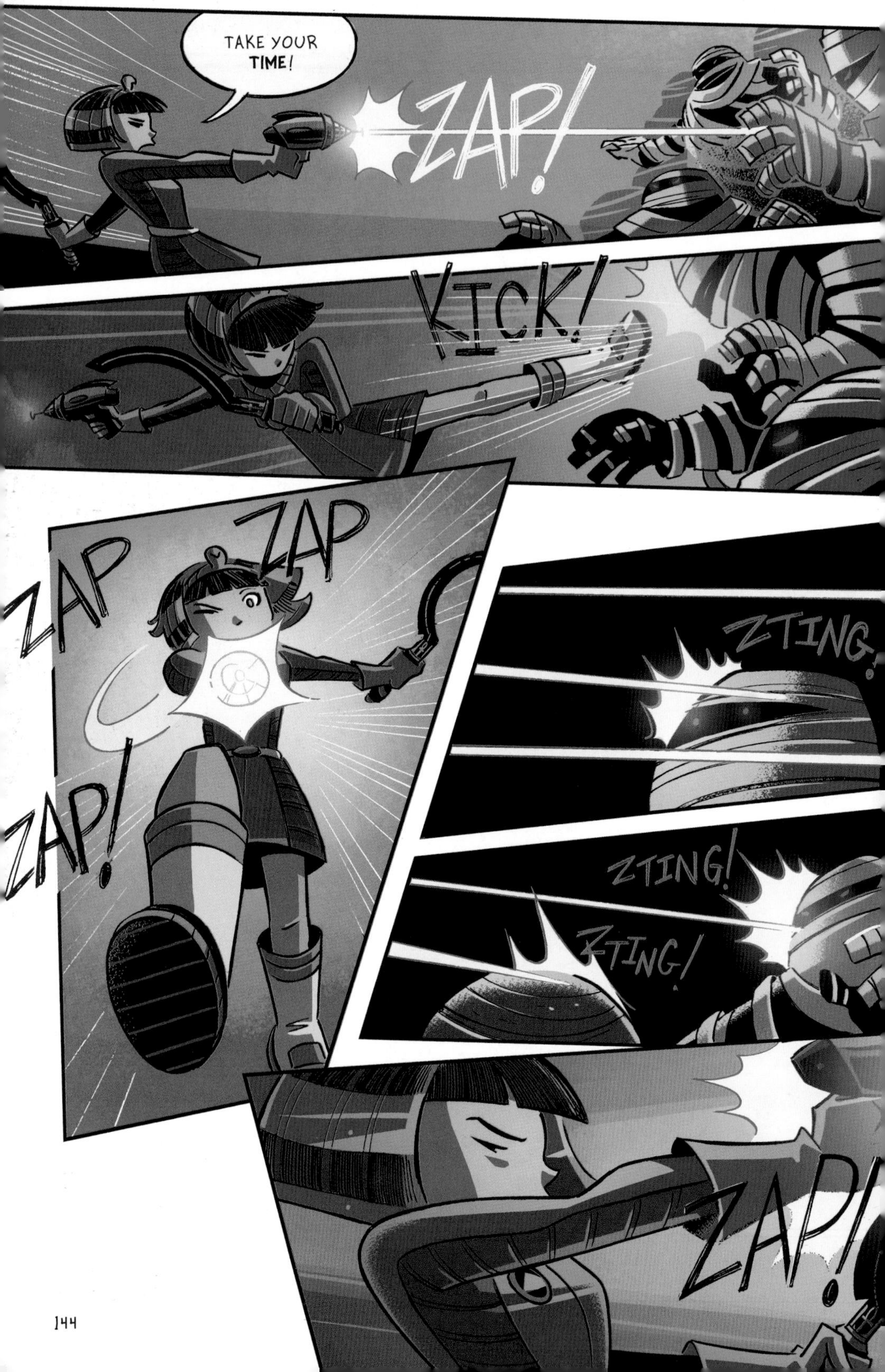
TAKE YOUR TIME!
ZAP!
KICK!
ZAP
ZAP
ZAP!
ZTING!
ZTING!
ZTING!
ZAP!

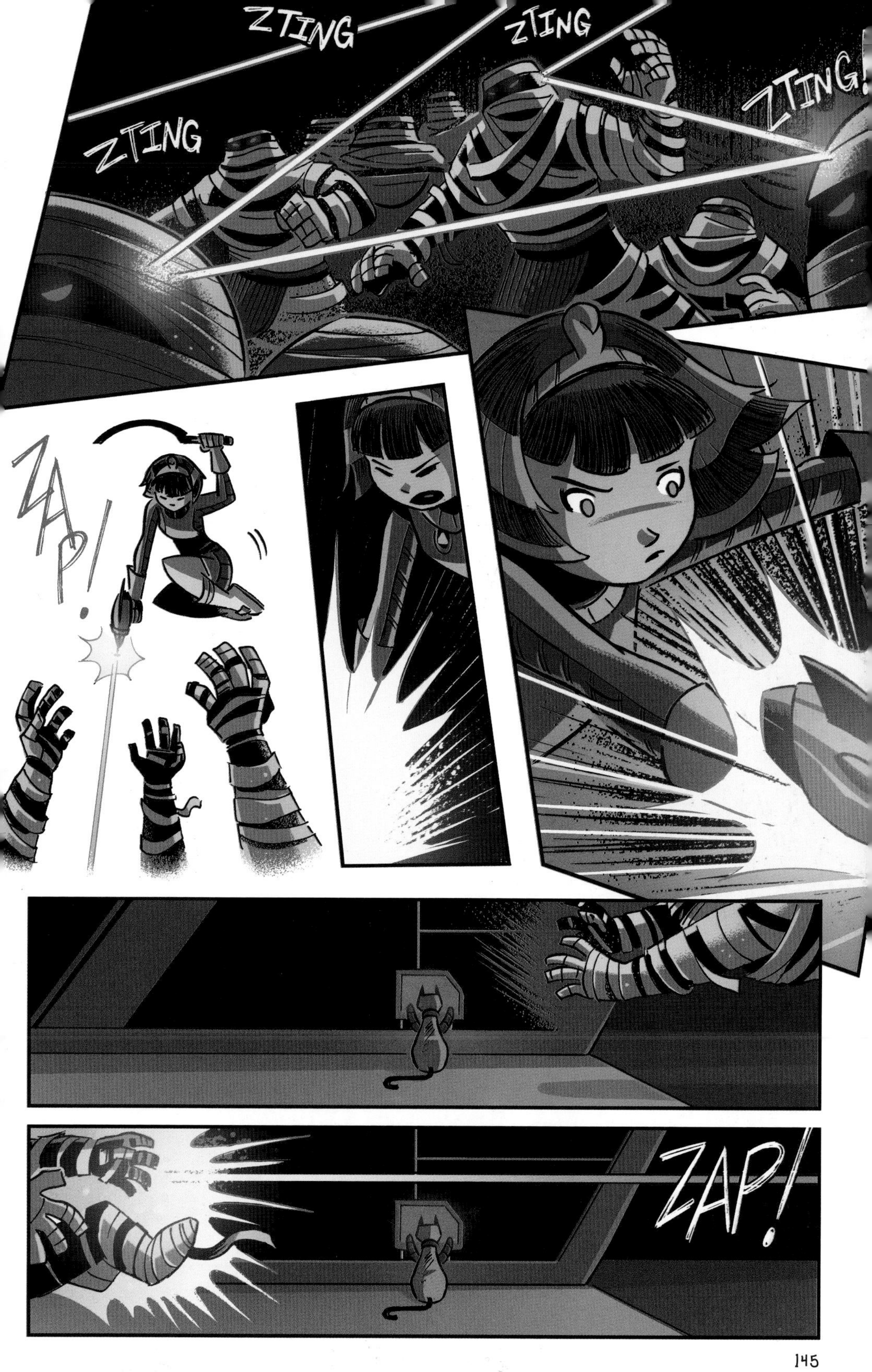
ZTING
ZTING
ZTING
ZTING!
ZAP!
ZAP!

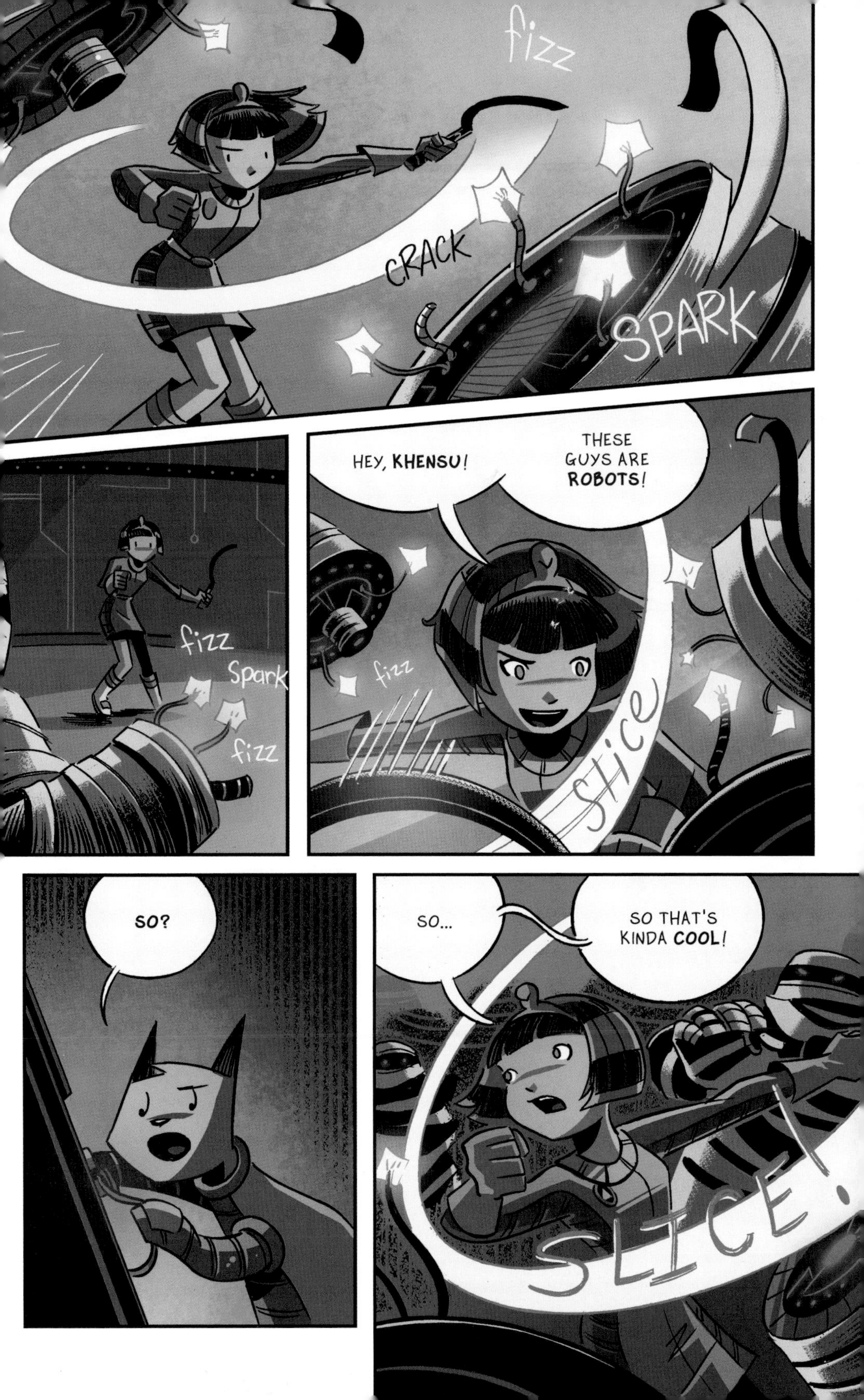
fizz
CRACK
SPARK
fizz
Spark
fizz
HEY, KHENSU!
THESE GUYS ARE ROBOTS!
fizz
SLICE
SO?
SO...
SO THAT'S KINDA COOL!
SLICE!

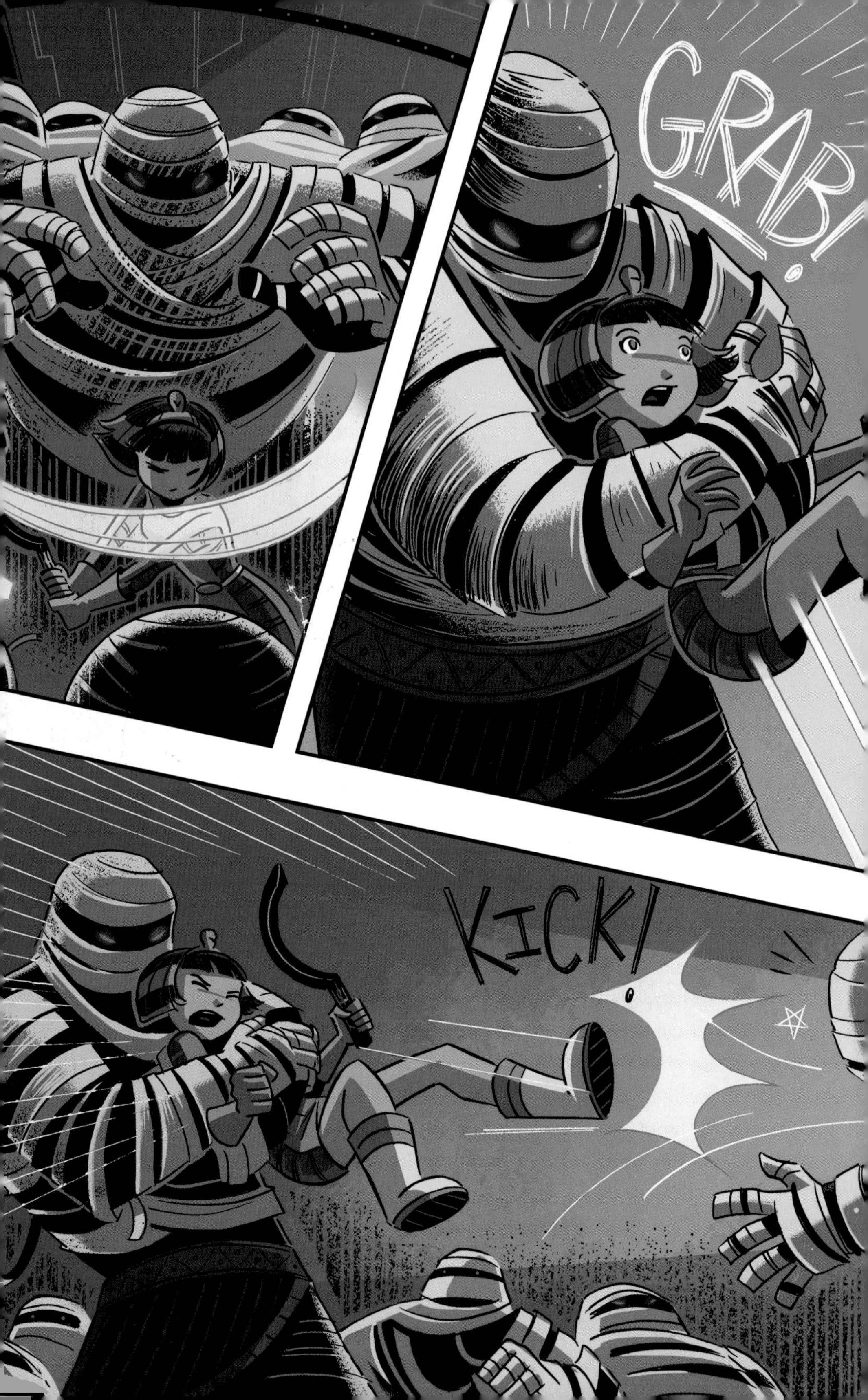
GRAB!
KICK!

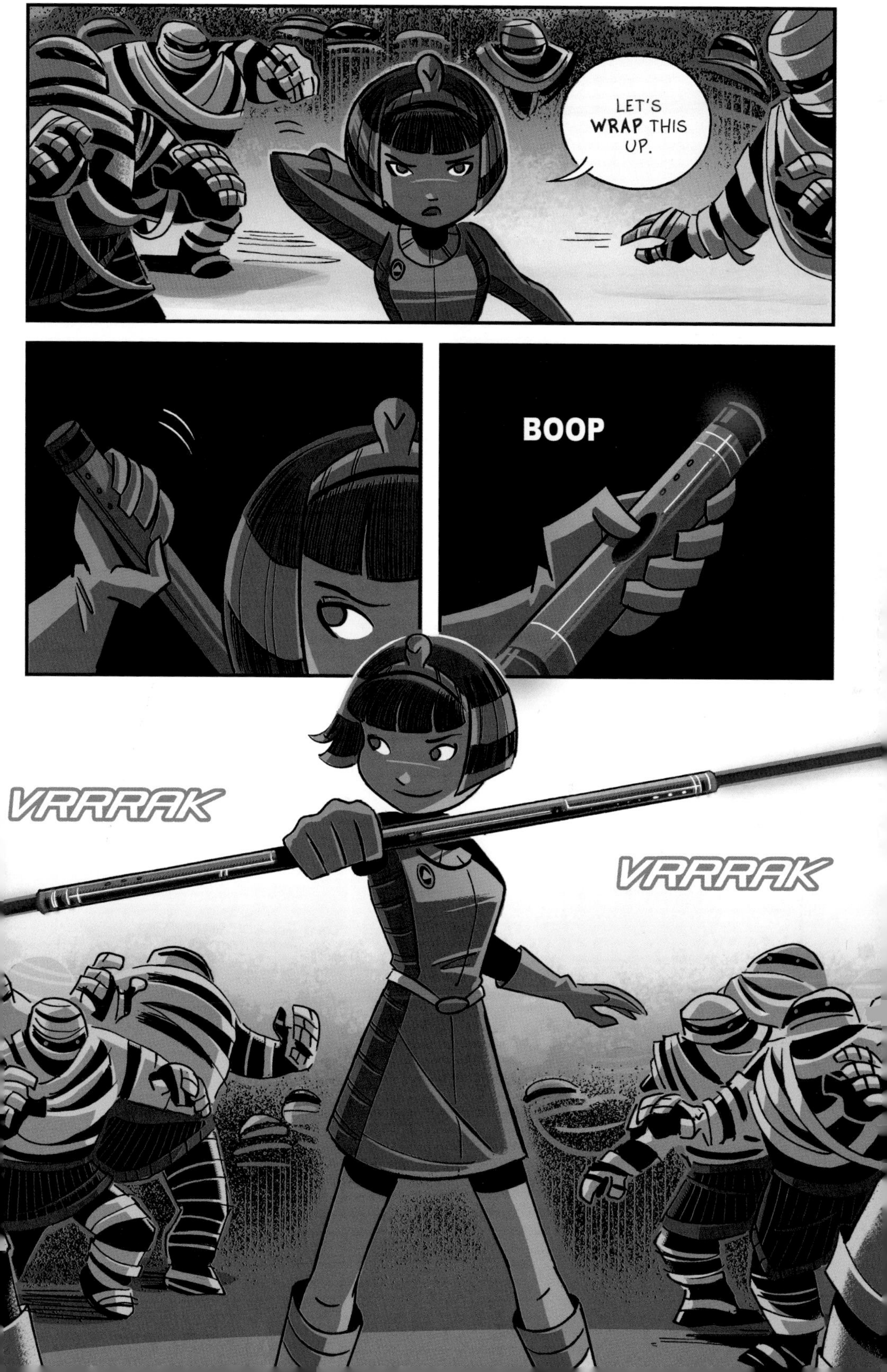
LET'S **WRAP** THIS UP.
BOOP
VRRRAK
VRRRAK

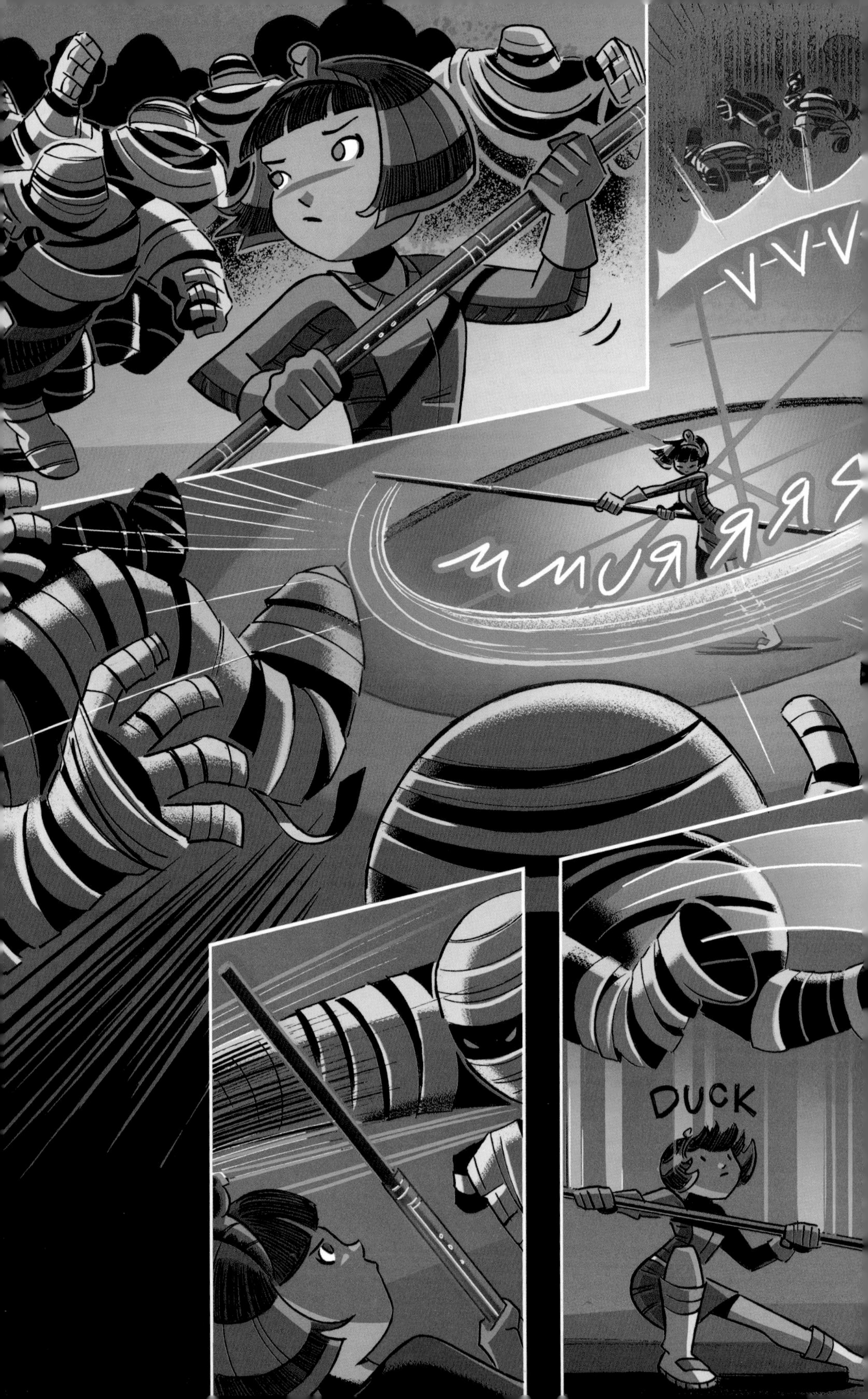
DUCK

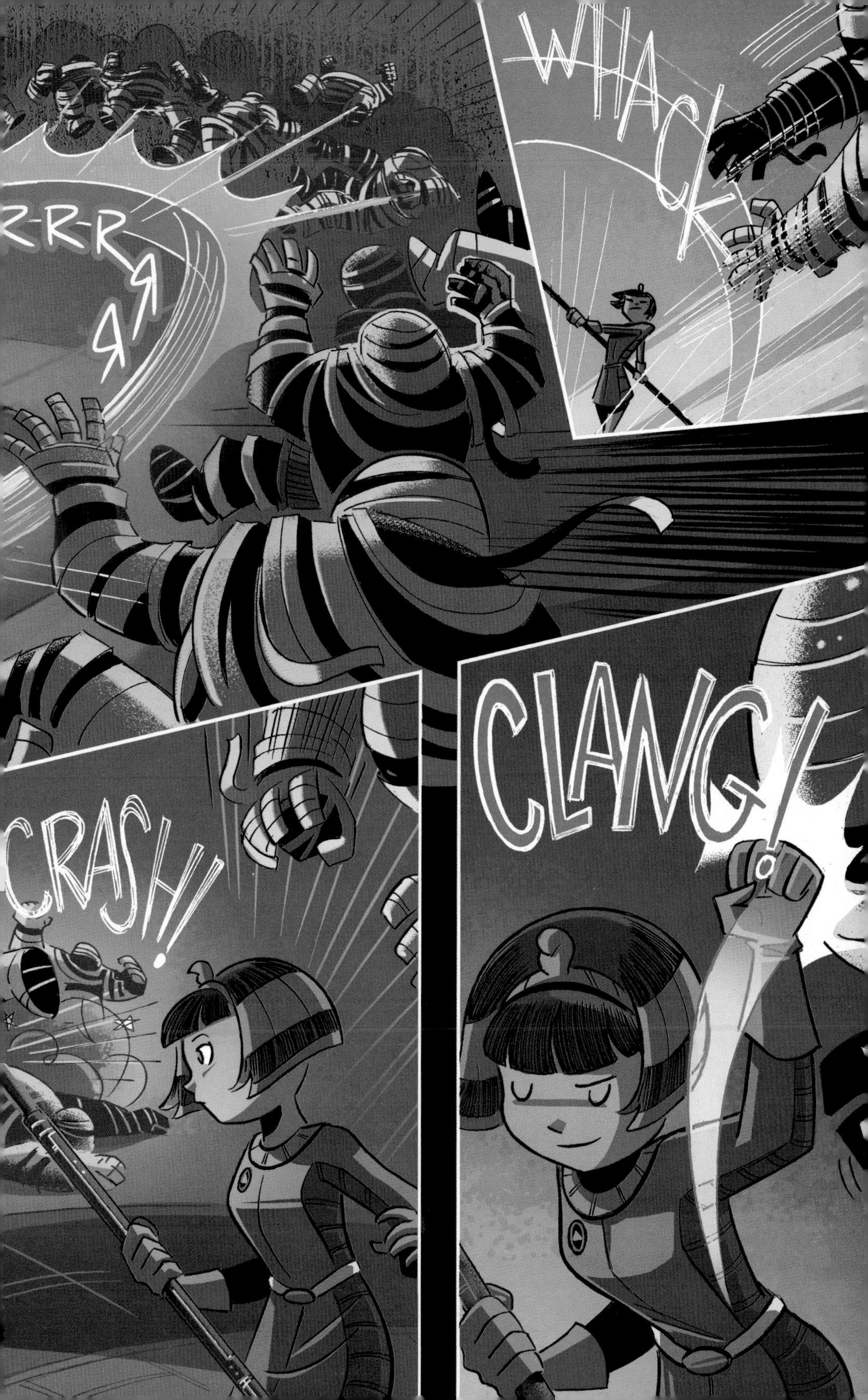

R-R-R R R R
WHACK
CRASH!
CLANG!

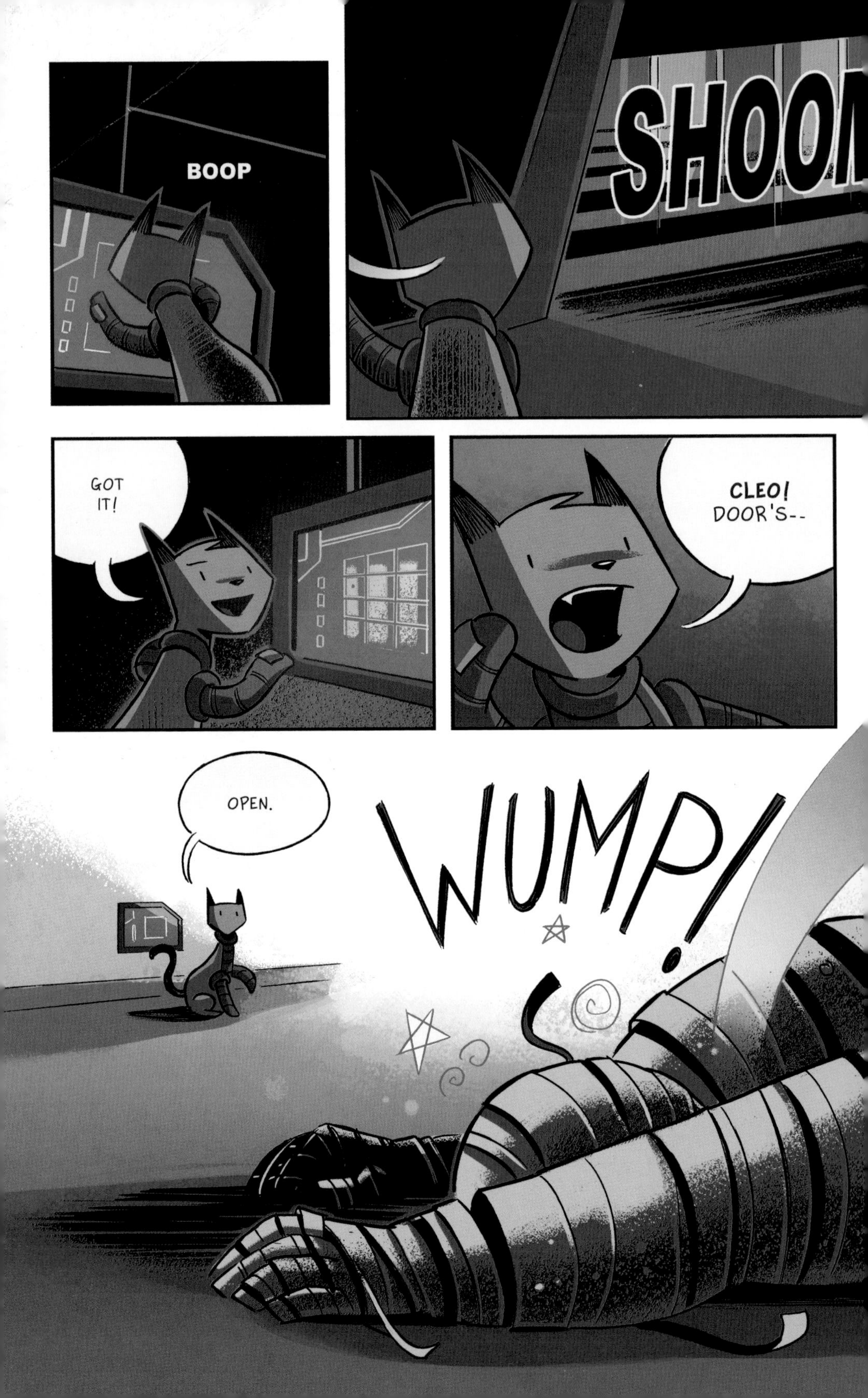
BOOP
SHOOM
GOT IT!
CLEO! DOOR'S--
OPEN.
WUMP!

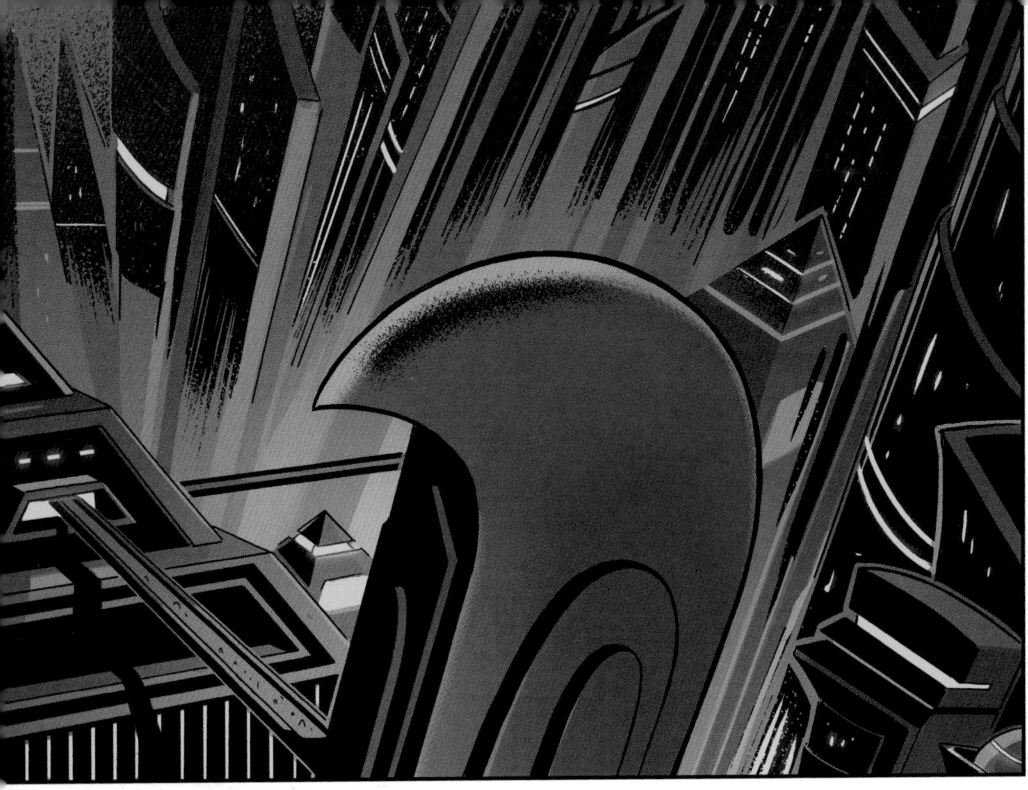

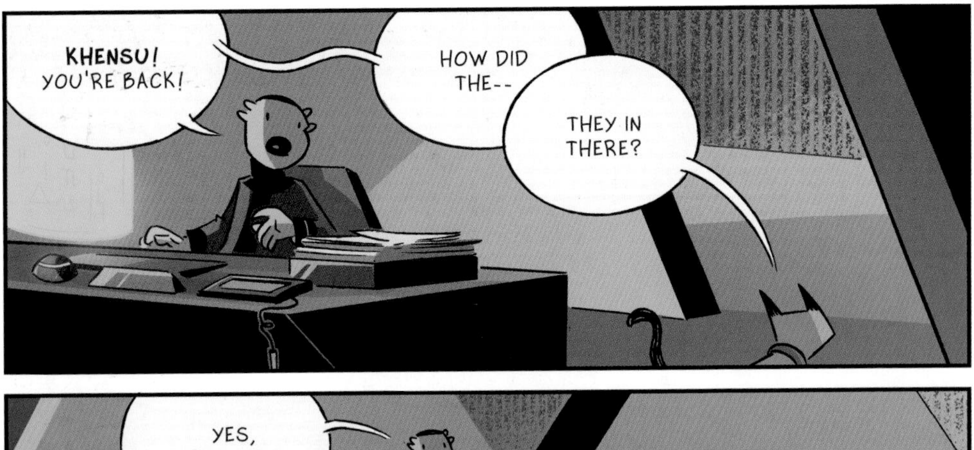
KHENSU!
YOU'RE BACK!
HOW DID THE--
THEY IN THERE?

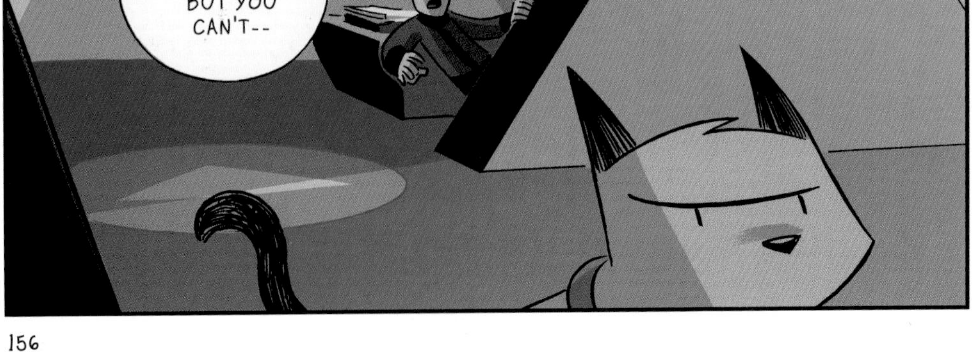
YES, BUT YOU CAN'T--

SHUFF

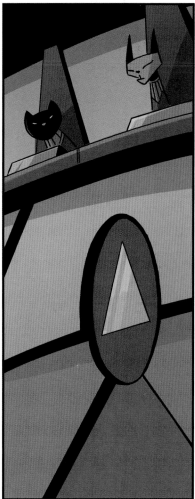

RUMORS...

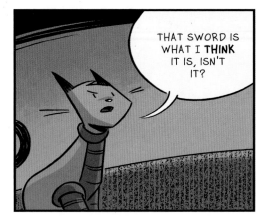

THAT SWORD IS WHAT I **THINK** IT IS, ISN'T IT?

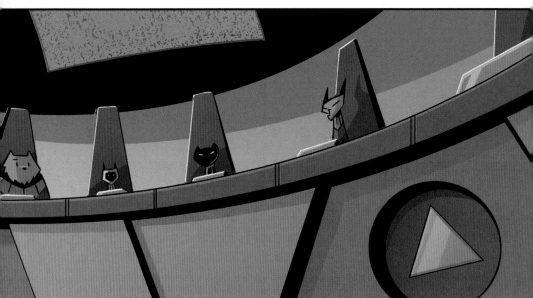

THE NEXT TIME YOU DECIDE TO SEND MY--MY **STUDENT** OFF TO SOME **DEATH TRAP** JUST TO PROVE SOMETHING WE **ALREADY**--

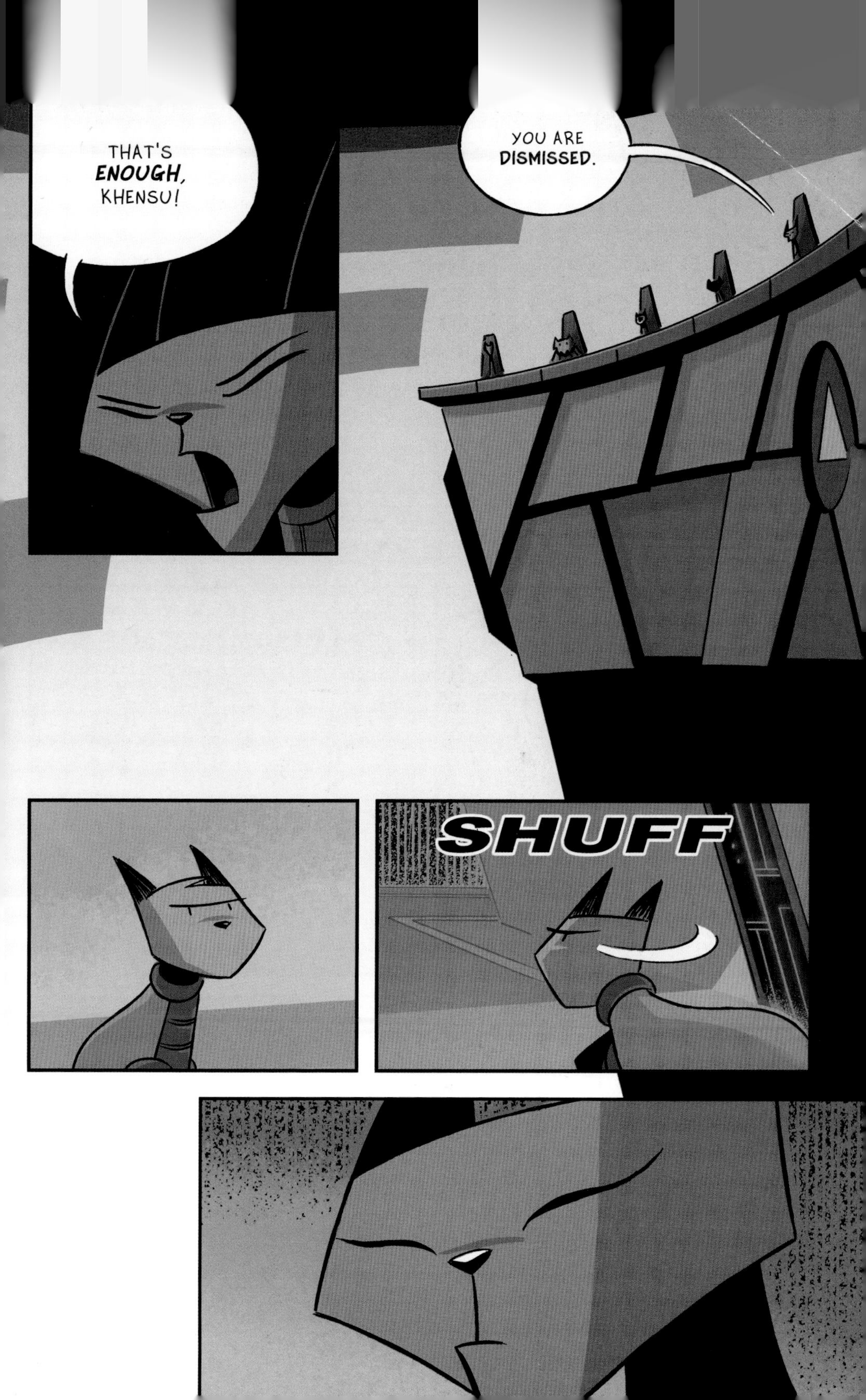
THAT'S ENOUGH, KHENSU!
YOU ARE DISMISSED.
SHUFF

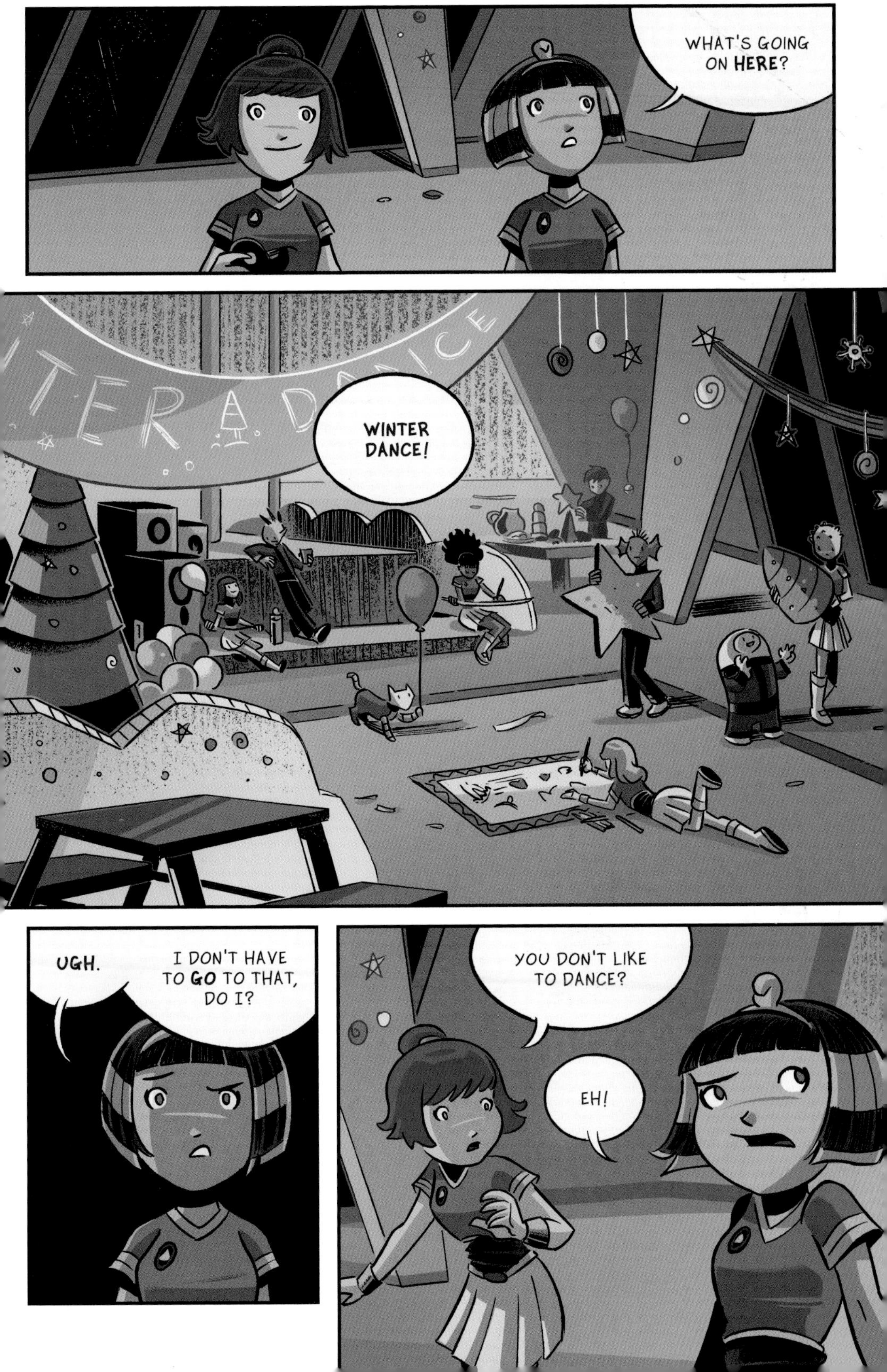
WHAT'S GOING ON HERE?
WINTER DANCE!
UGH.
I DON'T HAVE TO GO TO THAT, DO I?
YOU DON'T LIKE TO DANCE?
EH!

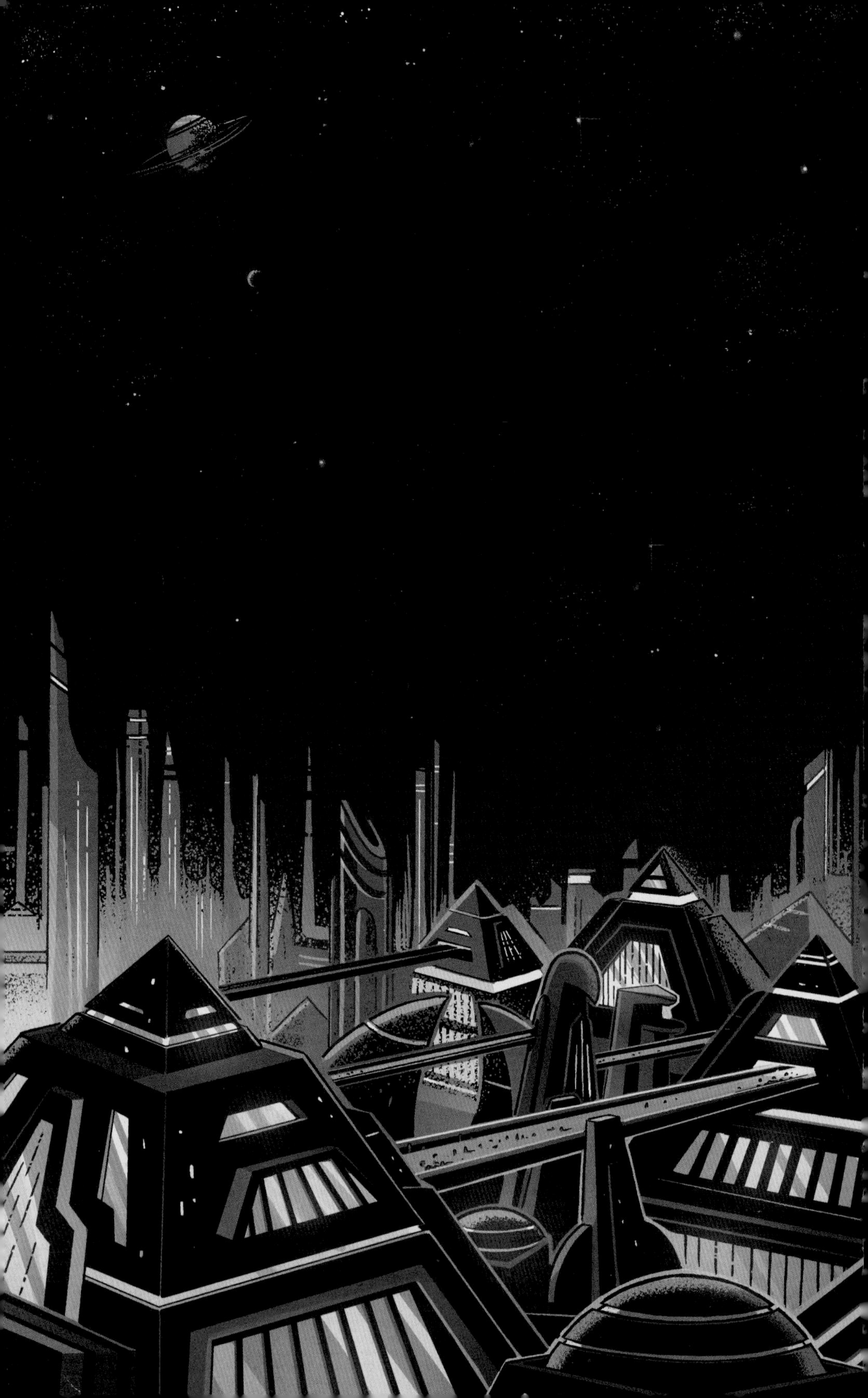

ACKNOWLEDGMENTS

If not for the following individuals, this story would have been lost in space:

First and foremost, to the love of my life, Jen Maihack, whose patience and support throughout this entire creative process has been extraordinary. Also, for suggesting that Cleo's bike look like a sphinx.

To my family and friends (you know who you are!), I don't mention often enough how much your support means, but hopefully you realize it all the same.

To Cassandra Pelham, Phil Falco, and David Saylor, for not only taking a chance on me, but also pushing me past my comfort zone to create a much better graphic novel than I ever would have on my own.

To the incredible Judy Hansen, for leading me through the crazy and often scary world that is literary publishing! I continue to look forward to your guidance.

To the amazing eyes and expertise of Stephen McCranie, Sarah Mensinga, Wes Molebash, Michael Regina, and Josh Ulrich. Expect me to keep asking for your advice!

To all those who have supported *Cleopatra in Space* all these years — both on the web and off. Your importance cannot be overstated enough.

Lastly, I'd like to thank my two cats, Ash and Misty. They are pretty useless and actually were more detrimental than supportive in the creation of this book, but I felt their companionship should still be

ABOUT THE AUTHOR

A graduate of the Columbus College of Art & Design, Mike Maihack spends his time drawing pictures of cats, superheroes, space girls, and just about anything else he can think of that might involve a ray gun or two. He is the creator of the popular webcomic *Cow & Buffalo*, illustrator of the all-ages card game Goblins Drool, Fairies Rule, and has contributed art and stories to books like *Parable*; *Jim Henson's The Storyteller*; *Cow Boy*; *Geeks, Girls, and Secret Identities*; and the Eisner and Harvey award-winning *Comic Book Tattoo*. Mike lives with his wife, two sons, and Siamese cat down in the humid depths of Lutz, Florida.

Visit Mike online at www.mikemaihack.com and follow him on Twitter at @mikemaihack.

AVAILABLE NOW . . .

CLEOPATRA IN SPACE

BOOK TWO
THE THIEF AND THE SWORD

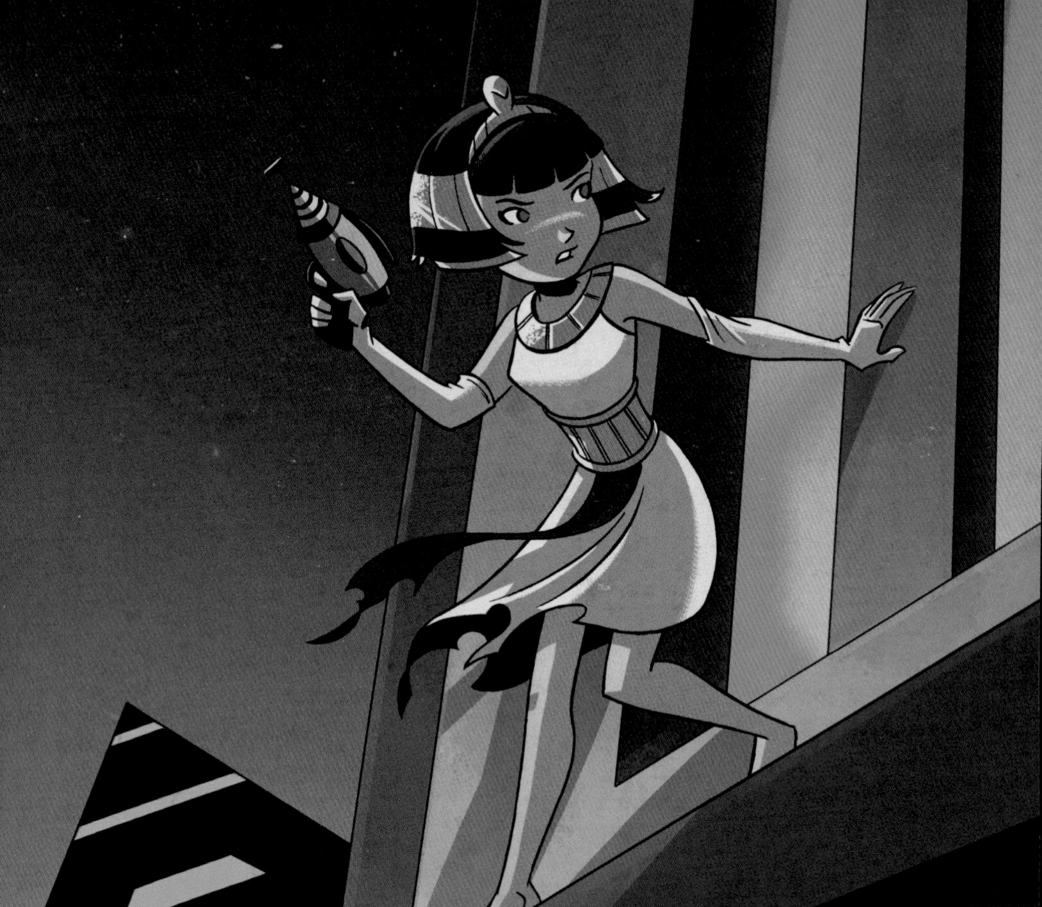

Things are going well for Cleo until she fails a training exercise, her friendship with Akila is threatened, and a mysterious boy who's working for the enemy shows up at Yasiro Academy. Find out what happens in Cleo's next adventure!